# I KISSED
# SHARA
# WHEELER

# CASEY McQUISTON

I KISSED SHARA WHEELER

MACMILLAN

First Published in the US 2022 by Wednesday Books,
an imprint of St. Martin's Publishing Group

This edition published in the UK 2023 by Macmillan Children's Books
an imprint of Pan Macmillan
The Smithson, 6 Briset Street, London EC1M 5NR
*EU representative:* Macmillan Publishers Ireland Ltd, 1st Floor,
The Liffey Trust Centre, 117–126 Sheriff Street Upper
Dublin 1, D01 YC43
Associated companies throughout the world
www.panmacmillan.com

ISBN 978-1-5290-9943-0

3 5 7 9 8 6 4 2

A CIP catalogue record for this book is available from the British Library.

Printed and bound by CPI Group (UK) Ltd, Croydon CR0 4YY
Designed by Devan Norman

FOR PEPPER,
MY BEST GIRL

Dear Reader,

If you come to this story from the South or from a Southern Baptist or Evangelical Christian background, you may recognize some of the culture it describes. Much of it is approached with humor, because sometimes you really do have to laugh. And though Chloe Green doesn't believe, her point of view isn't the only one you'll encounter in this book. There's room for the good parts and the bad, the funny and painful and everything in between, because that's what life as a teenager is—especially in Chloe's pocket of the world. To explore all of this, *I Kissed Shara Wheeler* includes elements of religious trauma and homophobia.

For more information, visit caseymcquiston.com.

IT STARTED OUT WITH A KISS . . .

**–THE KILLERS**

**1**

Chloe Green is going to put her fist through a window.

Usually when she has a thought like that, it means she's *spiritually* on the brink. But right now, squared up to the back door of the Wheeler house, she's actually physically ready to do it.

Her phone flashes the time: 11:27 a.m. Thirty-three minutes until the end of the late service at Willowgrove Christian Church, where the Wheelers are spending their morning pretending to be nice, normal folks whose nice, normal daughter didn't stage a disappearing act at prom twelve hours ago.

It has to be an act, is the thing. Obviously, Shara Wheeler is fine. Shara Wheeler is not missing. Shara Wheeler is doing what she does: a doe-eyed performance of blank innocence that makes everyone think she must be so deep and complex and enchanting when really, she's the most boring bore in this entire unbearably boring town.

Chloe is going to prove it. Because she's the only one smart enough to see it.

She wanted to *enjoy* her prom night after an entire year chasing early admission deadlines and her spot at the top of the class of '22. It took weeks to thrift the perfect dress (black chiffon and lace, like a sexy vampire assassin), and it was supposed to be a perfect prom. Not *the* perfect prom—no dates, no corsages—but *her* perfect prom. Just her friends in fancy outfits piling into Benjy's car, screaming Lil Yachty in a room with a chandelier, and collapsing into a Waffle House booth at one in the morning.

But thirty minutes before the prom court was announced, she saw her: Shara, rosy lips and a waterfall of almond-pink tulle, brushing past refreshments on her way to the door. Chloe had been watching her all night, waiting for a chance to get her alone.

Except when she got to the door, Shara was gone, and when student council president Brooklyn Bennett got up on stage to crown Shara as prom queen, she was still gone. Nobody saw her leave, and nobody's seen her since, but her white Jeep is missing from the Wheelers' driveway.

So here Chloe is, the morning after, makeup smudged around her eyes and hair crunchy with hairspray, ready to break into Shara's house.

She finds the spare key inside a conspicuously smooth rock with Joshua 24:15 engraved on it. *As for me and my house, we will serve the Lord.*

The whole drive to the country club, she imagined the look on Shara's face when she saw Chloe at her door. The big, shocked green eyes, the theatrical gasp, the dawning realization that her little stunt for attention isn't going to work out the way she planned because Chloe is a hot genius who can't be fooled. The sheer satisfaction was going to power Chloe through finals and probably like, the first two years of college.

But when she sticks her head through the open door and scans the Wheelers' enormous kitchen, Shara's nowhere.

So, she does what anyone else in her position would do. She shuts the door behind her and does a sweep of the first floor.

Shara's not here.

Okay. That's fine. But she's definitely *somewhere*. Probably upstairs, in her room.

In the upstairs hallway, a half-open door reveals a bathroom that must be Shara's. Beige-and-pink wallpaper, porcelain countertop lined with rosewater skincare products and a bottle of her signature nail polish (Essie, Ballet Slippers). Chloe hovers at the doorway; this isn't her objective, but there's a flower-patterned silk scrunchie next to the sink that she's never seen before, no matter how many AP classes she's spent glaring at the back of Shara's head. Shara exclusively wears her shiny blond hair down. That's like, her thing. She must put it up to wash her face at night.

Irrelevant.

Chloe pauses at the next door. It's slightly ajar and marked with a hand-painted pink *S*.

It'd be a lie—a huge, Willowgrove-Christian-Academy-football-budget-sized lie—to say she's never envisioned what sort of perfection incubator Shara Wheeler climbs inside when she goes home every day. A tank of goo to preserve her dewy complexion? A professional hairstylist on retainer? Where does Shara go when she's not having picturesque Starbucks dates with her quarterback boyfriend or spinning out suspiciously good comparative lit essays? Who is she when, for once, nobody is looking?

Only one way to find out.

She kicks the door open, and—

The room is empty.

Shara's room is, of course, a nice, normal room. Suspiciously plain, even. Bed, dresser, nightstand, vanity, bookshelf-slash-desk combo, eggshell lamp with a silver chain. There's a dried homecoming corsage on the windowsill and a tube of Burt's Bees lip balm in a seashell dish on the dresser, alongside a bottle of lilac body spray and a pile of bookmarked paperbacks for school. The walls are a simple biege, with framed photos of her family and her boyfriend and her flock of identical pointy-elbowed, flowy-haired friends with perfect Glossier faces.

Where's the Glossier Gang now? Nursing their prom hangovers, Chloe guesses. Clearly, none of them are here looking for clues. That's the thing about popular kids: They don't have the type of bond forged in the fire of being weird and queer in small-to-medium-town Alabama. If Chloe tried to ghost like this, there'd be a militia of Shakespeare gays kicking down every door in False Beach.

Why isn't Shara here?

Chloe clenches her fists, steps inside, and starts with the desk.

If there's no Shara to interrogate, maybe her room has some answers. She peers through the contents of the desk and shelves, looking for Shara's *Gone Girl* calendar with days of the week marked by "gather supplies" and "frame Chloe for my murder." All she finds are college brochures and a box of pink stationery monogrammed with Shara's initials—thank-you cards for the imminent flood of graduation checks from rich family. No incriminating diary pages crammed in the wastepaper basket, just the cardboard packaging for some lip gloss.

Jewelry box: nothing notable. Closet: clothes, a carefully organized shoe rack, prom and homecoming dresses zipped inside tidy garment bags. (Who uses *garment bags*?) Underwear drawer: half-empty, enough modest petal-soft things gone for a week or two. Bed: over the tucked-in ivory quilt, a neatly folded Harvard T-shirt. God forbid anyone forget that Shara got into her first-choice school, with offers from basically every other Ivy in the country.

Chloe releases a hiss through her teeth. This is just a bunch of perfectly normal stuff, suggesting the perfectly normal life of a perfectly normal girl.

She doubles back to the vanity, opening the drawer. Tubes of lip gloss line up neatly in almost identical shades of neutral pink, most half-used, labels rubbing off. At the end of the row, one is brand-new, so full and shiny it could have only been used once, if ever. She recognizes its packaging from the wastepaper basket.

When she twists the cap off, the scent hits her just as hard as it did the first time she smelled it: vanilla and mint.

The window opens.

Chloe swears, drops to the carpet, and crawls under the desk.

A pair of black Vans appears on the windowsill, bringing with them the skinny frame of a boy in distressed jeans and a flannel. He pauses—she can't see his face, but his body twists like he's checking that the coast is clear—and then drops down into the room.

Dark curly hair with caramel highlights, light brown skin, long and straight nose, a jawline both square and delicate like fishbone.

Rory Heron. Willowgrove's answer to every brooding bad boy from every late '90s teen drama. The most eligible bachelor amongst the stoners-skaters-and-slackers rung of the social ladder. She's never had a class with him, but she's heard he doesn't attend them much, anyway.

She watches as his eyes track the same path she did—the

dresser, the bed, the pictures on the wall. After noticing he's kicked the corsage off the sill and onto the floor, he picks it up with gentle fingers and examines the dried buds before returning it to its place. Chloe's eyes narrow. What is Rory Heron doing here, in Shara's bedroom, fondling her corsages?

Then he turns to the desk, sees her, and screams.

Chloe lunges to her feet and slaps her hand over his mouth.

"Shut *up*," Chloe hisses. Up close, his eyes are hazel-y brown and wide open in alarm. "The neighbors could hear you."

"I *am* the neighbors," he says when she releases him.

Chloe stares at him, trying to reconcile Rory's whole persona with the extreme uptightness of the False Beach Country Club. "You live here?"

Rory glares. "What, I don't look like I could afford to live here?"

"You seem like you'd rather die than live here," Chloe says.

"Believe me, it's not by choice," Rory says, still scowling, but in a different flavor now. "You're—Chloe, right? Chloe Green? What are you doing under Shara's desk?"

"What are *you* doing climbing through Shara's window?"

"You first."

"I—I, uh," Chloe stammers. Rory's entrance startled some of the fire out of her, and now she's not sure how to explain herself. Her face starts to heat; she wills it to stop. "I heard she ran away last night."

"I heard the same thing," Rory says. He talks with the same kind of studied disaffection that he carries himself with, shoulders slumped and impartial. "Did you—do you know where she is?"

"No, I just—I wanted to see if she was really gone."

"So you broke into her house," Rory says flatly.

"I used a key!"

"Yeah, that's still breaking and entering."

"Only if I commit a crime."

"Okay, trespassing."

"What do you call climbing through her window, then?"

Rory pauses, glancing down at the toes of his Vans. "That's different. She told me she was leaving her window unlocked."

"Not an invitation, dude."

"Jesus Christ, I told you, I'm her *neighbor*. People like, ask their neighbors to check on their stuff while they're gone all the time. It's a thing."

"And that's what you're doing?"

"I wanted to make sure she was okay."

Chloe pulls a skeptical face. "I've literally never seen you speak to her in my life."

"You don't even know her, do you?" Rory counters. "What are *you* doing here? Why do you care if she's gone?"

Why does she care? Because she and Shara have both spent every day of their high school careers dedicated to the singular goal of graduating valedictorian, and the only thing Chloe has ever wanted as much as that title is the satisfaction of knowing Shara Wheeler can't have it. Because Shara Wheeler has everything else.

Because if Shara's really gone, that's a forfeit, and Chloe Green does not win by default.

Because two days ago, Shara found her alone in the B Building elevator before fifth hour, pulled her in by the elbow, and kissed her until she forgot an entire semester of French. And Chloe still doesn't know why.

"Why do *you* care?" she snaps back at Rory.

"Because I—I get her, okay? Her stupid-ass friends don't, but I do."

"Oh, you *get her*." Chloe rolls her eyes. "So that makes you qualified to lead the search party."

"No—"

"Then what does?"

There's another pause. Rory shifts his weight from one foot to the other. And then he looks down at the desk, raises his dark brows, and says, "That."

When Chloe follows his gaze, she finds an envelope sitting innocuously in a pink letter organizer. Shara's cursive spells out Rory's name on the front.

*Rory's* name?

Rory's arms are longer, but Chloe reacts faster. She snatches the envelope up and opens it with one finger, taking out a piece of that pink monogrammed stationery, and reads Shara's flawless cursive out loud.

> Rory,
> Thanks for the kiss. If you thought I never noticed you, you're wrong.
>
> XOXO
> Shara
>
> P.S. peach100304
> P.P.S. Tell Smith to check the drafts. Chloe should have the rest.

"You *kissed* her?" Chloe demands.

Rory looks ready to dodge a punch, which he might want to save for when Shara's actual boyfriend finds out. "*She* kissed *me!*"

The anger comes screaming back, and Chloe grinds out, "When?"

"Last night. Before prom."

"Where?"

"On . . . the mouth?"

"*Geographically,* Heron."

"Oh. On my roof."

Shara kissed Rory. And now Rory is standing here, in her room, defending her to Chloe, because he—oh God.

She's the girl next door, and he's in love with her. That's what this is. How absolutely, annoyingly predictable.

"Well, don't get too excited," Chloe says. "She kissed me too."

Rory stares. "You're fucking with me."

"I'm really not," Chloe tells him. "At school, on Friday."

He squeezes his eyes shut, starts to run a hand through his curls, then stops himself before he can mess up the way he arranged them.

"Okay, so, this"—he gestures between the two of them and the room at large—"makes more sense."

A miserably awkward silence settles like a cloud of jock B.O. in the school gym on a pep rally Friday. Chloe bares her teeth to speak—

The front door opens downstairs.

"Hell," Chloe says. She checks the clock on the nightstand: 12:13 p.m. Rory made her lose track of time.

"You're gonna have to take the ladder," Rory says, already on the move.

"Shara fucking Wheeler," Chloe mutters, and she launches herself out the window so violently, she almost misses the first rung.

On the ground, Rory puts the ladder on one slight shoulder and clumsily tries to move it back to the fence. He really is just a very nice face on top of a broomstick, physically speaking. She gets why so many junior and sophomore girls are obsessed with his hot-surly-guy-with-the-guitar-in-the-school-parking-lot vibe, but it's sad to watch him lift something.

"Here," she says, reaching for the other side. He grunts unhappily but doesn't complain.

They climb into his backyard, which is as pristine and lush as the rest of the country club. Back in California, Chloe had never been inside a country club with a subdivision in it, sprawling acreage with a manned gate like a golf course bouncer. She had to pretend she was someone's nanny to get in.

"Okay, screw it," Chloe says, wiping at her leftover eyeliner. The back of her hand comes away black. "What does the peach thing mean? From the note?"

"I have no idea," Rory says.

"Then we'll tell Smith everything tomorrow at school and see if *he* knows."

Rory makes a face. He looks ridiculous, standing inside a gated community pretending to be some kind of dirtbag indie softboy.

"*We?*" he says. "You want to *tell Smith* you kissed his girlfriend?"

"Don't you want to know what she's doing? Where she is?"

"Why don't we just wait until she comes back and ask her?"

"What makes you so sure she's coming back anytime soon?" Chloe demands. "What if she has some kind of—some kind of secret second life in another town, or some sugar daddy she's holed up with, or something? What if she doesn't come back before we all leave for college? What if she ghosts everyone forever? What if you spend the rest of your life wondering why, in the name of God, Shara Wheeler kissed you?"

Rory, whose eyes have been narrowing more and more the longer she talks, tucks in one corner of his mouth and says, "She really got you fucked up, huh?"

"Bye," Chloe says, turning on her heel. "I'll do it myself."

"Wait," Rory calls after her.

She stops.

"When tomorrow?"

"First thing," Chloe says. "Football Physics is first hour."

"Great." He unlatches the gate for her. "I'll get my affairs in order."

"Why didn't you ever audition for spring musical? You're so dramatic."

"Not my thing."

They stand there, Chloe's keys jingling in her hand, Rory looking like he's going to start writing depressing poetry about Shara any second. Or whatever his deal is. It feels alarmingly like she's just been assigned to the world's worst group project, and she can't imagine the addition of Smith Parker will be an improvement.

"Um." Chloe clears her throat. "Maybe . . . don't tell anyone else? About Shara kissing me? I don't know if I should've . . . well, anyway, I don't think it should be spread all over school unless she tells people herself."

Rory shakes his head. "I wasn't gonna tell anyone."

Satisfied, Chloe lifts her chin and whips around, forcing the gate open. "See you at school tomorrow. You better show up. I know where you live now."

"Threat received," Rory says with a sullen salute, and she shuts him behind the gate.

She crosses the front yard of the Heron house and rounds the corner to a copse of trees and an elaborate fountain in the shape of a very ugly dolphin, where she parked her car.

In the driver's seat, she finally lets her body relax the way it only can when she's really, truly alone. Her shoulders slump.

Her keys slide out of her hand and onto the floor mat. Her head drops against the steering wheel. The miniature lucky cat on her dashboard waves at her, nonplussed.

She's been kissed and ditched by Shara Wheeler. And she's not even the only one.

But . . . that lip gloss. Vanilla and mint. It's absolutely, 100 percent the lip gloss she was wearing when they kissed. Chloe would never, ever forget that scent.

Which means Shara bought it specifically to kiss Chloe with.

Proof that Shara does, when she's home at night in her powder-blue room, brushing her hair and painting her nails and winding a rubber band three times around a stack of study cards, think about Chloe.

And *that* feels a bit like winning.

# FROM THE BURN PILE

PLEASE DO NOT REACT AUDIBLY if Madame Clark picks this one up and reads it out loud like she did with Tanner's ranking of girls' butts I will literally kill you

Okay. So.

Shara Wheeler just kissed me. Like literally just now on my way to fifth hour.

AGAIN PLEASE DO NOT REACT you are calm you are a placid lake you are my moms after a pitcher of hemp tea

I was taking the faculty elevator shortcut, and she got on, and then she kissed me, out of NOWHERE.

And I think I kissed her back??? She's hot! I panicked! She may be the bane of my existence, but she also looks like she lives in the hills of Sweden and spends all her time embroidering flowers on linen shirts like an extra in *Midsommar*. She looks like she smells nice and I'm here to report that she does in fact smell nice, like lilacs, except for her lip gloss, which was vanilla and mint. Like, what *else* am I supposed to do when a girl like that is about to kiss me? Anyone would have done the same thing.

ANYWAY. She kissed me, like really kissed me, like <u>KISSED</u> me, and then she was GONE.

What does it mean??? Shara Wheeler is the most tragic heterosexual to ever cram herself into a Brandy Melville crop top. She was obviously just screwing with me. This is mean straight girl behavior. Right???

What do I do????

Lilacs, Geo. LILACS.

# 2

The first thing Chloe saw when her moms' Subaru crossed into False Beach city limits was Shara Wheeler's face.

That's not just what it felt like—although it does seem like Shara Wheeler is everywhere, all the time. It was literally looming forty feet wide over the interstate between a Waffle House and a Winn-Dixie under a swampy gray sky: a pretty blond girl with a pretty smile, holding a stack of textbooks and a protractor.

JESUS LOVES GEOMETRY! the billboard declared, which struck Chloe as a bit of a bold claim. A CHRIST-CENTERED EDUCATION AT WILLOWGROVE CHRISTIAN ACADEMY!

There are a total of five high schools in False Beach, and Willowgrove is the only one with a decent AP program and a theater department with the budget to do *Phantom*. As a fourteen-year-old literary nerd neck-deep in a goth phase, those seemed like the most important things a high school education could offer her. Her mom went to Willowgrove back in the '90s, and she tried to warn her what it was like, but Chloe was insistent. If this was her only option, she could put up with the Jesus stuff.

"What kind of name is False Beach?" Chloe asked her mom for the five thousandth miserable time that day as they glided under Shara's billboard. It was a question she'd been asking since her mom first told her the name of her hometown.

"It's a beach but it's not," her mom answered, same as always, and her other mom flipped a page in *The Canterbury Tales,* and they kept driving out of the California sunset and into the buttcrack of Alabama.

False Beach sits on the wide banks of Lake Martin, which gives the slight illusion that it might be a beach town like Gulf Shores or Mobile down on the coast, but it's not. It's four hours inland from the Gulf of Mexico, closer to Atlanta than to Pensacola, nearly smack in the center of the state. The lakeshore isn't even sandy, because the lake isn't a real lake. It's a reservoir made in the 1920s, surrounded by marshy banks and woods and cliffs.

It's just a town by some water where nothing interesting ever happens. And, in what Chloe has learned is the nature of small towns, when one thing *does* happen, everyone knows about it. Which means by Monday morning, all anyone wants to talk about is where Shara could have gone.

Frankly, it's not *that* different from every other day at Willowgrove. Here, Shara Wheeler is like Helen of Troy, if she were famous for being both beautiful and too tragically, terribly brilliant for her small town, or Regina George, if her brand was logging double the school-mandated volunteer service hours.

Shara Wheeler's so *pretty.* Shara Wheeler's so *smart.* Shara Wheeler has *never* been mean to *anyone* in her *life.* Shara Wheeler has the voice of an angel, actually, but she's never auditioned for a spring musical because she doesn't want to take the spotlight away from students who need it more. Shara Wheeler is the football team's good luck charm, and if she misses a game, they're doomed. Last year, there was a whole movement of freshman girls eyelash-gluing their own Cupid's bows to re-create Shara's signature naturally full, upturned upper lip. It's a miracle nobody has put her likeness on like, the side of a butter container yet.

Today:

"I heard nobody's seen her since prom night."

"I heard Smith broke up with her and she lost it."

"I heard she ran away to build houses for the homeless."

"I heard she's secretly pregnant and her parents sent her away until she gives birth so nobody finds out."

"That's literally a plotline from *Riverdale,* idiot," Benjy calls after a passing sophomore. He sighs and carefully lays his folded Sonic uniform polo for his after-school shift at the bottom of his locker.

Chloe scowls at the mirror on her locker door. Annoying that her life should *also* have to revolve around Shara Wheeler right now.

"You good, Chloe?" Benjy asks.

"Of course I'm good," Chloe says, straightening her shiny silver collar pins. Georgia describes her interpretation of the uniform as "doing the most." Chloe describes it as "please let me feel one sweet hit of individuality before it's squeezed out of me by lunch." It's whatever. "Why wouldn't I be good?"

"Because you only did one eye."

"What?" She checks her reflection again. Left eye: expertly executed eyeliner wing in Blackest Black. Right eye: naked as a newborn baby. "Oh my God."

She whips a liner pen out of the emergency makeup pouch in her locker. It's been in there so long, she has to scribble on the back of her hand to get it going. She never thought she'd need it.

"Anyway," Benjy says, picking their conversation back up. "I told Georgia that we have to do movie night at her place this week because Ash wants to watch that *Labyrinth* movie your mom mentioned, and if my dad walks in and sees David Bowie's junk in white spandex, he is going to have some questions that I'm not interested in answering. So, we're—" He breaks off. "Um. Why is Rory Heron coming over here?"

A tiny figure appears over Chloe's shoulder in the mirror, right under the blunt edge of her bob but growing closer: Rory, looking deeply affronted at having to set foot on campus before third hour.

"I owe him money for a class gift for Madame Clark," Chloe lies quickly, finishing off her wing and capping the pen.

"Have fun," Benjy says, and then he's off to first hour.

Chloe shuts her locker and turns to face Rory. "Glad I don't have to go back to the country club."

Rory blinks. "You know your whole deal is like … exhausting, right?"

"Thank you," she says. "Come on."

She picks her way through the morning crowd to the physics lab, zeroing in on the one around whom every other football player seems to orbit. Smith Parker: Shara's boyfriend, quarterback, victim of a tragic first-name last-name, last-name first-name situation.

She remembers the day Smith and Shara got together. Homecoming week junior year, when the entire school was consumed by the bizarre Southern ritual of paying a dollar for the student council to send your crush carnations. Chloe was forced to be Shara's lab partner in AP Chem that year, and Shara had crossed out Chloe's chemical formula to write her own—Chloe's was right—when two dozen carnations were dumped all over their lab notes. Every single one was from Smith to Shara, and they've been a Willowgrove power couple ever since, which, honestly? Carnations aren't even that nice of a flower.

As far as Chloe is concerned, Smith isn't much better than the other football d-bags, all of whom she's obligated to dislike on principle. When most of last year's tuition went to stadium renovations and the cheerleading coach is teaching civics, Willowgrove's priorities are pretty obvious. Every game Smith wins yanks more cash out of arts programs, the only place for students with *actual* talent.

Up close, Smith Parker is . . . not quite as huge as Chloe thought. He's more tapered than bulky, more like a dancer than a football player. He's one of the few athletes Chloe considers good-looking instead of thick-necked hot-ugly: high cheekbones, striking brown eyes with sharp inner corners and arched brows, dark brown skin that somehow remains clear during football season. He's tall, even taller than Rory. Did he grow somehow since before prom? Has he always been this square-jawed and triangle-shaped? He's like an SAT geometry problem.

"Smith," she says. He doesn't respond at first, still yelling down the hall at one of his teammates—and, really, football season ended four months ago, can they find another personality trait?—so she tries again. "Smith!"

When he finally looks, it occurs to her that Smith Parker may not even know who she is. He definitely at least knows her as that weird queer girl from LA with two lesbian moms, like everyone else does, but does he *know* who she *is*? Her reputation for leading the Quiz Bowl team with an iron fist could be meaningless to him. Has Shara told him that Chloe is her only rightful academic nemesis?

"What's up?" Smith says. He glances beside her to Rory,

who is retracting into his uniform sweatshirt, and does a little chin nod.

Chloe purses her lips. "Can we talk to you for a second?"

Smith looks over his shoulder to where Ace Torres is at the door to the physics lab, slapping palms with yet another football guy. It's common knowledge at Willowgrove that first-hour senior physics is dumbed down and graded on an extreme curve to help student athletes keep their GPAs up.

"I really gotta get to class," he says.

Chloe releases a hiss. "It's Football Physics."

"I know," Smith says, "but—"

"And it's the last month of school," Chloe points out. "Nobody cares if anyone's late, least of all you."

"Look, I had a long weekend," Smith says, turning to her. This time, she can see heaviness around his eyes. She wonders how he spent his Sunday—probably cow tipping with the boys or something. "Can y'all just—"

Rory blurts out, "I kissed Shara."

Smith freezes. Rory freezes. Untipped cows on the edge of town freeze.

When Smith speaks again, his voice is low. "What?"

"I mean, uh," Rory says. It's almost funny, the way all his class-cutting, shoe-gazing edginess shrinks into nothing. Boys are so embarrassing. "She, uh—before she left, we, um—"

"He kissed Shara. And so did I," Chloe says, stepping up like the Spartacus of people who have kissed Smith Parker's girlfriend. "I mean, she kissed me, if we're being specific. But I kissed her back."

Smith stares at her face, then at Rory's, then Chloe's again.

"Y'all think this is funny?" he asks. "Because it's not."

"It's a little funny," Chloe notes.

"It's not a joke," Rory insists.

If Smith knows anything about Willowgrove's lower social ranks, he should know that Chloe and Rory have never so much as shared eye contact in the hallway, much less a conspiracy to prank the quarterback. The entire ecosystem of Willowgrove depends on rigid divisions between each social stratum. Smith has to know she wouldn't be upsetting the natural order if she didn't absolutely have to.

A muscle in Smith's jaw twitches.

"Well, that pretty much sucks to hear," Smith says. "Why're you telling me?"

"Because we need to talk," Rory attempts. "All of us."

Chloe takes a more direct approach. "Rory, show him the note."

"What note?" Smith says.

Rory grumbles but swings his backpack around and unzips it. It's covered in Thrasher patches and pretentious buttons and contains precisely zero schoolbooks.

"She left us that," Chloe says when he gives Smith the card. "Do you know what the last part means?"

Smith stares at it for a long minute, then he folds it closed and calmly hands it back.

"You like her, don't you?" Smith says to Rory. "Still?"

Chloe glances between them, at the pinched set of Smith's mouth and the unhappy crease between Rory's thick eyebrows. She doesn't usually credit too many complicated feelings to teenage boys, but there's definitely some kind of messed-up history there. The Shara Vortex.

"Kind of," Rory says, in the voice of a boy who climbed through Shara's bedroom window the day before.

Smith nods with grim satisfaction and turns to Chloe.

"What about you?"

Chloe blinks and lowers her voice. "I barely even *know* her. I have no idea why she kissed me. I just want to beat her to valedictorian."

Smith considers that and nods again. Chloe is starting to suspect she doesn't get jocks at all.

"I don't know what peach means," Smith says, "but the numbers are my locker combination."

Smith Parker's locker is a mess.

It at least smells better than the other football players' lockers, but it's crammed with textbooks and overstuffed notebooks and more books than he could possibly have to read for a regular English class. There is also a surprising number of cosmetics: tubes of moisturizer, hair ties, dark brown concealer, pomegranate lip balm. He shoves those behind a box of Little Debbie oatmeal pies.

"Really, dude?" Chloe says, nodding to the pies.

Smith shrugs. "Gotta keep my calorie intake up."

As Smith searches the mess, Chloe stares at the picture on his locker door. It's Smith and Shara at the homecoming dance last fall, him in a generic button-down-and-dress-pants combo, her in *that* dress.

Chloe didn't go to homecoming, but she saw Shara's dress on Instagram like everyone else alive. It was only a blue silk slip with a modest neckline, but it stuck to her like water, and she wasn't wearing a bra. For a whole week, nobody at school would shut up about it. *BBC News at 9*, the headlines: GOD'S FAVORITE DAUGHTER SHOWS ONE HINT OF NIP.

She glances over at Rory to see if he's looking at the same thing, but he's focused on Smith, who's yanked something out from behind his Gatorade stash.

"Hold up," Smith says. "I didn't put this in here."

It's a bag of candy, and there's a second card from Shara's stationery tied neatly to it with a pink ribbon. Smith's name is written on the envelope.

"Peach rings?" Chloe asks.

"She always gives a pack to the cheerleaders who make my game day treat bag," Smith says. "They're my favorite."

"Still?" Rory says.

Smith glares. "What?"

"Peach rings are just kinda middle school," Rory says with a shrug.

"Are you gonna open it or what?" Chloe butts in.

Smith sighs and pulls the card out, and Chloe skims it over his shoulder before he has a chance to pull it away.

Smith,
I think that, maybe, the problem is that I don't know how to tell you the truth. Maybe that's why I had to do this. I don't know how to tell you, but maybe I can show you.

    I promise I'm okay. Don't be too mad about the kisses. It wasn't their fault.

                                        XOXO
                                        Shara
P.S. You're not done with the P.S. from the last one yet. Make sure Rory holds on to it. Shouldn't be hard.
P.P.S. Tell Chloe it'll come to her.

"I have no idea what this is supposed to mean," Smith says, lowering the card to his side. Rory tilts his head sideways to squint at the words.

"You don't think she's been like, Liam Neeson Taken, do you?" Chloe asks.

"No."

"So, she would have left on purpose, then?"

"I guess."

"Maybe she's fleeing the scene of a crime? Maybe she *killed* someone."

"Doubt it."

Rory straightens up and cuts in: "Do you even care?"

Oof.

Smith pauses, then shuts his locker.

"Wanna try that again?"

"I mean, I don't know," Rory says. "Aren't you gonna dump her for SEC groupies after graduation anyway? That'd make this pretty convenient for you."

"Yikes." Chloe exhales.

Smith bites down on the inside corner of his mouth, nodding slowly with his chin like Rory is an eighty-five-pound kicker on a visiting team. Then he pulls out his phone, unlocks it, and holds it out.

It's open to his call log, and every single entry—ten calls in the last two hours alone—are the same. Shara, Shara, Shara, Shara, Shara.

"Me and Ace drove around every square mile of False Beach looking for her yesterday," Smith says. "We checked everywhere she likes to go to see if maybe she was at the Cinemark on Houghton or Sonic or the park with all the magnolia trees by the Dick's Sporting Goods, and she wasn't at any of them. I was out there for *hours.* So, yeah. I care."

The look on Rory's face is a blinking cursor at the top of a blank Word document, so Chloe takes the opening.

"Then you need us," she tells Smith. "Obviously this is . . .

some kind of puzzle Shara set up for us, and we all have a piece of it. Once we solve it, we'll know where she is."

Smith finally breaks his glare at Rory to look at her.

"Where's *your* piece?"

"I'm working on it," Chloe grouses. "But there's no point in finding it if we can't all agree we're in this together."

Smith's attention snaps back to Rory. "You're cool with that?"

"Look, I don't want to give a shit about this, but I do," Rory says, having finally recovered. "If Shara keeps mentioning the three of us, it probably means we're all supposed to be here, so like, whatever. I'll do it."

"So will I," Chloe says. "Which means if you want to know where your girlfriend is, you gotta get over the fact that she kissed us. Like, quickly."

All around them, the rest of Willowgrove is filtering into first hour, and every single one of them takes a second to stare as they pass. Chloe Green, the one who scored a 35 on the ACT. Smith Parker, the saint who led Willowgrove to the state champ title two years in a row. And Rory Heron, best known for flooding the bio lab on purpose. The three of them occupying the same spot is ripping a hole in the Willowgrove space-time continuum.

Smith is visibly doing some mental calculations. It's obvious he and Rory would rather do just about anything than spend another second in each other's company, which means Chloe's life is about to be a nonstop tornado of egos, but she can deal with it as long as they get her to a fair victory. Like Willowgrove, it's a necessary evil.

"I'm in, I guess," Smith says. He glances sidelong at Chloe. "I get what Shara meant about you."

Chloe blinks. "What did she say about me?"

"Don't worry about it."

"Fine," Chloe says, definitely worrying about it. "If there's anything we need to know, like if she said or did anything unusual lately, you should tell me."

"Us," Rory corrects her.

"Us," Chloe agrees.

"The only thing lately," Smith says finally, "was that she kept saying she couldn't hang out because she had homework. She does that a lot, but it was like, a *lot* of homework. So, I guess . . . maybe she was doing something else."

"Did she seem . . . unhappy?" Chloe asks.

"It's hard to tell with Shara sometimes," Smith says. "Sometimes, she just like, dips. Like she won't respond to texts for a whole weekend, or she'll put her phone on airplane mode, no explanation, and two days later it's like nothing happened."

"And what do you do?" Rory asks. "When she dips?"

"I never had to do anything before," Smith says. "She always came back."

**Group Chat Including Chloe Green,**
**Smith Parker, and Rory Heron**

sending this to create the chat. please don't reply unless you have new SW info.

Smith
ok

Smith I literally said not to reply.

Smith

**sorry**

Chloe changed the name of the chat to "I Kissed Shara Wheeler"

Rory

Smith

**hell no**

Smith deleted the name of the chat

**idk why you're mad when it's factually accurate**

# FROM THE BURN PILE

Contents of one of Rory's tapes, unspooled.
Marked with a green sticker for "personal."

I kissed Shara Wheeler.

It went like this: I don't believe in prom as an institution, but it's still kind of morbidly fascinating, so I climbed out of my window to sit on the roof and watch everyone get out of their rented limos at the clubhouse across the golf course. And that's where she found me. She hiked up her dress, climbed the trellis by the dogwood tree onto the roof, said "hi," and then she kissed me. And then she was gone again.

It didn't exactly feel like the earth-shattering moment I always thought it would, mostly because I was just . . . confused.

I sat there and watched Smith pull up to her house the way I've watched him pull up to her house a million times since sophomore year, smiling so wide, I could see how white his teeth are from the roof. He took pictures with Shara in front of her house like nothing had even happened.

Brooklyn Bennett posted a passive-aggressive Instagram story this morning about how the student council spent half their prom budget on a balloon drop for a prom queen announcement that never happened. Jake saw Ace at Sonic and Ace said Smith told him that he went to get Shara's stuff from purse check, and she was gone before he got back to the dance floor. Everyone's heard about it by now. Nobody knows where she went, or why.

But I kissed her.

# 3

In her bedroom Tuesday afternoon, Chloe winds a silver chain around her finger and thinks of California.

Before freshman year, Chloe had only visited False Beach a few times. She always found it unbearable—no In-N-Out, no boba, only gas station Polar Pops and an Olive Garden with a two-hour wait on Fridays because it was the fanciest restaurant in town. (There have been rumors for years that a P.F. Chang's is coming, but Chloe still thinks that's a little too adventurous for False Beach.)

But when her grandma got sick and it was obvious she wasn't getting better, her mama gave up her spot in the cast of the LA Opera and Chloe gave up her middle school friends and her twice-weekly sashimi for False Beach. That was four years ago.

Four years since she asked a girl in freshman bio why the chapter on sexual reproduction was taped shut and met Georgia, a Willowgrove student since kindergarten. Three and a half years since she ditched her goth phase and Georgia started keeping their five-year post-Willowgrove plan posted up in her locker. This year, Chloe and Benjy finally bullied

Mr. Truman, the choir teacher, into choosing *Phantom* for the spring musical, and the two of them played Christine and Raoul, respectively.

And, it's been four years since Chloe walked into her first class at Willowgrove and saw the girl from that billboard seated in the front row, highlighters lined up neatly. By the end of the day, she had heard: (1) That's Shara Wheeler. (2) Shara Wheeler's dad is Principal Wheeler, the man enforcing Willowgrove's archaic rules. (3) Her family has more money than God. (4) Everyone—*everyone*—loves her.

Even Georgia, always unimpressed by Willowgrove in her own quiet way, said when Chloe asked that first week, "Yeah, honestly, Shara's cool."

Shara's *not* cool. California was cool. Living in a place where it didn't matter if everyone knew about her moms was cool. Shara is a vague mist of a person, checking all the right False Beach boxes so that everyone thinks they see a perfect girl in her place. What's cool about that?

(No, Chloe still hasn't found her own note from Shara. Yes, she has checked everywhere, including the pocket of the oxford that was pressed up against Shara's cotton polo when they kissed.)

Chloe drops the delicate chain back into the drawer and shuts it, glaring at the bathroom mirror. Why is she looking at the only person in town immune to Shara Wheeler?

"You are cursed with flawless judgment," Chloe says to her reflection.

In her room, she kicks a stack of college admissions booklets aside to reach her backpack. The hunt for her Shara note will have to wait for a couple of hours. She's got a date with her French 4 final project, a full essay about uprisings in France from 1789 to 1832, which is due in three weeks. Georgia's her partner.

"Mom, Titania ate my underwear again," Chloe says as she sweeps into the kitchen.

Chloe's mom, who is still wearing her work coveralls and shoving something enormous into the freezer, grunts out, "Sounds like a problem for someone who leaves their underwear on the floor, not me."

"That's the third pair this month. Can I have some money to go to Target tomorrow?"

Titania, the house cat in question, is perched on top of the refrigerator and surveying them both like a tiny panty-eating lord. She's tempestuous and vindictive and has been a part of the Green household almost as long as Chloe has. Chloe's moms like to blame her for Chloe's personality.

"Check the change jar," she says.

Chloe sighs and begins counting out quarters.

"What is that?" she asks, watching her mom rearrange frozen vegetables to make room for the mysterious icy bundle. "Did you kill someone?"

"Your *mother*," she says as she finally manages to cram the thing in, "has requested a Southern feast when she gets home from Portugal this weekend. A very specific one." She pats the hunk of meat once and turns to Chloe, a bit of short, dark hair falling over her forehead. She used to have Chloe help her dye it blue, but she's kept it natural since the move. "This, my child, is a turducken."

"You lost me at *turd*," Chloe says. "But continue."

"It's a chicken stuffed inside a duck stuffed inside a turkey."

"Where did you even get that?"

"I know a guy."

"That's . . . upsetting."

Her mom nods and shuts the freezer. "My wife is a woman of refinement."

Because Chloe and her mom were both miserable about the move, her West Coast mama resolved to be aggressively positive about discovering the South. She bought a red Bama shirt to wear in her vegetable garden and a matching set of houndstooth luggage for her work trips abroad. She even put up a framed photo of Dolly Parton on the kitchen windowsill. It's a whole thing.

But her favorite activity has been seeking out every possible Southern delicacy. Back home, the most Alabama thing about their kitchen was the pitcher of sweet tea Chloe's mom always kept in the fridge. Now, her mama has insisted on learning how to fry chicken thighs and green tomatoes, sampled each item on the Bojangles menu, and become a regular at every soul-food joint in town.

And apparently, she's going to make Chloe eat some kind of nightmare poultry matryoshka, which is even worse than when she roasted a chicken by shoving a can of Miller Lite up its ass.

"I'm gonna walk across that stage to get my diploma and keep walking until I hit a city with a Trader Joe's," Chloe says.

"Hey." Her mom folds her arms as she peers across the kitchen at her. "Is this normal baseline Chloe curmudgeon behavior, or are you cranky because you miss your mama? Is one mom not good enough for you?"

Chloe shrugs it off, gathering up her purse and keys from the table by the back door under one of her mama's abstract paintings of boobs. "I'm fine."

"Or is it whatever has been making you act weird since last week?"

"I'm *fine!*" Chloe snaps. "You try wearing bikini bottoms as underwear and see how pleasant you are!"

"Okay. But, you know. If you need to talk about anything.

Girls, boys, whatever. The end of senior year brings up a lot of emotions for everyone. I know you're—"

"Bye!" Chloe calls as she breaks for the door. If she slams it fast enough, she's sure the ghost of Shara can't follow.

It takes fifteen minutes to drive to the center of False Beach from Chloe's house, and absolutely nothing of consequence but a Dairy Queen is passed along the way.

What the locals call "downtown" is a single main street lined with historic redbrick buildings and two-story shops pressed up against one another with iron balconies and Southern small-town charm. It all leads up to a white courthouse, towering with cast-iron pillars and a wide town square at its feet, Civil War era. There used to be some ugly Confederate monument at the square's center, but two summers ago someone pulled it down in the middle of the night and rolled it into Lake Martin, which is the only cool thing that's ever happened in False Beach. Last year, the city council held a contest to choose a new town mascot and installed a bronze statue of the winner: a rearing deer with huge antlers named Bucky the Buck.

Chloe takes a left at the square and parks in front of Webster's Ice Cream right as the bell tower chimes five o'clock in the evening.

Belltower Books, so named because it sits inside the base of the tower, is pretty much the only place in False Beach worth being. It's small, only two cramped rooms plus a third that requires a climb up a ladder and special permission, with books piled high on every available surface, like the floor, or the shelf above the toilet, or the top of a terrarium containing a fat iguana. Every hour on the hour, the bell in the tower echoes through the walls of the store, rattling all the way down to the front desk, where Georgia's dad sits in his aviator glasses and listens to The Eagles.

She finds Georgia perched on the top of the ladder with a paperback, the bottom half of her uniform traded for rolled-up gray sweats and Tevas. The two of them look a lot alike—brown eyes, thick eyebrows, angular jaws—but Chloe's aesthetic is more dark academia and Georgia's is more back-packing granola baby butch. They even have almost the same short, dark hair, but Chloe has blunt, decisive bangs, while Georgia doesn't care who sees her forehead.

Georgia is the kind of person who enters a room like she's stepped inside it a thousand times, knows where everything is, including the exits, and isn't worried that anything could have possibly changed since the last time she was there. She's too tall to look small, too gentle to be imposing, too smart in ways that have nothing to do with chemical formulas or antiderivatives to care about her GPA. One time, in their creative writing elective, Chloe was assigned to describe a person with one word. She chose Georgia and described her as "sturdy," like a tree, or a house.

It's a miracle that someone like Georgia coalesced from the primordial ooze of Alabama. Life would be unbearable without her.

Chloe reaches up and taps twice on the side of Georgia's ankle. "Whatcha readin'?"

Georgia flashes the cover without looking up from the page: *Emma*.

"Austen? *Again?*"

"Look." Georgia sighs, apparently finished with the passage she was on. She never speaks when she's mid-passage. "I tried one of those literary contemporaries Val suggested—"

"Please don't call my mom *Val*."

"—and the thing about books these days is, a lot of them are just not that good."

"And yet you want to write a book these days."

"The trick is," Georgia says, shutting her book, "I will simply write a good one."

"I don't get the Austen thing with you," Chloe says as Georgia slips between the rungs of the ladder to the shag rug below. "I always found Emma annoying."

"The book or the character?"

"The character. The book is fine."

Georgia leads the way to the front desk, announced by the echoing clangs of the water bottle she always carries as it collides with bookshelves and chairs. Georgia's mom waves from across the store, headphones on as she does inventory.

"Why is Emma annoying?" Georgia asks.

"Because she's manipulative," Chloe says. "I don't think she really makes up for everything she does to everyone else by the end."

"The point of the book isn't for her to make everything right. It's for her to be interesting," Georgia says, slipping behind the desk for her things. "And I think she is—she's this girl trapped in the same place she was born, so bored with what she's been given that she has to play around with people's lives to entertain herself. It's a good character."

"Sure, okay."

"Also, it's romantic. 'If I loved you less, I might be able to talk about it more.' Best line in Austen's entire body of work. And I've read them *all*, Chloe."

"How many of them have you read?" Chloe deadpans.

*"All of them."*

Chloe laughs, eyeing the books behind the counter.

"Anything new in the ol' CMFC?"

While Georgia rereads Regency classics, Chloe's favorite stories are the ones where the headstrong young woman on a cinematic journey to master her powers falls for the monster who's been antagonizing her all along. Georgia knows this, so she curates a stack of books behind the counter for Chloe and adds to it every time they get something Chloe might like. She affectionately calls it Chloe's Monster Fucker Collection.

"One," Georgia says. She plucks a battered paperback off the top of the stack—one of those '80s high fantasies with a loinclothed, mulleted elf on the cover. Her mama has a million. "Fairy princess on a heroic quest ravished by evil elf mercenary. Straight though."

Chloe sighs. "Thanks, but I'm maxed out on male villains for the month," she says.

"Thought so," Georgia says. She chucks it toward a box of secondhand books to be shelved. "Still on the hunt for the megabitch of your dreams."

"It doesn't *have* to be an evil queen," she says. "It's just *preferred*."

While she does like boys, she generally finds the traits of a compelling villain—arrogance, malice, an angsty backstory—tedious in a man. Like, what do hot guys with long dark hair even have to be that upset about? Get a clarifying shampoo and suck it up, Kylo Ren. So your rich parents sent you to magic camp and you didn't make any friends. Big deal.

"If the girl's going to end up with a dude who's a monster," Chloe says, "it needs to be—"

"Phantom," Georgia finishes for her as they head outside, because she's heard it five hundred thousand times.

"Monster on the outside, but on the inside, he cares about her career goals!" Chloe says. "Call me old-fashioned, but a man's place is in the basement, preparing vocal exercises for his more talented wife."

"You are as insane as the day I met you," Georgia says. "All I want is a nice girlfriend in a cottage where we have philosophical conversations over scones or something."

"And I support you," Chloe says, "in making that your retirement plan when you're like, thirty and tired of living in New York with me."

"Thanks so much," Georgia says, sliding into the passenger seat. "God, I'm starving."

"Same," says Chloe, whose appetite has made a quick turnaround from turduckens.

"Taco Bell?" Georgia says, like always.

"God, my left boob for a Shake Shack," Chloe says as she cranks up the engine. "This town is so depressing. I bet nobody in city limits other than you, me, and our parents even knows who Jane Austen is."

"My parents have kept a bookstore open here for twenty years, so I'm pretty sure the average False Beach resident isn't *that* illiterate," Georgia points out. "You know, Shara Wheeler came in for *Emma* a couple months ago."

"Ew."

"I can say her name. She's not Beetlejuice."

"She's not," Chloe agrees. "She's worse."

In terms of popular after-school locations for social gatherings, the Taco Bell three minutes from campus is Willowgrove's Met Gala. It's where you go to see and be seen. It's where every sophomore gets their first after-school drive-thru when they score their license. Last fall, Summer Collins and Ace Torres were rumored to have had an explosive breakup in the parking lot that ended in a Baja Blast to the face.

It also means that about half the part-time staff is composed of Willowgrove students whose parents forced them to get a job. The drive-thru cashier on Tuesday nights is a Willowgrove junior named Tyler Miller with a tragic haircut and a trombone on lease from the school. Taco Bell has been Chloe's Tuesday night tradition with Georgia ever since last summer, when her mom fixed the engine on her old car and handed over the keys, so she's spoken to Tyler more times through a crackly speaker than she has on campus.

When she pulls up to the window, he nearly fumbles her change.

"Um, hang on," he says after passing over her order. "There's something else."

The window shuts.

She shoots a confused look at Georgia, who checks the bag, then shakes her head and shrugs.

The window reopens, and Tyler clumsily hands something over.

"I'm, um, supposed to give this to you."

It's a sealed envelope. A pink one.

Sirens wailing in her head, she snatches the card and flips it over. Her name is written on the front. She stares down at it: the gentle arcs of the *H,* the perfect loop of the *O.*

She whips back to Tyler. "You couldn't have given it to me at school?"

"I—she—she brought it here last week and told me specifically to give it to you the next time you came through the drive-thru," he says.

"Who did?" Chloe demands.

His voice comes out shaky when he says it, like it's the name of an angel, "*Shara Wheeler.*"

"And you just *did it*?"

"That's the first time Shara Wheeler has ever spoken to me in my life," he tells her dreamily. "I didn't even think she knew I existed."

"Oh my God," Chloe says, and she slams on the gas.

Chloe,
Your mom graduated Willowgrove with my parents. You know that, right? I remember them talking about it at the dinner table the summer after eighth grade.

"I heard Valerie Green is moving back. Remember, she got suspended for coming to school with blue hair? She's married to a woman now. They want to send their daughter to Willowgrove."

Before your first day, I took the file out of my dad's office. Saw your entrance exam. You did pretty well, huh?

I've been curious about you since before I met you, but the way things work at Willowgrove, I never could get close enough to figure you out.

High school's almost over. Now or never, right?

XOXO

Shara Wheeler

P.S. turtledove316@gmail.com

Rory finally picks up on the fourth try.

"For what possible reason are you calling me?"

"Where are you?" Chloe demands, throwing a taco wrapper into the bag. She called him as soon as she dropped Georgia off at Belltower with a flimsy excuse, right after she heard back from Smith.

"I'm . . . at my friend's house?"

"Which friend?"

"Jake."

"Who's Jake?"

"Uh, Jake Stone?"

"Stone the Stoner?" She knows him—well, knows of him. Benjy almost got suspended once for happening to be in the boys' bathroom when Jake was caught vaping in there. Stringy blond hair, unpopular lo-fi SoundCloud music, future owner of a neck tattoo. "Okay, good, then you're not far from your house."

"How do you know where Jake lives?"

"Benjy lives on his street," Chloe says impatiently. "False Beach really isn't that big. Anyway, I'm on my way to your house, and so is Smith."

She can practically hear Rory's eyes go wide over the phone. *"Why?"*

"Because I'm absolutely dying to play a few holes of golf," she says. "I got my Shara note, obviously."

"Where?"

"Don't worry about it," she snaps. She cuts a sharp left, waving off a guy in a truck who honks at her.

"Why do we have to meet at my house?"

"Because it's equidistant from Belltower and Smith's house," Chloe says. "She gave me an email address. I think that thing from your note is the password. Now can you please call the front gate for me? My car is a piece of crap and the mall cops are gonna be suspicious."

"Okay, okay, Jesus, I'll meet you there."

She hangs up and chucks her phone into the empty passenger seat.

She can't believe Shara didn't give her a puzzle of her own to solve. Smith got a secret code, and Rory got a hint about the open window, but Chloe didn't even get a *chance* to prove she's smarter than whatever stupid riddle Shara could come up with for her. Her note was literally handed to her. It's *insulting.*

She'll come back to what was actually *in* the letter later, and the small silver key she found in the envelope. What the hell could it even be a key to?

When she parks outside Rory's house, hers is the only car on the street. Smith is leaning against the mailbox, staring across the driveway at Shara's house like she might pop out of the bushes any second. Rory arrives next, annoyed and surly in some kind of vintage '80s convertible in cherry red.

"Are your parents home?" she asks him.

He brushes past her to unlock the door. "Does it matter?"

"I mean, I'm not the one who'd have to explain this to them."

Rory shrugs. "My mom and stepdad are in Italy for the week."

"Casual," Smith comments under his breath.

Rory's house is nice, technically. Like an HGTV special on all the different ways to interpret beige. It reminds her of shopping for houses with her moms and walking into an open house where everything had been staged so obviously that you could tell no one actually lived there. But this is a lived-in version, complete with a wedding picture above the fireplace: two smiling middle-aged white people and a bored kid that could be Rory from five years ago.

"Where's your computer?" Chloe asks.

Rory glares at her from beside a vase of artificial hay. "In my room."

"Okay."

She's halfway to the second floor before she hears Smith behind her, followed finally by Rory. Upstairs, she doesn't need to guess Rory's bedroom door—there's one with a stolen stop sign affixed to it, and Rory's friends are known for their pastimes of leaning moodily against brick walls and low-level vandalism. She lets herself in.

If all the color has been drained out of the rest of the house, Rory's room is where it went. The shelves are stuffed with action figures, the double bed covered in a deep-purple bedspread and discarded flannels, the walls plastered with prints of weird abstract art. Beside a tower of red Vans sneaker boxes, there's a Leon Bridges tour poster and a turntable on a cabinet spilling vinyl records onto the carpet. She recognizes a few of the sleeves from the music curriculum her mama enforced growing up: Prince, Jimi Hendrix, B. B. King.

Under a dogwood-shaded window, there's a desk with a silver MacBook and an analog tape recorder with a pile of color-coded tapes, surrounded by a scattering of guitar picks and coiled guitar string. All the actual guitars are up a ladder in a lofted sitting area full of bean bags—and damn, those are a lot of really expensive guitars. One entire wall is painted with black chalkboard paint and covered in sketches and notes from friends. Chloe counts at least three different hand-drawn penises.

A bulletin board is hung over the dresser, bursting with photos and scraps and ticket stubs. She can see a shot of Rory laughing at a concert with a handsome salt-and-pepper-bearded Black man who must be his dad, and another with a college-aged guy sporting a Morehouse College sweatshirt, tied-up locs, and the exact same hazel eyes as Rory. There are a bunch of cards signed DAD, the kind of two-line note you include in a care package that says more than a letter could. It's weird to see so many pictures of Rory smiling, especially when real-life Rory is scowling three feet away.

"How many street signs have you stolen?" Smith asks, eyeing the collection of metal in the corner by the desk.

"More than this. Jake has some at his house." He must see judgment when he glances at Smith, because he rolls his eyes. "Chill. We only steal the signs of things named after some old racist. It's not my fault that's all of them here."

"This is . . ." Smith says, craning his head to get a better look at the sparkly red Stratocaster up in the loft. "Dope."

It is, admittedly, a cool room, the way Rory's car is admittedly a cool car.

Rory leans against the ladder and shrugs. "Don't sound so surprised."

"I'm not *surprised*," Smith says, immediately on the defensive, "I'm just *saying*."

"I don't need your opinion."

"No, just my girlfriend's, apparently."

"You're mad because you're finally having to confront the fact that being a big deal in high school isn't gonna get you whatever you want forever."

"I'm pretty sure I'm mad because my girlfriend cheated on me with you."

"Maybe there's something I have that you don't."

"What, a rich stepdad and a house in the country club?"

"More like taste," Rory says. "Interests. The ability to care about things that aren't jock itch."

"Yeah, it's probably that delightful personality of yours, man."

Chloe squeezes her eyes shut and tries, as hard as she can, to remember why exactly she's subjecting herself to this shit-show.

An image immediately fills her mind: Shara with her brand-new-lip-gloss smile, leaning across the counter to give Tyler Miller a pink envelope. Shara putting everything in place to show Chloe she was already ten steps ahead, that she guessed Chloe's exact moves before Chloe had even caught her scent.

"Okay!" Chloe snaps, and Smith and Rory pause midroast, mouths still open. "Hello! I *also* kissed Shara—which both of you seem to keep forgetting about—and I, personally, would like to know why, so can we please do what we came here to do?"

After a pause, Smith is the first to grumble, "Okay." Rory makes a sound like his molars are stuck together.

"Rory," Chloe says briskly, "what's the password?"

He gives her a hearty glower, then extracts a Moleskine from the mess on his desk and lets it fall open to the center, where a pink card has been tucked.

"Thank you," Chloe says. When she reaches for it, she glances down at the pages around it, which are covered in jagged, handwritten lines. Some of the words look like they might rhyme at the end. "Oh my God, you *do* write sad poems about Shara."

"Don't look at those!" Rory says, snapping the notebook shut.

"I wanna see," Smith says, craning his neck for a better look.

"Fuck both of y'all," Rory grumbles. "Chloe, *you're* the one who just told us to focus."

"Right," she concedes. She drops into the chair at Rory's desk, opening his laptop and laying out her card next to Rory's. She can sense Smith hovering behind her. He's probably reading what Shara wrote to her. Good. She's tired of being the only one who knows Shara isn't who she pretends she is.

"Hey, wait—" Rory starts as she opens up a browser window.

"Don't worry, I'm not gonna look through your search history," Chloe says, pulling up Gmail and typing in the email address from her note. "I can guess."

Smith and Rory crowd together, leaning in to watch Chloe finish pounding out the password. She hears the soft thump of Rory elbowing Smith in the ribs and pretending it was an accident.

There's nothing in the inbox when it loads, not even a promo email in the spam folder.

"The drafts," Smith recites. "Check the drafts."

There's one email in the drafts folder, unsent. The subject line says, *BRB*.

Chloe sucks in a breath as she clicks it open.

> Hi,
> This is Shara. Of course it's Shara. You already know that.
>> I had to leave. I promise it'll make sense soon.
>> I'm sorry I haven't told any of you how I really feel about you. I'm still not sure how. This is the only way I could think of.
>
> XOXO
> Shara
>
>> P.S. Chloe, the next card is for you. It's somewhere you go almost every day. Until then, you're keeping your vows, and I'm hiding in the brakes.

"What is this?" Rory asks. "This—this doesn't explain anything."

"A clue," Smith says. "The postscript is another clue."

"How do you know?"

"Because this is what Shara does," he says. "It's like . . . little hints. She can't just let you in. You have to figure out your way there."

"So, she wants us to find her?"

"I think so. It sounds like Chloe has to do it."

"Chloe?"

"Chloe, do you know what it means?"

Chloe can hear their voices overlapping, struggling to get her attention, but she can barely make out the words through the ringing in her ears, growing louder and louder the more she imagines Shara sitting at her dainty little vanity and typing out her smug little email and knowing she could get Chloe to read it. That she could lay out all the pretty pieces of a puzzle and have the three of them fighting over who would get to put it together first.

Of course. *Of course* Shara gave her this instead of an explanation. *Of course* Shara cast herself as the main character of her own personal John Green novel. And now the rest of them are supposed to be happy getting shuffled around like stupid little chess pieces, because Shara kissed them, and it's her board.

The problem is, Shara counted on Chloe being like Smith and Rory and everyone else at Willowgrove, waiting for her to notice them and magically make them interesting or smart or cool. Chloe knows better. She's kissed Shara Wheeler, and it changed absolutely nothing.

She pushes away from the desk and storms out, ignoring Smith's confused shout after her.

She's going to beat Shara at her own game. And then she's going to destroy her for it.

# FROM THE BURN PILE

WILLOWGROVE CHRISTIAN ACADEMY
CODE OF CONDUCT

Issued to: Chloe Green

First page of manual torn out and
replaced with a sheet of loose-leaf paper
covered in handwriting

1. All students must be capital-S Saved.

2. If not capital-S Saved, you must accept responsibility for any and all smear campaigns against your character, probably led by Emma Grace Baker (i.e., "I heard Chloe Green isn't Saved, I'm praying for her.").

3. No student may smoke, drink, dance, or have sex, which means half the students are smoking, drinking, dancing, having sex, and lying about it. Pills are fine. If you're on the football team, just ask Emma Grace's dad to write you a prescription.

4. Technically, since dancing is Sinful and Horny (same thing), there is no Willowgrove Christian Academy Homecoming Dance or Willowgrove Christian Academy Prom. There is, however, a prom hosted by a group of Willowgrove parents and unaffiliated with the school, which everyone attends at an off-site location.

5. Love God first, love Shara Wheeler second.

# 4

Sometimes, when Chloe is stressed, she pictures herself in another life.

Not as somebody else. She imagines herself in a universe where she gets to be cool and super hot and everybody appreciates how capable and smart she is, like if she were a vampire hunter in Edwardian England. It's a coping strategy, okay?

She tries to calm down as she drives to school by imagining herself at a fancy banquet, whipping up silk skirts to reveal a dagger strapped to her thigh before she flicks it across the room, straight into the wall an inch from vampire Shara's face.

It doesn't work; she pulls into the student parking lot in what her mama likes to call "an absolutely foul mood." Ash is late, as usual, but Georgia and Benjy are already there, leaning up against the fender of Benjy's Mustang. They carpool, since Georgia's parents can't afford to get her a car.

"You look like something crawled up your ass," Benjy tells Chloe when she slams her car door behind her.

"This should help," Georgia says. She hands over Chloe's usual Starbucks order: iced matcha latte with two pumps of brown sugar syrup and one pump of vanilla. The closest False Beach will ever get to boba. She takes a long sip, but it does nothing about the five hundred screeching bats inside her brain, all named Shara Wheeler.

When she glances up, Georgia is studying her face, and Chloe forces a smile. She's not eager to explain what happened after the Taco Bell drive-thru last night, and the angrier she acts, the sooner Georgia is going to ask.

All her friends know how she feels about Shara. Benjy was in honors world history when Chloe and Shara both chose Anne Boleyn for their midterm presentation and Shara scored five points higher by passing out homemade rose marchpane cookies like a Tudor tooth fairy. Ash let Chloe practically squeeze the bones in their hand to dust when Shara got called up in chapel as Junior Class Student of the Year, an award for which Chloe was disqualified due to "personal conduct." It's kind of a running joke among the four of them: Chloe and her bitter nemesis, a perfectly nice girl they all like.

If she told the rest of her friends about the kiss—which she won't, because of her complicated feelings on Shara's privacy—they'd probably throw her a Kissed the Hottest Girl in School party, which would make her want to die. And if they knew about the clues, they'd flame her in the group chat for letting herself get sucked into Shara's deranged side quest, which would make her want to kill them. So, keeping things to herself is for everyone's safety.

"Any news on the roommate front yet?" Chloe asks, knowing it's a safe bet to change the subject. Benjy and Ash are going to Bama and RISD, respectively. Ash is sharing their dorm room with an internet friend they met in a free Catboy company on their *Final Fantasy XIV* server, but Benjy is still waiting to hear what type of guy he's been stuck with.

Benjy takes the bait. "Not yet. My new fear is that he'll be a hot straight guy. I cannot spend my first year away from home with an unrequited crush on a guy who wears neckties to football games."

"Maybe he'll have cute friends," Chloe suggests.

"I don't have high hopes for the gays of Tuscaloosa," Benjy says.

"It's gonna be great," Georgia says. "You'll either meet a guy who owns five seersucker suits or a guy who wants to drive you around on the back of his ATV, and either way, you get to have a whirlwind romance under a dramatic canopy of oak trees."

"Are you gonna write me a coming-of-age movie or what?" Benjy asks her. "I'm ready to put Timothée Chalamet out of work."

"Sorry, I don't do screenplays," Georgia says, taking a swig from her water bottle.

"Did y'all apply for your cool NYU apartment yet?" Benjy asks them.

Chloe nods. "We don't get assigned until July though. I'm just glad I don't have to live with a random."

"Uh-huh," Georgia hums.

"I—" Benjy starts, but he cuts himself off. A black Jeep has parked three spots down, and Benjy tries to turn a glare into a polite smile as Ace Torres climbs out. Ace spots them and offers his trademark shit-eating grin.

"Hey, Benjy!" he says with a wave. "Chloe, Jessica."

He lumbers cheerfully off toward the courtyard where the jocks congregate before school, whistling to himself.

"Three months," Georgia says, gesturing with her water

bottle, which clangs against Benjy's headlight. "For three entire months, I was stage manager and he was Phantom, and he still can't bother to learn my name."

Benjy releases a sigh like the bearer of a centuries-old feud. "What do you think goes on in that head?"

"I always picture a cute little hamster running on a wheel," Chloe says.

"But it's wearing an itty-bitty letterman jacket," Benjy adds.

Georgia asks, "What did the hamster letter in?"

"Javelin," Benjy says. "I'm surprised he remembers *my* name. God forbid people think we're friends."

"Do you *want* to be friends with Ace Torres?"

"No," Benjy says haughtily. "I'm just saying; it's one thing to steal a role that doesn't belong to you"—here, he pauses to emphasize that *he's* the one who deserved the role—"and it's something else to steal it and then act like it never happened."

Chloe watches as Ace enters the courtyard and pulls Smith into one of those bizarre, sideways bro-hugs. Because *of course* Ace's best friend is Smith Parker, which means Smith came to the matinee performance of *Phantom* last month, which means he brought Shara, which means Chloe had to do an entire show pretending not to notice Shara front and center with her judgy face and shiny hair and—

She doesn't realize how hard she's squeezing her matcha until the lid pops off.

The bell rings, and Chloe shrugs off another look from Georgia and leads the way to B Building. They split at the double doors—Georgia's first hour is calculus, Benjy's is history—and Chloe heads straight down the hall to Mrs. Farley's AP Lit classroom.

By the girls' bathroom, Mrs. Sherman is at her usual post,

permed and scrutinizing passing students like the Eye of Sauron but with clumpy mascara. Chloe waves with the tips of her fingers as she passes, making sure Mrs. Sherman gets a good, long look at her nonregulation black nail polish. That should do it.

In her seat, second row center, she pulls out her binder and sets it on the smooth, cool surface, then lays out all three of the novels they've been discussing, one on top of the other so their spines form a pleasing column. Almost enough to distract from Shara's empty seat in front of hers.

Every morning of the past year, she's deliberately beaten Shara to Mrs. Farley's class. She figured out early on that English is Shara's best subject, which means every bit of extra credit counts. If she can get an additional 0.5 percent participation grade from being two minutes earlier, she's going to. She is not repeating the junior year travesty of losing her lead in Ms. Rodkey's class by a single point.

And because she's always in her seat before Shara, she always has to watch what happens when Shara enters a room.

There's this stupid thing that people always say about girls in murder documentaries. *She lit up a room when she walked in.* Chloe used to think it was what people said to make someone sound better when they felt bad about what happened to them, or maybe a trick of the brain, a misinterpretation of the glow a person takes on in your memory once they're gone.

But then she met Shara, who glides into every room like she's on a parade float, beaming and waving and tossing her hair. Every morning, Shara walks into Mrs. Farley's class, and every morning, people stop what they're doing to see what shade of lip gloss she's wearing that day. It's the same whispery feeling that fills a room when a teacher announces it's movie day, and every time it happens, Chloe feels like the only one who'd rather be talking about last night's homework than watching *The Crucible*.

Today, though, the seat in front of hers never fills.

With five minutes to go in the period, she checks the clock over the whiteboard, then shuts her binder and packs it up.

To her left, Brooklyn Bennett leans over and whispers, "What are you doing?"

Nobody loves rules like Brooklyn, student body president, head of the debate team and Model UN, editor in chief of the yearbook—basically a list of extracurriculars with a skirt on. Chloe has to admire her fanatical tunnel vision, but if *she's* high-strung, Brooklyn Bennett is a $20,000 viola.

"Chill, Brooklyn," Chloe whispers back. "I'm getting out early."

"Why?"

"You'll see," Chloe says. "Any minute now—"

Right on cue, the intercom sounds.

"Chloe Green, please come to the office. Chloe Green to the office, please."

Brooklyn stares at her. Chloe shrugs, picks up her bag, and waves goodbye to Mrs. Farley.

It's gone like this once a week since sophomore year: She gets dress coded and winds up in Principal Wheeler's office getting lectured on the importance of "respecting guidelines set in place to minimize distractions in the classroom" by the end of first hour.

Freshman year, she adjusted to Willowgrove by making problems on purpose, but nobody showed up to her GSA meeting, and she got suspended for bringing free condoms to school in protest of the abstinence-only sex ed policy. The lesson she learned: Nobody at Willowgrove actually wants

anyt...
wonderful change, not eve...
out until after grad and a...
minds, it wasn't worth jea...
an expulsion.

So, since then, she's settled...
platforms taller than one inch, socks th...
knee but below the hem of her skirt, pentagra...
dered into the collars of her oxfords, dark li...
year, Ash got famous on TikTok for making ea...
of everything they could find, and now Chloe...
rotation of gummy worms and hot sauce packets...pre-
served fruit slices to dangle from her earlobes. Just enough
to push back.

It's a track record that made it too easy to get Mrs. Sherman to report her this morning. When a beautiful, blond
small-town princess disappears, surely a full-scale FBI man-
hunt led by Wheeler himself must follow. Screw the cards,
screw the key—the fastest shortcut to Shara is to know what
they know, and the fastest way to do that is to get herself into
the principal's office.

On the way, she pops into the bathroom by the chem lab
to check her reflection.

Sophomore year, she stopped here before chem every day
to tidy up her makeup and shake out her hair. She was stuck
with Shara as a lab partner fall semester, and random classmates were always coming up to their lab table with pathetic
excuses—like, no, Tanner, Shara doesn't have time to help
you with step five. Chloe started touching up before class in
self-defense.

Sophomore year was also the one time it appeared possible that she and Shara could be friends.

...ond semester, after Shara ...t Chloe still sat
...y weren't lab partners any... ...all-time best subject—
...ara in precalc. It wasn't ... ...
...ly had to work for ... ...ninety-eight average. One day,
...t a test back with her answer to a conic sections problem
...sed out in red. Shara turned around and confided that
...d missed the same one.

The next day, Shara asked if she'd had a hard time with
... homework, and then Chloe became the person Shara
...ked to in the few minutes before class. For the first time,
...e got a glimpse of what other people must see when they
look at Shara. It was easy to look into those round, innocent
eyes and infer kindness when there was nothing else there.

Until a Friday morning, when they were supposed to be
reviewing their own midterm study guides and Shara asked,
"Do you get number seven?"

She scanned the problem—a question about finding the
length of the latus rectum of a parabola, which was exactly
the concept she'd spent an hour the night before trying to
nail.

"You, um," she said, "you have to find the equation of directrix first."

"Are you sure?" Shara said. "Can you show me?"

Shara leaned over Chloe's scratch sheet with her pencil,
hair falling over her shoulder, and she followed Chloe's suggestions until she started doing something backward and
Chloe grabbed her wrist to stop her.

Her thumb pressed into the soft flesh on the inside of
Shara's wrist, just below the palm. She could feel Shara's pulse
racing.

Shara shook her off, but it was enough for Chloe to figure out what was going on. She was lying. She'd known since freshman year that Shara was a liar, but in a few weeks, she'd managed to forget.

Chloe looked up from the paper and said, "You already know how to do this, don't you?"

When Shara met her eyes, their faces were inches apart. She didn't flinch. "Do you?"

"Of course I do."

"Then show me." Shara's face was smooth and unreadable, except for the incremental raise of her left eyebrow, which said, *prove it*.

That's what the popular kids at Willowgrove do: They pretend to be your friend for a chance to make you look stupid. She must have noticed what Chloe was struggling with and decided to rub it in her face.

Chloe snatched the paper out from under Shara's hands and told her to figure it out herself, and that was the end of that.

Now, Chloe finishes straightening her collar and heads to the principal's office.

She winks at the receptionist, Mrs. Bailey, as she signs in. Mrs. Bailey shakes her head in that familiar way, like, what a shame that such a brilliant student can't also be a nice, polite, straight young lady.

What's the point? They have Shara for that.

"Wheeler, man, you already know what's up," a gratingly familiar voice says from the short hall that connects the principal's office to reception. "But hey, I'll talk to you later, okay?"

Out strolls the poster boy for thick-necked, hot-ugly football players: prom king Dixon Wells. He flashes a flirtatious smile at Mrs. Bailey. Why are popular guys allowed to wander around during class like they're friends with all the teachers?

"See you later, my lady love."

"*Oh, stop it, Dixon,*" she says in a high-pitched voice that suggests she doesn't want him to stop at all. She turns to Chloe and drops her voice an octave. "You can go on back, sweetie."

Chloe takes her seat in Mr. Wheeler's office, a small room with all the trappings of a Good Old Alabama Boy: mounted trout, wraparound Oakley sunglasses with camo Croakies on the bookshelf, photos of himself as a Willowgrove senior in his football uniform. He was quarterback of the Wolves' first state champ team, and it's still his proudest accomplishment twenty-five years later. That and telling teenagers they're going to hell.

She knows the office well enough that if there's anything out of place, anything that would point to where Shara's gone or if she's even gone at all, Chloe will spot it.

"Chloe Green," a deep voice drawls.

Mr. Wheeler looks the same as usual, all chin and beach tan like he should be giving fishing tours on a fifty-foot yacht. He drops a pile of folders on his desk and takes a seat in his creaky leather chair.

"Mr. Wheeler," Chloe says back.

"I was hoping to see you in here less now that you've almost graduated."

"You know, I actually think I might miss our weekly meetings," she says. "What can I help you with this time? Ready to finally update the English curriculum? I have a lot of ideas."

He stares calmly back at her. Mouthing off at Wheeler isn't even that fun because he never gets that angry, unlike Mrs. Sherman, who Chloe will probably send into cardiac arrest one day. Wheeler just looks tired.

"I'm glad you have a sense of humor."

"Only got a few more weeks to use up the rest of my material."

"You know," Mr. Wheeler says, "people aren't going to give you as many chances as I do out there in the real world. You should remember that."

"Sure," Chloe says. He's said it nearly every time she's been in here, but if she's learned anything from her mom, it's that the real world is where people who hate high school go to be happy. "So, what's the infraction this time?"

"You already know," he says. "Mrs. Sherman said you were practically showing off your nail polish to her."

"I thought she might like it."

Wheeler sighs, rubbing his brows with his thumb and forefinger. "Why do you keep doing this, Chloe?"

"You seem stressed," Chloe says, seeing an opening. "Any particular reason?"

"Excuse me?"

"Just, you know," she says. "I noticed Shara wasn't in first hour today."

She's not sure what she expected, but it's certainly not the way Wheeler chuckles.

"Rumors going around already, huh?" He takes out a sticky note and jots down *sermon on gossip*. "You know, you try your best to lead your flock, but sometimes they wander right to the cliff anyway."

"What does that mean?"

"It means that gossip is against God's will, and so is lying," Wheeler says, putting his pen down. He shakes his head, offering Chloe a white-toothed smile. "Shara's visiting family. That's all. I hate to disappoint y'all, but there's really no story here."

It's a good lie, and he's good at delivering it, which isn't surprising, since he spends his whole life telling students God cares about spaghetti straps. It's almost believable.

"It's not gossip as long as it's for a prayer chain," Chloe says. "What family? Do they live here?"

There's a pause a millisecond too long, and she sees something flash in his eyes the way she has a few times before, when she catches a crack in his fake geniality—something like contempt, or maybe even fear. She swears she's seen it once in Shara's eyes, too, that day in precalc. That's okay. She's spent a long time converting that into energy. She's like a plant that's learned to photosynthesize spite.

"Look, Chloe," he says. "I'm gonna level with you. You get away with more than most people could get away with at this school. Do you know why that is?"

She thinks, *Because you can't afford to expel the example of academic excellence that you dangle in front of parents of prospective students for tuition money, and you need a new pool.*

She says, "No, I don't."

"Because you have potential, Chloe. You are an exceptional student. You set the curve in all your classes. You work harder than almost any student I've ever seen at this school." He leans back in his chair, springs groaning ominously. "And I would hate to see all of that go to waste because of the choices you make between now and graduation."

She presses the toes of her shoes into the floor. She's pretty sure that's a threat to not dig any deeper.

"Am I getting detention?" she asks in the politest tone she can manage.

Wheeler considers this. Chloe stares at the framed photo on the desk: Mr. Wheeler and his beautiful wife and daughter in white linen and khakis, smiling up from the deck of a sailboat with the name *Graduation* etched in cursive on the stern.

Chloe wants to pinch Shara's little blond two-dimensional head off.

"Not this time," Wheeler says. "You're free to go."

"Thanks," she says, and she leaves without looking back.

She got what she came for though. When Wheeler took out his Post-its, he jostled the stack of folders on his desk, and Chloe saw the corner of a pink card peeking out. Shara's stationery.

Shara left her parents a note, just like the rest of them.

She really is gone, and not even Wheeler knows where she is.

# FROM THE BURN PILE

Personal essay exercise: Smith Parker
Prompt: What is a moment in your life
      that you felt truly yourself?

When I was twelve, I threw my first real touchdown pass. My dad used to take me out in the backyard and tell me I could have one lap around the yard on his shoulders for every time I got the football through the tire he hung from our tree. The summer before third grade, we had to come up with a new system, because I was getting so good, he almost threw out his back. Dad played football at Bama, but he never got to start.

I love football because I love football, but I also love football because my dad loves football, and I love my dad.

That day, at the end of the second quarter, right before halftime, I threw a perfect pass to Ben Berkshire, right at the one yard line, and he scored.

I'll never forget the way Dad jumped out of his seat or the look on my mom's face or how much my little sister, Jas, cheered for me even though she didn't understand the game. I barely remember the rest of the game—the next thing that stands out is the bacon cheeseburger Dad bought me on the drive home. But the way the leather felt against my fingers when I let it fly? That was the first time I knew what I wanted to be.

# 5

Chloe enters the choir room for lunch with a peanut butter sandwich in her lunch bag and murder in her heart.

Today, she's greeted by the sight of Benjy, one foot planted on the scuffed tile floor and one pointed over his head, gripping his leg with his left hand, which would be startling if it weren't such a classic Benjy ambush. Being friends with him is like being friends with a very loud pretzel.

Chloe dumps her backpack on the floor while Georgia claims a seat on the risers next to Ash, who's hunched over their sketch pad with a charcoal pencil, squinting at Benjy.

"Business or pleasure, Ash?" Chloe asks.

"Final art portfolio," Ash answers, blending a line so vigorously that their dangly Dorito earring almost falls out. "I'm short two figure drawings."

"I thought she was going to let you sub in that painting series you did of lizards that came to you in a dream," Georgia says.

"She changed her mind. Apparently it was 'disturbing' and 'something to be discussed with my parents,'" they say with a shrug. "Benjy, can you move your head like, fifteen degrees to the right, but your nose five degrees to the left?"

"I can't move my nose independently of my face, Ash."

"You can try."

"My leg is tired," Benjy whines.

"Chloe?" Ash prompts.

Chloe nods. "I got it."

She reaches up and grabs Benjy's ankle to prop it up, and he grunts in relief. Between dance and all his shifts roller-skating at Sonic, Benjy is freaky strong for his size, but even he has his limits.

When Chloe first met Benjy, he was sort of the pet of the senior musical theater girls, always carted around by his older sister to rehearsals like a poodle in a handbag. But *they're* the seniors now, and things are different. Being super talented exempts him from a certain amount of bullying, but the order of Willowgrove operations states that being super gay, even if you haven't actually *told* anyone that you are, cancels a lot of that out. These days, he mostly gets harassed by fake-friendly jocks in the hallways to do eight-counts on command. Chloe can't wait for those guys' future girlfriends to drag them to see Benjy on Broadway one day.

"*Anyway*," Benjy says, "as I was saying before, the whole thing is kind of a vibe."

"What whole thing?" Georgia asks, unpacking a Tupperware of spaghetti from her backpack.

"The Shara Wheeler thing," Benjy says. "I mean, it's been days, so she's like *gone* gone, right?"

Chloe's heart clenches reflexively into a fist.

"I heard her parents haven't reported her missing, so she's like, *somewhere*," Ash says. "But nobody knows where."

"I *know*, that's what's so cool about it," Benjy goes on. "Like, disappearing into the night in a ball gown? There's something totally old Hollywood, tragic starlet, Lana Del Rey about it, and I'm like, kind of obsessed—*ow, Chloe!*"

Chloe, who didn't notice her grip growing tighter and tighter on Benjy's ankle the longer he talked about Shara Wheeler, relaxes her fingers. "Sorry."

She glances instinctively to Georgia, who is already waiting to make eye contact with her. She mouths, *Isengard?* Their code word for, *Do you need to be rescued?*

Chloe rolls her eyes and shakes her head.

"As your teacher, I'm obligated to tell you that gossiping about a missing person isn't very Christian," Mr. Truman says, emerging from his office with an overstuffed folder of sheet music.

Like a lot of Willowgrove teachers, Mr. Truman was born and raised in False Beach and never left. He knew Chloe the second he saw her on his roster because he graduated Willowgrove in '96 alongside her mom and Shara's parents. Chloe once found him in her mom's senior yearbook, looking like the coolest kid in the show choir. Her mom was more in the woodshop grunge crowd, but Mr. Truman remembers her.

Chloe can't imagine why in the world Mr. Truman would spend his whole life at Willowgrove on purpose. Every teacher has to sign a "morality clause" saying they won't drink or express political opinions or be gay, and while Mr. Truman has never *said* he's gay, he *is* a single fortysomething choir director with an extensive collection of slouchy sweaters. Some of the sweaters even have elbow patches. Like, come on.

"As our teacher, you probably got all kinds of administrative intel about what's actually going on with the missing person," Benjy points out, "and you are obligated to tell us, because we're your favorites."

"Not technically missing," Ash points out.

"Not technically my favorites," Mr. Truman says. "I don't have those."

"Uh-huh," Benjy says. "That's why I taught half the sectionals last semester, for free. Because you hate me."

"That's called field experience; it's for your college applications," Mr. Truman clarifies. "If you'll excuse me, I have to go plead my case to the administration for the fifteenth time this month to hire someone to fix the piano."

"I told you, it's the strings," Benjy says.

"I know, but *someone* lost the key to the lid lock, so I also have to convince them to hire a locksmith."

"Okay, first of all, *I* did not lose the key. It went missing from *your* office," Benjy says. "Second of all, I told you that installing a padlock on a piano was barbaric and you didn't listen."

"I wouldn't have had to put a padlock on it if y'all would stop opening it up when I'm not looking."

"That also was not me," Benjy points out.

"All right, well," Mr. Truman concludes. "Wish me luck."

He heads for the door, but pauses at the risers, examining Ash's sketchpad.

"That's . . . huh." He tilts his head sideways. "Did you make Benjy's head—?"

"A fried egg?" Ash says. They nod serenely. "Yeah. Isn't it cool?"

"You're a visionary," Mr. Truman says, hand over heart, and then he's out the door.

"You drew me as an *egg*?" Benjy demands, dropping his leg so fast that Chloe narrowly avoids a roundhouse kick to the nose. "I thought this was figure drawing."

"It *is*," Ash insists. They flip their sketchbook around to show their work, which is a gorgeously detailed study of the human form topped off with a sunny-side-up egg where Benjy's head should be. "It's my *interpretation* of figure drawing."

"I'm not posing for you anymore."

"I already drew you."

"Well, erase it."

"No, I like it," Ash says simply. "It's my art. I don't make you un-choreograph your Nicki Minaj songs."

"Hard to argue with that one," Chloe notes, and Benjy sighs hugely and retreats to the piano bench.

"Benjy," Georgia says. "Play us a song."

It works; Benjy's scowl immediately transforms into a smile. There's probably not a single thing Benjy loves more than someone asking him to play a song.

Back when they still had spring musical rehearsals, a handful of them would hang back afterward and Benjy would take requests. Chloe would sing along, then a junior in a supporting role would pick out a harmony, and eventually some strange quiet freshman would join in. It usually lasted fifteen minutes before Mr. Truman sent them home, but sometimes it would feel like hours on the tile floor with her back against Georgia's back and her head tilted on Georgia's shoulder so she could project her voice to the ceiling.

She smiles, the memory replacing Shara's mysterious whereabouts and suspiciously healthy cuticles in her mind. Ash puts down their sketchbook and joins Benjy on the piano bench. It's always funny to see them next to each other, because they have almost the exact same mullet-y haircut, one ginger, one brown. If the dress code allowed, they'd probably have given each other undercuts by now.

"There it is," Benjy says, backtracking over the last few keys with his left hand. One of them brings a mysterious noise with it, like an angry little bee somewhere inside the piano, the one Mr. Truman was complaining about.

He twiddles with a few keys around the middle of the key-board, searching for the faint buzz again, but what Chloe hears is one familiar note out of the jumble. What is it about that note?

*Somewhere you go almost every day.*

*Keeping your vows.*

*Hiding in the brakes.*

Wait.

Wedding vows.

*I'll run from thee and hide me in the brakes.* That's a line from *A Midsummer's Night Dream*, and *Midsummer* is where the wedding march comes from, not the here-comes-the-bride one but the other one, and Shara mentioned vows—

"Benjy," Chloe says. "Do you know the wedding march?"

"I have played all of my straight cousins' weddings," Benjy says wearily, "so, yes."

"Play the first note."

He does—that solid, resounding middle C—and Chloe hears it. The vibration of one of the interior strings against something flimsy, like paper.

"Huh," she says. She does not fly across the room and rip the top off the piano and fling it out of the way like Smith throwing a touchdown pass, but she very, very badly wants to. In her head, she is punching the entire thing apart with her bare hands. In reality, she purses her lips and says, "That's weird."

If she's right, and the thing inside the piano is what she thinks—Jesus, Mr. Truman said it's been acting up since *last month.* That would mean Shara's been crawling around leaving clues for *weeks.* Who *is* this girl?

When the bell rings for the end of lunch, she waves her friends off the way she always does to hang back for her sixth hour, Girls Select Chorus. As soon as the door shuts behind them, before Mr. Truman or any of her classmates come straggling in from lunch, she crosses to the upright piano.

The silver key from Shara's card is already in her pocket, just in case, and when she pushes it into the padlock on the piano lid, it's a perfect fit.

Guess that explains who stole the piano key.

Carefully, she eases the case open and peers down into its guts, all its dozens of levers and mysterious pieces, and there, paperclipped to one of the strings, is an unpleasantly familiar pink card.

*And leave thee to the mercy of wild beasts.* That's the rest of the line.

Junior year. AP Lang. Chloe and Shara were paired up for a project—involuntarily, of course. Ms. Rodkey split the class up in twos and forced them to memorize and perform a conversation from one of the plays they covered in their Shakespeare unit. She'll never forget Drew Taylor in his tube socks stammering through King Lear.

She remembers pushing her desk together with Shara's, glaring when Shara's skirt had the audacity to cross the invisible barrier between them and brush her knee. She remembers Shara smiling brightly at the teacher over the printed list of sample scenes before turning to Chloe and saying, "We're doing *Midsummer.*" Like she was the only one who got to decide. Like Chloe hadn't grown up listening to her moms recite *Twelfth Night* at each other over morning coffee.

She remembers their argument—Chloe wanted to do Olivia and Cesario meeting, Shara wanted Demetrius and Helena in the wood—and the way Shara's fingers were warm on the back of her hand when she reached over to point out the lines she didn't like. She remembers wanting to throw her copy of *Midsummer* at Shara's perfect, polite face, but that they did, eventually, agree to do it.

They met in the library after school and read lines at each other for an hour, Shara's cheeks going pinker and pinker with quiet anger the more Chloe recited without glancing at the page. Chloe chewed on a smile, off-book. It was obvious which of them was going to do better on the assignment. For once, it didn't matter that Shara had gotten her way.

She remembers the way Shara left in a huff, swinging her backpack over her shoulder, and then walked into class the next day with every word committed to memory. Chloe stood at the front of the room as Shara recited in her sugary drawl, *I'll follow thee and make a heaven of hell,* and she stared at Shara's face, at the pearl studs on her earlobes and the lock of hair tucked there behind her ear and her lip balm catching the light from the window when her mouth moved, and she willed her to miss a line, just *one line*. She didn't, and in the end, they were graded as a team anyway.

Chloe reaches inside the piano, slips the card out from between the strings, and opens it.

On the top flap of the card, Shara's written out another quote from *Midsummer*. Chloe knows this one from memory too. Hermia and Helena.

As if our hands, our sides, voices, and minds,
Had been incorporate. So we grew together,
Like to a double cherry—seeming parted
But yet an union in partition—
Two lovely berries molded on one stem;

On the other flap, the note is addressed to her:

*Chloe,*

*Being the principal's daughter does have at least one perk: a master key makes everything easier. Mr. Truman seems nice, though, so I did feel a little bad.*

*Glad you figured this one out. I stayed up all night memorizing our scene, but this was the one I really wanted to do. It's such a nice image, a double-stemmed cherry. I think we're like that. You always seemed to be right next to me, even though we never could get that close to each other. But then, I don't have to explain metaphors to you, do I?*

*XOXO*

*S*

"So, you're back in?" Rory says when they meet behind the gym after seventh hour.

"I was never officially out, and this isn't *Ocean's 8*," Chloe tells him. "Though if it was, I would be Cate Blanchett."

"Never saw it," Rory says, examining his cuticles. Then, so quietly she's not sure she's meant to hear it, he adds, "I'm Rihanna."

Smith's still reading over the postscript at the bottom of the Post-it Shara left in *Midsummer*. It's addressed to him.

*There are a couple more things I need you to know about me*, it says. *I left a photo of us in the last place you kissed me. Maybe it'll help.*

"The last place I kissed her?" Smith says incredulously. The three of them are maintaining a careful two feet of distance like they're saving room for Jesus at a homecoming dance. Smith looks at Rory while Rory looks down at his feet, then

Rory looks up, and Smith dedicates himself to studying the toes of his Air Forces. Chloe longs for last week, when she'd never had Shara's mouth on hers and her biggest problem was finding a sticky bra for prom.

"You don't remember the last place you kissed her?" Chloe asks.

"No, I do," Smith says. "It was at Dixon Wells's house when we were taking prom photos."

"Okay, so," Rory says, "ask him if you can come over and look for it."

"It's not that easy," Smith says. He rubs a hand over the buzzed hairs on the back of his neck. "Dixon is kind of an asshole."

"Yeah," Chloe agrees. "No joke."

"I thought he was your friend," Rory says.

"Dixon is a guy I hang out with," Smith tells him. "That's not the same thing."

"What are you saying?" Chloe asks.

"I'm saying that if I ask to come over to look for something Shara left there, he's probably gonna be a dick about it and want to know what it is, and if he finds out my girlfriend cheated on me with *both* of you, he's *definitely* gonna be a dick about it."

Chloe takes a second to think about that one. Shara may have dragged them into this, but she doesn't deserve for the school's most unapologetic d-bag to know she kissed a girl. Even if Chloe doesn't care about Smith's reputation, she does care about that. Like, in a general moral sense.

"Okay," Chloe says. "So, how else can we get into Dixon's house?"

"He's throwing a party tomorrow night," Smith says. "I'll look for it then."

"You need help," Rory says. "Dixon lives across the golf course from me. I've seen his house. It's basically a small country."

"You could—well, one of you could come with me. Two might be pushing it. He gets weird about people he doesn't know showing up. If we want to keep this to ourselves, only one of you can come."

"She wrote it on my note," Chloe says quickly. "I'll go."

# FROM THE BURN PILE

### VALEDICTORIAN SPEECH: DRAFT #3

Good morning, friends, family, faculty, and my fellow graduating class of Willowgrove Christian Academy 2022. I'm Chloe Green, and I'm so honored to be representing our class as valedictorian. It was a tough fight to the top, and I'm thankful to each of you whose hard work encouraged me to work that much harder.

Unlike almost every member of this graduating class, I didn't grow up here in False Beach. I grew up in southern California, near an actual beach. Moving here for high school is the first time I've lived among so many people who care this deeply about college football, who have never in their lives eaten a sushi roll, who believe bootcut jeans are still acceptable to wear in public. In fact, from the moment I arrived at Willowgrove, I was confident that I would spend the next four years of my high school career counting the days until I could escape this place, which has the spiritual aura of a Mountain Dew bottle filled with dip spit in the tour bus cupholder of a Christian rock Lynyrd Skynyrd cover band

Annotation from Georgia:

It's a graduation, not a roast. Consider making a list of things you actually like about False Beach, if possible.

# 6

The last thing Chloe wants to do, definitely at this moment and maybe ever for the rest of her life, is spend her Friday night watching Dixon Wells slobber all over a beer bong with Shara Wheeler's boyfriend.

It's not that she doesn't enjoy parties, or large groups of screaming people, or Saturday nights that get a little sloppy. It's very well-documented by Benjy's Snapchat stories that she enjoys all those things. She even once almost got French-kissed by Tucker Price from the Quiz Bowl team in his parents' saltwater jacuzzi. Straight A's and being capable of having fun are not mutually exclusive.

But a party full of the type of people popular at Willow-grove is not Chloe's idea of fun, especially when it's hosted by Dixon Wells. Dixon is a particular variety of affable jerk prevalent in Alabama: the type who insists it's okay for him to make offensive jokes because he's not *actually* racist/sexist/ho-mophobic/transphobic/whatever so he doesn't *actually* mean them, but aren't the jokes *so* funny? *Dark humor.* Of course, the student body voted him prom king over Smith, who seems boring but at least decent.

Dixon's house has one of those curved driveways out front like it should have valet service. Cars Chloe recognizes from the school parking lot line the street: Jeep, Jeep, Jeep, Range Rover, Jeep, jacked-up truck, jacked-up truck, jacked-up truck. She slots her hand-me-down Camry in behind an F-150 with a lift kit that belongs in the Australian outback.

I'm here, she texts Smith.

She waits five minutes, then another five, but Smith doesn't text back. Fantastic. She can hear the party raging in the backyard, but she doesn't want to walk in alone.

She can do this. She's wearing her heaviest ankle boots, the black ones with the big rubber treads and the three-inch heels. Benjy calls them her mankiller boots. She can do anything in her mankiller boots.

She closes her eyes and reels through a dozen alternate, fearless versions of Chloe, landing on an image of herself as a ruthless queen with a million yards of bloodred velvet pooling around her, stomping around a palace with a vial of poison and incredible hair. That'll do.

She opens the door, plants her mankiller boots in the Wellses' impeccably groomed front lawn, and immediately gets her heel trapped in a patch of mud.

She yanks herself loose and, only slightly pink in the face, stomps off.

The backyard is enormous, with a massive trampoline and a redbrick outdoor kitchen with a marble island and a gas grill that probably cost more than a semester at Willowgrove, which isn't cheap. Even the grass looks expensive. Nobody seems to be wearing actual clothing, only soggy T-shirts or swimsuits or cut-off shorts. She feels overdressed by having shoes on.

She peers across the wide pool full of screaming girls in

bikinis on linebacker shoulders, trying to pick Smith out of the crowd.

Every person she passes stops what they're doing to watch her walk by. She straightens her shoulders and stares ahead, same as when she stood on stage in front of the whole school and put her heart into singing "Think of Me." Eyes up, chin out, pretend that nobody is taking out their phone to do a mean Snapchat story about it.

"Chloe Green!" someone yells, and God, she hopes it's Smith. She whips her head around—

Nope, it's Ace Torres, shaggy dark hair dripping chlorine everywhere and that disconcertingly wide grin. Her jaw clenches automatically.

He reaches her in two enormous strides, looming like a wet bear with a slice of pizza. "Chloe! You're here! That's so crazy!"

Technically, Ace is harmless, and she wouldn't have any reason to hate him more than the average meathead Willowgrove boy if he hadn't imposed upon the most important spring musical of her high school career. She always thought Mr. Truman was above stunt-casting a football bro, but he practically had a stroke when Ace managed to sing four bars at tryouts.

"Yeah, I'm as surprised as you are," she says, dodging a drop of pool water.

Ace laughs. "Dude, I miss seeing you guys at rehearsal."

"You could still hang out with us," Chloe points out.

"I kinda get the feeling you don't actually want that," Ace says. Chloe blinks at him. "But it's cool! You're here now! Dope! Are you here with somebody?"

There's no easy answer to that, but she goes with, "Smith invited me."

"That's what's up," Ace says. "He needs more friends!"

She glances around the party, which seems to include more than a quarter of their grade and sizable delegations of the sophomore and junior classes. There are so many bodies in the pool, it's impossible to tell where one naked trapezius ends and another begins. "Is this not enough friends?"

Before Ace can answer, he catches sight of someone over her shoulder. "Hey, Smith, look who's here!"

And there's Smith, emerging from the snack table. As soon as his eyes land on Chloe's face, they dart guiltily to his pocket, where his phone must be.

"Hey, Chloe, uh, glad—glad you made it," Smith says.

She sighs, not wasting any more time. "Hi. Can you show me where to get some water?" She glares at him pointedly until he takes the hint.

"Oh, uh, yeah, it's right inside, over here," he says, turning to lead her toward the house.

"Bye, Chloe!" Ace calls after them. "Don't leave before upside-down margaritas!"

"What in the name of God is an upside-down margarita," Chloe hisses at Smith as he opens one of the massive French doors.

"You don't want to know."

There's nobody inside except for a couple of juniors making out on a couch, and Smith sidesteps them neatly and leads her into the kitchen.

"Holy *shitballs*," Chloe swears when she steps into it. The marble island is nearly the length of her entire bedroom at home. The stainless steel refrigerator looks like it could fit a human body. Maybe two.

"Yeah." Smith adds in a rush, "Look, I'm sorry I missed your text. I was talking to Summer about the whole Shara thing, and they used to be best friends until they had some weird falling-out this year that they both refuse to tell me anything about, and it's all—"

"It's fine," Chloe interrupts. "Tell me where I'm supposed to be looking."

Smith leans on one of the six leather barstools lining the island, thinking. The more time she spends with him, the more she notices that he doesn't carry himself like all the other football players out in the yard. He's big, but he's graceful. He doesn't walk from room to room as much as he flows through them.

He's wearing a Willowgrove football T-shirt with the sleeves torn off and a pair of swim trunks patterned with little pink flamingos. She spares exactly one second to find them charming.

"So," he says, "I was with her the whole time we were here for prom photos, except when she went to the bathroom."

"Where's the bathroom?"

Smith pulls a face. "I think there are five of them. Six if you count the one in the pool house. So, she could have passed through pretty much any part of the house to get to one."

Chloe groans. "I'm really getting sick of these country club mansions."

"I know," Smith agrees.

They split up—Smith takes the pool house and the finished basement, leaving Chloe the first and second floor. She works her way across the ground floor first, through spare rooms and game rooms and rooms that seem to have no use except adding square footage to the already astronomical square footage. She stumbles across what appears to be a man cave, the kind she and her moms heckle on HGTV—just a huge room full of nothing but a massive TV and a lot of tacky Bama decor.

On the second floor, she finds Dixon's room, which is a study in the worst of teenage boyhood. Chloe *likes* boys and their defined jawlines and crooked smiles, but the pile of sweaty laundry in the corner makes her want to quit them altogether. She squeezes a test shot of the spray-on deodorant on the dresser and gags. This time next year, Dixon Wells will be cracking open a cold one with the rest of Kappa Sig before his lawyer dad gets them off the hook for some *Dateline*-worthy hazing. Gross. There's no way Shara set foot in this room.

To be honest, it's not only hard to imagine Shara in Dixon's room; it's hard to imagine Shara doing *any* of this.

The Shara that Chloe has spent four years alongside has always seemed like a passive, quiet thing. You hear stories about her weekends feeding the homeless or tutoring fifth graders or being an eyebrow model in Japan, but you never actually see her *do* any of it unless she posts a gorgeously composed photo to her 25,000 Instagram followers. She just floats around, never a hair out of place, wearing a uniform skirt that somehow looks shorter on her than everyone else but sits exactly at regulation length. She doesn't get her hands dirty.

Chloe's fingers twitch for the silver chain in her bathroom drawer. She's always suspected there was something wrong with the math of Shara, but she's never been able to prove what. And considering she can't even picture Shara here, sneaking around someone else's house with a fistful of clues and a plan to skip town—she's never felt further from the answer.

She's about to find Smith and tell him it's a bust when she sees it.

On the landing between the first and second floors, tucked behind a stack of books and a fake plant, beneath a stuffed deer head, there's a pink card.

She snatches it up and rips it open.

Inside, the first thing she finds is a polaroid of Shara and Smith smiling by the pool, the sun setting behind them. Shara's in her pink prom dress, and Smith looks slightly uncomfortable in his tux but holds on tight to Shara's hand. Chloe flips it over so she doesn't have to look at them as she reads the card.

> Smith,
>
> I have to tell you something about this picture. I look happy, right? What I was thinking in this moment was, "We're not going to make it to Graduation."
>
> P.S. Check the records, Rory. Chloe should know where they are. The key is already there, where I am.

Outside, she slips past the defensive line shotgunning White Claws and toward the pool house. The side door is slightly ajar—Smith must still be in there—and she reaches for the handle—

She tries to take another step, but she can't. The heel of her boot is stuck, *again,* this time in a puddle of sucking mud between two of the pavers leading to the door. She tugs, but the ground tugs harder.

This far back in the yard, the sounds of the party are muted enough that she can hear Smith's voice from within the pool house, and she opens her mouth to abandon her pride and ask him to pull her out of the lawn, but first, another voice speaks.

". . . fine," Chloe makes out. "Don't worry about it."

She doesn't spend much time around people likely to be at a Dixon party, but it's easy to assign a face to the voice. Summer Collins, softball star and homecoming court member. Pretty, popular, in Chloe's AP Bio class, the only Black girl in the class of '22. Her older sister famously came out as a lesbian two years after graduating, and her dad's rich because he owns the car dealership across the road from Willowgrove.

"Remember eighth grade?" Smith's voice asks. "When we had to take care of that bag of flour for life sciences?"

"Yeah," Summer says, "I dropped it out of my mom's car and exploded our baby all over the driveway the first night I had it."

"Remember how your mom took us to the store to find the exact brand of flour and replace the bag, and we brought it to class, and I freaked out because I thought everyone could tell—"

"And you narced on us to Mrs. Young? Yeah, how could I forget? We *failed*. That's the only time I've ever gotten a bad grade on a science project in my life. I was pissed."

"Do you ever . . . I don't know, feel like that sometimes?"

Hell. Chloe drops to one knee and starts clawing at her boot laces, attempting to free herself before she can accidentally hear any revelations about Smith Parker's internal life.

"Feel like what?" she hears Summer ask. "Pissed at you?"

"No, I mean, like . . . like you were *switched* or something, but you look the way you're supposed to look, and you're still flour, so why should it feel like you're wrong?"

"*Oh*," Summer says. "Actually—"

With a final heave, Chloe manages to dislodge her foot, but the momentum sends her tumbling forward, through the doorway, and onto the polished concrete floor of the pool house. Right at Summer's feet.

Summer and Smith both freeze, red Solo cups in hand,

staring down at her sprawled out with one shoe on.

"Okay, well," Chloe says, "someone should really look into the safety standards of this house party. Lawsuit waiting to happen."

"You good?" Summer asks as Smith extends a hand to help Chloe up. "You shouldn't drink more than one if it's your first time."

"Appreciate it, but I don't drink," Chloe says. Smith pulls her to her feet with the full force of his biceps, which almost sends her tumbling all over again, and now she's embarrassed *and* motion sick. "Was looking for Smith. Hi, Smith."

"Hey," Smith says. He raises his eyebrows unsubtly at her. "Did you find the bathroom?"

"Yeah, I found it," she says.

Summer looks them over, arches an eyebrow, and shakes her head. "Is there still pizza left?"

"Uh, I think so," Chloe says.

"Finish this later?" Summer says to Smith.

"Uh," Smith says, "I mean, it's fine."

Summer shrugs, leans out the open door, then quickly ducks back in. "Looks like Ace got upside-down margaritas started. Somebody's gonna get their teeth knocked out and you only have one chance to be able to tell that story."

"Uh, actually," Chloe attempts, "I was gonna—"

But Summer is gone, and Smith is right behind her.

"—go home," she finishes to no one.

That's what she should do. She can send Smith a photo of Shara's note from the comfort of her bedroom, where nobody is going to end the night throwing up in the pool and having to fish their retainer out of the filter.

She steps into the doorway and leans down to recover her shoe from the lawn.

Although . . . maybe this *is* where she needs to be. *Know thy enemy,* et cetera. Four years of looking at Shara from the outside hasn't gotten her anywhere, but this could be her chance to climb into Shara's skin for a night and see her from the inside.

"Shara absolute nightmare Wheeler," she sighs to herself.

She pulls off her other boot, squares her shoulders, and walks barefoot into the party.

# FROM THE BURN PILE

Passed notes between Benjy Carter
and Ace Torres

Written on the back of a page
from the *Phantom* script

yo do you think Chloe hates me? :(

I think you need to be worrying about that note at the end of "Point of No Return"

TRUE TRUE do you think Truman will let me wear my lucky socks on stage they help me sing better

not historically accurate but I do think he would say yes if you asked

NIIIIICE

# 7

Upside-down margaritas, apparently, is the name of a party game with no winners and a very basic set of rules. Dixon stands at one end of the yard while a football bro pours tequila and margarita mixer directly into his mouth, and then two more football bros grab him by his outstretched arms and throw him across the yard.

"That's it?" Chloe asks Summer as Dixon goes careening head over ass into a pile of pool inflatables. "That's not a game. That's a concussion."

"It's usually more of a face-first impact than blunt force to the head," Summer points out from beside her. She has really nice dimples, Chloe notices, and little silvery charms sparkle in her braids. "I wasn't joking about losing teeth. You should ask Tanner to take his fake ones out for you. It's his favorite party trick."

Chloe stares at Tanner, the guy holding the margarita mix. "The crash zone is a new addition, then?"

"At least they're not driving out to cow pastures to do it anymore," Summer says. She leaves to refill her drink, and Smith sidles into the space she leaves behind.

"Where'd you find it?" he asks, voice low.

"Does it matter?" Chloe says.

Smith sighs. "I guess not. What does it say?"

"I don't think you're gonna like it."

Smith takes a second with that. Then he releases a low chuckle and shakes his head.

"Okay," he says, "tell me later."

She nods, and Smith waves over another two cups of Coke for them, and the party rolls on.

Chloe watches jocks fly across the yard and lowerclassmen play ping-pong on the outdoor kitchen island and wonders how Shara fits into it all. Does she sit primly on the edge of the jacuzzi like Emma Grace Baker, her silver cross necklace dipping down between her bikini cleavage? Does she swing her hips to the beat with Mackenzie Harris and the other dance team girls? Does she elbow in with the guys like Summer?

Maybe she does what Chloe's doing—trying not to think about homework and instead, letting the noise and the sugar high and Smith's warm presence at her side convince her that she could learn to enjoy this.

Ace's turn for upside-down margaritas comes right as somebody switches the playlist from SoundCloud rap to The Killers, and she watches Smith watch him fly across the yard, missing the inflatables entirely. Ace staggers to his feet with sod stuck to his bare chest and margarita mixer dripping down his chin, and Smith laughs so hard, he almost chokes on his pizza. This is Smith unguarded, she realizes—she never even considered he might have his guard up around her.

Ace bounds over, slinging his arm around Smith's shoulders and wiping his face on Smith's shirt.

"Man, I love this song!" Ace announces, shaking his shoulders in gratitude to the playlist. "You know what's funny? By the end of the song, he never says if he's jealous of the guy or the girl."

Chloe arches an eyebrow at him. "I'm surprised you know it."

"Chloe," Ace says, smirking, "*everyone* knows 'Mr. Brightside.'"

She stares at him and Smith. They're being so nice to her. Like, suspiciously nice. She wonders if this is that sneaky type of shittiness, the mocking, popular-kid fakery. But it's impossible to look at Ace's big dumb cabana-boy-at-Margaritaville face and Smith's wide, pretty smile and see bad intentions.

"You're up," Smith tells her.

"No," she says. "No way. I don't drink."

"Bro," Ace says, "I don't either. I did mine with the mixer."

She squints at him. "But you seem drunk."

Ace shrugs. "That's just my personality. Come on."

And the next thing she knows, she's being whisked away to a corner of the yard, where some girl from the track team takes one of her arms and Ace takes the other.

Summer steps in front of her, margarita mixer in hand.

"Keep your arms and legs loose and you'll be fine," she says, almost businesslike.

"Have you done this before?" Chloe asks.

Summer snorts. "No, I'm smart." She tilts Chloe's chin up with her free hand, raising the jug of mixer. Chloe has to respect a girl who gets straight to the point. "Open up."

And then Chloe's flying across the grass.

She gets a second of airtime, lime burning in her sinuses and a flash of starry sky, before tumbling into a pile of donuts and palm trees and red-white-and-blue popsicles. For a moment, all she can see is neon vinyl, and then she flails out onto the wet ground.

There's silence, until she pulls herself to her feet and raises her arms over her head, opening her mouth wide to show that it's empty, and the onlooking crowd erupts into cheers.

So, Chloe parties.

Ace yells about ordering more pizza, Smith and Summer pull her up to dance on the ledge of the hot tub waterfall, juniors document everything for Snapchat, and Chloe parties. At some point, by complete accident, she ends up in the pool fully clothed, and Smith pulls her out and wraps his letterman jacket around her shoulders. She fishes the card out of her skirt pocket and dries it off on the backup quarterback's T-shirt before tucking it safely away again.

She slips in and out of the crowd, into the area where the softball team is watching the Auburn game on an outdoor TV. Summer leans her head on the shoulder of a teammate and laughs, and a memory hits Chloe: Shara, at a pep rally last football season, huddled on the other side of the bleachers with her friends, confetti in her hair and Smith's football number painted on her cheek, laughing.

She pictures the two cherries from *Midsummer,* her and Shara sitting side by side in class after class, taking the same notes and then walking out into the hallway in opposite directions. How many times has Shara worn Smith's jacket like this? She looks down at her fingertips peeking out of the too-long sleeves, her bitten-down nails, and imagines Shara's perfect, pastel pink manicure.

This is Shara's life, and for half a second, it feels like it could be Chloe's too. A girl with a perfect academic record and more friends than can fit in one pool.

"Nah," she overhears from a nearby group. Dixon, talking too loud as always. His light brown hair has dried from the pool in the way he favors for school: flipping out in every direction like he just took off a football helmet. "I'm telling you, we can do it with four-wheelers."

"Where are we gonna put it, though, man?" Tanner asks him.

"We can borrow a trailer to haul it. My dad has like, five."

"There's no way we don't get caught though."

"If we do, we'll make Mackenzie call her dad."

"What are you guys talking about?" Chloe interjects, too curious to ignore them.

Dixon looks at her like she's something that crawled out of the robotic pool vacuum before switching on a wide grin. "This one yours, Smith? Shara's only been gone a few days. That's cap."

"She's my friend," Smith says. "And you're not using 'cap' right."

"Tell her to mind her business."

"You were basically yelling," Chloe points out. "I didn't realize it was a secret."

"They're talking about the senior prank," Smith tells her. "They want to steal the Bucky the Buck statue from the town square."

"*Dude,*" Dixon yells. "The point of a prank is that it's a *secret*!"

"You talked about it in front of Shara last week, and her dad's literally the principal," Smith says. He holds his hands up, letting out a laugh. "It's no big deal, man. She's chill."

"That's it?" Chloe says. "A statue?"

"It's—we're not just gonna steal it," Dixon says. "We're gonna bring it to school and leave it in the middle of the courtyard."

"I mean, it's fine," Chloe says. She shrugs Smith's jacket down to her elbows so she can rearrange her wet T-shirt. "You could do better though."

Dixon laughs and sidles in next to her, putting an arm over her shoulders.

Chloe's body goes stiff.

"I'm willing to let that slide due to the Rachel Rule," Dixon says with an overly friendly smile.

"Bruh," Smith says, suddenly looking panicked. The guys surrounding them are snickering. "Don't."

"What's the Rachel Rule?" Chloe asks.

"It's a rule the seniors made last year for Rachel Kennedy, who was a huge bitch but still got to come to parties because she had huge boobs," Dixon says. He's looking down now. At her chest, and her wet shirt. Her hands clench into fists at her sides—ever since she sprouted D-cups in tenth grade, a guy staring at her chest has never ended well. "So, as long as you keep wearing that, the Rachel Rule says you can stay."

It's impossible that the party stops, or that sirens start screaming in the distance, or that every drop of Chloe's blood actually rushes to her face, but it feels like it.

She wrenches herself out from under Dixon's arm.

"What did you say?"

"What?" he says. He looks around at his friends, who are laughing behind their hands. "You know that's how everyone knows you, right? 'Who's Chloe Green?' 'Oh, she's that girl from LA with the huge boobs.'"

All Chloe manages to say is, "Wow."

"It's a compliment! Look, before they came in, everyone just called you a lesbian, so I'd call this an upgrade. You should be proud of them!"

Smith steps in, touching Dixon on the shoulder. "Dixon, man, shut up."

"Come on, she knows what she looks like! It's a joke, man!"

"You're being a jackass—"

"No, no, it's okay," Chloe says. "I do know what I look like. And one day, when Dixon's fifty and his second wife has left him because he's a balding middle school football coach with the personality of a frozen meatloaf, and his kids hate him because he's never expressed an emotion that's not impotent rage or horniness, he's gonna look back on senior year of high school and realize that being prom king was the only thing he ever achieved in his life, and that at his absolute peak, before everything went to shit, that girl from LA with the huge boobs still wouldn't have slept with him."

She wraps the jacket around herself and storms out of the yard, snatching up her boots on the way. She throws open the gate and keeps going, away from Dixon and the other guys whooping after her like she's the hired entertainment.

What was she even *doing*? Some popular kids were nice to her one time and she forgets everything she's ever known about the Willowgrove food chain? She's not Shara. These people mean nothing to her. The whole point of beating Shara is proving she can win in the way that matters. She always knew she'd never win the Willowgrove way.

Infuriatingly, embarrassed tears prick at the corners of her eyes.

"Chloe, wait up—"

Smith freaking Parker and his future-Heisman-winner speed.

She whips around in the middle of the front lawn, boots swinging wildly from her hand by their laces. "You should have let me handle it. It was humiliating enough without you swooping in to save me."

"I wasn't—ugh," Smith groans. "Okay, fine."

"I don't understand why you hang out with assholes like him. You clearly know better."

Smith pulls a face. "Do you like everyone who's in the spring musical with you? Is there not a single dickhead that you put up with on the Quiz Bowl team because it's easier to do that than make things weird?"

"That's different," Chloe says. "Our dickheads aren't homophobes."

He rolls his eyes. "Do you really think Dixon Wells has never been racist to me? You think I don't hate his guts? But I was stuck with him on the team for four years, and I'm stuck with him until we graduate, and there's pretty much nothing I can do to change that. You pick your battles. He's not worth it."

She remembers what Ace said earlier about Smith needing more friends. *Hanging out with someone is not the same as being friends with them.*

"What are you doing?" she asks as Smith takes out his phone.

"I'm texting my sister to come pick me up," he says. "It's her turn with the car, and I'm tired."

She sighs. "You want a ride?"

In the car, Chloe puts Bleachers on low and Smith leans against the passenger window.

"Can I ask you something?" she says after a few minutes of quiet. Smith turns to her, and their eyes lock for a second, brown on brown. "What do you see in Shara?"

Smith's expression turns wry. "You for real right now?"

"I'm curious, okay? Indulge me."

Smith sighs. She senses him close his eyes without having to look at him. "This is gonna sound weird, but she's kind of like . . . my best friend."

Chloe's brow furrows. "Isn't that what everyone says about their girlfriend?"

Smith folds his arms, and Chloe sees his bare forearms reflecting a passing streetlight and realizes she's still wearing his jacket.

"I mean I feel more comfortable around her than I do around almost anyone," Smith says. "I'm not thinking about what everyone expects me to be. Sometimes we don't even have to talk. It's just like, an understanding. But at the same time, there's always more going on in her head than you can ever guess, and she'll never tell you exactly what it is. You still have to figure her out."

"Sounds to me like she's kind of frigid."

"Yeah," Smith says, and he smiles at her. "Because you're so much fun yourself."

"I am, actually. I'm a blast."

"What about you?" Smith asks. He leans his head back on the headrest. "What do you see in her?"

"I have no idea what you're talking about," Chloe says. Her cheeks feel warm. She adjusts the AC dial. "She's the one who kissed me."

"But you're here," Smith says. "You came to this party even though you'd obviously rather be anywhere else. You decided to look for her."

Chloe's fingers tighten on the steering wheel. "Just because I'm queer doesn't mean I'm in love with every beautiful girl who pays attention to me."

"I didn't say you were in love with her."

"It was implied."

"So you think she's beautiful?"

"A *mole* would think she's beautiful, Smith. That's not an indicator of anything except that I have a pulse."

They're pulling into Smith's neighborhood now. He doesn't live in the country club like Shara or Rory or most of the popular kids—he lives one subdivision over from Chloe, one of fifty identical houses in a development that, according to her mom, didn't exist ten years ago. False Beach is like that: country clubs, trailer parks, and retired cow pastures outfitted with cookie-cutter houses that still smell like fresh paint.

She glances over at Smith, expecting to catch another amused smile, but Smith looks thoughtful. "For the record, you being gay wasn't what made me think you were in love with her."

"I'm not gay." She bristles. "I'm bisexual. That's a thing."

"I know it's a thing," Smith says doggedly. "I just didn't realize you were."

"Well, I am."

"Okay, cool."

A pause. Smith waits.

"And I'm not in love with her," Chloe grinds out. "She's the only person in this school who can keep up with me, which is . . . unexpected. She surprises me. Okay?"

"Yeah," Smith says. "She can be surprising."

Chloe puts the car in park in front of Smith's house and admits, "And she's hot."

"Yeah, she's hot."

"Why does she smell like—"

"Lilacs?"

"*Dude,*" she groans, and Smith laughs. "Is this weird?"

He thinks about it. "I feel like . . . it should be, but it's not?"

A muscle in Smith's jaw flexes before relaxing into its smooth right angle. Usually the only people in False Beach who are this cool about her being queer are other queer people.

Hm.

"How do you think Rory would answer that question?" Smith asks.

"I don't know," Chloe says. "You should ask him."

Smith reaches out and boops the dashboard lucky cat on the nose with one finger.

"Maybe."

"What's the deal with you and him, anyway?"

Smith shrugs. "He's in love with my girlfriend. I feel like the deal is pretty obvious."

"To be honest, you don't really strike me as the jealous type," Chloe points out. "Like, you seem fine with me."

"It's different with Rory."

"Because he's a guy?"

"Because Rory used to be my best friend."

Chloe's head whips around.

"What? *When?*"

"Back in middle school," Smith says, still focused on the lucky cat's waving paw, "when I first started at Willowgrove. We had the same homeroom, and we clicked, I guess. Him and Summer were the first two friends I made. And then I joined JV football, and Rory decided he was too cool to be friends with a dumb jock or whatever, and we kind of drifted. We haven't really talked since. It sucked."

"Does Shara know? About the two of you?"

"She was there the whole time," Smith says. "Rory's always had a crush on her. And he's still pissed that I'm dating her, even though all that stuff was a million years ago. Like, you should have seen his face the first time he looked out his window and saw me picking Shara up for a date."

"But she picked you," Chloe says. "Why does it matter?"

"It's hard to explain," Smith says. His brow pinches. "I haven't talked to him since we were fourteen, but I haven't been able to get rid of him either. It's like he was always gonna come back to mess things up for me, and now he has."

The whole thing sounds kind of dramatic to Chloe, until she remembers the feeling in her gut the first time she saw Shara, like the universe had dropped a personalized time bomb into first-hour world history. Maybe some people are supposed to hate each other.

"I guess that's fair," she says.

Something settles into the air between them, an unsteady truce. They have almost nothing in common outside the fact that they've both kissed Shara Wheeler, unless there's something else.

After he climbs out the passenger side, Chloe rolls down the window and yells, "Hey!"

Smith pauses on the curb. "What?"

"You forgot this," she says, shrugging out of his jacket and holding it toward him. He leans back through the window and takes it. "Card's in the pocket."

"Thanks," he says.

"Congrats on being the only member of the football team I would save in a fire."

Smith folds the jacket over his arm and laughs. It's a warm sound, like sunbaked earth under bare feet. She doesn't have to wonder what Shara sees in him. It's objectively obvious.

# FROM THE BURN PILE

From Georgia's composition book
for Creative Writing, junior year
Assignment: Describe a person with one word

There's a girl with brown eyes who reminds me of the first book I ever loved. When I look at her, I feel like there might be another universe in her. I imagine her on a shelf too high for me to reach, or peeking out of someone else's backpack, or at the end of a long wait at the library. I know there are other books that are easier to get my hands on, but none are half as good as her. Every part of her seems to have a purpose, a specific meaning, an exact reason for being how and what and where it is. So, the word I would choose to describe her is "deliberate."

Annotation by Chloe:

Who is this about????

# 8

"Sorry," Chloe's mom says, folding her arms across her chest. She leans against the side of the truck, where the logo of her welding company is painted in black. "You went to a party *where* last night?"

This is how it always goes with Chloe's moms. They talk about *everything*, so every secret feels huge. She lasted until Sunday morning, then folded on the ride to the Birmingham airport.

"Dixon Wells's house."

"Why does that name sound so familiar?"

"Because he's a douchebag of nuclear proportions. I'm sure I've complained about him before."

"And this was when you said you were with Georgia?"

"No," Chloe hedges, "I said I was going out with a friend. Which was true because I went to the party with a friend. Well, technically I met him there, but we went together."

"Playing pretty fast and loose with the concept of truth there, junior. Do you want to tell me why you went to the house party of an atomic asshole?"

"Nuclear douchebag."

"Sure."

Since she knew she'd end up breaking, she already has her story. The whole hunting-down-her-academic-rival thing is too complicated to explain, and if she claims she wants to make peace with the Willowgrove elite as a graduation good-will gesture, her mom will probably rush her to the ER for a head injury.

"I'm in a group project with a football player in my Bible class," she says, "and I needed to tell him to stop blowing me off and do his part."

"Ah, yes." Her mom grimaces. "Mandatory Bible class."

Bringing up Bible class always works. Her mom isn't any happier than Chloe is to be stuck in False Beach, which is the main reason Chloe can't be mad at her for dragging them here. Resenting Willowgrove has been a bonding activity for them these past few years.

"Yeah," Chloe says. "Coach Wilson takes time away from his busy schedule of training the baseball team to inform six classes of seniors every day that premarital sex is a sin and homosexuals are an abomination. It's great."

Her mom looks like she has something to say, but then the automatic doors slide open and there's her mama, look-ing the same as ever in a pair of loose linen overalls, tugging along a suitcase full of opera gowns. She has Chloe in her arms in a second, scooping her up and burying her fingers in Chloe's short hair.

"Oh, sweet girl," she says in Chloe's ear. Chloe feels her throat go tight. She coughs into her mama's shoulder. "I missed you so much."

"Did you get grayer?" Chloe asks into her hair.

"Probably." She releases Chloe, then turns to Chloe's mom, gathers her up at the waist, and gives her a long, open-mouthed kiss like they're on the bow of the freaking *Titanic*.

"Okay, okay," Chloe says. "We're still in Alabama. Let's go."

On the way home she recounts the story of Dixon's party. She does get in trouble for lying, but the extent of her punishment is having to endure a thirty-minute lecture from her mama about the importance of open communication within a self-policing community, even one as small as a family of three. Chloe checks Shara's Instagram for updates and says "uh-huh" in all the right places. There's nothing new, just the same purposefully curated grid of warm-toned fake candids.

When she's done with Shara's Instagram, she returns to her group chat with Smith and Rory, where they've been discussing the postscript on Shara's latest note. Chloe's sure the word "records" is a reference to Rory's music collection and wants to do a search of his room, but he responded via perturbed voice note this morning that he's perfectly capable of looking on his own and neither of them are allowed back in his room ever again.

?????, Chloe texts, which the others know by now is her way of demanding a status report. Rory replies with a middle finger emoji.

At home, they eat the accursed turducken, over which her mama describes her hotel in Portugal and its fancy balconies and the room service custard tarts. After dinner, there's homemade cheesecake with sugared cherries on top, which reminds Chloe of *Midsummer* and Shara, and then she's itching to take her phone out and check Instagram again.

She drops her plate in the sink and heads for her bedroom.

"Hey, where are you off to?" her mama says, brushing a long lock of graying hair back into her braid. Her mom grunts past her in the hallway, hauling an armload of blankets out of the master bedroom. "We're renting *You've Got Mail*."

"Yeah," her mom says as she dumps everything on the couch. "Aren't you gonna watch Tom Hanks put an adorable indie bookstore out of business with us?"

And God, she missed her mama, she really did.

But . . . Shara.

"I have a huge paper due on Monday," she says.

Her mama pouts. "Why did I raise you to be so responsible? I was supposed to raise you to be an anarchist."

She shrugs. "Dropped the ball, I guess."

Down the hall, she flips on her light and flops onto the bed.

If she were in her old room, she'd know what to do about Shara. It was easier to think there.

She loved the apartment in LA. It was right on the edge of the city, a three-bedroom on the fourth floor, and she still has the layout committed to memory. The single bathroom, the hall closet Titania liked to hide inside, the pink wingback chair in the living room. To the left of the kitchen sink, there was an antique hutch her moms salvaged from an estate sale and painted mint green. Her room had a sliding glass door to a tiny balcony and views of the skyline. When she was ten, her moms finally let her have the key to it, and she never felt as cool and adult as she did while reading books on a beach towel on her own private balcony all summer long.

The house here in False Beach is only slightly bigger than the apartment, but it feels too big, somehow. She misses hearing her neighbor's daily routines through the walls and getting sweet tea from the kitchen without losing the Bluetooth connection between her headphones and her laptop. She misses her old room, the lavender-yellow-green layers of paint as she got older and the spot on the closet door where she stuck a *Legend of Korra* poster and never got the tape off. It's hard to learn everything you know about life in the same room and then pack everything up one day and never see it again.

They've tried to make her new room as Chloe as it can be. They painted the walls green and strung up lights around the ceiling, and above the metal bars of her headboard, they hung a giant framed print of her favorite taco truck from their old neighborhood. There's no balcony, only a window facing the sideyard next to the AC unit, but her mom built a wooden bench the width of the sill so Chloe could read in the sun.

It still doesn't feel like home though. After her grandma died sophomore year, Chloe hoped they'd go back, but there was her grandma's house to sort through and sell, and the estate to settle, and then it was too late to finish high school somewhere else.

Titania hops up on the bed, and Chloe pats her between the ears.

One of the things her moms say Chloe inherited from Titania is the way they both need something to scratch at, a place to dull their claws so they don't tear the house apart. That's something Willowgrove has on the hippie schools she went to in California: a chance for her to compete.

It's why she can't stop poking around the place where Shara's supposed to be. As long as they've both been at Willowgrove, Chloe finally had someone to fight for dominance, and that gave some kind of reason to life here. It's not like Shara is *that* important; it's just that, without her, Chloe's not sure what the point of anything is.

Her friends, she recalls suddenly. That's the point of her life here. Georgia and Benjy and Ash, her friends she was supposed to spend Friday night with before Shara got in the way.

She rolls over, picks up her phone, and FaceTimes Georgia.

"'Sup," Georgia answers after two rings.

"Geoooo," Chloe says back.

The shot is backdropped by the overstuffed shelves of Bell-tower. Georgia's wearing her favorite T-shirt, an off-white tee with a picture of Smokey Bear surrounded by woodland creatures and the slogan *Be careful, there are babes in the forest,* and she's chugging from her emotional support water bottle. The store must have gotten a shipment of new releases—that's the only reason she'd go in when the shop's closed on Sundays.

"You know, I'm really glad you landed on your gay aesthetic," Chloe tells her. "Aspiring park ranger looks great on you."

"Thanks," she says. "I don't know why it took me so long. I guess I didn't realize being a Girl Scout and being gay could be the same thing."

"Remember your 'Hey Mamas' phase," Chloe says.

"*Please,* that was like, *one week,*" Georgia groans.

In the year since Georgia first told Chloe she liked girls, she's cycled through a half dozen different lesbian aesthetics trying to figure out which one was her. First was tying her hair up and wearing Nike sports bras and researching face exercises to sharpen her jawline, then it was high femme red lipstick and drawn-on tattoos, next were ripped jeans and thrifted leather jackets, and exactly once, she considered cutting off her hair entirely and trying out for the soccer team. In the end, Chloe's mom gifted Georgia a carabiner for her seventeenth birthday, and she chopped off her hair above her shoulders and it all came together.

"Where have you been?" Georgia asks. "I texted you like, three times last night to see if you were coming to Ash's for movie night."

Chloe winces.

"My mama came home from Portugal today," she says.

"My mom's been going nuts cleaning the house. She roasted an actual turducken. It's a whole thing. How was the movie?"

"We got sidetracked doing a mozzarella stick tasting."

"A what?"

"Benjy drove us around and we picked up mozzarella sticks from every place in town. Then we ranked them on a scale of one to ten for flavor, presentation, structural integrity, and dipping sauce."

"Oh my God. I'm so mad I missed that. Did you average the results at the end? Who won?"

"Chloe, we're gay. We can't do math."

"Okay, well, next time I'll come and make a spreadsheet."

"This is why we need you," Georgia says. "Once in a generation, there is born a bisexual who can do math. You're the chosen one."

She switches the call to her laptop and slides Georgia's face to the side, opening up Chrome while Georgia describes how Ash almost threw up in a bush because they keep insisting they're not lactose intolerant even though they obviously are. Georgia and her do this a lot—sitting on FaceTime for hours while they work on homework or scroll silently through their phones. What she loves most about Georgia is how she's only ever felt completely comfortable in her company, even when she's pissed off or stressed or insecure or weird. Everything's easy with Georgia.

"Did you ever figure out what that card was about?" Georgia asks. "The one Shara left for you at Taco Bell?"

Ah. That's why everything's easy with Georgia. Because she can read Chloe's mind.

"Popular girl wants attention, I guess," Chloe says. Her hands fidget on the keyboard, and somehow she's pulling up the burner email account Shara left for them. Hm. Well, since she's here, might as well check the drafts. Maybe there's something new since the last five times she checked. "Who cares?"

"Uh, you, like three days ago?" Georgia points out. "Like, a lot?"

"I thought you were sick of me complaining about Shara," Chloe says. She doesn't find any new drafts, but the editing timestamp on the one in the folder says someone logged in this morning. Suspicious.

"I mean, kind of," Georgia says. "But getting kissed by Shara Wheeler is the most interesting thing that's happened to either of us in a long time, so I'm kind of invested."

"It wasn't even a good kiss," Chloe lies spectacularly. "Anyway, that's Smith's problem now."

"Fine, starve me."

She could tell Georgia the truth. She thinks about it, even. Georgia knows every other one of her secrets. But she feels fiercely protective of this one, even with Georgia—*especially* with Georgia. She's not sure she wants to hear Georgia's take on this situation. Georgia is the light on the dark side of Chloe's moon, and sometimes Chloe doesn't want to see what's going on over there.

"Do you have time to talk about something real quick?" Georgia asks.

"Is it about the French project?" Chloe says, praying for a change of topic. "Because I promise I am doing tons of research on the June Rebellion."

"Watching *Les Mis* doesn't count."

"I don't see why not."

"Madame Clark specifically said we can't use it as a source."

"Fine, then I'll do other research. Like reading *Les Mis*."

"Look, as long as you write your half of the paper, I don't

even care. I just want this year to be over."

Chloe nods. "I will. Can you send me your notes so far?"

"Yeah, hang on."

Georgia's face disappears momentarily, and then there's the ping of an email.

As she opens her inbox, she considers sending Shara an email enumerating all the ways she's pissed Chloe off, but there's no way Shara would take the bait. She's not responding to Smith's texts or her friends' Instagram comments, only communicating through cryptic notes. Everything has to be a guess, a backward word you can only see by holding it up to a mirror. She won't respond to something so obvious.

"Ooh, color-coded," Chloe says, opening the Google Doc Georgia sent her. "I see you took my suggestions."

"Yeah, well, at this point, fifty percent of my human interaction is in Google Docs, so I needed some structure."

Willowgrove has a strict no-phones-on-campus rule, but most students have workarounds. One of the most popular: creating a Google Doc and giving your friends editing permission, so everyone can type in it like an unofficial group chat. It looks like schoolwork, and if a teacher gets too close, you delete everything.

Something changeable, something easily hidden . . .

"Chloe?" says Georgia, and she jumps.

"Sorry, I spaced," Chloe says. "What were you saying?"

Georgia frowns, tucking her hair behind her ear. "I was reminding you that it's due on the twenty-sixth."

"I know," Chloe assures her, even though somehow she thought it was the twenty-eighth. "I'll even come to school in full French revolutionary cosplay the day we turn it in. Really sell it."

"Cool, I'll be Marie Antoinette," Georgia says. "We can roll in a guillotine and do a whole historical reenactment. Anyway, there's something I—"

"Actually," Chloe says, clicking to create a new document. She has an idea. "I gotta go do something. Pick this up later?"

"Okay, tomorrow?"

"Yeah, definitely," Chloe says. "Loveyoubye."

She hangs up and copies the URL for the doc, pastes it into a blank email, puts the burner account into the address field, and hits send.

She imagines Shara getting that ping on her phone. Maybe she's in a hotel with a stolen credit card, bundled up in a fuzzy white robe with a fake ID and cash fanned out on the nightstand, skimming her lips on the rim of a champagne flute. Maybe she's locked away in some cabin in the woods, thumbing through her copy of *Emma*. Maybe she's on a beach in Gulf Shores getting her toes licked by a college sophomore named Brayden.

Wherever she is, she'll see the notification. And then she'll open the email and see the link. And then she'll click on the link, and she'll see the document Chloe created and the three words typed at the top of the page.

**Where are you?**

# FROM THE BURN PILE

Lab report in Chloe's AP Chem binder

Chloe Green & Shara Wheeler
Mr. Rowley
4th Hour
11/2/20

## Acid-Base Titration

Objective: The purpose of the lab is to calculate the concentration of NaOH using a titration with 10 mL of 1.5M HCl.

Procedure: First, we added 50 mL of an unknown concentration of NaOH to the buret and recorded the starting volume for NaOH. Then, Shara told me to add 10 mL of 1.5M HCl to the Erlenmeyer flask because I'm her lab assistant apparently. Then she told me I was doing it wrong. I suggested she do it herself if she cares so much. She inquired as to why I was getting "so defensive." (It should be noted that she was not wearing her hair back per lab rules. While this was not an issue for this particular lab, it is a liability and a distraction, and the rules apply to EVERYONE. I always wear my safety goggles.) Next, I added 2–3 drops of phenolphthalein to HCl.

# 9

Of all the weird parts of life at Willowgrove, chapel day was the hardest for Chloe to get used to.

Once a week, classes shift to an abbreviated schedule to make room for a compulsory hour-long service in the sanctuary on campus. Usually it happens on Wednesdays, but since they also have part of this week off for Easter, it's a special Monday chapel day.

There's a praise band of Willowgrove upperclassmen plodding through Christian rock songs, then a sermon, usually led by a teacher or Principal Wheeler himself. Sometimes a student will be moved by the Spirit to do a shaky fifteen-minute personal testimony at the microphone, like the time Emma Grace Baker explained that her diabetes has brought her closer to Jesus.

Before Willowgrove, the closest Chloe had ever been to church was listening to her mama practice Mozart, and chapel day has made sure she won't ever be back. Sermons have ranged from "Halloween is Satanic" to "a sophomore sent her boyfriend nudes and he forwarded them to all his friends, so now we are going to do a very shame-y talk on modesty and then next week she's going to switch schools while her boyfriend experiences exactly zero consequences." Once, the Spanish teacher got up with an easel pad, drew a diagram of two stick men on a deserted island, and told them the fact that humanity would go extinct on that island was proof God doesn't want anyone to be gay. Occasionally, the school hires actors to do a skit about bullying.

Chloe turns to Georgia as they file into the sanctuary.

"What do you think it's gonna be this week?" Chloe asks her.

"Probably something festive, like a table read of the *Passion of the Christ,*" she says. She's fidgeting with her hair, pinning it behind her ear.

"Remember last year when they had that cop come and try to scare us about drugs, but he ended up telling us exactly how many ounces of weed you can carry without getting arrested?"

"Iconic."

"Hey, Chloe," says a voice, "can I talk to you real quick?"

When she turns, it's Smith who has found his way to her in the crowd. He's wearing his letterman jacket, and Chloe almost has to admire his commitment to jock flexing. It's eighty degrees outside.

Georgia eyes him under a skeptical brow, then Chloe, then the letterman jacket, then Chloe again. *Isengard?*

Chloe shakes her head.

"Be right back," she tells Georgia, and she slips into the current with Smith.

"Is this about the party?" she asks once they're out of Georgia's earshot. "I promise I won't tell your friends you secretly hate them."

"I don't hate *most* of my friends," Smith clarifies. "But that's not what I was gonna say."

"Oh my God, hi, Chloe," Mackenzie Harris says. Smith has been absorbed into the popular-seniors pocket of the crowd, and Chloe's along for the ride like an unfortunate barnacle. "You look really pretty today. Is your makeup different?"

She punctuates the question by turning to Emma Grace and exchanging a raised-eyebrow, too-big smile, the kind of popular girl move that immediately gets Chloe's skin crawling.

"*Anyway,*" she says to Smith, who manages to look somewhat apologetic. "You were saying?"

Smith leans down, closing enough of their height gap that he can lower his voice.

"I was reading Shara's note again last night, and it hit me that maybe we're thinking about the wrong kind of records. What's another place that Rory has *records,* that Shara would have a key to?"

*Records—?* Oh, of *course.* Why didn't she think of that? She's only sat on the other side of the desk having her own file waved threateningly in her face approximately one billion times.

"Wheeler's office," Chloe concludes. "She meant his *student* records. Wait, are you saying you want to break into the admin offices?"

Smith holds up both hands, calloused palms out. "*Nooo* way. I'm not going anywhere near that."

"What happened to 'I'll do anything to find my girlfriend'?" Chloe asks, cocking a brow.

"I can't risk getting caught," Smith says, and he adds, as if anyone has ever forgotten that Shara got recruited by Harvard and Smith got recruited by Texas A&M, "I signed with *A&M,* Chloe."

"Isn't that kind of an insurance policy though? Like, I don't know anything about football, but I'm pretty sure Wheeler can't put a famous quarterback in the Willowgrove recruitment brochures if he expels you before you get to start."

Smith shakes his head. "It's bigger than that. You know I already have my own page on the ESPN website? I'm gonna get an article written about me if I *breathe* wrong. It's a miracle they haven't found out about Shara, and I'm not about to push it."

"Okay, fine," Chloe concedes, "so what are you saying? You want *me* to do it?"

"Um," says Mackenzie's too-friendly voice beside her. "I was gonna sit there."

Chloe looks up and realizes, to her horror, that they've moved into the pews, and she's trapped in the middle of the Shara crowd. Mackenzie's smiling that fake smile, but she doesn't sell it the way Shara does. She has shark eyes.

Chloe glances toward the last pews, where Georgia is sitting wild-eyed between Ash and Benjy, looking ready to mount a Navy SEAL extraction mission.

"I don't want to be here either," Chloe tells Mackenzie.

"Then, um, leave?"

"I—"

*"Shhhh."*

It's Emma Grace this time, shushing her from three seats down. Chloe doesn't know when the praise band wrapped up, but suddenly she, Smith, and Mackenzie are the last three people standing in the entire sanctuary. At the altar, Principal Wheeler has stepped behind the microphone.

"Ms. Green, can you please sit down and be respectful, sweetheart?" he says into the mic. A ripple of giggles breaks out, and Chloe feels her face flush. She wants to shout that Smith and Mackenzie were standing too, but they've already sunk into their seats. She drops down between them and slumps low enough for her face to disappear.

"Good morning, everyone," Wheeler says. He takes the mic off the stand and paces across the stage in that way he likes to do, like he's a cool, casual dude talking about super relatable topics for teens. "I wanted to say a few quick words before we pray today. I want to remind y'all what the Bible tells us about gossiping. We're all tempted every day to talk about each other, but Ephesians 4:29 says, 'Do not let any unwholesome talk come out of your mouths, but only what is helpful for building others up according to their needs, that it may benefit those who listen.'"

On the projection screen above the altar, the Bible verse pops up in white letters on a blue PowerPoint slide. She remembers the note he jotted down in his office last week when she saw the card in his files. *Sermon on gossip.* Of course this was coming.

"I've been hearing that a lot of you have been gossiping about a member of the senior class who happens to be my daughter," he goes on, immediately sucking all the air out of the sanctuary like a caught trout getting vacuum sealed for the freezer. "In fact, one of you took it upon yourself to personally ask me about it."

Smith's chin twitches, and Chloe sinks even lower until she's eye level with the hymnal tucked into the back of the next pew.

She stares at the hymnal. The hymnal stares back.

The only days she likes Bible class are "spiritual devotion" days, when they get to go to the sanctuary and do free-range contemplation on God. She usually spends the hour crawling under pews with her friends, sharing vending machine snacks and hushed laughter. One of those days, about a month ago,

Chloe left her favorite pen behind and had to sneak in between classes to retrieve it, only to find Shara.

The overhead lights were off, so the afternoon sun fell across the sanctuary in slashes through the tall, thin windows, and there Shara was, halfway illuminated in one. Even from the other side of the church, Chloe recognized her by her delicate quarter profile and the way her blond hair fanned behind her shoulders. She was by herself, her fingers resting on the spine of a hymnal in the next pew, and her head was bowed like she was praying.

Chloe left without her pen. She didn't want to be alone in a room with Shara and God.

"I know you're all very curious," Principal Wheeler goes on. "When you care about someone, and they're part of your community and your fellowship, it's natural to worry about them. But it's never okay to spread rumors, or to tell lies about another person. And if the Lord is calling someone to be somewhere else for a time, that's nobody else's business. All right?"

Chloe counts the rows quickly—it's the same pew. The hymnal might be the same hymnal Shara touched that day.

Wasn't it suspicious, actually, that Shara was in the sanctuary by herself? Praying in public is basically a competitive sport at Willowgrove—why would she be sneaking around to do it, unless she had something to hide?

Something like a little pink card?

They haven't found any clues that point toward the sanctuary yet, but if they're already hidden, and she can guess a place one might be, she can take a shortcut off the trail.

She slides the hymnal from the pew and shakes it upsidedown—Emma Grace makes a face like she's kicked a puppy named Jesus down a flight of stairs—but no card falls out.

"I want to remind y'all that here at Willowgrove we have a zero-tolerance policy for bullying, and bullying can come in many forms," Wheeler says. "And one of them is gossip. So, if you're going to spread a rumor about someone, think real hard about whether it's really, really worth it. And then do the right thing."

After an excruciatingly long pause, Wheeler leads the student body in prayer and then passes the mic to the guest speaker for an unnecessarily grisly lecture on the crucifixion. Smith shifts in his seat, pressing his fist into his chin. Chloe crosses her arms and wishes she were in the back row exchanging harrowed eye contact with Georgia instead of feeling Mackenzie's bony elbow in her side.

Afterward, Smith grabs her arm before she can make a break for it.

"Ask Rory about the office," Smith says. "He's good at stuff like this."

When the lunch bell rings, Chloe clears out of French before Georgia is done zipping her backpack and heads in the opposite direction of the choir room.

Willowgrove does have a cafeteria, but most students don't actually use it. The high schoolers disperse into unofficial designated areas of campus for lunch: freshmen against the brick cafeteria exterior, sophomores on the steps of the sanctuary, juniors in the courtyard, and seniors with the prime real estate of the benches outside C Building.

She passes Smith, perched on the armrest of a bench, surrounded by the same people she was trapped between two hours ago during chapel. Mackenzie turns to Emma Grace and says something behind her hand, and they dissolve into laughter. Chloe glances at Smith, hoping for a lifeline of annoyance.

But Smith's attention is on something in the distance, and she follows his line of sight to find exactly the person she's looking for: Rory, pointedly avoiding the rest of the grade by situating himself inside the campus live oak. One good thing about the weird, jealous feud between Rory and Smith: As long as she can find one, she'll find the other.

The live oak is massive and technically off-limits to students, since its lower branches are perfect for both easy climbing and filing a lawsuit when you break your arm. For what it's worth, she thinks, Rory *does* look like a cool rule-breaker lounging up there on a bough.

He's not alone either. There's also Jake Stone, the infamous Stone the Stoner, and on the branch above Rory, there's April Butcher, most often spotted cruising around the parking lot after school on a longboard like girls Chloe used to see at the Santa Monica Pier. The only indication that she cares about anything at all is the fact that she's on the marching band's drumline.

"Yo, Chlo," Rory calls down to her as she approaches.

She squints up at him and the acoustic guitar in his lap. "How'd you get a guitar up there?"

"The tree provides," April answers for him. She unwraps a Tootsie Roll pop and puts it in her mouth.

"I'm assuming you come bearing Shara news," Rory says, plucking a melancholic chord.

Chloe stares up at April and Jake, both exuding an air of disaffection that suggests they'd rather be hotboxing Rory's Beemer right now.

"They know about the Shara thing?"

Rory furrows his brow. "They're my friends. Of course they know about the Shara thing. Did you not tell your friends about the Shara thing?"

"You're like," Jake says from his tree nest like a lightly blazed owl, "taller than I thought you were like, up close."

"Thanks?" Chloe says, and then she pulls herself up to a low branch and explains Smith's theory about the clue and the office. "He doesn't want to help us with this one, though, so it's just us."

"Oh." Rory's next chord goes unpleasantly flat. He glances up, and Chloe knows he's looking at Smith, and that Smith is now trying to pretend he was squirrel-watching. "Figures."

Chloe barrels on. "Can we talk logistics? I've spent a lot of time in Wheeler's office, so I know the layout pretty well."

"So have I," Rory points out.

"You—" Right. She forgot she has that in common with Rory. She spares a thought for how much butt warmth they've unknowingly shared via Wheeler's office chair over the years. "Well, I've also spent a lot of time at school after hours for rehearsals and club meetings, so I know that—"

"Every door in this school is on a timer and locks automatically at 5 p.m.?" Rory finishes for her. "Yeah, I know."

"How?"

Rory shrugs. "You ever heard of this thing called loitering?"

"Okay," Chloe says, "so, then—then you know that there's no way to get in or out of the building outside of school hours without a key, and there's no way to get to Wheeler's office during the day without going through Mrs. Bailey and five other administrators, so basically our options are to get a key or evacuate the entire campus, which seems kind of extreme but I'm not *totally* against it—"

"Or we could hide somewhere inside C Building until everyone goes home," Rory suggests simply.

"That *would* work," Chloe agrees, "except all the inside doors would still be locked."

"Wait," Jake says. "What's your friend's name? The one who looks like you but with better vibes?"

"Her vibes are fine, dude," Rory says. "Don't be shitty."

"Thank you," says Chloe, whose vibes have never been complimented before. "Um, do you mean Georgia?"

"Yeahhh, that girl," Jake says. "Isn't she a library aide? I always see her when I'm skipping sixth hour."

"Yeah, she is," Chloe says. "Why?"

"Well, then she has a key."

"To the *library* office," Chloe points out. "Not the *principal's* office."

"Right," Rory says, drumming his fingers on the fretboard of his guitar. "But you work backward from what you have." He jerks his chin up toward the top of the tree, which brushes up against the side of C Building. "The library office, it's that window, right?"

Chloe looks up through the branches to the second-story window covered in Easter egg stickers and lined with books. She knows it well; Georgia sometimes lets her sneak in her overdue books to avoid late fees.

"Yeah," she confirms.

Rory does a contemplative lip bite. "Pretty short jump."

"Okay," Chloe says, "so we can get out of the building. But there are still at least three locked doors between that window and Wheeler's office, unless you can like, walk through walls."

"What about through the ceiling?" Rory asks.

"Dude," April says, her jaw dropping so fast, her Tootsie Roll pop plummets to the ground below. "Do you mean—"

Rory smirks. "That's *exactly* what I mean."

"*Without* us?"

"There's no way it could be all four of us," Rory says. "Way too risky. You guys have to be the support team from the parking lot. Jake?"

"But it's our *dream*!"

"*What* are you talking about?" Chloe demands.

Rory tilts his head back, settling it against the tree so his curls crumple up at his crown and his jawline goes all model-y, his eyes slipping closed like visions of perfectly executed pranks are dancing in his head. He answers, in the wistful voice of someone announcing a long-awaited fantasy: "The air ducts."

# FROM THE BURN PILE

Passed notes between Tucker Price
and Tyler Miller

Written in the margins of
an American History study guide

dude i hooked up with the Mistress of Pain herself last
night at the Quiz Bowl party

Chloe Green????? what happened?

made out in the hot tub

wow haha did you like it

it was fine I guess? kinda thought I would be more into
it than I ended up being

Passed notes between Tyler and Ash


Scribbled in one corner of a still-life
drawing exercise in art class


Aren't you friends with Chloe Green?

yeah why? btw yr interpretation of the
assignment is rly cool, those grapes look
really anguished. great job!

Do you know if she likes anyone?

she does but she doesn't know it yet

wtf is that supposed to mean

why are you asking?

Because my friend Tucker told me
he made out with her in his parents
jacuzzi and I was just wondering if
she liked him

ohhhh the one with the nose on Quiz Bowl?
why doesn't he ask her himself?

bc Chloe Green is terrifying??? also pls don't tell her I asked. or him, actually.

genuine question: are you in love with Tucker? full support if so, his nose is very interesting to look at

What??? No?????? He's my friend??????????

then why are you asking about Chloe, and why do you care if he finds out

Forget it!!!!!

# 10

Rory is terrible at pretending to study.

"Can you at least like, look at a note card?" Chloe mutters across the study tables. They've been sitting ten careful feet apart for an hour and a half now, trying to look like two casual classmates who happen to both be spending their after-school time in the library and are certainly not going to abscond into the HVAC system as soon as the opportunity arises.

Rory scratches the back of his head and ignores her. He's got his black Converse propped up on the nearest chair and a small tape recorder on the table in front of him. Chloe suspects he thinks it makes him look cool and alt and analog, but she's seen that exact recorder on the Urban Outfitters website for $90, and he's listening to it with $200 AirPods.

*Chloe* at least has her AP European History notes out. If Ms. Dunbury sniffs them out before they get a chance to put their plan in motion, it'll be Rory's fault, not hers.

She closes her eyes and pinches the bridge of her nose, imagining Shara somewhere far away, in a corset, surrounded by cake. Gotta stay focused. The guillotine won't drop itself.

At long last, Ms. Dunbury retreats from the front desk

into the library office, and Chloe hears the pops of a fork stabbing through plastic and the beeps of a microwave. A Lean Cuisine, definitely. That gives them three minutes.

"*Hey*," she hisses at Rory. When he doesn't respond, she stands and plucks out one of his AirPods. "Let's go."

They gather up their bags and slip silently to the back of the stacks, to the AC vent in the ceiling over the nonfiction section. She passes her backpack to Rory, and while he's hiding their stuff among the musty throw pillows of a reading corner, she pushes a cart of returns up to the shelf below the vent.

When she looks over at Rory, he's stripping off his uniform polo.

"Whoa, *what* are you doing?"

"The less uneven parts of your clothing to get caught on something up there, the better," Rory tells her, now in his undershirt. "I've watched a lot of YouTube videos about this, okay? Trust me."

Chloe groans but doesn't waste time arguing—she whips her oxford off and chucks it at Rory, who crams it alongside their stash and then gets down to business.

She's never seen Rory do anything with urgency before, so it's kind of incredible to watch him spring into his element like a cat burglar. He levers himself off the book cart with one foot and scales the shelves the rest of the way up in one fluid second, and then he's soundlessly popping the vent off and pushing it upward into the ceiling before Chloe has finished straightening out her undershirt.

"You gotta go in first," he whispers to her, hopping down.

"What? No, you have to go first and pull me up."

"Chloe, look. I didn't ever want it to come to this, but we have to be honest with each other." He closes his eyes gravely.

"You can lift more than me. It makes more sense for *you* to help me up."

"Oh," Chloe says. "Okay."

Feeling quite pleased with herself, she follows the same route Rory did up to the opening in the ceiling, silently apologizing to the sanctity of libraries and to Millard Fillmore when she kicks his biography. She sticks her head into the dark hole, hooks her elbows over the ledge, and pushes off the bookshelf with both feet. It takes a helpful nudge from Rory, but she makes it.

The air duct is . . . well, an air duct. It's not nearly as well-lit as they always are in movies, just a long, dim, narrow metal box, like a coffin made of space blankets. The library vent seems to be at the end of a short branch off the main trunk, because a few feet ahead, a slightly wider duct intersects with this one and stretches perpendicularly into the darkness.

Chloe is very completely inside the ceiling of the school. Like, she is up there. No arguing with that.

"Shara fucking Wheeler," she mutters, as she twists around on her stomach until she can see Rory below.

But when Rory tries to use the cart for a boost, some ancient, rusted screw decides to give up the ghost, and the entire top shelf breaks off with a grinding, metallic crash.

Two dozen hardcovers avalanche to the floor, clattering against one another and smashing open with pulpy slaps against the bookcases. Across the library, there's the sound of the office door being thrown open, followed by the portentous stomp of Ms. Dunbury's orthopedic sneakers.

"What are y'all doing back there?"

"Shit," Rory hisses.

"*Oh my God*," Chloe gasps. She's going to be ripped straight out of the ceiling and into a permanent suspension. She glances at the grate resting inside the duct, wondering if she can drag it over fast enough to seal herself in.

But when she looks back down, she sees Rory, knee-deep in books and visibly calculating a hundred ways he could still outrun the law, and she stops.

"Come on," she whispers, extending her arm down to Rory. "You can make it."

She doesn't know if it's true—the library's not that big—but she can't leave an enemy of the Willowgrove Code of Conduct behind.

"Heyyyy, Ms. Dunbury!" says a sudden, jovial voice from what sounds like the library entrance. "How's my favorite librarian doing this fine afternoon?"

Rory exhales. *"Smith."*

"Mr. Parker! What are you doing here?"

"Just finished training. Gotta stay in shape for the fall, you know what I'm saying? I was stopping by my locker when I saw the library was still open and I thought, 'Man, when's the last time I checked on my girl Debbie?'"

Ms. Dunbury giggles. A diversion. Damn, he's good.

"What is he doing?" Rory mumbles to himself.

"Saving your ass," Chloe hisses. She waves her hand at him. "Let's go!"

With a parting glance at Smith and a shake of his head, Rory scales the bookcase in one breath and grabs hold of Chloe's arm with the next. Together, they haul him up into the duct, and as soon as his last foot is in, he crawls over Chloe to pop the vent back into place.

They're both momentarily silent, piled on top of each other, illuminated only by thin slats of light through the vent.

"Oh my gosh, you have so much to carry," Smith says. "Can I help you?"

"Oh, I couldn't ask you to—"

"With all due respect, Ms. Dunbury, what is the point of these protein shakes I drink if I can't carry some books?"

"Oh, you're an angel," Ms. Dunbury says, predictably melting. The microwave dings, forgotten. "I see why Shara's so sweet on you."

"Ha, yeah."

"How is she, by the way? I heard she's off taking care of her sick aunt. That's our Shara, isn't it?"

"Uh-huh," Smith says. "Got your keys? Great, let's go."

The doors close, and half a second later, Chloe can barely make out the click of the automatic lock.

"Was that incredibly convenient timing," Chloe says, squinting at Rory in the dark as he clambers off of her, "or did you tell him what we were doing?"

"I may have stopped by his locker after seventh hour and mentioned that *some of us* were actually going to be trying to find his girlfriend after school today."

"You know what," Chloe says, "it worked out for me, so, can't complain."

They take stock of their surroundings: the tunnels extending in different directions, the specks of light from vents, the low *whoosh* of air.

"Do you hear that?" Rory asks.

Chloe listens: a muffled, faint sound of music playing, echoing down the ducts to their left.

"Sounds like it's coming from the admin office."

"No," Rory says, pointing right, "the office is that way."

"No, that way is the chem lab." She points left. "*This* way is the office."

"But—but we're—it's—"

She points more emphatically. "That way."

Rory grumbles but crawls to the left, and Chloe follows. After about ten feet, the duct splits off to the right, and Rory takes the fork and keeps crawling toward the noise. Another few yards, and he reaches another vent and peeks through it.

"We're over the hall," he says, his quiet voice reverberating back to her. "You were right. The office should be straight ahead."

"Told you."

"Shut up," Rory says. The music's getting louder the farther they crawl. "That sounds like—"

*. . . straight up, what did you hope to learn about here . . .*

"It's Matchbox Twenty," Chloe confirms. Someone is in the admin offices, burning the midnight oil to the greatest of late '90s top-40 rock. As long as Wheeler's office door is shut, they shouldn't have a problem. "Keep going."

After what feels like days dragging herself along sheet metal on her stomach, trying to keep her shoes from banging around and pretending nothing small and leggy could possibly crawl up her skirt, listening to the distant music switch from Matchbox Twenty to Hootie & the Blowfish, they take a left into another duct and reach the next vent. Rory checks it.

"Admin reception. Almost there."

The closer they get, the more details Chloe adds to her fantasy of dropping into Wheeler's office like a jewel thief, somersaulting through lasers, maybe having a French accent. She wonders if Shara has any idea how far Chloe would go to beat her. Maybe that's why Shara hid a card here in the first place—to see if Chloe had the brains and the nerve to find a way.

Nice try, Shara. If there's one thing Chloe's good at, it's tests.

"Fuck," Rory curses suddenly.

"What?"

"Shhhhh."

He's peering down through the vent. It sounds like they're right over the source of the music.

Rory scrubs a dusty hand over his face and whispers, "Well, the good news is, we found the right vent."

"It's Wheeler, isn't it?" Chloe guesses. "He's working late."

"Yeah." Hootie & the Blowfish fades out, and they both hold their breath until Matchbox Twenty picks back up. It's really not a very creative playlist. "At least we have a sound buffer."

"God, why is he still here? What is he doing? There's no way his job is that hard. All he does is cut the arts budget and misinterpret the Bible. How many hours can that possibly take?"

Gingerly, Rory wriggles his phone out of his back pocket and starts a call. "April. We— Yeah, the ducts are everything we thought they would be. Yeah, it's just like *Die Hard*. Yeah—uh, but you guys are gonna have to chill in the car. It might be a while."

"Hey, Chloe," Rory says. "Wanna see something cool?"

It's been two and a half hours. One-hundred and fifty minutes of lying in a dusty air duct over the administrative offices, listening to the Spin Doctors. Chloe texted her moms that she'd be out late studying with Georgia, but she probably should have sent them her final farewell, because she's definitely going to die here.

They've scooted back far enough in the duct system to find an intersection where they could lie head-to-head instead of feet-to-face, suffering in silence under the glow of Rory's phone flashlight.

"Rory, if you show me that dead mouse again, I swear to God I'm gonna make you eat it."

"Not that," Rory says. "This."

He puts his thumb and forefinger inside his nose, and for one hideous second she thinks he's about to show her something his sinus cavity created, until a shiny piece of silver catches the light from his phone. He's flipped down a hidden septum barbell.

"You have a *secret nose piercing*?"

"I told you it was cool," he says. "April did it."

"Don't you have like, money? You could pay a professional who won't give you a staph infection."

"That would totally kill the vibe," Rory says. "And my *stepdad* has money, not me."

"So he's the one who buys all your nice guitars?" Chloe asks, remembering Rory's collection of glittering Strats. "I grew up around musicians. I know what those things cost."

"My mom buys guitars for me because she knows I like them, and she feels bad for making me move into the country club so she could marry some douchebag lawyer and ditch me for trips to Cancun. My dad calls them 'guilt-tars,' which I also hate, but I like my dad."

"Ah," Chloe says. From this angle, the phone light catches on his curls in the places where he's bleached them, and she imagines him huddled in the bathroom with April and Jake and a bleach kit the same way she and her friends gathered around the sink to help Ash cut off all their hair. "Okay. Well, the piercing is cool."

"Thanks."

"You should wear it to school."

"I wear it to school every day."

"I meant visibly."

Rory shrugs, his shoulders sliding up and down the sheet metal. "Yeah, I don't know. If you're gonna break rules, I don't really see the point in dress code violations. Low-hanging fruit. Draws too much attention. Doesn't even inconvenience anyone that bad."

Chloe frowns. "Feeling subtweeted right now."

"Why do you do it, then?"

"I guess because ... I already know people are going to be staring at me, and that teachers are going to find some reason to punish me, so at least this way I control *why*."

"Fair enough."

"Also, I look fucking cool. And the dress code is stupid."

Rory smirks. "I'm with you on the last part, at least."

"And ..." Chloe goes on. "I mean, it's probably also that I can't really break any bigger rules than that, because then I'd actually be risking valedictorian, and I can't risk that."

"Aren't you kind of risking it right now?" Rory asks, gesturing with one hand to their whole insane situation.

"This is different," Chloe insists. "Nobody's ever gonna know we did this. And we're doing it so I can find Shara before grades are finalized and make her come back. I didn't work my ass off for the last four years *not* to see her face when she loses."

"Jesus," Rory says. "Is that really the only reason you're doing this? Valedictorian?"

"Better than trying to get in her pants."

"That's—" Rory blinks a few times, like she's managed to unsettle him. "That's not how I see Shara."

"Then how?"

He considers the question, then rolls over onto his side

and says, "What was middle school like for you?"

"What does that have to do with anything?"

He smirks. "Humor me."

"Okay," she says. "Um, grew five inches, started taking high school English, briefly got into cosplay. Best friend was this girl named Priya who taught me how to do my eyeliner, but we haven't really kept in touch. Told my moms I was bi when I was thirteen and they weren't even surprised. Realized I was weird but that I kinda liked it."

"Yeah," Rory says. "So, for me, it sucked ass. My parents split up. I had no friends. I was this awkward, ugly kid who liked poetry but hated reading it, so I got really into music instead, but I couldn't read guitar tabs either so I had to learn from YouTube, and *then* I had double jaw surgery in eighth grade to fix my underbite, *and* I was the only Black kid in the grade other than Summer, who was way too cool to hang out with me. I was roasted every day of my life. Dixon Wells used to call me Snore-y Rory because I had really bad asthma and sometimes I would breathe weird during tests."

"His name literally has the word 'dicks' in it," Chloe says, "and that's the best he could come up with?"

"I know," says Rory, whose face in profile is such a work of art that she should have guessed someone designed it on purpose. "So, seventh grade, Smith shows up. Said my Naruto backpack was cool. He was my first best friend, or whatever—my *only* friend, unless you count my older brother. He'd help me with my homework and with writing down my songs, and I was like, maybe high school won't totally wreck my shit. But then he ditched me, and everything sucked again. My dad took a job in Texas, and my brother left for college, and my mom got remarried so we had to move—but when I looked out the window of my new room, I saw a girl next door reading a book, and it was Shara fucking Wheeler."

"And you thought she was going to solve all your problems," Chloe guesses.

"You don't get it, Chloe. Shara has been the ultimate girl since I was in kindergarten. And that's not my opinion—literally everyone I've ever met thinks Shara Wheeler is the ultimate."

Chloe grinds her molars together. "I'm well aware."

"What I'm saying is, everyone said she was the dream girl, so I grew up believing it," Rory explains. "She's the only girl I've ever thought about. Like, it *had* to be her. So, I thought if Shara Wheeler ever looked over the fence and noticed me, if that was all I had going for me, it would be enough. Because it would be *her*."

She does kind of understand what he means. If Willowgrove is the whole world, and every person in it sees themself as the main character of their own story, and Shara is the mandatory leading girl, she's either the love interest or the antagonist. Chloe made her choice. Rory made his.

"But then," Rory goes on, "I got my braces off, and I realized I could use a tape recorder to keep track of my songs, and my face finally figured its shit out, and I made a couple friends, so I got over it. Or thought I did. Until this one night, when Smith pulled up to Shara's house with her in the passenger seat. I wasn't trying to look. I was sitting at my desk, working on a song. But that little ceiling light in his car caught my eye, and when I looked, it was like they were inside a snow globe or something. And they kissed, and I—it felt like someone had punched me in the stomach. And it all came back."

For some reason, she's reminded of her first memory of Shara and Smith together: a pile of carnations on the lab table,

Shara holding one to the tip of her nose and breathing in deep while Chloe tried to finish the experiment on her own.

"Is that what you write songs about?" Chloe asks. "Shara?"

"Sometimes," Rory admits in a low voice. "Sometimes they're about like, being jealous or sad or afraid something's wrong with you. Or whatever."

Chloe never really thought Rory was *that* serious about music, because he doesn't act very serious about anything, but the lilt of his voice when he talks about songwriting reminds her of Benjy talking about a new piece he's learned. Maybe she should introduce them sometime.

"That sounds cool," she says.

Rory smiles softly, shyly. Chloe smiles back.

She thinks of what he said about his dad and remembers the bulletin board in his room.

"You and your dad," she says. "You're close?"

"Yeah," Rory says, still smiling. "He's really fucking cool. He's a museum curator."

"Why didn't you just go with him when he moved?"

"My parents were afraid my grades would get even worse if I switched schools. So Mom got school months and Dad got summers."

"That must have been hard."

"Yeah, well," Rory says. "Life sucks sometimes."

She tries to transpose awkward middle school Rory over the one she knows. Must have been one hell of a shock for Smith when his ex–best friend showed up hot on the first day of freshman year—

The music from Wheeler's office cuts out.

They listen to the muffled noises below: a pause, then a door opening and closing, then another farther away. Ten seconds. Twenty seconds. Nothing.

"I think he left," Chloe whispers.

"Move it, Green," Rory says, and he takes off down the duct.

Over Wheeler's office, Rory pulls the vent up and lowers himself out feetfirst, narrowly avoiding the keyboard and papers as he drops onto the desk. Wheeler's left the overhead light off, but the desk lamp is still on, so Chloe has to squint to see where to land when she jumps down behind him.

They split up, Chloe pacing the perimeter of the office while Rory opens each drawer of the desk. Chloe recites the clue in her head: *The key is there, where I am.*

Where *isn't* Shara? Even in Chloe's first visits here, the Shara of it all was suffocating, like a Bath & Body Works candle in a sickly sweet scent that someone left burning too long. She'd sit in the chair opposite the desk getting lectured and wonder, is this where Shara hides between the final bell and National Honor Society? When Shara was a kid, did she crawl under her dad's desk, absorbing the essence of Willowgrove through the gray carpet? This is another episode of, *Has Shara picked up that book? Touched that stapler? Printed a major works data sheet on that printer?*

She's checking the bookshelf when she notices, wedged between two different memoirs of Republican senators, something pink.

It's not with the records, but it's definitely one of Shara's cards.

She glances over her shoulder—Rory's occupied with the contents of the desk drawers.

She can have this one to herself for a second. Just her and Shara.

She slides it out.

*Mom & Dad,*
*I'm fine. If you want to find me, I'm sure you can.*

*S*

This must be the card Chloe saw that morning she got herself called in. One line. Two sentences, twelve words. That's all Shara left for her parents. If it were Chloe, she'd get about fifteen minutes out before her moms pulled up in the truck and dragged her to Webster's for sundaes and group therapy.

She slips the card back into its spot on the shelf and turns to the desk, where Rory is checking under the blotter.

"Anything?" Chloe asks him.

"No key," Rory says.

And then Chloe's eyes land on the picture.

The framed photo of Shara and her parents on their sailboat, the one that's always bothered her because it faces out, for the benefit of visitors instead of the actual dad sitting at the desk.

*Where I am.*

Chloe snatches up the frame and flips it around, and there it is: a small key, taped to the back of the frame, under the hinge of the stand so it's invisible from the desk chair. Shara hid it right in front of her dad's face.

"I got it."

She rips the key off, and when she puts it into the lock of the filing cabinet, it's a smooth slide. She twists, and there's the satisfying, hollow thunk of the lock opening.

"Perfect, this is the senior drawer," Chloe says to Rory, already thumbing through files. "If it's here, it's probably in your folder, but we should check mine and Smith's too. Come help me."

Rory finally closes the desk back up and comes to hover at the side of the cabinet, staring at the tabs on the files. "Um."

Chloe glances up. "What, this is your thing. Don't get shy now."

"Not that," Rory grouses. "I—the letters are really small."

"What?" Chloe slides Smith's file out, moving forward to the G–H section. "Do you need glasses?"

"No," Rory says. "I just think you should do this part."

She pauses, holding Rory's file, which is thick from what must be fifty pages of detention slips and complaints from teachers about how he doesn't try in class. She remembers the way Rory wordlessly handed her Shara's card in his room instead of reading the password to her, and the different inks in his songbook, like it took him days of fits and starts with different pens to get it all down. The directions in the ducts, the tape recorder—

"Ohhhhh," she says, realizing at once. "You're dyslexic."

Rory stares at her. "What?"

"No time, explain later." She spots the correct label sticking out of the drawer and points to it. "Mine is that one, with the purple tab."

He passes Chloe her file, and she spreads all three out on the desk. As expected, the card is in Rory's. Picture-ready pink, sealed in its envelope and paperclipped to a middling progress report.

Chloe opens it, and this time, she reads Shara's words out loud.

Hi Rory (and also Chloe, I'm assuming),
Glad to see you've gotten this far. By my estimation, it should have taken you about a week and a half from prom night, based on

when Dixon's next house party was scheduled. Of course, that depends on if I'm right about Chloe being fast enough to find the note I left in the choir room before the party, but I know she is. And I know the card at Dixon's house should have been exactly where I put it, because before I left, I texted him that if it was moved, I would tell Emma Grace and Mackenzie that he's been feeling up both of them behind the other's back.

And, well, I really do hope you've already found that one, because on Friday morning Emma Grace and Mackenzie are getting an anonymous Instagram message anyway. That's one thing about me nobody knows: I don't actually care about keeping my promises.

Keep going. You're getting closer.

XOXO

S

P.S. I've heard you can take your heart back, but I don't think you can. Up close, with the light in your eyes, all you can see is what's right in front of you.

"She was *blackmailing her own friends?*" Chloe says as soon as she's finished reading.

"I'm, uh, honestly more worried about how she predicted the exact day we'd be here," Rory says.

"And sabotaging her friends' relationships," Chloe goes on. Vindication zips up her spine like a chill, and she can't stop herself from smiling down at the card.

She *knew* there was a reason she didn't like Shara, but she never had any concrete evidence against her, until now.

And if this is the first piece, there could be more where it came from.

"I'm like, kind of starting to wonder if we should be . . . afraid of her?" Rory says.

Chloe ignores him, reading back over the postscript, zeroing in on the first line. She knows that phrase. But what does it—

From the front entrance of the offices, there's the unmistakable sound of a door opening. The hum of a man's voice carries through the walls, half-remembering the chorus of a Dave Matthews song.

"Oh my God." Chloe is paralyzed on the spot. For the second time this evening, panic erupts in her chest like a Disneyland New Year's Eve pyrotechnic show, whistles and flashes and sparklers spelling out YOU'RE SCREWED, CHLOE GREEN in the sky. "Ohmygod ohmygod ohmygod—"

Rory, who has already swept the files up off the desk and started cramming them back into the cabinet, whispers at her, "Don't freak out."

"What is he doing!" Chloe wheezes. "He should be home watching NCIS!"

"Chloe."

"Oh my God, Smith was right, we shouldn't have done this—"

"Chloe!" Rory says again, grabbing her shoulders. "The more you freak out, the more likely we are to get caught." He gives her a little shake, and her anxious brain rattles unpleasantly. "Chill. This is the fun part."

He's got to be kidding. "The *fun* part?"

"We've all got our own ways to have fun in False Beach, right?" Rory pushes her up onto the desk. "You get horny for books—"

"Very reductive way to describe being interested in literature," Chloe points out hysterically, reaching for the ceiling with numb hands. She can hear the jingle of keys in the hallway.

"—and I get away with shit," Rory finishes. "So get up in that ceiling and get away with this."

She closes her eyes, takes a huge breath like she's jumping off a high dive, and heaves herself up through the vent hole. Rory's right behind her, and he manages to catch the vent cover with the toe of his sneaker and push it back over the opening just as the office door opens below.

Wheeler pauses in the doorway, a Jack in the Box bag in his hand and a suspicious furrow creasing his forehead. Chloe's insides are Pop Rocks.

He walks over to the desk and picks up the framed family photo, which Chloe left where it fell in her panic. He frowns, then licks his thumb and rubs a smudge off the glass in front of his own little photographic face before returning it to the desk, face out.

And then he sits down at his desk, takes out a burger, and turns the music back on.

"Let's go," Rory says to her.

She leads the way this time, retracing the route back to the library, down through the vent—Rory grabs their bags and shirts—over the pile of books they left behind and through the dark stacks, past the study tables, over the front desk, to the door of the library office.

"Turn around," she says.

"What?" Rory asks. "Why?"

"The key's in my bra. Don't look."

"I promise you, I do *not* care."

"Just do it!"

"*Fine,*" he groans, doing a theatrical ninety-degree turn so Chloe can fish the key out from between her boobs.

With the door unlocked, they're almost to sweet freedom. Rory texts April and Jake while Chloe unlatches the window and throws it open. The sun has gone down since they climbed through the first vent.

"You know what I just realized?" Chloe sticks her head out to estimate the distance between the sill and the tree. Not as close as it looked from the ground, but there's a big, sturdy-looking branch a couple of feet below, and if she lands right, she should be able to shimmy down it to the trunk. "This is the second time you and I have thrown ourselves out a second-story window for Shara Wheeler."

"She has that effect," Rory says, and then he climbs over the sill and disappears into the night.

"Shit," Chloe whispers after him.

She jumps, and after a lot of maneuvering and swearing and scrambling and scrapes on her arms from tree bark, they hit the ground running. They bank around the side of the building, cursing through a copse of thorny bushes, and break free to the ditch separating the faculty parking lot from the service road alongside it.

Jake's car is waiting with the back door open. Chloe launches herself into the backseat full of Bojangles bags and energy drink cans with a crunchy, rattling crash. They take off before Rory's even done pulling it shut behind him.

There are five electric seconds in which the only sounds are the roar of the engine and Chloe catching her breath, and then Rory releases a low whistle, and Jake laughs and cranks up the radio.

Chloe laughs too, loud and breathless, adrenaline blazing in her veins. Rory was right. She got away with it. It was one of the most terrifying things to ever happen to her, and it *was* fun.

Ten minutes out from school, Jake pulls into Sonic and tips the roller-skating waitress ten dollars for four slushes, and they take off again, speakers going tinny from the boom of the bass as April shoots her straw wrapper at Rory.

It's not much—Chloe knows this. It's just car windows rolled down, the blue-and-white glow of a Walmart in the distance, the smell of wet pavement under the tires, the hum of neon from a Dairy Queen, the same radio station as always blasting a rotation of the same fifteen songs. But she thinks she's starting to understand what it means to be from here, because she could swear the bright red burn of artificial cherry is the best thing she's ever tasted.

She leans out into the wind and tips her head back, opening her eyes to the stars, and thinks maybe everything in the world really can fit inside False Beach city limits.

Shara has that effect.

# FROM THE BURN PILE

Extracted from the back of Brooklyn's
accordion folder (the pink one, not the
green one)

## Student Council Meeting Minutes
## January 19, 2022

1.  Call to order by Brooklyn Bennett, Student Council President

2.  At 11:37 a.m. in Room C204

3.  12 members, 1 advisor, 1 guest present

    a.  Guest: April Butcher, lounging in the last row, practicing a drum solo on a desk; unclear if aware student council meeting taking place

4.  Minutes of the previous meeting read by Bailey Hunt, Student Council Secretary

Motion to approve the minutes

Moved by Rhett Taggert

Seconded by Julie Tran

Motion carried

5.  Officer's report

    a.  Treasurer's report

        i.   Nothing to report

        ii.  April Butcher (not a member) suggests adding more spicy items to the vending machines

        iii. April Butcher is not recognized by the chair

6.    Standing Committee Report

   a.    Senior Executive Committee
      President Brooklyn Bennett declares the formation of a subcommittee of the Senior Executive Committee: the Prom Planning Committee, which would not be officially recognized by the administration due to dancing (a sin) but will choose theme and decorations

      i.   April Butcher proposes *Teen Mom 2* as a prom theme

      ii.   April Butcher is again not recognized by the chair

      iii.   April Butcher is asked to leave the meeting by Secretary Bailey Hunt

      iv.   April Butcher eats half of the sandwich President Brooklyn Bennett's packed for lunch

      v.   April Butcher is removed from the meeting

# 11

Monday afternoon, Chloe is sitting on the floor of the choir room, tapping the eraser of a No. 2 pencil against a sheet music study guide. It feels ridiculous to be transcribing quarter notes into block letters when everyone in the room has been sight-reading since sophomore year. Everyone in Mr. Truman's sixth hour, Girls Select Chorus, knows that the final exam is a technicality.

"Y'all know if they would let me count the spring festivals for the grade, I would," Mr. Truman tells them.

She's not thinking about sheet music though. She's thinking about the note in Rory's file, the postscript at the end. *Take your heart back.*

The reference is easy. Her brain filled in the rest of the lyric as soon as she got home: *When you find that once again you long to take your heart back and be free . . .*

"Think of Me" was her big solo in *Phantom;* she'll probably have every line seared into her brain until she's dead.

But she can't figure out why Shara would specifically use that song as a reference unless there's something more to it. Like maybe Andrew Lloyd Webber's birthday corresponds to her coordinates. Or she's starting a new life with a man named Raoul. Or she left to get a nose job and is recuperating in a subterranean labyrinth beneath an opera house in France.

She thinks about junior year, when she was Sonia in *Godspell*. At least there weren't any football players in that cast, so she didn't have to see Shara's face while she was doing a G-rated burlesque act about the teachings of Jesus. When she's on stage, she's always thankful the spotlight's too bright to see the audience beyond the first row.

*Up close, with the light in your eyes, all you can see is what's right in front of you.*

She drops her pencil.

The front row of the auditorium. Where Shara sat to watch Chloe in *Phantom*.

Mr. Truman shrugs when she asks to go to the bathroom, and she books it toward C Building instead. Rory is easy to find—she's learned that he usually skulks around the back staircase for his study hall hour—and she fires off her theory.

Rory nods. "We should probably get Smith for this."

"I don't know where he is for sixth hour," Chloe says. "God, the fact that they don't let us have *phones*—"

"Spanish," Rory says.

"What?"

"Smith's in Spanish right now."

Chloe squints at him. Rory squints back. The speed with which he recited Smith's schedule goes unaddressed but not unnoticed.

"Can you get him?" Chloe asks.

Rory heads off with a fake story about Smith being needed in the principal's office and returns with him in tow, as well as—

"Why is Ace with you?" Chloe asks, eyes narrowed. Ace smiles.

"We ran into him in the hall on the way here," Smith says, sounding only slightly annoyed.

"If y'all are skipping, I want in," Ace says.

Chloe sighs. If Rory's friends are involved, she guesses Smith's might as well be too. She wonders, momentarily, if she should have just told Georgia, instead of lying about an overdue book to get the library key, or if Benjy could understand this elaborate Shara production better than Chloe if he got the chance—

No, Rory's and Smith's friends don't count. It doesn't matter if they know, because they think she's weird anyway. *Her* friends will clock how far off the rails she's going, and that'll make everything even more complicated.

"I don't even care anymore," she says, and takes off for the auditorium.

Inside, Smith leads them to the front, where he and Shara sat for the matinee, and the three of them split up. Rory climbs onto the stage and inspects the bottom of the curtain while Chloe folds down the first row of seats one by one, but it's Smith who finds the envelope stuck with a magnet to the metal leg of seat A21.

They all gather around—except for Ace, who stopped at the entrance for a Powerade from the vending machine—as Smith opens the envelope. This note is a long one. They've been getting longer and longer, Shara's handwriting on the cards shrinking smaller and smaller. Smith reads out loud.

Hi,
Me again. Not sure which of you is reading this, but I'm sure all of you will at some point. Good

job with the song lyric, Chloe, since I know that was you.

Smith, you sat right there, one seat over, rolling your program up in your hands because you were so nervous for Ace. You told me you didn't think he could do it, that you'd never heard him sing before. You were afraid he was going to humiliate himself in front of the entire school, and then your jaw dropped when he sang his first line. I really do admire that about you—the way you root for other people. You didn't know that I already knew he could sing, that he told me his mom raised him on Stephen Sondheim soundtracks. You didn't know that's the reason Summer doesn't talk to me anymore—because she caught us.

Chloe, I remember your dress. God, they put you in that nightmare of a frilly white costume gown, more a robe than anything, absolutely hideous, tied at the waist. You should sue. You looked straight into the spotlight. You were avoiding my eyes, weren't you? Do you remember dropping the beginning of a line? (Don't worry, I don't think anyone else noticed.) You must have spent so many hours perfecting the delivery, internalizing the rhythm, and I felt it skip right on past you and your open mouth. You missed a cue by about a second and a half. I squeezed the armrest so I wouldn't smile.

This is what I've been trying to tell you.

XOXO

S

P.S.

*Rory, I haven't forgotten about you. Sometimes I think about last fall, when you had detention and the game got called for rain. Did you think I didn't know you were watching?*

Before Chloe has a chance to react to what Shara wrote about her, Ace saunters up the aisle, chugging Mountain Blast.

Smith folds the card shut and says to him, "Summer caught you with Shara?"

Ace chokes.

"Oop," Rory says. He hops up on the edge of the stage to watch the show.

Ace wipes a dribble of fluorescent blue from his chin. "She—she told you that?"

"She wrote it," Smith says. He holds up the card. "In here."

"I—it wasn't like *that*—"

"Then what was it like?"

If this were two weeks ago, Chloe would be worried she might have a jock-versus-jock Thunderdome deathmatch on her hands. But she's gotten to know both of them a bit since then, and they're two of the least confrontational people she's ever met—especially Smith. Once, when she was looking for him after school, she found him in the bio lab, poking around at the bean sprouts. Another time, he saw her with a book of poems and told her his mom was a spoken-word poet back in the '90s, and that she gave him a Danez Smith collection for his birthday.

So yeah, this is more likely to end in tears, which might be worse.

"I mean, Summer did, technically, break up with me because of Shara, but—"

"Man, if you've been pretending to help me all this time when you—"

Ace holds up both hands in front of his chest. "She was helping me practice for spring musical auditions, okay?"

What.

"What?" Chloe interjects.

"What?" Smith asks, eyebrows near his hairline.

"It's—it's stupid." Ace sinks down into one of the folding seats, running a hand through his floppy hair. "But I've always wanted to try out for spring musical. Always. But it scared the shit out of me, because like, what if I wasn't any good? Or what if I was good, and Dixon and them roasted me for being into showtunes until graduation? And then it was senior year, and it was my last chance, and Truman was doing rehearsals before auditions, and I almost went to one, but I kept thinking, what if I don't get the part? What if I don't even get cast, or they make me like, a tree, and then everyone knows I really wanted it but I wasn't good enough? But I remembered that Shara used to play piano in the talent show when we were kids, so I asked if she could help me with the sheet music. And we started meeting up at my house after school to work on my audition song."

He looks up at Smith and raises his hands helplessly, letting them drop back into his lap. "That was it, I swear."

Never, not in all the evenings after school blocking scenes with Ace in the choir room, not even when she had to practice kissing his big mouth, did it occur to Chloe that Ace didn't audition as a joke.

Smith looks skeptical.

"You're telling me Summer dumped you over that?"

"No, Summer dumped me because I blew off a date to practice, and when she came by my house that night, she saw Shara coming out of the front door and freaked out."

Smith shakes his head, incredulous. "Why didn't you just tell her what y'all were doing?"

"Because Shara said if I ever told anyone she helped me with the music, she'd report me to her dad for smoking weed."

"Okay, now that I don't understand," Chloe butts in. "Shara loves it when people know she's done a good deed."

"I don't know," Ace says. "But she was dead serious. I believed her. And like, Summer is *so* dope, but I can't get expelled right before I graduate. I'll lose my scholarship."

"So," Smith says. He crosses back toward Ace, his hip brushing Rory's knees as he passes. Rory absently reaches down to touch his own knee as he watches. "You . . . you tried to pull a *High School Musical,* basically."

"Yeah."

"And Shara blackmailed you for it."

"Wouldn't be the first person she's blackmailed," Rory points out.

Smith rubs both palms over the back of his head.

"You could have told me before you asked Shara for help," he says finally, softly. "My sister could have helped you. You know she's good at that stuff. And I know everyone else we know has to be all no-homo about everything, but I kinda thought I'd made it clear we're not like that. I mean, I showed you my Sailor Moon collection."

"I know."

"I told you I shared clothes with my sister until I was thirteen."

Chloe leans in. "Quick question: necessity or preference?"

"It's not like that," Ace says, ignoring her. "You're the only one I *didn't* think would judge me. I was afraid of being bad."

"Well, you're not. You were pretty fucking great, actually."

Ace grins at that, wide as ever, and he's on a beach in Tahiti again, all palm trees and coconuts with tiny umbrellas. Chloe doesn't know how he does it.

"Thanks."

"Okay, well," Rory says, apparently bored. He hops down from the stage. "Congratulations on being best friends forever. Can we go get the next note before seventh hour?"

"I don't know where it is," Smith says.

Rory sighs. "I do."

The next card is in the football stadium. Shara's tucked it inside a plastic sandwich bag to protect it from rain and taped it to the underside of a row of bleachers so high up that Chloe has to climb onto Rory's shoulders to retrieve it. Rory looks and sounds like he's about to snap in half from the effort.

"You know, you could have counted the rows, climbed up to that seat on the topside, and reached through the gap in the bleachers," Smith points out as Chloe clambers down Rory's back. "That's probably how Shara put it there."

"A suggestion we could have used two minutes ago," Rory grunts.

Smith shrugs, clearly fighting a grin. "Yeah, but it was fun to watch."

Hi, Rory & company,
There was a football game last fall that got postponed due to lightning. They tried to play, but by the end of the first quarter, everyone was soaked, and nobody wanted to be out there

anymore. Smith, I met you right here, under the bleachers, and I kissed you. On the drive home, you looked out through the rain at a red light and told me it was the first time in a long time that it felt right.

It's so stupid how my dad makes students work for free at the concession stand as a form of detention, isn't it, Rory? You looked miserable, and that was before you even saw me kiss Smith right in front of you. I know you saw, because I knew you were there, watching the same way you watch from your bedroom window, turning away every time somebody looks.

Jealousy is a funny thing. We spend so much of high school consumed by it, hating that another person has something we don't, wishing we could taste what it's like to be them. To take that feeling out of your hands for a second and pass it to someone else is a relief.

So, I guess that's why it felt like I meant it.

XOXO

S

P.S. Chloe, I would offer you a basic question with a simple solution, but I know that wouldn't satisfy you. Still, it might be fun to see your reaction.

Smith, who finally seems to be nearing his limit, turns to Rory when he's done reading.

"Where did you find the first note?" Smith asks him.

Rory frowns. "What?"

"The first note y'all showed me from Shara. It was for you, wasn't it? Where was it?"

The question must catch Rory off guard, because he doesn't hesitate before admitting, "In Shara's bedroom."

"Oop," Chloe says, in Rory fashion. If it were up to her, Smith would never have known either of them set foot inside the Wheeler house.

"You told me you never hooked up with her." It's not an accusation; he sounds different than earlier, when he thought Ace might have been hooking up with Shara. He's reviewing the facts, realizing he's missing something.

"I didn't," Rory confirms.

"So how did you get in her room?"

There it is.

"It was—I was—" Rory starts, and then he visibly realizes that he needs an alibi he doesn't have. He panics and points at Chloe. "She was there too!"

"Really, dude?" Chloe groans. She thought they had a no-snitching policy between them. "At least I used a key. *You* climbed through her window with a *ladder*."

Smith's eyes widen. "You did *what*?"

"Shara told me she was leaving her window unlocked!" Rory insists. "She obviously wanted me to use it, hence the note with my fucking name on it!"

"See, this is what I'm talking about," Smith says, waving the card in Rory's face. "You're always in my shit! Every time I go to Shara's house, there's Rory in his window like a fucking Elf on a Shelf. You're always just—just *there*."

"I live there! I'm allowed to be at my house!"

"You screwed this whole thing up for me! It's supposed to be me and Shara, and instead, it's always me and Shara and *you*, and I know you hate me for dating her even though I knew you liked her, but—"

"That is *not* what my beef with you is."

"What, am I supposed to act like I wasn't there when we were thirteen and you told me Shara was the only pretty girl in school?" Smith says. "Like, do you think I'm dumb?"

"I think you act like a lot of shit from when we were thirteen never happened."

"What's *that* supposed to mean?"

Rory opens his mouth, thinks better of it, and closes it. "Forget it. You know, if your relationship is ruined, that's your problem, not mine. I'm only in Shara's life as much as she wants me to be."

"You don't know shit about what Shara wants!"

"Neither do you, obviously!"

"Hey!" Chloe finally interrupts. "Chill!"

Smith and Rory stop, their faces inches apart. She was going to let them go at it—seems overdue, anyway—but she can't take this anymore. Neither of them deserves the blame for Shara's nuclear fallout.

"This is ridiculous," she says. "What's the common denominator here? Smith, Rory didn't *make* Shara kiss you in front of him. Neither of us *made* her kiss us and skip town. Rory, that note literally says she wanted to make you jealous, because she knew you liked her and she liked the attention. I mean, come on! None of this is because of any of us. It's *Shara*. Stop pretending she's a saint! Read the notes! She's playing both of you, and you're *letting her*."

She stands there under the bleachers, looking from Smith to Rory, waiting for the thing she's been wanting this whole time: for someone to see Shara the way she's always seen her. The bell to end sixth hour rings. None of them make a move to go to seventh.

"I don't understand," Smith says finally, sounding defeated. "Everything she's done the past few weeks, everything she's saying she did in these notes . . . it doesn't sound like her. And I don't understand why she did any of it, or why she's telling me, or why she's telling me like this. And I guess I'm starting to worry that I . . . I don't know. Maybe Rory's right. Maybe I don't know her like I thought I did."

It should feel like the round of applause on closing night, like after a fifth-grade birthday party when her moms proclaimed in the car that all the other parents wished their kids were doing as well in school as Chloe.

But Smith looks sad, and Rory looks annoyed and embarrassed, and it's not as satisfying as it was supposed to be.

"My beef with you," Rory says finally, to Smith, "is that you ditched me for the football guys, who you *knew* were total assholes to me."

"I didn't ditch you for the football guys," Smith says, voice raw and earnest, "*you* ditched *me* because you didn't like that I joined the team, even though I *told* you the whole reason my parents sent me to Willowgrove was to play football."

"That is not what happened," Rory grumbles.

"It's how I remember it."

"Well," Rory says, "I remember it different."

"Okay, well." Smith shrugs. "Whatever."

"Whatever."

"Are we good?" Chloe asks.

"We're good," Smith says.

Rory looks at Smith for a long moment, then crams his hands into his pockets.

"Whatever."

Later, she spends the remainder of seventh hour rewriting lines of Shara's last note from memory in the margins of her

AP Calc notebook and wondering why exactly this doesn't feel the way she thought it would.

Somewhere, in a different classroom, Smith is confronting the fact that this girl he's spent two years projecting a high school sweetheart onto is distant, not because she's too complex, but because she didn't want him to see who she really was. Rory's probably already slouched in the driver's seat of his car, wondering if the girl next door ever existed at all.

Chloe already knew these things. But of all the possibilities she considered for the real Shara, she never seriously thought "evil genius" would be the one that fit.

Shara wrote in Smith's note that she wanted to show him the truth, and that's exactly what she's doing. She's not an angel. She's the type of girl who hurts her friends on purpose and breaks her promises and leaves the people who care about her the most without even saying goodbye.

She gets why Shara would want Smith and Rory to know— what's the point of wanting and being wanted in return if the person they want isn't truly you? She still doesn't get why Shara decided to tell *her* though.

But now that she knows . . . well, she hates to admit it. She really does. But this Shara, the one spelled out on pink stationery, is a million times more interesting than the fake one. Like, no contest.

It's kind of a bummer she's the only one who sees it that way.

# FROM THE BURN PILE

Passed notes between Ace Torres
and Shara Wheeler

Scribbled on the back of Bible worksheet titled
"Armoring Yourself with the Lord"

Hey Shara!

I'm trying to study, Ace.

Cool, I was just wondering if you were free this
afternoon for practice

We've practiced twice already this
week.

I know, but I'm still not sure I have that last
note down

You do. You sound good. Also, I
have an essay due tomorrow.

Really?? You think so??? I mean, I guess if you
think I'm ready, it's just that tryouts are next
week and every time I think about it I feel like
I'm gonna blow chunks

Please never, ever use that expression again.

Sorry!!!! I'm just really nervous!!!

I'll be over at 4.

# 12

The bleachers note changes things.

Smith and Rory, who heretofore were both operating under the impression that they could win Shara if they made it to the end of the trail, really seem to be struggling with the idea that the princess in the tower might be more of a dragon. They stop sniping at each other and start exchanging a lot of morose looks while Chloe does all the work on the clues. She practically has to drag them to the next one.

As for Chloe . . . well, it's not that Chloe forgets how to think about anything other than Shara Wheeler. But nothing else seems half as interesting, which isn't her fault. Honestly, maybe other things should try harder.

"Are you coming tonight, Chloe?" Ash asks.

Chloe blinks, startled out of thought. She looks up at Ash two seats over on the choir risers, holding different sizes of fishing lures up to Benjy's earlobes to test out which one they want to make into earrings while he begrudgingly sits still.

"What?" Chloe asks.

"Me, Georgia, foraging in the park by Winn-Dixie," Ash

says. "Georgia got that book about mushroom identification? I told you about it last week and you said you'd think about it?"

"Oh," Chloe says. She honestly can't quite remember that conversation, but she pretends she does. "Yeah, I can't. I have too much homework."

Georgia squints at Chloe over her lunch, and Chloe feels bad. She does. But there's only one thing she wants to do right now. She promises herself that she'll find time to hang out with Georgia over the weekend.

The rest of the week brings three more clues, one each day. Each one contains a new revelation, some evil deed Shara's kept locked away. Chloe rips a sheet of graph paper from a notebook and makes a table to track them from memory.

| Card # | Location | Pertinent contents |
|--------|----------|--------------------|
| 1 | Shara's desk | Password to burner email |
| 2 | Smith's locker | Instructions to check drafts |
| 3 | Taco Bell drive-thru | Burner email address, implicit threat that she can predict my every move |
| 4 | Inside the choir piano (note: stolen key included) | Stayed up all night to memorize scene from <u>Midsummer</u> so I wouldn't humiliate her in front of whole class |
| 5 | Dixon's house | Planned to break up with Smith |

| 6 | Wheeler's office | Blackmailed Dixon to cooperate, backstabbed him anyway |
| 7 | Auditorium (first row, under seat) | Cast a hex upon me during Sunday matinee, broke up Ace and Summer |
| 8 | Football stadium (under bleachers) | Used Smith to make Rory jealous on purpose because she thought it would be fun |
| 9 | Chem lab (chemical storage closet) | Manipulated student council secretary to rig homecoming court vote so she would lose in upset to Emma Grace Baker because she was "worried about overexposure" |
| 10 | Rory's roof (tied to a rock) | Faked flu on National Signing Day so she wouldn't have to be in Smith's livestream |
| 11 | Shara's gym locker | Spent last summer at home reading with phone on airplane mode while everyone thought she was on mission trip to Nicaragua |

Every single card is another pink shot of satisfaction. She collects them in the makeup pouch at the bottom of her locker like it's a crime scene evidence bag, cataloging all the things she suspected Shara was—dishonest and calculating and fake—and a million others she never could have otherwise proven. Vindictive. Destructive. Mean. An absolute wrecking ball bitch, swinging in silence from a divertingly beautiful crane.

So Chloe is gaining momentum, and Smith and Rory are losing it. Morale is at a record low in the "I Kissed Shara Wheeler" group chat.

"Okay, the last note says there are directions to the next one in a club photo one of us took with her for the yearbook," Chloe says, dropping her tray on the table at the Taco Bell near school. "It has to be the National Honor Society photo she took with me. That's the only extracurricular any of us have in common with her. I just don't know how to get access to it."

Smith braces a hand against his forehead and contemplates his life, as well as his taco order, which he hasn't yet settled upon.

"So . . . this isn't even a clue to find the next note," Smith says. "It's a clue to find another clue to find the next note."

"Come on, chin up," Chloe says. "We gotta be almost there. I have a feeling she made this one harder because it's the last one."

"I don't know how much more I want to know," Smith says as Rory drops an overloaded tray on the table.

Chloe rolls her eyes and unwraps her quesadilla. "God, you guys are so *boring*. We're putting together like, the psychological profile of someone who is either going to be the president of the United States or a full-on serial killer."

Rory begins separating burritos and tacos from his pile of food and setting them down in front of Smith, who finally tears his attention away from the menu.

"What's this?" he asks.

"I got you food."

Smith raises his eyebrows. "What did you get me?"

"I don't know," Rory mumbles, "whatever you usually get."

"You remembered?"

Rory scowls. "They don't have the Grande Soft Taco anymore, so I got you two soft tacos and a side of nacho cheese. You just have to make it yourself. Or whatever."

"Oh. Did you get—?"

"A spork?"

"Yeah."

"Obviously." Rory dedicates himself to picking apart his nachos.

"You want me to Venmo you?"

"It's fine."

"Oh," Smith says. Rory looks up in time to watch Smith's smile break out across his face. It's really something to see, Smith's smile. It comes out of nowhere and hits like an earthquake, absolute and devastating. "Thanks, man."

"You're welcome," Rory says, blinking like he's looking into the sun.

"Wow," Chloe observes. "A friendship reforged."

Rory's scowl immediately returns. "Fuck off, Chloe."

But Smith hums happily as he unwraps the first taco, and the curl of Rory's lip softens.

Meanwhile, Chloe digs through Shara's entire Instagram feed yet again for anything she might have missed. She doesn't find any new leads, only small surprises that amount to nothing. An unfamiliar angle that exposes a birthmark on the top of Shara's shoulder. A well-camouflaged line from a Mary Oliver poem in a caption. There's this one photo of Shara sitting next to Summer on a pier, both wearing sunglasses and smiling wide, and when Chloe zooms in, she can see the faint outline of a book in the tan on Shara's stomach, like she fell asleep reading in the sun. All pieces of the puzzle, but none that complete it.

She checks the Google Doc she sent to Shara's burner a dozen times a day, but it never changes. Always Chloe's same three words, awaiting Shara's answer. The most recent editing date at the top of the page will sometimes change, but no words ever materialize.

Still, she's gaining ground. She's got all these clues, these secrets. She knows she's closing in.

If Shara were an SAT question, she'd be one of those confusing logic puzzles. Critical reasoning with no obvious answers to rule out. Simple, straightforward words arranged in a strange, winding order, something to get lost inside until you realize you're way behind on time and you're going to have to bubble in C for the last four problems.

If Shara leaves town on the highway traveling west at sixty miles per hour, and Chloe spends the next three weeks chasing after her, at what speed will Shara be traveling when they collide?

Time never moves correctly during the last few weeks of school, but especially not at the end of senior year. They're standing before the end of school uniforms and major works data sheets and asking permission to pee, and everything feels exhausted and giddy. The spiritual frequency of the entire senior class is two in the morning at IHOP after the spring musical's last show.

It seems impossible that Shara was standing across a dance floor in her pink gown only a couple of weekends ago.

By the same messed-up laws of time, it feels like ages since she last saw Georgia outside of school when she drives to Bell-tower with Starbucks late Saturday afternoon, even though it's only been a few days.

Georgia's at the front desk sorting through a box of literary fiction, and she gladly accepts the iced coffee Chloe hands her.

"Anything good this week?" Chloe asks.

"Not unless you're into marriage dramas about straight

white people who can't stop having affairs," Georgia says.

"I'm good," Chloe says. "Let me know if you have any horny monsters though."

"You know I'm always on horny monster watch for you," Georgia says. She glances around, making sure they're alone before she adds, lower, "And lesbians with swords."

It's not as simple for Georgia as it is for Chloe, being queer. Georgia isn't sure how her parents will take it, much less her entire extended Southern Baptist family. The first time she came over to Chloe's, she stood across the room staring at Chloe's moms making dinner together for so long that Chloe worried she might be homophobic. It wasn't until later, when they were on her bedroom floor cutting pictures out of magazines to stick to their notebooks, that Georgia quietly mentioned she'd never seen a married lesbian couple in real life, and Chloe figured out what was going on.

Chloe leans in to help unpack the box.

"Where've you been all week?" Georgia asks. "We were supposed to work on the French paper on Thursday."

Chloe winces. "Crap. Were we?"

"We were," Georgia says. "I went ahead and wrote the first three pages."

"I got the last three, then," Chloe says. "I promise."

Georgia nods. "Okay."

"And I promise I'll make it up to you one day when I'm a hotshot editor and you're my most prized author and we're taking the literary world by storm."

"All right, all right."

"*And* I promise to give you more than your share of space in our fridge next year," Chloe says. "You can store foraged mushrooms to your heart's content."

Georgia fusses with the barrette holding back her hair.

"Yeah. Um, there's actually something I wanted to talk to you about," Georgia says.

"Hm?"

She glances over Georgia's shoulder, at the shelves behind her. The Austen section, specifically, where Shara must have stopped a few weeks ago when she came in to buy *Emma*.

Wait. Why would Shara come here, of all places, to buy a book?

"I've been—um, what are you doing?" Georgia calls after her, but Chloe's already across the room and at the shelf, opening an illustrated edition of *Pride & Prejudice*. She should have ransacked the whole Austen selection as soon as Georgia told her the story.

"I just realized I—" Shara must have seen Georgia reading Austen at school and figured that if she bought a book by the same author, Georgia would mention it to Chloe. She pulls *Persuasion* next, but there's nothing inside either cover except book smell. "I think I left something in one of these books."

"What?" Georgia says, putting down the hardback she's holding. "Why?"

"I, um, was gonna buy it but I changed my mind," Chloe lies, shaking out *Northanger Abbey* to no avail.

"You don't remember which one?" Georgia asks, audibly perplexed.

The last one Chloe tries is a hardcover of *Mansfield Park*, and there, tucked into the front flap, is a pink card. And inside the card is a piece of loose-leaf, folded three times.

"Found it!" she says, tucking both into her pocket before Georgia can see. "But, oh, crap, I just remembered I'm—I'm supposed to be doing puzzle night with my moms, so sorry, gotta go!"

She's out the door and in her car before the entry bell finishes jingling behind her.

Parked in the driveway at home, she reads the letter for the third time. It's by far the longest one Shara's left behind, and it's addressed only to Chloe. She can't stop touching the pen strokes on the paper.

Hi, Chloe,

Nice one. I was a little worried the book would get sold before you found this, but I figured <u>Mansfield Park</u> was a safe bet. And let's be honest . . . the books aren't exactly flying off the shelves here.

Anyway. Would you be surprised if I told you I asked Mr. Davis to make us lab partners in chem?

What if I told you that I pretended my shoe was untied so I could wait outside Mrs. Farley's room until I saw you walk in on the first day of school this year? What if I told you the truth, which is that I made sure to brush three fingers across the top right corner of your desk before I took the seat in front of you, and I sat there for an hour trying to picture the look on your face when I did it?

What if I told you that, in the three years of English classes we had together before that one, I would sit across the room from you and think about all the ways I could ruin your perfect record? I tried reporting you for uniform violations, but that never seemed to stick. Sometimes I'd picture breaking into my dad's office and figuring out a way to change all your 99s to 89s. Sometimes I'd dream up a whole conspiracy to frame you for plagiarism. I even thought about slashing your tires the night before the AP exam (not my most Christlike moment, I'll admit).

Sometimes, when I was feeling especially creative, I would imagine how I could make you fall in love with me. As soon as I knew you liked girls, I saw my way in. I could drag my fingertip along the curve of your jaw, I could almost kiss you in the library. I could break your heart so exquisitely, you'd forget you ever cared about winning. It's always been so easy, making people love me. I was sure I could do it to you.

I tried, sophomore year. You remember precalc? I pretended not to understand something because I knew you didn't either. It was supposed to get me close enough to you to bring out every trick I know. But you figured me out. You're not like anyone else. The same tricks don't work on you.

I think that's where this started to go wrong for me. There are things that don't make sense about me. I don't know if I belong here. How can that be possible, to feel estranged from a place where everyone loves you? To owe your life to a place and still want to run? I've been trying and trying to figure out what it is about me that makes me feel this way and why it feels so deep and so big that it must be most of me, the skin stretching between my knuckles and across my shoulders and then the bones under them too.

*Knowing that I couldn't have you if I wanted*
*to—that stings almost the same. It's almost the*
*same feeling. They're right beside each other.*
*What do they have in common?*
    *I'd prefer if you kept this one to yourself,*

                                                    *S*


When Chloe was in sixth grade, she won the California
state spelling bee.

It wasn't easy—not because she had any trouble spelling,
but because her school didn't believe in "creating a competitive environment for students." At nine, she came home with
a stern note for forcing her friends into an underground fight
club of timed math quizzes during unstructured play time.
They were not going to be pitting kids against one another in
the spelling bee qualifier rounds.

But she saw the previous year's winner on the local news
and refused to let it go until her moms had figured out how
to get her independently qualified and she had crushed every
other eleven-year-old in the state with the final word, "dip-
somaniac."

The moment she set foot on Willowgrove's campus, she
signed up for the Quiz Bowl team. She joined the French
Club on the promise that there would be tests at the conven-
tion and started quietly tracking the highest grades in each of
her classes, and she discovered that her only real competition
was Shara.

This letter is finally, *finally* proof that Shara has always
seen her the same way. They're equals. That's what she's
thinking as she drags her fingertip down the crease of the
paper.

But she's also thinking about Shara researching how

Georgia's dad is the owner of Belltower. That Chloe likes to spend her afternoons there with the books.

Did she figure out Chloe's plans that weekend so she could come by the shop when Chloe wasn't tucked into a corner with *Little Women*? Did she check the street for Chloe's car? How many times did she write the note out before she settled on the exact loops in Chloe's name? Did she sit on her ivory quilt and plan a whole day around creating this moment, right now, Chloe sitting here with this letter, thinking about Shara thinking about her?

It feels even more intimate than the Shakespeare passage in the piano. Willowgrove is where Shara is—was—every day, but Belltower is Chloe's. Shara doesn't have a key. She had to walk through the doorway that Chloe repainted last summer and make polite small talk with Chloe's best friend.

She thinks about the ends of Shara's hair brushing her desk in precalc and the flutter of a pulse under her fingers. If Shara was really in control of that play, if that was all it meant to her, why was her heart beating so fast?

The deeper she gets into this, the more she pictures the hours Shara spent on it. On Smith and Rory too, yes, but Chloe's the one who got a whole letter on loose-leaf paper addressed only to her. There's no clue leading to or from this one. Her kiss was the one Shara bought brand-new lip gloss for.

The postscripts on the cards always allude to something that only one of the three of them can translate, but when she lines them up next to one another, something doesn't match. The clues for Smith and Rory usually reference a specific memory, but the clues for Chloe reference art. Not just any art—books found at Belltower, Shakespeare, *Phantom*. She specifically picked Chloe's favorite things, wrote riddles in Chloe's own language, and hid them in Chloe's favorite places. Like Chloe is special.

She wonders.

What if this is why Shara wants Chloe to know who she is?

What if that kiss on the elevator was more than the first phase of a plan?

What if Shara's more than an evil shitbird? What if Shara is an evil shitbird who's *in love with her*?

"Chloe, thank God you're here," her mama says when she finally stumbles inside. She holds up one of the thousand puzzle pieces spread across the kitchen table. "Would you describe this color as honey or amber?"

"It's yellow," she says.

"Thank you!" her mom says. "It goes in the yellow pile!"

"But the yellow pile has five subsections, Val."

"You're making this way harder than it needs to be, Jess."

Thankful for the cover of distraction, Chloe slips off to her room. She snatches her laptop off her desk, balancing it on one hand while she unzips her skirt and shimmies it to the floor. She's so desperate for one more piece of Shara, her whole body feels itchy. Her Google Doc is instantly open, and—

There, at the top of the page, in small gray letters: Last edit was seconds ago.

When her eyes fly to the space under her three words, Where are you?, there's a green cursor holding steady. She hovers over it until the name of the person editing the document pops up: SW.

Shara's there. Shara's in the doc right now. For the first time since prom, they're in the same place at the same time.

Chloe's foot gets caught in her skirt, and she yelps and topples sideways to the carpet.

When she recovers her laptop from the floor, the cursor is gone—wherever Shara is, she must have realized Chloe had logged on and closed the window as fast as she could. There's nothing new in the document, only the same blank stretch where Shara's cursor vanished. But the timestamp at the top still says the last edit was seconds ago. She was *so close*.

But—wait. There shouldn't be anywhere for Shara's cursor to rest if there's nothing below Chloe's words.

Crumpled at the foot of her bed in her underwear, Chloe hits the command button with her thumb and the A key with her middle finger to highlight everything on the page.

Shara typed in white text. Invisible ink.

Beneath Where are you? she's written a single line.

Come on. There are a million more interesting questions you could ask.

"You bitch," Chloe exhales, and she types out, Fine. Why did you leave?

A pause. Chloe finally kicks her skirt off her ankles and holds her breath. Then a little SW appears in a bubble at the top of the document. Shara must have edit notifications on for the doc—God, why didn't *Chloe* think of that?

Another sentence unfolds across the page, in black this time.

I don't think you actually want me to make it that easy. And then, What are you thinking about right now?

You, she types out automatically, before remembering Shara can see it and hastily adding, 're running out of time to come back. AP tests and finals are next week.

She waits.

Thanks for reminding me, Shara types. What's the last note you found?

It was a letter, actually, Chloe types. The one you left me at Belltower and asked me not to show anyone.

A second passes, and another, and then Shara's cursor disappears.

# FROM THE BURN PILE

Note from Chloe Green to Shara Wheeler,
written on the back of a major works
data sheet on *The Great Gatsby*

Found this on the floor of Ms. Rodkey's class—thought you might want to keep it. The stuff you wrote about the symbolism of the green light sounded kind of personal.

# 13

Shara ghosts the doc for the rest of the weekend after finding out Chloe read the letter, and Chloe knows her theory is correct: Shara is in love with her.

How *embarrassing* for Shara.

All these years, Shara's been sitting in her room, brushing her hair in front of her vanity mirror and thinking about how Chloe could be unraveled. Shara, Shara actual Wheeler, is obsessed with *her*. Willowgrove's perfect little daughter of Christ wants the weird queer girl with too much eyeliner.

Even if Chloe doesn't want Shara back, she *does* want to be a sharp-beaked little bird making a nest in that pretty head. If the next note is anything like the last, she needs it. Like, for entertainment purposes.

At least she has an idea of how to get it.

"The theater end-of-year party is tonight," Chloe says on Monday when she catches Smith at his locker. She doesn't remember when she learned Smith Parker's locker number by heart, but she adds it to the list of ways Shara has derailed her life in a matter of weeks.

"Okay," Smith says.

"Brooklyn's coming, and she's supposed to be taking pictures for the yearbook, so she'll have her camera there, and we can check the memory card for the club photos," Chloe goes on. "Everyone who did *Phantom* is invited, including Ace, so all you have to do is convince him he should actually show up—"

"He's going."

"That's the spirit. Show him who's boss."

"No, I mean he already told me he's going."

Chloe blinks. "What?"

"Yeah, I think he's looking forward to it. He bought a new shirt."

"I—uh, okay. Well, then, you can just figure out an excuse to come with him. And then when Brooklyn's doing the senior number, you can get to her camera."

Smith sighs.

"We're close, Smith," Chloe reminds him. "You deserve answers. We all do."

Smith chews on his thumbnail. "Okay. I'll be there."

"Let's go, let's go, the seven-layer dip ain't gettin' any fresher," Mr. Truman says as he waves students into the gym like the emcee at the Kit Kat Club. "No, Taelynn, it's fine that your mom didn't put lime juice on the avocados like I told her last time and now they're already brown— Hi, Chloe, you have a fire in your eyes tonight and I hope it's for theater."

"It's definitely for something," she says.

"Great, no further questions."

Chloe has been looking forward to her senior theater party since freshman year, when she sat wide-eyed on the floor of the gym watching the senior leads from that year's spring musical (who were basically celebrities to her at four-teen). The self-appointed keeper of tradition, Mr. Truman invented an iconic Willowgrove theater ritual when he played Conrad in *Bye Bye Birdie* in '96 and performed the entire clos-ing number as Rosie at the end-of-year party. It's evolved over the years; now, as custom dictates, it's Chloe and Benjy's turn to swap roles and lead the seniors in an over-the-top, gender-bent performance of the titular number.

Benjy, who takes nothing more seriously than an oppor-tunity to commit to a bit, waylays her by the folding table of two-liter sodas and snacks.

"You're like, thirty minutes late," he says. "Did you get the blocking notes I sent you? Do you know your lyrics?"

"Benjy, I have known the words to this song since I was in utero," she says. She mentally flips through the contents of her emails—she's sure she skimmed Benjy's plan for the num-ber, but it's been mostly overwritten in her mind by Shara in her Google Docs.

She wants to be here, in this moment, doing this thing she's been dreaming of her whole high school career. But she's also here because she needs to know where to follow Shara next.

She forces her hands to reach for a cupcake instead of her phone. "Did you bake these?"

"Please," he says. "As if I have time. I— Wait. What is Ace doing here?"

He's looking over her shoulder at the entrance to the gym, where Ace has appeared in all his lumbering glory.

"He was Phantom," Chloe reminds him. "He got an invite."

"Yeah, but he wasn't supposed to *come*. He's not supposed to act like any of us exist," Benjy says, his expression going pointy and sour. "I planned our entire number around him not coming. What, are we gonna have *two Christines*? Like a bunch of *idiots*? *And* he's going to screw it up because this whole thing is a *joke* to him."

Chloe touches his shoulder in what she hopes is a calming way. She's usually the one getting calmed down, so she's not quite sure she's doing it right. Hand goes like this?

"Okay, don't tell anyone I told you this, but it turns out Ace Torres is like . . . actually really into musical theater."

"What are you talking about?" Benjy snaps. "He was messing up his lines all the way up to tech week. I don't know if he ever even read the script or just memorized the movie."

"I know," Chloe says. Even she can't believe she's saying this. "But I think that was because he was nervous. He practiced for weeks before tryouts."

"He told you this? Since you're friends with Smith Parker now, for some reason? Who is . . ." He frowns as Smith materializes behind Ace, looking decidedly awkward. ". . . Also here?"

"It's a long story," Chloe says. "But . . . please don't kill me . . . I *think* Ace may have actually . . ." She retracts into her shoulders like a turtle. "Deserved the part?"

Benjy looks at her like she's been replaced with a clone. "Chloe."

"I'm not saying you didn't!" Chloe immediately clarifies. "Or that he deserved it more! But he's . . . he's not as bad as we thought he was. You should ask him what his favorite Sondheim is."

He's still glaring, but he at least doesn't seem like he might jump her. "You've changed."

"Don't be so dramatic."

"We're literally at a theater party right now."

"Okay, everyone!" Mr. Truman yells, rolling a rack of tragic-looking secondhand gowns and tuxedo jackets into the gym. "Costumes! Makeup!"

"I'll ask," Benjy says. "But for the record, there is a wrong answer."

"I know there is," Chloe says, and she races him to the racks.

The gym connects to a back hallway, where two locker rooms sit across from the choir room, and once everyone finishes fighting for costumes, they disperse to get changed. It takes about five seconds for the girls' locker room to transform into a near-perfect re-creation of the night *Phantom* closed. Makeup kits exploding over benches, someone pulling out a Bluetooth speaker and putting on the soundtrack, bobby pins somehow already everywhere. Three junior girls commandeer the sinks, climbing up to sit inside the bowls with their sneakers braced against the mirror to do their contour up close.

When Chloe tries to explain what she loves so much about high school theater, even though she'll probably never set foot on another stage after graduation, she always ends up at this: the chaos of backstage. Sitting on the dressing room floor in a sweaty wig cap eating a box of McNuggets someone's mom dropped off, accidentally catching a glimpse of a cute lead's underwear when they're quick-changing behind a towel in the wings, ranking the smelliest character shoes in the chorus, and the delirious, unsupervised hours between the morning and evening shows on a Saturday.

So much of Chloe's life at Willowgrove is spent in absolute control to compensate for being different, but not here, not in this glittering shitshow.

"What color did you get?" Chloe asks Georgia, eyeing her own tux with extreme skepticism.

Georgia holds up hers, a shade of powder blue that looks right out of *Hairspray*. "Brought my great-uncle's prom tux from home. Knew it would come in handy someday."

"You *genius*," Chloe says. "Mine looks like somebody died in it."

Brooklyn brushes by, fussily tying her hair back. Her tux is draped over her arm, and it's one of those camo monstrosities that are distressingly common in Alabama. "At least you didn't get the Shotgun Wedding Special."

Chloe retreats to a corner to pull on her tux, which also affords her the opportunity to check her phone without anyone asking her about it. Still nothing new from Shara.

"Did you see that Ace actually came?" she overhears one of the senior girls from the chorus say to another.

"No way. Really?"

"Yeah, and he brought Smith Parker with him."

"Oh my God."

They sound skeptical but not hostile, so Chloe kicks aside a confusing twinge of protectiveness. Since when did she start looking after jocks?

Once she's buttoned up, she makes her way back to the full-length mirror. It could certainly fit better, but the dark gray doesn't look as funeral home as she feared it might on her, and honestly, that's kind of a vibe for *Phantom* anyway. She tugs on her sleeves, swishing her cape—some purple crushed velvet abomination that her mom unearthed from an old Halloween costume—and scrutinizing her reflection. It could be worse.

Over her shoulder, a stall door squeaks open, and Georgia emerges in her powder-blue tux.

"Does it look okay?" she asks. "Ash helped me take it in a little."

Chloe turns around to look at her and gasps.

The pants have been hemmed and tapered into cigarette pants that end right at the top of her Vans, and she's rolled the sleeves of the jacket up to her elbows. Her short hair is shoved back and messy, which makes her look at least three years older.

"Geo," she says, "you look so fucking cool."

She blushes. "Really?"

"You look like Kristen Stewart at the Oscars."

"*Kristen Stewart?*" she repeats, blushing harder.

She steps up to the mirror and turns left and right, checking her jawline in the reflection, then smooths out her lapels with visible coolness.

"Can you—um—" She turns to Chloe, who's still holding her phone. "Can you take a picture and send it to me?"

She eyes Georgia. She's not really a selfie person, or a posting photos of things that aren't dogs or books on her Instagram person. "Who are you sending it to?"

"Nobody," she insists. "I just want to have it."

Chloe shrugs and lines up the shot: Georgia with her hands in her pockets, one hip cocked, looking effortless and confident and honestly pretty hot.

Right before she hits the button, an email notification pops up at the top of the screen: SW edited your document.

Shara, back within reach.

"Chloe?" Georgia says.

"Sorry, sorry!" Chloe snaps the shot quickly. "Here, I'll send it to you."

She fires off the photo to Georgia, and then ducks into a stall and opens up the doc. It takes ages, since the locker rooms are basically a dead zone for cell service, so she climbs up on the toilet seat to boost her signal.

Under the last thing she wrote, new words finally appear.

**Well, what did you think of the letter?**

She slaps her phone against her chest and stares up at the water-stained ceiling, screams and laughter and music and gossip fading out under the deafening volume of Shara's nerve.

**I think you made your point pretty clearly,** she types, thumbs jabbing at the keyboard. Shara's cursor is waiting for her response. **Though I'm surprised you actually showed your hand.**

Shara types back immediately.

**You figured it out, then. I knew I wasn't overestimating you.**

Chloe rolls her eyes. Of course Shara wants to play it cool, like she didn't write a whole letter about how she's in love with Chloe and then disappear when Chloe read it. Shara Wheeler, always running away and pretending it was all part of her plan.

**What I can't figure out is why you had to do it like this,** Chloe types. **Seems like a lot of work for something you could have done from your desk in Mrs. Farley's class. I've been right here the whole time.**

This time, Shara takes longer to start typing. Chloe stares at her cursor and imagines her on the other side of it, tucking her long hair behind her ear and frowning down at the keyboard.

**That's the problem,** Shara types. **I was too close to realize that you're special. Took a while to figure out how to get you where I want you.**

"Chloe!"

Chloe startles so hard, her foot almost goes straight into the toilet.

"Yeah!" she shouts back, jumping down. Her voice comes out strangled, so she clears her throat before she opens the door. "What's up?"

Georgia's waiting for her on the other side of the door with a fistful of lipsticks and a quizzical brow. "Do you have a minute?"

"Yeah, of course," she says.

"I need to—"

"Bring those to Ash?" Chloe says, pulling the lipsticks out of her hand. "Got it."

"Wait—"

"I know," Chloe calls over her shoulder, already at the door. "No direct application! I'll tell them to use a brush."

In the choir room, Ash has set up an approximation of the makeup station they had for *Phantom*. They're a bit of a legend within the theater program for being a wizard with a Morphe brush. They transformed Ace's face into a complete horror show for *Phantom* with nothing but liquid latex, wet Kleenex, and a YouTube tutorial in unsubtitled Russian.

"Georgia wanted me to bring these to you," Chloe says, dropping the lipsticks in Ash's lap.

"Oh, really?" Ash says. "That's nice of her."

Most of the guys are still changing, but Ace is sitting cross-legged on a riser with a full contour and green eyeshadow. Nearby, Smith is watching raptly.

"You look cool, Ace," Chloe says.

"Thanks," he preens. "You do too. The cape is dope."

"You're a good sport," she says, half-distracted, already pulling out her phone.

"I let Mackenzie put lipstick on me when we borrowed cheerleader uniforms for the homecoming pep rally, but this is like, so much cooler," Ace says.

"Hold still, I'm almost done," Ash says.

"Oops." Ace freezes, and when he speaks again, it's through his teeth and a locked jaw. "Sorry."

In the doc on Chloe's phone, Shara hasn't typed anything else. Chloe lets the last four words settle in her stomach. **Where I want you.**

She types back carefully, **Where is that?** And then hides her phone before Smith can catch on.

When she looks up at Smith, though, he's not paying attention to her at all. He's still watching Ash put the final flourish on Ace's eye makeup.

"Okay," Ash says, putting down their brush. "You can go change now."

"Thanks, Ash, you're so cool," Ace says, and he gets up and lumbers out, leaving Ash blinking owlishly after him.

"Do you think, um," Smith says, "do you think you could put some on me?"

Ash turns, and now Smith is the one getting blinked at.

"But you weren't in the spring musical."

"I know," he says. He touches his hair, then the side of his face. "But it looks fun."

Ash considers it and shrugs. "Okay."

Smith scoots into Ace's spot, and Ash examines his face from a few angles before picking out a handful of pigments from their kit.

"Are you gonna do a costume?" Chloe asks Ash. "I think all that's left on the rack is probably way too big for you. You'll have no shape."

"That works for me," Ash says. "My ideal body is no body at all."

Chloe snorts. "Just a head floating above a sexy void."

"That's so gender of me," Ash says, beginning to chisel out Smith's cheekbones. Another buzz from her phone. Another edit to the doc.

**Exactly where you are,** Shara has written. There's a pause, and on a new line, she adds, **If you know what this is about, why are you still talking to me?**

It takes her nearly a full minute to decide what to say. Smith and Ash are talking quietly, but she's not taking any of it in. It's like Shara is sitting right here on the chair next to her, reflected beside her in the big mirror on the back wall, watching Chloe's mouth for the next thing she'll say.

**Because I still don't know where you are,** she finally types.

Shara responds, **The next one should get you there.**

**And then what?**

"I'm really sorry if this is a stupid question," Smith says to Ash, "and you don't have to answer it, but . . . the thing you said about gender. Can you explain the whole nonbinary thing to me?"

*That* finally pulls Chloe back to the present. Ash's brush pauses over Smith's half-glittery eyelid.

It hasn't exactly been a smooth coming-out process for Ash, or even really much of a coming out at all. Their parents don't know, and the Willowgrove faculty would probably go into collective cardiac arrest if a student asked for their dead-name to be dropped from class rosters. But last year, one of their TikToks about weird earrings went viral, and everyone in school saw their pronouns in their bio, so that was pretty much it.

Chloe can see them doing the same math she did with

Smith at Dixon's party, but under his long lashes, Smith's eyes are warm and curious. A faint memory returns to Chloe: Smith, shoving hair ties and concealer toward the back of his locker.

"When you first started at Willowgrove, back in middle school, you had to tell all your teachers to call you Smith, right?" Ash asks. Their brush starts moving again. "Because it's not your first name?"

"Yeah. It's my middle name. Mom's last name before she got married."

The answer surprises Chloe. She arrived at Willowgrove after Smith, so she always assumed Smith was his first name.

"What's your first name, then?"

"William."

"Your parents named you Will Smith?" Chloe interjects.

Ash ignores her. "And when did you start going by Smith?"

"When I was a little kid."

"Why don't you go by William?"

Smith shrugs. "I don't know. It just doesn't feel right. Like, Smith feels like my name, but William doesn't."

"How do you know you're not a William?"

"I don't know. I just . . . do."

"Okay, so," Ash says. "That's how I felt about being a girl. When I was a kid, I thought I didn't like girly things, but then I got older and realized that I liked some girly things, but I hated that liking them made people *think* I was a girl, because on some level I always knew I wasn't one. So *then* I thought maybe I was actually a boy, because I wanted to be feminine the way boys can be feminine, but then I'd look at other boys and I wasn't one of them either. I knew I wasn't a girl, and I wasn't a boy. Like if someone yelled your first name at you. You might answer to it, but it wouldn't feel right, because that's not you."

"So, wait—why did you cut your hair, if you don't want to be a guy?"

Chloe winces, but Ash seems unbothered. "Because I'm still not a girl, so I don't like it when someone takes one look at me and automatically shoves me into the girl category in their brain. The hair helps."

"Okay, but I feel like that too, and I'm not nonbinary."

There's the slightest change in Ash's face. "What do you mean?"

"Like . . . I like my body, because it's fast and strong and good at football. But it also has to be a dude's body, *because* I play football. So like, maybe sometimes I wish it was smaller or softer or . . . *different* . . . but I don't really have a choice. And I can wear stuff like my letterman jacket and feel better because I could be shaped like anything under that, and I can imagine that maybe I'm not shaped like a dude sometimes. But that's not the same thing as what you're talking about, right?"

"Are there . . . times you don't *want* to be a dude?"

Smith's eyes are closed so Ash can keep working, but his eyebrows furrow above them. "Does it matter? I'd have to be a guy no matter what."

"You know . . . if being a guy feels like something you *have* to do, like it's an obligation or something . . ." Ash says carefully. "Maybe think about that."

Smith looks like he might have another question, but the choir room door flies open, and a dozen lowerclassmen come tumbling in, ready to have their makeup topped off by Ash's glitter stash.

"An orderly line would be appreciated," Ash yells over the burst of noise, and Smith glances over their shoulder to check his face in the mirror wall. Chloe sees him smile before she leaves.

"If this thing makes me break out from your leftover face juices, I'm gonna murder you," Chloe says, tugging at the mask covering one side of her face.

"I have great skin," Ace says. "Which you should remember from all the times you kissed me."

"I try not to think about that," Chloe says.

Ace's dress is a beaded floral confection that is straining dangerously across his chest and ends about four inches above his ankles. He looks like he's halfway into a werewolf transformation, and he is having a spectacular time. Chloe found him surrounded by chorus members, yelling the punch line of some joke she can't begin to imagine. He's a little sweaty, but he's got the spirit.

"I love kissing people," Ace says. "It's like, a hobby of mine. I would describe myself as a make-out hobbyist."

"That's nice," Chloe says, checking her phone.

"I've kissed like, all my homies."

Chloe glances up. "Even Smith?"

"Especially Smith." Ace grins, wide and ringed with lipstick, and then he catches sight of something over Chloe's shoulder and his eyes go wide. "Speaking of, holy shit."

She turns, and over the heads of dragged-out, cupcake-cramming theater kids, there's Smith.

His lips are lined in dark purple, fading into a soft lavender at the center. His cheeks are hollowed out with shadow and the bones dusted up top with iridescent highlighter that makes them glow sharp and high on his face. And his lids are glossy, his lower lash line dotted with big flecks of glitter. Chloe can't help staring, not because he looks strange, but because he looks . . . natural. It's a subtle drag, and it suits his face like he put it on himself. Something about his shoulders looks lighter.

He spots Chloe across the crowd and smiles a nervous smile, and the glitter under his eyes catches the grimy light from the overheads and turns it to stardust.

Two seniors descend upon him, whisking him into the party, and Chloe wonders if Shara ever imagined this as one of the outcomes of her plan.

In her hand, her phone buzzes. Shara's reply: Then I guess it's your turn to surprise me.

Soon, someone kills half the lights, and someone else cues up the backing track on the sound system, and the seniors shuffle into their places. The lowerclassmen pile on top of one another on gym mats with plastic cups of Sprite and smears of lipstick on their chins, and Mr. Truman climbs atop a row of bleachers with his phone horizontal, ready to film the whole thing so the seniors can have it for posterity. She notices Brooklyn handing her camera off to a sophomore before she joins the rest of them, and she makes eye contact with Smith, who nods. He shouldn't have any trouble sweet-talking it away from her, not looking like that.

"Don't screw this up for us," Benjy hisses to Ace in the final second of anticipatory silence.

Chloe tucks her phone into her suit jacket and shakes out her cape. For the last time in her high school career, it's curtain call.

Inexplicably, she kind of wishes Shara were in the front row again.

The organs start blasting, and Chloe steps to the center of the floor and sings.

* * *

"Did you get it?" Chloe asks Smith the second the performance is done.

"Yeah," he says, "but I'm not sure what it means."

He shows her a picture on his phone of the back of Brooklyn's camera, where the National Honor Society photo is zoomed in on Shara. Seniors get the privilege of doing their extracurricular photos with silly concepts and gags, so instead of a posed group shot, it's a dozen of the grade's highest GPA holders in Mrs. Farley's room, surrounded by the classroom stash of board games.

She remembers taking this photo. She's on the left side of the frame with Georgia, pretending to fight over a game of Uno. Brooklyn's sitting primly in front of Connect Four, while Drew Taylor makes a show of studying a chess board. Shara's at a desk across the room, alone, her elbow propped up on the board game SORRY!.

In the picture, Shara's holding something in her hand. Chloe zooms in on Smith's phone screen, squinting to make out the details.

It's the SORRY card, the one that tells you to send an opponent back to the starting space on the board.

"*Back to start . . .*" Chloe mumbles.

All of this started with three kisses: Chloe, Smith, Rory. They've been to Dixon's house, where Shara last kissed Smith, and the roof where she kissed Rory. The only place left, the only kiss they haven't revisited, is Chloe's.

She passes the phone back to a confused Smith. "I know where to go."

Cape flying, she barrels out the back door of the gym and past the choir room, down the hallway full of spare lockers and closets, around the corner, and through the open door where the back of A Building connects to the elementary classrooms on the first floor of B Building.

Walls of crayon-colored pictures of beach balls and construction paper wishes for a happy summer break blur out in a muted rainbow—a stray teacher's aide yells something after her—and then she skids to a stop at the faculty elevator. It opens as soon as she calls.

Inside, nothing looks out of place. She checks behind the handrail before hiking up her suit pants and climbing on top of it to check the light fixture on the ceiling. It's not until the doors slide shut that she sees it.

There's a smear of pink nail polish on the lip of the inner doors, right where they meet.

Freshman year, when she got the campus tour from Georgia, she learned the secret of this elevator. If you stop it between floors and pry the inner doors apart, the inside of the outer doors is covered in thirty-six years of Willowgrove student graffiti. She and Georgia left their initials in Sharpie.

She jams the button for the top floor, counts the seconds, and on "two" she yanks the emergency stop.

When she wrenches the inner doors apart, the message is three feet tall and just as wide. It must have been here, hidden and still drying, when Shara pulled her close and kissed her.

On top of hundreds of signatures and lewd scrawls, there's a heart painted in pink nail polish. And inside it, Shara's daubed four cursive words.

I already told you.

Chloe checks three times to make sure she's read it right.

No postscript. No clue. No more confessions. Not even a direction to look next.

It's the end of the trail. This is where it was always leading: nowhere.

# FROM THE BURN PILE

Maybe I just want to be Smith.

Not like, the way most guys at Willowgrove wanna be him. I don't want to be the quarterback or anything. It's more like, looking over the fence at him and Shara and thinking about what Shara sees when she looks at him. The way he throws his head back when he laughs or how he carries himself like the human version of that "Lo-Fi Hip Hop Beats to Study To" thing on YouTube. The time he showed up at her door before school on a Wednesday morning with a Styrofoam box of pancakes because he wanted to bring her breakfast. I remember what it was like to see Smith up close like that.

So, I guess maybe I want to know what it's like to be that. To look in the mirror every day and see someone who knows exactly where they fit in, to be able to want—I mean, have—a girl like Shara.

I don't know. I don't know what else to call it.

# 14

Rory pulls up outside the gym ten minutes after Chloe texts the group chat. When Smith slides into the passenger seat, his lipstick has been wiped off, but the rest of his makeup is still there. Chloe watches from the back seat as Rory stares at him across the console.

"Don't say anything," Smith says, the glitter around his eyes shimmering in the dashboard light.

"I—I wasn't going to," Rory says. "I like it."

He puts the car in drive without another word.

Chloe tells them about the elevator and the nail polish note and then sits silently and waits for their reaction. Maybe it'll be a breakdown this time, or one of them will cry, or Rory will pull over to write the next great sad-boy anthem. Surely, if she's at her wit's undeniable end, they must be too.

Instead, Smith tips his head back and laughs.

"I don't know what I expected," Rory says, and then he's laughing too.

"*What* about this is funny?" Chloe demands.

"The whole thing," Smith says, shaking his head. "Like, I have to laugh."

"But she—"

"Do you wanna go get some snacks?" Rory asks.

"Damn," Smith says, "yeah, I do."

"But—" Chloe starts.

"Chloe," Smith says, "there's nothing we can do about it tonight."

She opens her mouth to argue, but then Rory is pulling into a gas station and she's the only one left in the car, fuming in her ill-fitting suit.

She glares out the window as Smith and Rory elbow each other toward the glass doors, which are emblazoned with a giant, peeling picture of a 99-cent corn dog. Shara could be anywhere, and they're getting corn dogs.

She sighs, opens her door, and yells, "Get some mustard!"

They drive, and they drive, out of town and up the hills until they reach a dirt road toward Lake Martin. The trees spread out and vanish into the dark the closer they get to the water, until the damp dusk opens all around them.

Rory parks on a cliff fringed with dense greenery and big, round rocks, and when he kills the headlights, Chloe can see over the edge into the distance, down to the sparkling water and the green and red dots of boat lights. The afternoon's rain left the ground soft and damp, the mossy trees dripping with leftover rainwater. Everything out here is green, green, green.

They climb up onto the hood of the car, Rory in the middle, and Smith passes out warm foil packets of corn dogs. Rory opens his and takes a deep whiff.

"You ever notice that greasy gas station food is like, the greatest smell in the world?" he says.

"Disagree," Chloe says. "The greatest smell in the world is when your mom brings home fresh cilantro from the grocery store and you stick your face in the bag and take the biggest huff of your life."

Rory wrinkles his nose. "Ew."

"Oh, you're a cilantro hater," Chloe says.

"He's a hater in general," Smith says. He glances over at Rory with a wink, like he's making sure Rory knows it's a joke. Chloe watches the moment bounce between them.

"Whatever," Rory says. "What do *you* think the best smell is, then?"

Smith considers it, swallows a bite of corn dog, and confidently declares, "My mom's chicken and gravy."

"Oh, man," Rory moans. "Chicken and gravy. I miss my dad's. I haven't had it since I saw him for Christmas."

"You should come over next time my mom cooks it," Smith says.

Rory misses the straw for his ICEE but gets it on the second try. "You know what else smells amazing? Sharpies. Like, a fresh one, when it's juicy."

Chloe lets out a laugh. "Did you just say juicy?"

"You gonna tell me a brand-new Sharpie isn't juicy?"

"Orange juice," Smith says. "That's the best smell. Or like, your hands after you peel an orange."

"Lilacs," Chloe blurts without thinking. She waits for Smith or Rory to react, but if either realize she's talking about Shara, they don't say. Cheeks pink, she hurries to add, "Or a really old book."

"Taco Bell nacho cheese."

"Sage."

"A standardized test booklet when you break the seal on it."

"That smell triggers my fight or flight," Rory says. "Pine-Sol."

Smith just laughs, but Chloe asks, "What? Why?"

"When I was a kid," Rory says, "I'd go stay over with my

cousins on my dad's side in Texas, and every Saturday morning my aunt would get up early and start cleaning the whole house. Loud as shit, always woke us up, but we'd all lay there pretending to sleep so we wouldn't have to help until she came and made us. So now that smell just makes me think of being in a sleeping bag on my cousin's floor, listening to my other cousin fake snoring and trying not to laugh so I wouldn't have to roll socks."

Smith, who's still laughing, says, "Wait, I got it. Friday afternoon in late October, after school lets out but before we start warming up for the game, when it feels like we're the only ones on campus and nobody can tell us what to do, and they're starting up the grills behind the concession stand, and somebody's burning leaves a mile away. Charcoal and burgers and smoke and wet grass and that little bit of nerves. That's the best smell in the world."

Chloe sighs, chomping into her corn dog. "God, to live in the mind of a jock."

"Sorry I'm not motorboating an encyclopedia from 1927."

"Okay," Chloe concedes, "but what about the worst smell in the world?"

"Definitely the bio lab on frog dissection week." Smith shivers. "So glad it flooded the week I was supposed to do mine."

"Because of the smell?" Chloe asks.

"Because I feel bad doing all that to a frog," Smith says. "Like, I don't know how he died! What if he had a family? What if he had like, dreams? What if he never got to finish *Breaking Bad*?"

"Smith," Chloe says. "It's just a frog."

"Don't get him started on frogs—" Rory says, like she's prying open a tomb Rory's tried to keep shut since middle school, but it's too late. Smith has gotten started on frogs.

"It's messed up!" Smith says, eyes wide, gesturing so emphatically he nearly backhands his ICEE into the bushes. "All frogs do is eat bugs that we hate and mind their business. They don't deserve all that. They're literally just vibing."

At that precise moment, a massive bullfrog lands on the hood of the car with a heavy thump.

"Oh my God, look!" Smith says as Chloe screams and Rory jerks away from Smith's new amphibious friend. "He heard me talking about frogs, and he came to see what's up!" He reaches down and pets the frog's back with one finger. "What's good, cuz?"

"Don't touch it!" Chloe says, shrill and horrified. "You don't know where it's been."

Smith snorts at her. "Man, you're really not from down here, huh?"

The frog hops away into the grass beside the car before disappearing behind a rock.

"Wait," Smith calls, clambering down to his feet, "come back!"

Smith follows the frog's flight plan into the night, corn dog in hand.

"Aaaand now he's gonna befriend a frog," Rory says, smiling like he can't believe it.

He settles his shoulders against the windshield and watches Smith's silhouette disappear into the moonlit greenery. There's no trace of Shara's mystery on his face, only a contemplative look as his laugh fades into the sounds of wind on water and scurrying little creatures in the mud.

But when Chloe leans back next to him and looks up at the stars, she's still thinking about Shara, somewhere under the same big sky like a gym-class parachute. The elevator, the pink script. Tonight was the first time she's been back to the place they kissed.

If asked, Chloe would insist she hasn't been avoiding the elevator. There are other shortcuts to French class, obviously. She'd never reconstruct her campus routes around what was supposed to be a straight girl playing some cruel joke on her. She doesn't even think about that kiss.

What she *has* thought about is how, if she hadn't left a French assignment in her car, she wouldn't have had to dash to the parking lot between classes, and she might have gotten to the elevator two minutes earlier and missed Shara entirely. If she'd hit the "close door" button faster, they'd have shut in Shara's face. It seemed so accidental, such a stupid, fleeting chance that she and Shara wound up on the same elevator at all.

But, of course, it wasn't chance. It was planned: Chloe's usual path to fifth hour, soft fingers around Chloe's wrist, vanilla and mint lip gloss. She didn't just *get* kissed—there was a second when she lost the plot completely and did some embarrassingly desperate leaning—but the *circumstances* of the leaning only happened because Shara planned them. Because Shara wanted it to happen.

If she'd known all this then, she wouldn't have let herself get left on an elevator. She would have yanked Shara back through the doors and made her fucking *deal with it*.

She turns to Rory.

"Can I ask you something?"

He nods, still watching the bushes rustle in the distance.

"Are you really not pissed at Shara?"

Rory blinks a few times, like he doesn't understand the question at first.

"To be honest?" he finally says. "It feels like . . . like I'm relieved she let me off the hook."

"Seriously?" Chloe asks, incredulous. "Haven't you liked her for like, *years*?"

"I guess," Rory says. "It's more that . . . there's never been another girl I thought about?"

Chloe crumples up her empty corn dog packet, then takes her cape off and shoves it behind her head as a makeshift pillow. "Can't relate."

After a long pause, Rory says, "I, um. I keep thinking about that, actually. The fact that it's only ever been Shara. You think that means something?"

Chloe furrows her brow at the sky.

"Like what? That you're meant for each other?"

In her periphery, Rory is shaking his head. "No, like . . . like maybe I talked myself into her, because when I looked at her and Smith together, I was so jealous, and she seemed like the right place to put it."

"She's not a place," Chloe points out. "Or an idea. She's a person."

"Yeah," Rory says. "But an idea can't want you back. And I'm starting to think that was kind of the whole point."

He glances away, and Chloe follows the line of his gaze across the clearing and down to the cliff's edge, where Smith is still rummaging through the underbrush, and of all idiotic memories, the thing that springs to mind is Ace at a party shouting about Mr. Brightside: *He never says which one he's jealous of.*

She thinks of Georgia tearing a magazine picture into pieces and chewing her bottom lip on the way to chapel. She thinks of her mom's jars of hair dye gathering dust in the bathroom cabinet, and of Mr. Truman filling a cart with bridesmaid dresses at Goodwill. She pictures Rory, raised by Willowgrove since kindergarten, sitting at his bedroom window as Shara and Smith kiss good night, feeling an anxious, shivery type of envy and cramming it into a shape that doesn't mean something's wrong with him.

Damn. Okay.

It's hard for her to wrap her brain around it sometimes—the idea that for most people from here, the stuff she hears in Bible class is reality. Who would she be if she hadn't been raised by two moms and a small army of gay middle-aged Californians? What if Willowgrove had always been her whole world, and the people in charge of it, who left their classroom door unlocked for her and cracked jokes with her like they saw her as a person, told her gently but firmly that she was wrong? That there was something inside of her—even if she hadn't named it yet—that needed to be fixed?

"You know," Chloe says. She keeps her voice low, her tone noncommittal. "It would be okay. If you didn't like Shara. If you didn't like girls at all." She lets the words settle between them, clinging to the shiny hood of Rory's car like the first drops of rain before a storm. Rory doesn't say anything, but he doesn't scoff or shrug it off or make a sarcastic joke. He keeps staring off into the trees, and after a few long seconds, he lets out a breath.

"Shit," he says.

"Yeah," Chloe agrees.

It's not fair, she thinks. Here she is, on a cliff in a thrifted suit with a glittery quarterback and the human embodiment of repressed homoerotic angst, and none of them have ever had the luxury of running away from what they are. Neither has Georgia, or Benjy, or her mom, or Mr. Truman, or Ash. Any of them.

Maybe it's hard to be Shara and love a girl. But why should *she* get to run? Why shouldn't she have to go through hell too?

Why should this be over because Shara said so?

# FROM THE BURN PILE

Personal essay exercise: Smith Parker
Prompt: What is a moment in your life
that you felt truly yourself?

When I was a kid, my mom used to tell me I was infinite the way the Holy Spirit was infinite. She'd say, "There's no beginning or end to your heart. That means you can be anything." She'd say there was God in that, and that expansion was godly.

I still feel endless sometimes. Like I might have what she saw in me, but in different ways. I feel like there are different sides of me, like I could be anyone and touch anyone and love like that kind of Holy Ghost love—everywhere and everyone. Most of my friends act like they know exactly who and what they are, like there's only one answer, but to me, that feels like putting a beginning and end on something that's not supposed to have either.

I went to a party with a bunch of people I didn't know, and someone put stars around my eyes, and I noticed stuff about my face I never noticed before. I saw myself in the rearview mirror of a person I've loved since I was thirteen, and I felt endless. Like, Holy Spirit endless. Maybe that's what it means to feel like myself.

# 15

This must be what a hangover feels like.

Chloe presses her aching forehead to her locker door, wondering if this is the work of gas station corn dogs or a Shara-related migraine. She wasn't even *out* that late—Rory dropped her off at her car before ten, and she was in bed by ten thirty—but she spent half the night reciting Shara's notes to her bedroom ceiling like Arya Stark with bangs.

She's throwing back the last can from her emergency espresso stash when she hears the heralding clangs of Georgia's water bottle against the nearby lockers.

"There you are," Georgia says, slightly out of breath. "You weren't in the parking lot. I was afraid I wouldn't find you before first hour to put everything together."

Chloe's stomach does a horrible swoop as Georgia unzips her bag and holds out her hand.

The last three pages of the French essay. Twenty percent of their final grade. Due today.

"Georgia, I—"

"I know, you specifically said no fun colors," Georgia says, holding up the file folder, which is magenta. "But it's the last file folder of my high school career, okay?"

"No, Geo." Chloe feels like she's going to throw up or cry or cry so much she throws up. "I forgot."

Georgia freezes. "What do you mean you forgot?"

"I mean I don't have it," Chloe says. "I didn't do it." She's never not done an assignment in her life. She was going to stay up late and do it after the theater party. She had it in her planner and everything—but then Shara—

"Please tell me you're joking," Georgia says.

"I'll—I'll skip first hour and go to the library and write it right now," Chloe says, already switching into efficiency mode, half of her panicked thoughts diverting into French. *Je suis absolutely screwed.* "I'll have it by fifth hour—"

"Forget it," Georgia snaps, and she gathers her folder and water bottle and jangles angrily off.

"Geo!" Chloe jogs to catch up, shouldering an onlooking freshman out of her path. Up close, Georgia's face is flushed, her thick eyebrows making an annoyed V. "Don't be mad at me! I'm gonna fix it!"

"It doesn't matter, Chloe."

"Of course it matters," Chloe says. "I'm not gonna mess up my GPA, or yours."

Georgia groans and sidesteps her, pulling off into an empty classroom. Chloe follows.

"I don't care about my stupid GPA, and nobody's going to care about yours after we graduate," Georgia points out. "You know that, right?"

"It's important to me," Chloe says.

"Well, it'd be nice if *I* was important to you," Georgia spits out.

*"What?"* Chloe stares at her. "Of course you're important to me! What are you *talking* about?"

"I've been begging you to help me with this project, and every time you blow me off for Smith and Rory and the rest of your new friends."

Seriously? *That's* what this is about?

"That's been happening for like, *four weeks.*"

"Yeah, the four most important weeks of our life so far!" Georgia says hotly. "You think I don't know you were at a party with Smith when you were supposed to be at our last movie night of senior year? You think I can't figure out where you are when you skip lunch with us? We spent four years talking about our senior cast party, and you left before it was even over! We were supposed to do this *together.*"

A hundred things jump up Chloe's throat. Arguments, defenses, the image of Georgia in a powder-blue tux. A memory of two fourteen-year-old girls on a living room rug reading Tolkien out loud with all the accents. She swallows all of them.

"You're gonna leave for New York and forget about me," Georgia says, quieter now.

"You're gonna be right there next to me the whole time," Chloe insists.

"No, I'm not."

"Of course you are."

"No," Georgia says again. "I'm not."

Above their heads, the bell rings. A terrible little voice in the back of Chloe's mind says she should wrap this up soon if she wants to finish the essay.

"What are you saying?"

Georgia bites her lip. "I can't go to NYU."

"We talked about the financial aid thing—"

"I'm going to Auburn."

No.

The plan has always been Chloe and Georgia and NYU. There's never been another plan. There's certainly never been a plan that involves—

"*Auburn?* As in forty-minutes-from-here Auburn?"

"The store's not doing great, and college is expensive, even with financial aid," Georgia explains. She looks away, glaring at a splotch of ink on the desk next to her. "My parents can't afford to keep anyone on staff anymore, but they can't do it by themselves. So I'm gonna stay home and help with the store and go to Auburn."

"Since *when?*"

"I decided last month."

"When were you going to tell me?"

"I've been trying to tell you for weeks! But every time I try to talk to you, you're busy or distracted or hanging out with other people, and I'm—"

"Georgia, you cannot spend your life in False Beach."

"God, you're still not even *listening* to me! Has it ever occurred to you that I might not completely hate this place?"

"We literally shit on this place every single day of our lives."

"No, *you* do," Georgia says. "Yeah, there's a lot about this place that sucks, but it's where I'm from. And honestly, sometimes I'm sick of you acting like you're so much better than it, like your family's not from here too."

"But you want to get out. You've spent the last four years telling me how much you want to get out."

Georgia turns away, wringing her hands. "What I want is . . . I want to fall in love. I want to have a big, dramatic, ridiculous love story, like a period piece, and my love interest is played by Saoirse Ronan and I get to wear a fancy corset.

I want to write books about the way that feels. And I don't know if I'll ever have any of that here, but I know what I'll lose if I leave."

"So you're staying?"

Georgia nods, still not looking at her. "I can't let Belltower close."

"You really think you can be happy here? Do you want to ask my mom how that's going for her?"

"I know, she left. A lot of people do. And that's okay! I get it! Everybody has to do what they have to do. But if everyone like us leaves False Beach, it's never gonna change. Someone has to stay."

"But why does it have to be you?"

Georgia finally lifts her eyes. "Because I can take it."

"That's *insane,* Georgia," Chloe says, throwing her hands up. "And what am I supposed to do? Go to New York by myself?"

"I don't know, Chloe, you seem fine without me."

*I'm not,* she wants to scream. *I won't be.*

"Fine," Chloe says instead. She breaks for the door, swiping at her eyes. "See you in French."

She skips first and second hour, stumbles through third and fourth, and brings her half of the essay to French, where Georgia takes it wordlessly and passes it up to Madame Clark. They don't talk for the rest of class, and when the bell rings for lunch, Georgia flounces out with Ash, and Chloe stomps off toward the gym.

Maybe she messed up, but it wasn't completely her fault. If she tracks Shara down, she can prove it.

Up in Rory's live oak tree, Jake and April are splitting a party-size cardboard tray of nachos, which is balanced so precariously on the bough between them that Chloe makes a point not to stand under it.

"Hey," Chloe says, gripping the straps of her backpack.

"Hey," Jake says through a mouthful. "You want a taco?"

"What?" Chloe says, but April has already reached into the plastic Taco Bell bag dangling from a branch and lobbed a soft taco at Chloe's head. It smacks her gently in the cheek and falls into her hands. "Um. Thanks. Where's Rory?"

Jake points with his vape pen—one branch up, on the other side of the tree, there's Rory. And next to him, perched more gracefully than should be possible for someone his size, is Smith.

"Oh," Chloe says.

She drops her backpack on the sprawling roots, shoves the taco into her oxford pocket, and starts climbing.

"Since when do you eat lunch here, Smith?" Chloe calls up to him. Across the courtyard, Mackenzie and Dixon and the others are still on their same bench.

Smith shrugs. "It's almost graduation. I mean, look at Ace."

He points, and she looks: Ace has wandered away from his usual spot and is having an animated conversation with one of the junior theater girls. Summer's nowhere to be seen either, she realizes.

She shakes her head and pulls herself up higher.

"Okay," she says, "about what Shara wrote on the elevator—*I already told you.* I think it means there's a clue in one of the notes that explains where she is, and we're supposed to figure it out and meet her there."

Rory swallows a bite of burrito and nods slowly. "Uh-huh."

"We should go back over the cards," she goes on. "Do y'all wanna do it now or meet up after seventh hour?"

Rory and Smith exchange a look, like they've recovered whatever unspoken language they must have developed when they were thirteen, which is nice for them and incredibly inconvenient for Chloe.

"What?" she demands.

"Chloe," Rory says. "If she wanted us to know, we would."

"But maybe we *do*," Chloe insists, "and we haven't realized it yet."

Another silent look between Smith and Rory.

"*What?*" she says again. "Are you actually *giving up*?"

"Look," Smith says. "I care about Shara. A lot. But I'm tired. And I'm starting to wonder if she ever wanted us to catch her at all. Like, maybe this whole thing was one big goodbye."

She shakes her head. "Rory?"

"I don't know what else we have to go on," he says. "Kinda feels like a dead end."

*A dead end?*

"Well, I might lose all my friends over this, and finals are next week, which means if she's not back by then, she won't even be eligible for valedictorian, which means my salutatorian will be Drew Taylor, which is just embarrassing," Chloe snaps. "He has a YouTube channel about why girls at Willowgrove are sluts for taking birth control pills. He doesn't deserve to come second to me."

"But you still win," Smith points out. "Isn't that enough?"

"No! It's not! Not if she *lets me* win!"

She jumps down, landing untidily on her feet and storming off toward sixth hour, spiking the uneaten taco from her pocket into the first trash can she passes.

She didn't ask for any of this. But she's going to finish it, even if she has to do it alone.

Georgia takes one look at Chloe outside her house and says, "You're kidding."

"Hang on." Chloe sticks her foot in the door so it can't be slammed in her face. "Please, listen for a second."

"All I do is listen to you, Chloe. That's the whole problem."

"If you just let me show you what's been up with me, it'll all make sense. I promise."

Chloe went straight to Belltower after school, but Georgia wasn't there, which is why she's standing on this tiny front porch with her makeup pouch, trying to prove that Shara's the one who ruined everything, not her.

"Fine." Georgia crosses her arms. "What's in the bag?"

"You remember how Shara kissed me?"

It takes a moment for the outrage to dawn on Georgia's face.

"Shara Wheeler?" Georgia says, eyes wide. "This is about *Shara Wheeler?*"

"Stay with me. Shara kissed me, and then she ran away, and then she left me that note. The one I got in the Taco Bell drive-thru."

"Uh-huh."

She unzips the bag and hands it to Georgia.

"She left notes for Rory and Smith too," Chloe says as Georgia starts pulling out pink card after pink card. "With *clues* in them, all leading to another clue, and another, and another. And they're in these ridiculous places. I'm telling

you, Georgia, it's been a full-time job finding them, that's
why I've been spending so much time with Smith and Rory.
I had to go to that Dixon party because she hid one there,
and then I had to break into the principal's office to get one
out of her dad's filing cabinet—I mean, it's like, unbeliev-
able. And every clue has a note from her, and every single
one proves that I was right about her. I mean, she's *evil*—"

Georgia stops shuffling the cards.

"Hang on," Georgia interrupts. "You said you broke into
the office? How?"

"I had a key," Chloe answers automatically.

"To the office?"

"Not exactly."

Georgia's eyes narrow. "When was this?"

"I don't know, like two weeks ago."

"Two weeks ago," Georgia says slowly, "as in, when I let
you borrow my library key?"

Uh-oh.

"I—I made sure I didn't get caught," she backpedals.

"Do you have *any idea* how much trouble you could have
gotten me in?" Georgia demands. Her face is going red in
patches the way it does when she's really heartbroken. "You
*lied* to me! You could have gotten me *suspended*!"

"I wouldn't have let that happen!"

Georgia throws the pouch back at her.

"Go home, Chloe."

"No—"

"You don't get to decide everything!" Georgia says. "*I* decided you're leaving! So, leave!"

She kicks Chloe's foot out of the way, curses under her
breath when her socked toes connect with Chloe's shoe, and
slams the door.

"Geo!" Chloe yells at the wood.

"Bye!" Georgia's voice shouts from the other side. "Go away!"

*"Georgia!"*

"Don't text me either!"

She calls Georgia's name one more time, but there's no answer.

Chloe spends the rest of Dead Week alone, nose-down in study guides, both hands a highlighter bloodbath.

Maybe she doesn't need her friends, who seem perfectly fine joking around in the parking lot before school without her, or Rory and Smith, or anyone. Maybe this is good practice for life after high school, when she'll have to rely on herself for everything. Only Chloe, eating lunch by herself in the library with Shara's cards and a mountain of exams. She has plenty to focus on. Willowgrove likes to consolidate AP exams and senior finals into the same week of early May, so next week is going to be hell, even if the finals for her AP classes are all perfunctory take-home exams that double as reviews for the real tests.

It's fine. Good, actually, since she's slipped in a couple of classes the past month, so she needs to catch up now. She can handle it. And she has nothing to feel bad about. All she's been doing is what she's had to do.

Shara's the one who *Gone Girl*'d herself because she's in love with Chloe. How is *Chloe* the crazy one?

The week ends—her last real week of school—and it's fine. She can handle it.

Valedictorian and her friends and Willowgrove and Shara and the whole world. She can handle it.

"I can handle it!" she snaps when her mama tries to pull a jar of chili oil out of her hands in the kitchen on Friday night. She's been struggling to open it for five minutes. She just wants to make some cup noodles and disappear into her room until Monday.

"Well, hello," says her mama, putting her hands on her hips in the way she does that says, *We're going to talk about this now.*

"I don't want to talk about it," she says immediately.

"Okay," her mama says. "Val!"

"Yeah?" her mom yells from the living room.

"Chloe is very angry about something and says she doesn't want to talk about it!"

"Please don't—" Chloe attempts.

"Oh, fun," says her mom, and then she's joining them in the kitchen, tucking a screwdriver into the kangaroo pocket over her overalls.

"I said I *don't* want to *talk* about it," Chloe insists.

Her mama nudges her onto one of the stools at the kitchen counter, and the two of them stand across from her with arms folded and calm, expectant looks. Maybe Chloe should feel comforted by this, but all she really feels is the anger bubbling hot in her chest, blurring her vision at the corners.

She knows neither of her moms will let it drop until she says something, so she sighs and opens her mouth to give them the stupid, infuriating details of her stupid, infuriating life—Georgia's cold shoulder, Shara, AP exams, finals, Shara, the thought of having to go to New York and start a new life all by herself when she was supposed to have her best friend in the entire world alongside her, every last thing about Shara Wheeler—

Nobody is more surprised than Chloe to hear her own voice say hoarsely, "Is there something wrong with me?"

Her mama flinches at the words, shaking her head. "Of course there's not."

"Okay, but," Chloe grinds out. She doesn't feel in control of her mouth anymore. Her voice comes out nauseatingly raw. "Are you sure? Like, am I a bad person?"

Her moms exchange a look.

"Where's this coming from?" her mom asks.

"I—I just need to know."

"You take care of yourself, and that's important," her mom says. "And you don't hurt anyone."

"But I *do* hurt people," Chloe insists.

"Do you do it on purpose?"

"No."

"Okay, then, you're human."

"But Georgia said I don't care about her, and I'm—if I'm so mean that my best friend doesn't even know I care about her, then—then what's *wrong* with me?"

"There's nothing wrong with you. You're just you."

"I'm not a nice person," she says.

"Chloe," her mom says, "your mama and I decided long before you were born that we would let you be whoever you are, no matter who that is."

"And if who you are is a snarling little Pomeranian with eyes like fire, then that's who you are, darling," her mama adds.

"Jess," her mom hisses. "What she means is that nice and kind are not the same thing. Plenty of people aren't nice at all, but they're kind. And that's what matters."

"Sometimes," Chloe blurts out, squeezing her temples between both hands, "sometimes it feels like I'm gonna explode, like everything I'm feeling is the first time anyone's felt it, ever, in the history of the universe, and then I get so *angry* when people don't understand that I'm walking around feeling like this and still doing everything I'm supposed to do and making As and getting into NYU and putting up with all of the Willowgrove bullshit. I—I can't even explain how I feel, and it feels wrong to say it without the right words, so I don't say it at all, but then nobody knows, and I'm mad that nobody knows, even though I don't even *want* them to know."

"To know what?" her mom asks gently.

"That—" Chloe says, but it sticks in her throat. "That it's *hard*. That I have to be like this, because it's all so fucking *hard*."

"I know," her mama says. "It's enough to get through it though."

"No, it's not," Chloe says, shoving away from the counter. "It's *not*."

Her moms try to drag her with them to Olive Garden for dinner, but Chloe finds the idea so depressing that she shouts through her bedroom door for them to go without her. Once she hears their car pull out, she rolls out of bed and trudges into her bathroom.

The silver chain is in the same place she left it, and she takes it out and holds it in the palm of her hand. It's a necklace, with a thin, ornate charm: a diamond-studded crucifix.

Cross necklaces are a status symbol at Willowgrove. If your parents can afford to buy you a dainty diamond crucifix before you get your learner's permit, you're somebody. Chloe's moms couldn't afford to get her one even if she wanted it.

Every popular girl who ever made Chloe feel like a freak

had one gleaming from the opening of her uniform polo.

Shara had one until halfway through freshman year.

Chloe had been sentenced to writing lines from the Bible in after-school detention, and she was avoiding it. She stopped in the empty library and hid behind a shelf in case anybody came looking for her.

That's where she saw Shara, staring at the wastepaper basket near the study tables.

She watched Shara hesitate briefly, biting one of her buffed pink nails with shiny white teeth before she swept her hair over one shoulder and unclasped the chain at the nape of her neck. She dropped it in the trash can, and she left.

Looking back, Chloe can't completely recall deciding to fish the necklace out. She'd overheard her moms the night before, arguing in low voices on the back porch about the cost of Chloe's tuition when they thought she'd gone to bed. Maybe she took it with some half-formed idea of pawning it like they do on the A&E shows her mama likes to watch. But she's never once thought about selling it.

Because Shara came back for it. Ten minutes later, she watched Shara burst into the library, go straight for the trash can, and grow more and more panicked as she pulled out bits of paper and vending machine candy wrappers. She turned the whole thing upside down and shook it, then gave up. She never even realized Chloe was there.

And Chloe was there the next week at the gym lockers when Shara put on a tearful performance of realizing she must have lost it running laps around the football field in PE. The entire PE class went out to search through the turf on their hands and knees, and Shara stood there and let them. Chloe got grass stains, but it was worth it to know that Shara isn't who everyone thinks she is.

She pulls the bag of cards out from under her bed, where it's been since Georgia threw it at her. If she can solve this godforsaken puzzle, she can finally prove it to everyone: that she's not a bad friend, that she's not crazy, that she was right all along and Shara is a fake bitch who can't handle her own secrets without making them everyone else's problem. And then she'll win, and everyone will *have* to forgive her.

She goes through the cards again and again, reading over Shara's handwriting, which she's come to know with a kind of intimacy that makes her want to lie down in the ditch behind her house and forget she ever knew there were girls like Shara Wheeler. There has to be an answer here. What could she be missing?

She's fingering the pen strokes on the card from Dixon's house when she feels it.

*The key is there, where I am.*

At the end of the line, the indentions in the paper feel different. She holds it up an inch from her nose and tilts it toward her bedside lamp until the light catches on the tiniest details. Now she sees it: little grooves under those last three words, like Shara laid a second sheet of paper over the card and dug in with a pen to leave the impression of nearly invisible lines. They underscore the last three words, setting them apart for emphasis. *Where I am.*

*Where she is?*

The key was taped to the back of the picture of Shara on her parents' sailboat. It was where Shara's image was, physically, in the office, but maybe it's more than that—maybe the photo was meant to tell her where Shara actually, literally *is*.

Chloe's sat in the chair opposite Principal Wheeler's

desk a hundred times, and she's memorized every detail of that photo. The number 15 marking the slip. The sign in the background announcing Anchor Bay Marina. Shara, smiling, angelic.

"I'm gonna kill her," Chloe says, and she reaches for her keys.

# FROM THE BURN PILE

Written on a sheet of loose-leaf in the
back of Chloe Green's physics binder

## VALEDICTORIAN SPEECH: DRAFT #17

Hi, everyone. I'm Chloe Green. You may know me as the girl who always volunteers to do her presentation in front of the class first. I'm proud to say I've never been the girl who reminded the teacher we have homework, though I have thought about it more than once, because, I mean, I did do the homework, and it took me a whole hour, and I know my answers are right, and I deserve a 100% participation grade, but who cares? It's fine.

You may also know me as the girl who beat Shara Wheeler for the prize of standing at this podium. I know most of you were probably rooting for her, but turns out, she doesn't always get what she wants. ~~By the way, her hair isn't even that great. It's just long. And I think~~

Annotation from Chloe:

Maybe slightly less personal???

# 16

Anchor Bay Marina is nearly silent, blue under a cloudless night sky with only the sounds of water lapping at the shore and the broad hulls of fancy boats. Wooden piers separate twenty individual slips, wrapping in a U shape around a squat boathouse that's closed for the night. Shara's white Jeep is tucked neatly into the back corner of the parking lot. Chloe's insides turn to jet fuel at the sight.

From the shore, she can't see where the Wheelers' boat should be, so she starts at the slip with the number one painted in faded white on a pylon and counts down the pier.

Slip 2, slip 3, slip 4.

Slip 7, 8, 9.

Slip 12, 13, 14—she rounds the corner—

In the weeks since Shara left, she's always looked the same in Chloe's mind: frozen in her ball gown, her hair spilling over her shoulders like sunlight and her lips stained a soft, berry red, remote and unreachable under a sparkling country club chandelier.

Now, waiting under the moon in the fifteenth slip, Shara looks like she tumbled right out of Chloe's memory. Mostly because, for some infernal reason, she's still wearing her prom dress.

She's sitting on the front of the sailboat like the smug figurehead of a voyaging ship, almond-pink tulle fanning out behind her on the deck and frothing over the sides of the bow.

Shara in the flesh. Not a line on a card or a picture in Smith's locker or a memory nipping at the back of Chloe's neck, but actual Shara, with her pointy nose and elegant shoulders and annoyingly innocent facial expression.

Chloe feels, more so than usual, like she might explode.

And then Shara opens her mouth and says, "I had a feeling you'd show up."

Yeah, explode. A full-on spontaneous combustion. Five million tiny, angry little Chloes raining down over the Anchor Bay Marina, all giving Shara the finger.

Now that she's standing in front of the boat, she can see that Shara doesn't look *exactly* like she did on prom night. Her face is scrubbed clean, her lips their natural pink. Her hair is tied up on top of her head with a scrunchie.

To Chloe's immense displeasure, her first thought is of the silk scrunchie on Shara's bathroom counter. This is her first time seeing Shara with her hair up. What a stupid thing to realize.

"I have to say," Chloe says, taking a step forward until the toes of her sneakers are hanging over the edge of the pier, "this is a little anticlimactic."

Shara raises an eyebrow. "What were you expecting?"

"Don't get me wrong. I'm not surprised you're just some boring bitch on a boat," Chloe clarifies, "but I guess part of me was still holding out for a plot twist. Is there a dead body in an ice chest around here somewhere?"

"You're the one who came all the way here to see some boring bitch on a boat," Shara says.

"I did," Chloe confirms. Her mouth feels unpleasantly

dry. Shara's exposed collarbones seem very confrontational. "So I can tell everyone where you've been."

Shara stands, lifting her dress as she turns away. She's not wearing any shoes, just socks with bumblebees on them. Sucks that bumblebees are going to be ruined for Chloe forever now.

"That's not what you're gonna do right now, though, is it?"

Chloe glares at the back of her head one more time for posterity. "You don't know what I'm gonna do."

"Sure," Shara says, and then she opens a white door in the center of the boat and disappears down a set of steps.

Chloe stands there, watching Shara's dress trail behind her until it whips out of sight.

"I'm not getting on your stupid boat!" she yells into the empty night.

She gets on Shara's stupid boat.

The stairs down into the cabin are a total death trap, which seems fitting. The first compartment is crammed with bins of equipment, bundles of rope, and a minuscule kitchenette. There's a tiny gas range, the kind her mom takes on camping trips, and a wide piece of wood on top as a makeshift countertop. Clif Bars, boxes of mac and cheese, plastic containers of trail mix, and a bag of clementines are arranged in a neat row like Shara's highlighters on Chloe's first day of school.

She wonders if Shara is always like this, or if she laid everything out because she knew Chloe was coming soon.

Ahead, the cabin opens into a small imitation of a room, two benches around a bolted-down table. A rose-gold MacBook rests next to a bag of individually wrapped chocolates and a notebook open to tidy notes. Chloe's been spending all her time chasing leads, and Shara's been eating bonbons on a boat in a ball gown.

She'd admire it if it weren't Shara, which means she has to hate it.

Shara's kneeling on one of the benches with her skirt gathered in one hand, tucking a book into the built-in shelf behind it. The hem of her dress is gray with dirt, and when she turns to face Chloe again, Chloe sees popped stiches at the juncture of the bodice and the skirt.

"Have you actually been wearing that for four weeks?" Chloe asks her.

"Ew," Shara says, sitting down. "Don't be gross. I packed other clothes."

She waves her hand toward the cabin entrance, and Chloe looks to her right and sees a small, tucked-away sleeping space. At the foot is Shara's school bag and two folded piles of clothes.

"So you're wearing that because . . . ?" Chloe asks, pretending not to examine the soft tangle of underthings, the same ones missing from Shara's dresser.

"Because I like to, sometimes," Shara says. "It does get boring in here."

"You know how else you could break the monotony of living on a boat?" Chloe says. She finally looks at Shara. The distance between them is tight, but she still manages to seem far away. "Not running away to live on a boat."

"That would actually be the most boring thing I could possibly do," she counters.

"Do you think this is cute?"

"I think it's fun. And kinda funny." She pulls the bag of chocolates toward her and takes one out, then looks at Chloe and tilts her head to the side. She sticks her bottom lip out in a pout. "You look mad."

"Of course I'm mad. You wasted a whole month of my life on your demented scavenger hunt that wasn't even *going* anywhere, while you've been luxuriating on a yacht like an oil baron—"

"This isn't a yacht," Shara says. "It's under thirty-five feet."

For some reason, that's the thing that finally makes Chloe snap.

"God, you're such an obnoxious narcissist, I don't even feel bad that you're in love with me."

Shara freezes, the foil wrapper of the chocolate still under her fingernail. Chloe gets a whole second of pure gratification before she says, "*What?* No. What?"

"You're in love with me," Chloe repeats. "That's what this whole thing is about. You ran away because you're in love with me and you don't want to deal with the consequences. Like, it's pathetic how much you're in love with me."

"Oh my God," Shara says, and then she actually *laughs.* "Is that what you think?"

"You—" Chloe says. Shara's bluffing. She has to be bluffing. "You literally told me in the *Mansfield Park* letter."

"Chloe, oh my God. Read it again. I told you what I was going to *do*. My plan was to make you obsessed with me," she says. She finally gets the chocolate unwrapped and throws it in her mouth. "Oh, this is so disappointing. I thought you had figured out what this was really about, but you *fell* for it."

Chloe rewinds their Google Doc. Was she—were they having two completely different conversations?

"No. No way. That doesn't make any sense. Why would you want me to—to be obsessed with you?"

It's time for the kick in the teeth—the flat reminder that this is the exact type of joke that straight girls like Shara inflict on girls like Chloe who have the misfortune of being queer in their line of sight.

But what Shara says is, "I didn't get in to Harvard."

It's such an abrupt and obvious lie that Chloe can't even respond. Shara getting accepted early to Harvard is the biggest part of the Shara mythos, the crowning achievement that proved she really was going to go out into the world and make False Beach proud.

"Bullshit," Chloe says finally.

"I didn't get in," Shara says again. She swallows her chocolate and folds her arms across her pink bodice. Her collarbones have taken on an air of the tragic now. She looks . . . like she might be telling the truth. "I bombed my interview. They rejected me. I haven't told anyone, not even my parents."

"But—but what does that have to do with kissing me, or the clues, or anything?"

"I *told* you," Shara says. She looks up at Chloe, face impassive. "Did I do too good of a job with that letter? Did you forget everything else in it? Come on, what is the one thing we both want, that I've been trying to figure out how to get since you showed up at Willowgrove?"

Chloe skims to the top of the letter in her mind, before all the stuff about making Chloe fall in love with her, to—

"You mean *valedictorian*?"

Shara smiles a pageant smile.

"This whole thing was pretty distracting, right?" Shara says. "I turned in my assignments for the last nine weeks ahead of time, but you've probably missed a couple deadlines, right? Dropped a percentage point or two?"

"You did this to—to *sabotage my chances at valedictorian*?"

Shara rolls her eyes. "Like you wouldn't have done the same thing if you'd thought of it."

"*Why?*" is all Chloe can say. "Why do you need it that bad?"

"Because it's all I have left."

"Are you kidding me?" she nearly yells. "You have *everything*. You—you have a town full of people who are obsessed with you, a boyfriend who loves you, a hot guy next door who would do anything for you, rich parents who can give you whatever you want, a million people lining up to kiss the ground you walk on—*what else do you need?*"

Shara lets her finish before she says calmly, "You know my parents have a security camera on this stupid pier? And they think I don't know they have a tracker on my car, but I do. They've known where I was the entire time I've been gone. I thought it would be funny, to see how long I could do this before they came after me, but the joke's on me. They're doing what they do every time I have the nerve to do or say or think something they don't like: pretending it's not happening until it goes away."

It's probably a play for sympathy, but Chloe's fists unclench a fraction of an inch.

"What about Smith, then?" she asks. "And Rory? What do they have to do with valedictorian?"

"Chloe. You're smarter than this."

"Stop screwing with me and answer the question, Shara."

Shara pauses, reaching for another chocolate. She doesn't unwrap this one. It rolls around in her palm as she thinks about what she's going to say. "You've seen the way they look at each other, haven't you?"

"What's that supposed to mean?"

"Smith didn't have any interest in me until he found out Rory moved in next door. Then, all of a sudden, he was asking me to homecoming, and he seemed all right, so I thought I'd give him a chance. But when he came to pick me up, I swear Rory almost fell off his roof when they saw each other, and

I got it. I knew what I was to them. You weren't around in eighth grade, but I saw what they were like together." Shara's still rolling the chocolate around in her hand, letting it go soft at the edges from her body heat. "They both think they love me, but I'm not the one they're here for."

The bleachers note. Shara said she kissed Smith to make Rory jealous, but if she knew how he felt—

She never said which of them he was supposed to be jealous of.

"Everybody wants to use me for something, Chloe," Shara says. "At least with them, there was something in it for me too."

"Like what?"

"Social capital and entertainment, mainly. But I'm bored, and high school's almost over, so I thought I'd point them at each other and see what happens." She drops the chocolate unceremoniously back into the bag. "And I knew the three of you would keep each other on the trail, so I wrapped everything up together. Two birds and all. Nice and neat."

"Smith would never use anyone like that," Chloe says. "You broke his heart."

She cuts her eyes over, like Chloe shouldn't have the right to say Smith's name in front of her, which is pretty rich, all things considered.

"I was always gonna break his heart."

"Why?"

"Because I can't love him back."

"Why not?" Chloe demands.

"I just can't, okay?" Shara finally snaps. She swats a loose strand of hair away from her face. "You're still not getting it. I *can't*. I can't be with Smith. I can't be what everyone wants. I can't go to Harvard. All I can do is win this one last thing, so *that* can be the way everyone remembers me, and they'll never need to know about the rest. And you're in my way, so I did what I had to. *That's* all I care about."

Chloe's experienced enough theater to know a rehearsed line when she hears one.

"Tell yourself whatever you want," Chloe says. "Won't change the fact that you're so scared of what people in some fucking nothing town think of you that it made you do all this."

She whips around and stomps up the steps, emerging topside into the wet night. Shara comes bursting up after her.

"Maybe I am scared," Shara yells at her back, "but not as scared as you are!"

Chloe rounds on her. There Shara is again, in her ridiculous Greek tragedy of a prom dress, her face sharp and hateful.

"What the hell is that supposed to mean?"

"You know what I do? When I'm scared?" Shara asks. "I look at myself in the mirror and find something to fix. Like I'm the gardeners at the front of the club trimming rose bushes into the right shape. I moisturize my face and I condition my hair and I think about what I can say to exactly which person tomorrow to make them believe what I want them to about me. But you—you march into school every day like you know everything and you're better than everyone, and that's how I know you're terrified. You *have* to decide that you're so certain about everything, because uncertainty scares the shit out of you."

"I cannot express how much none of this is about me," Chloe says.

"You said it was about being scared of what people think," Shara says. "I'm just saying, I'm not the only one."

Chloe, who is out of patience for Shara's maritime monologues on things she knows *absolutely nothing about,* takes a step toward her.

It's then that Shara does something to betray her entire performance: she flinches backward, tripping on the dirty hem of her gown, stumbling until the small of her back hits the boat's railing.

She's afraid to let Chloe any closer. Because she knows what'll happen. She knows what she'll do.

Chloe was right. Shara wants her. She just doesn't want to admit it.

Chloe takes another step. "You know, if this was really about valedictorian, there were easier ways. You could've had your dad kick me out, even. But that wouldn't have gotten you what you really wanted, would it?"

Shara tries to pull off an eye roll, but behind her back, she's fumbling for the railing with one hand. "I don't know what you're talking about."

Something hot curls around Chloe's heart, but the words feel featherlight, cool, a soft breeze on sweat.

"You wanted to know I was looking at you," she says. She's almost close enough to touch her. "You *liked* it, didn't you? You liked knowing I was thinking about you all the time."

"I told you. I thought it was funny."

"Maybe that's what you told *yourself,*" Chloe says. "But deep down, somewhere under all this bullshit, you kissed me because you wanted to."

"That's not true," Shara insists. "It didn't mean anything."

When Chloe leans in, she sees it: Shara's gaze flickering to her lips.

"Then why do you want me to kiss you right now?"

"I don't."

"Okay," Chloe says. "Then I won't."

She begins to turn away, but there's that familiar feeling: Shara's hand closing around her arm, pulling her in. Shara's eyes are wide and green and furious, and a helpless, strangled sound crashes into the back of her bared teeth.

When she kisses Chloe this time, Chloe's ready.

She knows exactly what she's doing when she twists her fingers into the loose wisps of hair at the nape of Shara's neck and kisses her back, hard. Her other hand grips the tulle where it fans out from Shara's waist and holds Shara's body up against hers like *see, we're a match,* and it works—Shara sighs and lets go of the rail to slide her palm over Chloe's cheek. The skin is cool from the metal; Chloe suppresses a shiver.

She doesn't give herself time to think about the way Shara's thumb brushes over her cheekbone or the way Shara's lips feel against hers. Instead, she breaks off, abrupt enough that Shara's left blinking and dazed, and God, finally Chloe isn't the one doing the embarrassing leaning. She's getting embarrassingly leaned *at.* Amazing. Top five Chloe moment.

"Told you," Chloe says.

And with one solid shove, she pushes Shara—prom dress and all—over the railing and into Lake Martin.

# FROM THE BURN PILE

Scrapped first draft of a journaling
assignment, eventually replaced with one
that had more precise wording
Hidden in the pocket of one of
Shara's five-subject notebooks

I don't really believe in journaling. Having my private thoughts written down somewhere seems like a liability.

If I have to, though, the main thing on my mind today is the way they made us memorize the parts of the tabernacle in seventh grade. It all seemed a little showy for me, but I could still draw you a picture: the Altar of Burnt Offerings, the Golden Lampstand, the Altar of Incense. I think a lot about the phrase "Most Holy Place." There's something I love about the idea of somewhere only one person is ever allowed to go.

Maybe they had the right idea, as far as secrecy goes. The loudest Christians I've ever met were the worst ones. I don't believe doing something in front of everybody makes it more meaningful, anyway. If anything, it makes it stop belonging to you.

Sometimes, when I walk into a church, I'm not sure I'm supposed to be there, even though it feels like home. Home hasn't always been a good place for me to be.

# 17

Chloe wakes up late the next morning to a text from Smith that says, hey, do you like MarioKart? Which, (a) why and (b) now she feels guilty for yelling at him the other day and (c) yikes, she has to tell Smith she kissed his girlfriend again. Double guilty.

She should be happy. She won. After all this time rearranging her life around Shara's game like a *Saw* knockoff, she finally has the power. She has Shara's secrets *and* Shara's heart. She can expose Shara's big fat Harvard lie to the whole school if she wants to. Shara's probably mildewing on her boat right now, looking soggily, tragically beautiful and wondering if she'll ever have a chance to kiss Chloe again, and Chloe should be satisfied knowing the answer is no.

Needs time to sink in. That's all.

The house is empty and smells like butter and syrup, which means her moms have had an early morning and are outside doing their little weekend projects. She slips on her mama's Birkenstocks and heads out to the garage.

"Morning, coconut," her mama calls out from a lawn chair. The garage door is open to the boiling morning, and her mama is sipping sweet tea in bikini bottoms and Chloe's T-shirt from a fourth-grade field trip to the San Diego Zoo, cropped under the boobs. "You missed breakfast. We made pancakes."

Chloe nods at the Bluetooth speaker at her feet, which is playing Pavarotti. "Rigoletto, act two?"

"Act one," she replies with a wink. Pavarotti always reminds Chloe of being a kid, swanning around the apartment in one of her mom's performance gowns like a contessa. "You feeling better? After last night?"

At first, she wonders how on earth her mama knows about Shara, before she remembers her meltdown in the kitchen. It's been a long twenty-four hours. A long month, really.

"Yeah," Chloe says. "I'm fine. Right now everything is . . . a lot."

Her mom, who has been banging around the undercarriage of her truck with a wrench, rolls out and looks up at Chloe from her creeper.

"Yeah," she says, wiping sweat off her brow and leaving behind a streak of grease. "Willowgrove gets to you sometimes."

Chloe frowns, shoulders tensing automatically. "That's not what it is."

"You sure? I got all morning if you wanna talk," her mom says, sitting up. "I lived through it, remember?"

"I'm fine," she says again, looking for an out. "I—I gotta go study though. Gonna meet up with some people from bio. Okay?"

"Okay, but come home for dinner!" her mama calls as she heads for her car. "I finally figured out fried green tomatoes! Finals-week feast!"

"Okay," Chloe agrees, avoiding her mom's eyes before she asks any more questions. Thank God she left her backpack in her car last night. Clean getaway.

She's restless all the way to Smith's house, jiggling her toes on the gas pedal and speeding through the yellows. She has to make this quick—she really *does* have to study—but she's also wired on seven hundred different emotions, none of which she's particularly eager to express to anyone.

When the front door opens, the person behind it is a tall girl Chloe hasn't seen before. She's holding a Switch and appears to be in the middle of a heated Smash battle.

"Hi, is Smith home?" Chloe asks, peering past the girl's shoulder at the small living room with crosses on the wall and a floral sofa set. This must be Smith's sister, Jas.

"Who are you?" she says without looking up.

"I'm Chloe. From school."

Jas's Mewtwo Final Smashes someone's Piranha Plant. "Okay, Chloe From School. Smith didn't say anything about a girl coming over."

"Mind your business, Jas," says a laughing voice, and then Smith is behind her, looking surprised in a sleeveless shirt and soft-looking gray shorts. She hasn't noticed until now that his hair's gotten a little longer.

He shoves the side of Jas's head with one palm and says, "Go away. And don't forget to plug that shit in when you're done. I got MarioKart with Rory tonight."

"You're such an asshole," she says back.

"Mom, Jas called me an asshole!" Smith yells.

*"Jasmine Parker!"*

"You *suck*," Jas says, glaring, and then she disappears as Smith laughs into his fist.

"I'm gonna miss that girl next year," Smith says.

"Is that why you texted me about MarioKart?" Chloe says. "Because of Rory?"

Smith shrugs. "I was gonna invite you."

"You two can hang out on the weekend without a

Chloe buffer," Chloe points out.

"I know, it's just . . . been a while," Smith mumbles. "Anyway, what's up? You look weird."

Right. "Can we talk?"

Smith nods. "You wanna come in?"

Chloe leaves her shoes at the door and follows Smith through the living room and down a short hall lined with framed photos: Smith in his football uniform with the national championship trophy, Smith's parents smiling on a cruise ship, his two youngest siblings in matching Easter outfits, Jas on stage with a microphone.

She's barely been there for three seconds when a pretty middle-aged woman with Smith's exact same eyes and curl pattern appears at the doorway.

"Smith," she says, "who's this?"

"This is Chloe, Mom," Smith says. "She's my friend from school. She was in the play with Ace."

"Just a friend?"

"*Yes,* Mom," Smith says, sounding mortified.

His mom nods, looking Chloe over. "There's brisket in the kitchen," she announces. She leaves with a point over her shoulder at Smith's bedroom door, sing-songing, "Door stays open!"

"Sorry," Smith says. "I'm not technically supposed to have girls in here, but they're starting to give up now that I'm almost in college. Also, you should probably take her up on that brisket, my dad smoked it this morning and it's amaz—"

"I saw Shara last night."

Smith stops.

He doesn't react at first, just looks at her for a long second like he's trying to figure out if she's joking. Then, satisfied that she isn't, he pulls out the desk chair and sits on a pile of discarded hoodies.

"I figured out where she was, and I went by myself," Chloe tells him. "I'm sorry. I'm *really* sorry. I know I should have told you, but I was—I was so *mad* at her—"

"Chloe," Smith says finally, holding up a hand. There's a speck of glitter on his thumbnail, like he painted it and then scraped it off. "It's fine. Did she tell you why she left?"

"She said she did all this because she lied about getting in to Harvard, and because she wanted to distract me so she could win valedictorian," Chloe rattles off. "*And* to force you and Rory to talk to each other, because she thinks you're only dating her because of him."

Smith doubles over, forehead to knees, and Chloe thinks he's taking the news hard until she hears him laugh out, "*Oh, thank you, Jesus.*"

"What?"

Smith straightens up again, still laughing. He swipes a hand across his forehead. "I thought I was gonna have to tell her myself. *Whew.*"

There's no way. She saw Smith's call log after Shara disappeared. He couldn't have faked caring that much. "You—what are you saying? She was *right?*"

"It's," Smith says, sobering with a wince, "complicated."

"I *defended* you!"

"Look, it only started that way!" he insists. "It was ... okay, so, freshman year, I went to a party at Dixon's house and found out Rory had moved in next door to Shara. And he didn't want to talk to me at school, but I realized I could still stay close to him, and I wanted to know he was okay. I was worried about him. The last few months we were friends, we talked a lot about how he was afraid his dad would have to move, and how his brother wouldn't be able to drive us around introducing us to music anymore because he was going to college. I knew it had to be rough for him. So I—I asked Shara to homecoming, so I could go over to her house and see him."

"You spent twenty dollars on carnations for that?"

"I wasn't sure she'd say yes," Smith says. "It was only supposed to be homecoming, I swear, but then I *liked* her. Like, as a person. She was cool, and I could be myself around her. And everyone liked us together, and it worked for both of us, and I felt so guilty about how it started, but it was too late to tell her the truth. And every time I said I loved her, I meant it, just, you know. Not like that. And I tried to forget about the Rory thing and be a good boyfriend, but he was—he was always *there,* and I couldn't think about her because I was thinking about him—"

"Oh my God," Chloe gasps, "you *are* in love with him."

Smith's eyes go wide. "Is that what Shara said? Am I— Does he—?"

"Uh-uh." Chloe holds both hands up to ward him off. "I am *not* getting involved with that side of this love quadrilateral. Go back to the story."

"Right," Smith says, shaking his head. Chloe is definitely not attending Smith and Rory's emotionally fraught MarioKart session tonight. "Anyway, next thing I knew, it'd been like, two and half years and Shara was my best friend other than Ace, and I realized she deserved to know before we decided what to do after graduation. So I told myself I was gonna come clean after prom, but then she dipped. And the worst part is, I was *relieved,* because it meant I could put the conversation off a little longer. That's why I didn't say anything after the note from Dixon's house."

Chloe tries to catch up. "What about the note from Dixon's house?"

"She told me where she was in that note," Smith says, rubbing the back of his neck. "The G in 'Graduation' was capitalized."

It takes a second for the memory to snap into focus: the name on the back of Wheeler's sailboat. *Graduation.*

Chloe, who's still processing the revelation that Smith and Shara have been in the Willowgrove version of a lavender marriage since sophomore homecoming, tries not to scream when she says, "*You've known where she was since Dixon's party?*"

"I know! I know! I'm an asshole!" Smith says. "You think I don't feel like shit? I feel like shit! But the longer it went on, the longer I didn't have to talk to her."

"But . . ." Chloe presses her fingers to her temples. "But she knew you'd figure that out. Why would she tell you so early?"

"I think," Smith says, "she wanted to give me the option to end the whole thing, but she trusted I'd let her do what she had to do first. We've always kind of gotten each other like that. Like, even with all of the stuff I've found out about her since she left, I still think that part was always true."

"So, you . . . you let me and Rory run around like idiots for weeks. We went in the air ducts, Smith. The *air ducts.*"

"I told you, I'm not proud of it. Of any of it. But . . . I don't know, Chloe. I kinda did want to let her do her thing," Smith tells her. "And not just because I didn't want to have the conversation, or because I felt guilty, or because I was starting to wonder who she even was. And not because it meant Rory was talking to me again for the first time since we were fourteen, though that was . . . definitely part of it."

Chloe shakes her head. "What other possible reason is there?"

Smith considers the question, folding his hand under his chin.

"The other day, after the theater party and the lake," Smith says, "I came home when everyone was asleep and pulled flowers out of my dad's garden. And I sat in front of my mirror and put them in my hair. Just to see how it would look. And it looked *dope*. So I thought about what Ash said, and some stuff I talked to Summer about, and what I'm supposed to look like and act like to play football, and what actually feels like *me*, and the way Shara used to look at me sometimes . . . I mean, yeah. Shara's done shitty things. That sucks. But at the same time, if you're not what Willowgrove wants you to be, and if your family believes certain stuff, it can make you kind of crazy. You know what I mean?"

The words "not what Willowgrove wants you to be" send Chloe's brain tumbling noisily away like Georgia's water bottle when she dropped it down the C Building stairs. Her ears start ringing.

Why does *everyone* keep bringing that up?

"I, uh. Okay. I actually have to go." She turns for the door, then pauses. "Um. Not because of you. You're doing great, with all the, um. Identity stuff. Also, pronouns?"

Smith bites his lip. He looks like he might smile. "Same for now."

"Okay, cool," Chloe says. "Um. Talk more later?"

She hasn't even told him about the kiss, but she has to go. She has to.

Maybe this was how Shara felt when she ran.

She doesn't know where to drive. She can't call Georgia. She's too restless to go home, too full of Smith's words, too afraid everything will catch up to her the second she stops moving.

It's not until she pulls up to the curb that she realizes she automatically followed all the turns and back roads to the empty lot.

When they moved to False Beach, her grandma was still living in the house Chloe's mom grew up in—a double-wide trailer on a stretch of road near the edge of town, out toward Lake Martin. Chloe remembers the smell of cigarettes and cinnamon air freshener, the hand-knit green and orange afghan on the armchair where her grandma would sit and watch tiny Chloe read *Redwall* during her few childhood trips to Alabama. Her grandma was mostly conservative, but a dogged commitment to Southern hospitality meant she was kind to everyone if they were her neighbor or her company. She didn't speak to Chloe's mom for three years after she came out as a lesbian, but when she heard about the engagement, she showed up in LA with a case of beers as an olive branch and her old wedding dress in a carry-on.

After the cancer, Chloe spent a week between sophomore and junior year in the trailer with her mama, boxing up old photos and putting furniture up on Craigslist so her mom didn't have to see everything empty. Then they sold the trailer and had it hauled off, and now all that's left is an empty plot of land with a faded FOR SALE sign stuck in the overgrown weeds.

Chloe kills the engine and walks out into the tall grass. The ground is wet from recent rain, though it always seems to be wet this close to the lake. She takes off her sandals and lets her toes touch the cool earth, feeling it give slightly under her weight, taking account of her.

Chloe Green was born in California. Her mom's egg, her mama's body, California soil. She grew up in a house full of Obama coffee mugs and Tibetan singing bowls and unofficial aunts who played cello in their living room after dinner parties. Before they moved here, she never felt anything about Alabama, and she certainly never imagined it could make her feel anything about herself.

But Alabama is in her, no matter how much she pretends it's not.

According to the introductory course Georgia gave Chloe on her first day at Willowgrove, there has been exactly one person who came out as gay while still a student in the thirty-six years since the school was founded.

There are a lot of versions of the story, because many people who graduate Willowgrove never fully escape the gravitational pull of its gossip. When Georgia first told it, she didn't know the girl's name, only that she graduated in the late '90s and came out as a lesbian in front of the whole grade on the senior retreat when everyone was sharing personal testimonies. Another rendition is that this mythical lesbian came to school with her hair dyed blue and got suspended for trying to recruit girls to her satanic sex cult. In a different version, she got busted for having a stash of *Playboy* magazines in her locker and is now married to a Florida senator.

But Chloe knows the real story, because that girl's name was Valerie Green.

She knows for a fact that her mom put a blue streak in her hair with bleach and Kool-Aid and told three friends from woodshop that she liked girls, and that, when the secret got out, the Willowgrove rumor factory stamped out a hundred iterations like candy bars. There were meetings with the guidance counselor and the principal and the pastor, in which she was encouraged to finish high school somewhere else until she assured them that none of the rumors were true, and then months of everyone talking about it anyway. It was the main reason she ran west as soon as she could and didn't come back until she had to.

Chloe's mom told her all of this before the move.

"You can go wherever you want to go," her mom said,

stroking her hair as they sat in a pile of moving boxes. "We'll find the money. But I want to protect you."

"I'll be fine, Mom," Chloe said confidently. "Besides, there's no way it's the same now as it was like, twenty years ago."

She told herself it didn't get to her. She knew who she was. Her moms love her, her friends love her, she *knows* who she *is,* and she's never bought into the bullshit notion that people like her are made wrong, not for a second. It's an unpleasant sting when a teacher tells her to stop trying to use Bible verses to prove that the love between her moms can't be wrong because it says right there that God is love and all love is of God, but—no. No, as long as she can go home at the end of the day and see the two women who raised her sitting on either side of the kitchen table, she knows it's not true.

But that's not accounting for the time in between.

That's not accounting for Mackenzie Harris refusing to change in front of her in the locker room, or the teachers who give her As but never use her work as an example for the class, or the shitty jokes about her moms. That's not accounting for Wheeler's vendetta against her or the way it sometimes feels like everyone's just finished laughing about her when she walks into a room. There's the initial sting, and there's the moment she walks through the door of her house and feels it fade, but there's all this time in between when she's furiously maintaining her GPA and stomping through the hallways and breaking small rules to feel like she's done something to deserve the way people look at her.

She was so sure if she didn't believe any of it, it couldn't hurt her.

Was Shara right? Has she really been afraid this whole time? That rage between her ribs, the thing clawing out of the muscle of her heart—what if it's always been fear, waiting in her marrow, cut loose the first day of freshman year?

What if Willowgrove got to her after all?

At 2 p.m. on Sunday afternoon, Chloe's phone lights up on her nightstand. She holds her place in her AP Bio study guide with her finger and checks it.

shara.wheeler has started an Instagram Live.

No way. Absolutely no way is she going to look. She won. She's done.

One second passes, and another.

She throws her notes to the foot of the bed and reaches for her phone.

The video is an empty shot of the cabin of Shara's parents' sailboat, exactly the way Chloe remembers it: the bunk, the stairs, the pink toothbrush in a cup by the miniature sink. She watches the number at the corner of the screen go higher and higher: 37 viewers, 61 viewers, 112, 249 and counting. Familiar names start popping up with messages. Summer Collins types out a string of question marks. Tyler Miller asks if he missed it already. April Butcher sends a series of skeptical emojis wearing monocles.

When the number hits 300—three-quarters of Willowgrove's high school population—Shara steps into the frame and says, "Hi."

Her hair's up, and her face is bare. She's wearing a baggy old T-shirt with a hole in the collar, tugged over on one side so that her collarbone pokes out. *Again* with the clavicles.

"Here's the thing." She sits and stares directly into the camera, chin up, eyes intent. Chloe's seen her make the same face before she aces an exam. "I lied."

Chloe feels herself lean closer to the screen.

"I lied about . . . a lot of stuff, actually. Pretty much everything. But let's start with the college thing: I didn't get in to Harvard. I mean, I almost did, but I absolutely tanked the interview." She holds up a slip of paper with the Harvard seal. "This is my rejection letter. So, there's that, but the other part of the lie is, I bombed the interview on purpose."

What.

"What," Chloe murmurs at her phone.

Shara pulls a shoebox into view—where did she hide that when Chloe was there?—and dumps it out on the table. Papers come cascading out, unsealed envelopes and rubber stamps.

"The truth is," Shara goes on, "the more I thought about it—about walking into my first day of classes at Harvard, where half the people in the room would be just as smart as me, and the other half would be smarter—I couldn't do it. I didn't *want* to do it. But I'd already made sure everyone knew about Harvard, so I decided to fake it. And then, of course, my dad wouldn't let me apply to only one school, so I sat at the kitchen table while he watched me apply to seventeen different colleges he picked out. Duke. Vanderbilt. Yale, Notre Dame, Rice—you get the picture. And when enough time had passed, I started faking acceptance letters too. Researched what they all looked like. Made a big deal out of getting the mail myself every day. I even bought a few welcome packets off eBay." She shrugs, offering the camera a wry smile. "Look, nobody can say I don't commit to something once I decide to do it, okay? It just wasn't Harvard I was committing to. And focusing on all this meant I didn't have time to think about what came after."

She pushes the box offscreen, and Chloe sees her eyes dart down to the comments streaming in. She shakes her head slightly and goes on.

"To be honest, it was easy. I've been lying my whole life—though I prefer to think of it as adapting. Working. As far back as I can remember, everybody told me I was pretty, I was perfect, I was a legacy, so I decided to be that, because it made my parents like me better and it made me feel safe. I lied to my family, to my friends, to my boyfriend, to people I barely even know, and I did it all to make people fall in love with something I made instead of someone I actually had to be. I still don't really get what's supposed to be bad about that—I mean, I *liked* being prom queen. I *chose* it. It made everything easier. What's wrong with doing what it takes to have an easier life? Why is it so bad to want to feel special, or loved, or accepted? High school feels like all there is sometimes, the whole world, and don't we all want the whole world to revolve around us? Isn't that what our parents say? Let me tell y'all, sometimes a pedestal is a very comfortable place to be, because at least up there nothing can hurt you."

She pauses, swiping a piece of hair out of her face.

"But anyway," she continues, "a couple months ago, when I saw the end of senior year coming, I decided to run away. I knew it was only a matter of time until people found out about Harvard if I stayed. I was gonna come back once everyone missed me, win valedictorian, and let that be the way y'all remembered me. I loved the picture in my head: Shara Wheeler, she had more important places to be, but she came back one last time to remind us she was the best. Nobody ever had to see all the pins holding the dress together, if you know what I mean.

"That was my plan. This wasn't ever part of it, but that was back when I thought I knew what all of my lies were and why I had to tell them. It hadn't really occurred to me that I was lying to myself too. I didn't know that part until two nights ago, and that's why I decided to tell y'all everything. I think maybe I needed so many secrets to keep this one locked up, and now that it's not locked up anymore, I don't need the rest."

Shara lays her palms flat on the table, looking right into the camera so intently that Chloe wants to look away, but she can't.

"The real reason I ran away isn't a reason at all. It's a person. I did all of this for her attention, and I told myself it was because I wanted to beat her, but really, I wanted to know she was looking at me. This part shouldn't be a surprise to her—she figured it out before I did. I guess she already won something, huh?

"So, that's the truth," Shara concludes. "All of it. I'm done lying. And if you hate me now, fine. Only two weeks left. I can take it.

"See you on Monday."

# FROM THE BURN PILE

Passed notes between Shara and Smith
Found in Smith's Free Enterprise notes

Do you wanna go out for dinner tomorrow?
It's my turn to have the car and Olive Garden
has unlimited soup, salad, and breadsticks on
weekdays 🙂

I can't, I have to study.

At your house?

I was gonna go to the library.

ahhh got it

Actually, I can do it at my house.
Wanna come over?

yeah!

# 18

Chloe is, as she often is, and as she has in fact been every single time she's thought about Shara since she first saw her on that cursed billboard, fuming.

She was in control. She had all of Shara's secrets. For exactly thirty-six hours, before Shara outplayed her. Again.

And now Shara's coming back, and Chloe's behind on her studying in three different classes because she's been wasting all her time and energy trying to win a rigged game.

It's Monday morning, and she's not waiting for Shara. She's sitting alone on the hood of her car in the student lot because Georgia still isn't speaking to her, because of Shara, and neither are the rest of her friends, because of Shara, so she's going over her AP Lit study guide by herself, and she's definitely not waiting to see Shara's white Jeep pull in for the first time in a month.

It's not Shara's white Jeep, but Rory's red BMW that purrs into the lot.

He's got the top down, Jimi Hendrix screaming out of the speakers, and Shara in the passenger seat.

Chloe's notecards hit the concrete.

Rory, the absolute traitor, is at the wheel in a pair of Ray-Ban sunglasses. All Chloe can do is gape as he pulls into the spot next to her and throws it in park. Gaping is all anyone's doing, actually—a ripple of shock that starts at the edge of the courtyard, where Emma Grace Baker drops her vanilla bean frap all over her Superstars.

Shara opens the door and steps out.

Her skirt's hiked up at least three inches above regulation length. Her face is bare. And her hair—the trademark Shara Wheeler wavy blond waterfall—has been chopped off just above her shoulders in a jagged line, like she did it herself with a pair of kitchen scissors over the bathroom sink, and dyed a shade of hot pink expressly forbidden by the Willowgrove dress code. When she runs a hand through it, her fingers are dye-stained.

"Hi," she says to Chloe over the sound of the guitars.

"Hi," Chloe says back.

They stay there. Chloe's brain is stuck replaying the last minute of Shara's livestream. The defiant tilt of Shara's jaw as she spoke, the burn of her eyes. *I wanted to know she was looking at me.* Here Chloe is, looking.

Finally, stiffly, Shara says, "Didn't want to miss any exams."

She turns and walks away, and like always, the whole world bends around Shara Wheeler. Everything goes slow motion. Obnoxious freshmen shut up. Marching band couples stop groping each other. April smacks Jake so hard that he expels a surreptitious vape cloud. Mrs. Sherman's overlined mouth goes so thin, it disappears. A football hits Ace in the side of the head and bounces away, completely forgotten.

Chloe watches Shara's skirt swish in perfect time to the music still blasting out of Rory's car and feels like she's losing her mind.

She rounds on Rory. "Really? *'Purple Haze'*?"

He shrugs. "It's a good song."

"Why are you *driving her around*?"

"Her parents took the steering wheel off her car, so she came next door and asked me for a ride. We talked. It's chill."

"It's chill? After everything she put you through, it's *chill*? I thought you weren't in love with her anymore."

"I'm not," he says. He slides his sunglasses down his nose and raises an eyebrow. "In fact, I think we might both be gay."

The only scene Chloe's imagination can supply at that moment is her own hand slamming down on a big red button to nuke herself and the entire campus from orbit.

"Useless." She scoops up her study materials and storms off to her first exam. *"Useless!"*

"Did you hear Shara's back?"

"I heard she faked getting into all those schools."

"You didn't *hear* that, she *told* you," Chloe mutters, shoving through the crowd toward her exam. Just like the first Monday after Shara left, it's impossible to go anywhere on campus without hearing her name.

"I heard she stole a boat and sailed to Mexico and back by herself."

"I heard Smith dumped her."

"Really? 'Cause I heard *she* dumped *him* because she's a lesb—"

A siren blasts through the morning buzz, sending students ducking for cover with their hands over their ears. In the center of the hall stands Principal Wheeler, holding a megaphone and visibly out of breath.

"Willowgrove students!" he shouts into the megaphone. "If you are not a senior, there is no reason for you not to be in your first hour classrooms, in your seat, ready for your morning prayer and announcements! If you *are* a senior, you should be reporting to your first exam! This is not a disco! You are not on summer vacation yet! If I see any students in this hallway in two minutes when the homeroom bell rings, you will be in detention this afternoon! I repeat, detention! Let's go!"

He lowers the bullhorn as everyone scatters, and then he turns and finds himself facing Chloe.

He looks absolutely awful. Hair askew, shirt buttoned wrong, dark circles under his eyes, all in all like a man who had a terrible weekend and is now having a terrible Monday. She wonders, briefly, how pissed he must have been when he checked Shara's bedroom this morning and discovered that his bundle of Christly joy had vanished again with nothing left behind but tumbleweeds of hacked-off blond hair. Now he's stuck running through the hallways with a bullhorn, trying to keep the stock value of the Wheeler name from dropping any lower.

He raises the bullhorn and says, over a squawk of feedback, "You too, Miss Green."

She does not say, "I kissed your daughter, twice," but she thinks it. She thinks it *hard*.

Instead, she smiles and salutes and marches off to her AP Lit exam.

Shara's already in her desk when Chloe gets to Mrs. Farley's classroom. The rest of the class is leaning across aisles and whispering behind stacks of notecards, and every last one of them is staring at the girl on the front row with the pink hair.

Before, when everyone in a room was staring at Shara, it made her more powerful, like the moon refracting sunlight. Now, if she notices it at all, she doesn't let on. Her eyes are straight ahead, fixed on her neat line of pens and pencils.

She doesn't look up when Chloe sits behind her, but her posture straightens slightly.

Mrs. Farley doesn't say anything to Shara when she passes out the exam booklets. Not a dress code notice, not a demand for a doctor's note for the month of class she missed, not even a disapproving look. Must be nice to be the principal's daughter. If Chloe said a bunch of gay stuff on Instagram Live and then showed up at school with pink hair and a too-short skirt, she'd be catapulted out of the building and probably into the dumpsters behind the cafeteria.

At least she finishes her exam before Shara does. She slides her papers smugly onto Mrs. Farley's desk, and that's it—her very last English exam of high school.

When she turns around and sees Shara in the front row, head down, diligently writing her essay, she remembers Shara's letter: three fingers on Chloe's desk the first day of class. She remembers that moment, how she sat there with her nerves sparking and watched Shara pull sharpened pencils from a pencil case out of her backpack, which was also annoying, somehow—always a thing inside a thing inside a thing with Shara.

So, on the way back to her seat, she leans in and touches the corner of Shara's desk with three intentional fingertips, light and short enough that anyone else could mistake it for an accident.

But Shara's not anyone else. Her chin snaps upward, and she looks from Chloe's hand to Chloe's face, pen frozen on the paper, a piece of streaky pink hair falling across the top of her nose.

The way her eyes flash at Chloe . . . it's not surprise. It's not confusion. It's bright, heady expectation, like she knew it was only a matter of time until this happened. Like she's been waiting since she sat down for Chloe to come up there and kiss her.

And that's when it clicks. Shara still thinks she gets whatever she wants whenever she decides she wants it. She thinks, because she got a makeover and stopped denying her crush, Chloe's going to fall into her lap. As if Chloe is going to be like everyone else Shara's ever met and make it *easy*.

She still has something on Shara: herself. She can make Shara chase her. She can be smart about it—let her think she might have a chance and then give her the first bottom-of-the-heart rejection of her entire charmed life. Chloe's spent four years trying to keep one thing out of Shara's hands. Now she can *be* that.

Really, Shara's original plan to break Chloe's heart wasn't a bad one. Shame to let it go to waste.

She gives Shara a small, tight smile and slides into her seat.

Chloe's plan for the rest of finals week is simple: One, make herself available to Shara. Two, do things that she knows Shara will be into based on past behavior. Nothing that would count as actual pursuit, but like, horny little traps. Three, lay it on so thick that Shara *has* to try something. Four, rejection, gratification, *glory*.

Shara pretty much does step one for her. The next few days, she seems to have suddenly developed a habit of being everywhere Chloe is. Chloe goes to ask her calc teacher a question, and Shara is waiting outside the classroom. Chloe unlocks her car, and Shara is two parking spaces over, pretending to be interested in Ace's tire pressure. Chloe hovers at the edge of the courtyard, watching her friends share a carton of Sonic tots and wondering if Ash ever finished their portfolio, and suddenly Shara is perched on the nearest flowerbox with her color-coded binder of study guides.

Chloe can only imagine Shara's strategy is similar. She's making herself available to Chloe, under the mistaken impression that Chloe hasn't yet fainted into her arms simply due to lack of opportunity.

She can use this.

When she stops at her locker for an emergency coffee, there Shara is, leaning against the next locker, trying to open a granola bar.

The choppy pink hair *does* look unfairly good on her. Against her defined features and her long lashes, it makes her look like a comic book character.

"How do you think you did on the calc exam?" Shara asks.

"Oh, you know," Chloe says. She swallows a mouthful, then holds Shara's gaze as she innocently swipes the side of her thumb across her bottom lip, the way she would if she were a girl in one of Georgia's Regency novels. Shara's fingers go stiff around the wrapper. "Pretty well. Implicit derivatives are actually pretty easy once you get the hang of them."

"No," Shara disagrees, staring at her mouth, "they're not."

"Hm. Maybe it's just me, then," Chloe says. "What about you?"

"What about me?"

"The exam," Chloe says. "How do you think you did?"

"Oh. Fine."

"Better than me?" Chloe asks.

One corner of Shara's mouth tucks in. "Maybe."

"Wanna make a bet?" Chloe says.

"What would I win?"

"You tell me," Chloe says. "I'm sure you could come up with something of mine that you want."

Shara finally succeeds in ripping her granola bar open.

"Yeah," Shara says in an explosion of granola crumbs, "probably."

And then she storms off.

That's new. Not the running away part—that's Shara's thing—but the indignant way she looked at Chloe before she did it, like Chloe had *betrayed* her, somehow. Like Chloe's done a crime to her, and the crime is "not taking her top off."

"Oh," she realizes out loud, "that's *fun*."

The next day, Chloe is punching in the number for a Three Musketeers and Shara's reflection materializes next to hers in the vending machine glass.

"Are you growing your bangs out?" Shara asks. "They look different."

Chloe sucks in a breath and turns to face her, relaxing her mouth into a soft smirk.

"I've been thinking about it, actually," Chloe says. "I kind of want to grow it all out so I can put it up if I need to. You know how you need to put your hair up sometimes?"

"Uh-huh," Shara says.

"Do you think I'd look good with long hair?" Chloe asks.

"I—" Shara begins. Her lip curls, and Chloe tamps down a laugh. "Sure. If you want."

Shara huffs and leaves again.

That afternoon, in front of the mirrors in the girls' bathroom, Chloe leans over the sink to fix the tip of her eyeliner wing while Shara perches on the next one.

"What brand of eyeliner do you use?" Shara asks.

"Why?" Chloe says, turning to her. "Do you want to try it?"

"Oh, that's—"

"I can put it on for you," Chloe says. "Come here."

"I'm good, actually," Shara says, jumping down. She tries to make a haughty exit, but her shoes squeak on the damp tile floor the whole way, which only seems to make her angrier.

When the door closes behind her, Chloe grins at her reflection.

She's always thought of herself as somewhere to the left of hot. Pretty, probably, but in a Gucci-campaign, teeth-too-far-apart, eyes-too-big way. But this thing with Shara—a girl who grew up the kind of beautiful most people never even see in real life, the kind of gorgeous it almost hurts to look at—it's like shimmering into new skin. Like being beamed into space and all her particles reassembling into someone who technically looks the same but is one version ahead of the last. She's a scrappy galactic rebel, and Shara is a star, and she's loading up a big-ass plasma cannon and leveling it right at Shara's heart.

Like, how could that *not* be the best thing ever?

On Thursday afternoon, after her AP Bio exam, she emerges from the classroom to find Shara at Smith's nearby locker.

It's the first time Chloe has seen them together since Shara got back, which is . . . weird. She's not sure what she expected—maybe Smith trying to fend her off with a chair like a lion tamer—but it certainly wasn't the sense of quiet ease that hangs around them. They stand the way they've always stood, angled into each other like two stretching plants, even after everything. She says something inaudible to him, and he laughs that sun-warm laugh of his.

First Rory, now Smith? *How* does she get to drop back into their lives like nothing happened? Even if Smith does feel guilty for dating her under false pretenses, she still did everything else she did.

A dozen lockers down, Ash is cramming their art kit—basically a fishing tackle box of polymer clay and googly eyes—into their locker. They glance up, and Chloe almost raises a hand to wave, but Ash pulls a sad face and turns away.

Right. Chloe's the only one who has to experience consequences for her actions. So far, at least.

She marches up to the locker two spots over from Smith's, where Brooklyn Bennett is sifting wide-eyed through her stacks of rubber-banded notecards.

"Hi, Brooklyn," she says, aggressively friendly. "What's up?"

"About to have a mental breakdown, that's what," she says. Brooklyn launches into a long, itemized list of all the questions she thinks she got wrong on every one of her exams, and Chloe plasters on a sympathetic expression and tunes it out, listening instead to Shara and Smith's conversation.

". . . just started talking again," Smith is saying quietly. "What if I mess this up, and he goes back to pretending I don't exist?"

"Right," Shara deadpans, "this whole time he's been minding his business and *not* leering at you from his bedroom window."

"I'm being serious, Shara," Smith says. "I think this is my last chance."

"*I'm* being serious," Shara counters. "I don't think you're going to run out of chances there."

Over their shoulders, Chloe can see the homecoming picture still stuck up on Smith's locker door. The blue dress, Shara's God-honoring nip shadows.

"I'm gonna go study in the library," Chloe announces loudly.

"Uh," Brooklyn says, startled. "Okay."

"Yep," she says. Two lockers down, she can detect the

slight shift in Shara's shoulders as she listens in. "Should be there all afternoon."

"Okay," Brooklyn says again. "Thanks?"

She leaves Brooklyn staring after her and books it to her locker. From the makeup pouch, the one she once used to hold Shara's cards, she removes something she brought to school earlier this week. It's an escalation, for sure. A real break-glass-in-case-of-emergency type of measure.

As much fun as she's had watching Shara blush and scowl and stare at her with those big spangly eyes, as addictive as it is to be so sweet to her that it splits like a sucked pepper-mint into shards that cut, as much as she knows she could keep twisting this around her finger until the heat death of the universe and never get bored, it's time. Somebody has to make Shara answer for something, and Chloe's going to do it. Warm that space cannon *up,* baby.

She checks her bangs one last time in the plastic mirror on her locker door, between a note from her mom and a photo strip of her and Georgia at the movies. God, if Georgia knew about this, she'd be so stressed out. Benjy would be game, though, he loves a scheme, and Ash would—

She shuts her locker and takes off for the library.

# FROM THE BURN PILE

Scrawled in the margins of
a sight-reading assignment

VALEDICTORIAN SPEECH: DRAFT #29

I would like to begin by addressing Principal Wheeler: Respectfully, sir, I'm going to find a way to ruin your life if it's the last thing I do.

# 19

It takes half an hour to edit her Euro history notecards down to the ones with potential for erotic subtext. Peninsula War? No. Corn laws? Absolutely not. Enlightened despot? Probably how Shara sees herself, but no. Would be really helpful if European history were less horrifying. She's going to have to lean hard on the religious stuff.

She's so absorbed in deciding whether Francis Bacon could possibly be sexy that she almost misses the sound of Shara entering through the side door of the library.

Her table is one of the secluded ones set aside from the main study area, so she has about a second and a half before Shara spots her. All at once, she kicks her backpack off the seat next to her, shoves her notes out of the way, flips her hair, straightens her shoulders, and, for the final touch, hooks her ankle around the empty chair and drags it a foot closer.

By the time she feels Shara's eyes on her, she's posed serenely over her notes with her face angled to catch the overhead fluorescents from the most flattering possible direction.

She hears Shara's sneakers pause on the carpet, then the soft *pat-pat-pat* of her approach, and Shara says from beside the table, "You know, if you wanted me to meet you here, you could have asked."

"Oh, hi, Shara," Chloe says, blinking up at her in fake surprise.

"You didn't have to drag Brooklyn into it," Shara says. "That girl is one Scantron bubble away from a nervous breakdown."

"I don't know what you're talking about," Chloe says, "but if you're in the mood to confront some stuff, there are a couple of other places you could start."

Shara bites her lip. "What's your last exam?"

"Don't you know?" Chloe asks.

Shara's lip turns creamy white under her teeth, then strawberry red when she releases it. She sits in the empty chair and begins unzipping her backpack, close enough that Chloe can smell lilacs for the first time since the sailboat. She tries not to get too lost in the memory of Shara screaming and splashing around in a wet cloud of pink tulle. Seriously, top five Chloe moment.

"European history," Shara finally concedes.

"And yours is Chem II," Chloe says. Shara blinks, like she really thought Chloe was stupid enough not to have learned her schedule too. "Have you gotten any better at limiting reactant problems since sophomore year, or do you want some help?"

Shara sets her binder down on the table. "Have you figured out the difference between Prussia and Germany yet, or should I call your flashcards out for you?"

"Actually," Chloe says, smiling. If this is how it feels to have a plan go perfectly, she sees why Shara likes them so much. "That would be really helpful."

And so, because refusing would mean accepting the

alternative—a deliberate and meaningful conversation about her feelings—Shara opens her hand and accepts Chloe's stack of notecards.

Chloe, of course, already has them memorized. She props her chin on her hand and gazes into Shara's flushed face as she recites the answers effortlessly.

"The Institutes of Christian Religion," Shara asks.

"Written by John Calvin, 1536. Says the Bible is the only source of Christian doctrine and that there are only two sacraments: baptism and communion."

"Defenestration of Prague."

"1618," Chloe says. "Protestants threw a bunch of Catholic officials out of a castle window in Bohemia. Started the Thirty Years War."

Shara glances up from the card.

"Do you know the officials' names?"

An obvious maneuver.

"Count Jaroslav BoDita of Martinice, Count Vilem Slavata of Chlum, Adam II von Sternberg, and Matthew Leopold Popel Lobkowitz," Chloe rattles off.

Shara, looking deeply put out, moves on to the next one. "Regicide."

"The killing of a king," Chloe says. "Or queen."

"Lucrezia Borgia."

"1480 to 1519. One of the most famous women of the Renaissance. Super hot. Blonde. Amazing hair. Smart, educated, accomplished, lots of politically strategic marriages, rumored to enjoy poisoning people. Often used in power plays by her father, Pope Alexander VI."

Over the top of the card, Shara searches Chloe's face for something. Chloe offers her another innocent smile.

"Keep going," she says. "You're doing great."

Shara clenches her jaw and flips to the next card.

"Botticelli."

"1444 to 1510. Leading painter of the Florentine Renaissance, sponsored by the Medici family, best known for *Primavera*, 1482, and *The Birth of Venus*, mid-1480s. Very distinctive style."

"In what way?"

The trapdoor. Shara just stepped right on top of it. Chloe pulls the lever.

"Well," Chloe says, "it was kind of about what his idea of beauty was. Especially women—he always painted women sort of flowing through space. Girls with an effortless sort of elegance, like they're weightless and solid at the same time. Do you know what I mean?"

Shara swallows and nods.

"And then like, this line." And here is where she does it: she reaches over and almost touches the hinge of Shara's jaw with her fingertip, skimming the length of her jawline to her chin. Shara holds absolutely still. "He would have painted it with a strong edge, because he liked really dramatic, defined contours."

She sits back and, before Shara has a chance to recover, tips her head to the side and casually pushes her collar aside, as if it were an accident.

It's kind of funny, she has to admit. She's a waif flouncing around Dracula's candlelit manor with her neck out, sighing, "*Ohhhh noooo,* look at my *poor exposed and vulnerable arteries,* wouldn't it be *absolutely tragic* if someone were to come along and *slurp them?*"

It works. Shara's gaze goes directly where she wants it to, right to the opening of Chloe's oxford, where the secret weapon is resting below the dip between her collarbones.

Shara's silver crucifix necklace.

"Is that—" Shara whispers. "Where did you get that?"

"What, this?" Chloe glances down, raising her eyebrows. "I found it in the trash, actually. Crazy, right? Why, does it mean something to you?"

*It's yours, Shara. Tell me it's yours. Own up to something for once in your life.*

"I have no idea how to answer that question," Shara says quietly, as if she's not sure whether to direct it at Chloe or herself or God.

"Are you sure?" Chloe asks.

Something warm ghosts over Chloe's skin.

On the table, on top of Chloe's piles of notes, Shara carefully, slowly, gently slips the smallest finger of her left hand into the space between the first two of Chloe's right.

This is it. Shara's going to look at her and say, "Oh, that's my necklace, you were right all along, you know me better than I know myself, all I did was lie until you," and then Chloe will say, "duh," and Shara will continue, "put your arms around me, you hot genius," and Chloe will let Shara kiss her, and together they'll dip into a quiet corner of the stacks so Shara can kiss her in the fiction section, M through R, and she'll touch the side of Shara's neck under her hair—

No. Wait. Not the plan.

She's going to let Shara lean in to kiss her, and then, when Shara's hanging there in that breath before their lips touch, she'll wince and say, "Oh, this is awkward, but I'm not really into you like that."

She drags her eyes from their hands to Shara's beautiful, anxious face, which is closer than it was seconds ago. She's looking at Chloe's throat, at Chloe's mouth when she angles it to mirror Shara's.

*Come on,* Chloe thinks. *Just say it's yours. Do something.*

Shara's lips part.

"I—"

She drops Chloe's notecards and pushes her chair out, sweeping her binder and bag into her arms.

"I have to go," she says. "Rory's giving me a ride home, and he— I'm supposed to meet him—"

Without another word, she whirls around and leaves the library as fast as she did that afternoon with *Midsummer.*

At home that night, her mom asks, "Where did you get that?"

She follows her mom's eyes to the opening of her shirt. Crap. She forgot to take Shara's crucifix off.

"Oh, um. I found it?"

Her mom looks skeptical. "That looks like it cost a couple grand, Chloe. Why are you wearing it?"

"I—okay, well, it's—" No way around this one, really. "It's . . . about a girl. It's her necklace, and I was trying to mess with her, so I kind of, uh. Wore it in front of her."

Her mama coos from the kitchen table, "Sounds like how I used to wear your mom's welding apron around the house when I was in the mood."

"Jesus *Christ.*" Chloe sighs.

"So *that's* what's been up with you," her mom says. "You got a thing for a Christian girl."

"I don't—"

"Look, I can't blame you—all those girls walking around with Jesus right over their boobs? Always seemed like entrapment to me when I was your age." She pats Chloe on the head. "Are you pretending to go to church now so you can date somebody's nice wholesome daughter?"

"It's not like that," Chloe insists. Her mama is already singing "Papa Don't Preach" under her breath. Chloe unclasps the necklace and gathers the chain in her hand. "See? Still the heathen you raised."

"You're always perfect," her mom says, pressing a kiss to her hair. "Tell me her name later. You need dinner?"

"I'm good," she says, reaching into the freezer for a few Uncrustables. "I'll eat while I study."

In her room, she spreads her notes across her bed and checks for anything she still needs to go over. She's about to start on the Bolsheviks when the motion-activated floodlights outside her window snap on.

She squints at her drawn blinds and wishes Titania luck escorting every last cricket off this mortal plane, but then she hears it: a faint metallic scrape at her windowpane. The sound of someone removing the screen.

She doesn't know how she knows, but she does.

She jumps out of bed and pulls the blinds up and there, kneeling outside her bedroom, nose inches from the glass, is Shara.

She's lost her uniform top since this afternoon, down to only her skirt and a white cotton undershirt under the glare of the floodlights. For one wild and gorgeous second, Chloe thinks she's here to do what she couldn't in the library. She thinks Shara is finally going to climb into Chloe's life and make this real.

Then she looks down at Shara's hand and sees the pink card.

For a moment, they're locked in a freeze-frame. Chloe imagines a movie camera spinning around them, from behind Shara's shoulders to Shara's stunned profile to the card's sweet, flowery monogram, into Chloe's bedroom under the whirr of the ceiling fan to the hot gasp she sucks in through her teeth, finishing on the blood that slams into Chloe's cheeks as she exhales, "*No.*"

She throws the window open and leaps through it so fast, she doesn't even touch the sill. One second, she's in her room, and the next, her entire body is outside the house and her ass and head and all four limbs are flying at Shara like a rampaging lemur on National Geographic, snarling and tumbling into the grass, the screen cartwheeling off into the night as Shara screams and rolls. *Both* of them scream and roll, kicking and thrashing until they crash sideways into the giant air conditioning unit on the side of the house, which is absolutely *roaring,* because in Alabama it's eighty-five degrees even at night—Chloe's elbow connects with something that might be a nose—Shara's fingernails are *sharp*—Shara throws her shoulder into Chloe's chest, flipping her onto her back—

"Stop!" Shara shrieks.

"I'm not doing this again!" Chloe screeches. She rips up a handful of grass and flings it in Shara's face, and while Shara's sputtering and spitting, Chloe wrestles her way back on top.

"Just take it!" Shara growls, wrenching her arm out from between them and holding up the card, which is crumpled in her fist now.

"No!"

"Take it!"

"You can't make mmmmf—!"

Shara, apparently short on options, crams the card into Chloe's mouth.

Chloe recoils, choking it out onto the grass—the cardstock slices the corner of her mouth, which is perfect, really, what is Shara if not a papercut in the mouth corner of Chloe's existence—and with a feral sort of yowl, she bites Shara's finger.

"Ow!"

"What is *wrong* with you?" Chloe yells. She jams her thumb into the vulnerable inside of Shara's thigh, and Shara relents for the duration of another *"ow!,"* long enough for Chloe to climb up onto her knees. With one hand, she pins the first wrist she can grab to Shara's stomach, and then—also short on options—she straddles Shara around the waist to hold her down.

Shara stops moving.

"Are you running away again?" Chloe demands. She's out of breath, her heart sledgehammering through her chest.

"I—" Shara starts. Above her head, her free hand falls limp on the lawn, palm open to the sky. "No, I—I wrote you a card."

"Oh my God, why can't you act like a *normal human person*?" Chloe says. "Why can't you do *one thing* that's not some fucking emotional manipulation gesture from fifteen million miles away? I'm not *doing* this with you anymore! All I have done for the past month is try to figure out who the hell you are, but I don't even think *you* know!"

"Chloe—"

"Do you think love is just someone arranging their entire life around whatever you want?" she continues, ignoring Shara, whose face is as pink as her hair. "Do you have any idea what you even mean when you say you want me? *No*, you fucking *don't*, because if you *did*, if it actually *meant something to you*, if it wasn't about how much you get off on someone being obsessed with you, if you were actually willing to confront anything about yourself or sacrifice anything that actually matters to you, you wouldn't be sticking notes on my window when I'm not looking! You would have kissed me when you had your chance in the library today!"

She doesn't realize how long they've been stuck there, motionless on the lawn, until the floodlights automatically switch off. Suddenly, she's looking down at Shara beneath her body in the lavender wash of the moonlight, feeling the rise and fall of Shara's breaths between her thighs.

Shara's unpinned hand is still loose above her head. It's just lying there, surrendered, wide open. Chloe is absolutely sick to death of waiting for her to use it.

"I told everyone," Shara says.

"Tell *me*."

"Chloe. Read the card."

"No!" Chloe snaps. "Say it to my face! Do this for real! Ask me on a *date* like everyone who has ever liked someone in the history of the universe!"

She gives Shara ten entire seconds to respond, but she doesn't. She stares up at Chloe, eyes wide, lips parted around nothing.

She releases Shara's wrist and jerks to her feet.

In her head, she's cast Shara in the role of a million different beautiful women laid low: Marie Antoinette in pastel silks, Lucrezia Borgia dripping poison, vampire queens and girls in space. Now, standing over her, she doesn't see any of them. She sees a girl with a kitchen-scissor haircut in a yard in the suburbs.

A month ago, she stood like this outside Shara's house and refused to believe Shara was gone, because she knew the myth was a lie. That there was nothing extraordinary about Shara Wheeler.

This is the real tragedy: Everything extraordinary about

her is trapped behind the myth.

"I have to study," Chloe says. "Go home, Shara."

On her way out of her last exam, Chloe hears a new rumor.

One junior tells another that some total narc of a sophomore walked in on two girls making out in the B Building bathroom. Five lockers down, two guys from the baseball team are muttering about how the girls got reported to Principal Wheeler, and he's going to suspend them.

She's hovering at the water fountain near the exit, trying to catch the name of the snitch she's going to make her new mortal enemy, when one of the double doors opens.

"*There* you are," Shara says when she sees Chloe, as if she hasn't known Chloe's exact whereabouts for months. She's backlit in the doorway with afternoon sun, a hot breeze swirling her hair around her face in rose gold.

Chloe groans. Shara cinematic-ass Wheeler.

"I told you to—"

Shara cuts her off: "It was Georgia."

Chloe's stomach twists. Georgia's name out of Shara's mouth can't possibly mean anything good.

"What? What was Georgia?"

"One of the girls from the B Building bathroom," Shara says. "I thought you should know."

"Georgia? With *who*?"

"Summer," Shara says, "but they only saw Georgia, so she's the only one who got reported."

"*Summer Collins?* They— Since *when*?"

"I don't know, nobody told me either," Shara says. "Summer hasn't exactly been dying to talk to me lately."

Chloe doesn't have time to react to that.

"Where's Georgia now?"

"The office," Shara says. "My dad's gonna call her parents."

Shara steps back, holding the door open. Her eyes are wide, eyebrows set in a dire arch. She's still catching her breath—she must have sprinted all the way across campus.

"There's time if you run," she says.

Chloe runs.

# FROM THE BURN PILE

Passed notes between Georgia and Summer
Found on the back of the instructions for
their geometry project, for which
they received a 95/100

Where do you want to meet after school to work on the project? I think Ms. Johnson's room should be open and she's chill

I'm supposed to go to work right after school, tomorrow?

Softball practice :( I could come to your job maybe? Where do you work?

Yeah that's fine! I work at Belltower Books

YOU WORK THERE??? that's so cool

it's no big deal haha, my parents own it!

You do see how that's cooler, right? OK, I'll meet you there.

# 20

Chloe crashes into the admin office's glass door like a dive-bombing pigeon.

When she throws it open, she doesn't hear it smash into the opposite wall or the alarmed squawk of the receptionist. She doesn't see anything but Georgia, sitting on one of the hideous carpeted chairs, waiting to be called back.

Their eyes lock, and Georgia's expression cycles from shock to confusion to anger and back in less than a second, before best friend mind-meld kicks in, and she mouths, "Isengard."

It's not too late, then.

Chloe keeps running straight to the principal's office, where Wheeler stops with his hand over the number pad of his desk phone, the receiver still pinned between his ear and shoulder.

"Ms. Green," he says, "if you want to meet with me, you can talk to Mrs.—"

"Georgia wasn't the one kissing a girl in the B Building bathroom," Chloe says, "it was me."

Wheeler stares at her for a long second. He puts the receiver down.

"Is that right?" Wheeler asks.

"Yes," she says, and for good measure adds, "sir." Ew. Hated that.

Wheeler studies her face, which she schools into something she hopes is contrite.

"Do you want to explain why a student reported Georgia Neale to me?"

"It happens all the time," Chloe says quickly. "We look alike, and we're always with the same people and doing the same things, and since last fall we even have almost the same haircut, and lowerclassmen are idiots, but—but I swear, it was me. I mean, Georgia's never broken a rule in her life, I'm the one who does that, so you can call my m—my parents instead and tell them what happened. But don't punish Georgia for what I did."

Wheeler contemplates this, leaning back in his tall leather chair with a creak.

"Sexually inappropriate conduct on campus is strictly against the Willowgrove student handbook," Wheeler says. "Normally, something like this would be grounds for suspension. But at this point, that'd just be sending you on summer break early, wouldn't it?"

Dread expands in a horrible bubble inside Chloe's gut, like she's ratcheting up to the big drop of a roller coaster. She knows where this is going.

"But when a wolf is after your flock, the shepherd has to make it clear that it's not welcome," Wheeler says. "Set a precedent. How about . . . a ban from the graduation ceremony?"

"Fine," Chloe hears herself say.

"That means no walking across the stage, no awards, no cap and gown, no pictures with your little friends." He pauses, folding his hands in front of him on the desk. "And, if you happen to get the grades for valedictorian, well ... I hope you didn't waste too much time working on a speech."

It hurts. Of course it hurts.

But Georgia's not ready for this, and that matters more. Every time she's ever made an enemy of Wheeler will be worth it for this.

"I'm gonna ask you again, Chloe," Wheeler says. "Are you sure it was you?"

Chloe swallows the burn in her throat and nods.

When she walks out to her car thirty minutes later, after a quick cry in the very bathroom where she's supposed to have committed the unforgivable crime of kissing a girl, Georgia is sitting against the front driver's side tire.

She remembers now, all the unfinished sentences of the last month. Georgia tried to tell her about Auburn. Maybe she was trying to tell her about Summer too.

"Are you okay?" Chloe asks.

Georgia sniffs and nods. "Are you?"

Chloe shrugs and holds out a hand. "Taco Bell?"

Georgia nods again, letting Chloe pull her up. "Taco Bell."

They walk into Belltower with two heavy bags of burritos and wave goodbye to Georgia's dad as he passes the night shift off to Georgia. If Chloe had been paying closer attention, she could have seen the signs. Georgia's been managing the store as much as her parents for the last six months. Of course she can't leave.

They climb up the ladder to the loft and settle amid the rare books, on the patchy rug that once sat in the living room of Georgia's house until her parents got a new one and recycled it for the store.

"Remember when I got my license," Chloe says, punching her straw out of its wrapper, "and I picked you up from your house, and we got Taco Bell and then went to Walmart and just walked around for an hour? Didn't you get fifteen flavors of Laffy Taffy?"

"It was Airheads."

"That's right. And I bought a Super Soaker."

"We were drunk on power."

"God, that was the best day," Chloe says with a sigh. "Why is the freedom to wander around Walmart unsupervised so intoxicating?"

"I don't know, man." Georgia laughs.

Chloe laughs too, and then she says, "I'm sorry," at the exact same moment Georgia says, "Thank you."

Chloe puts down her drink.

"You first."

"I just—" Georgia starts. "You really jumped on the gay grenade for me today. Thank you."

"Don't worry about it," Chloe says. "I'm . . . I'm sorry I wasn't around, and that I stole the key, and that I lied to you, and that I got so caught up in my own stuff that I let it make me a crappy friend. And for the French essay." She exhales. It really is a long list. "And I'm really, really sorry I didn't apologize to you until now. I would jump on a gay grenade for you every day of my life, and it sucks that I wasn't acting like it."

"I know you would," Georgia says. She pokes at her nachos and continues. "And I—I know I could have brought up how I was feeling earlier instead of blowing up at you."

"I kind of deserved to be blown up at."

Georgia makes a serious face. "Still."

"Well," Chloe says, "if our relationship is gonna be long

distance, we have to promise that we're gonna be better at communication, okay?"

"You're not still mad at me about Auburn?"

"I was never mad at you about Auburn," Chloe says. "Did you think I was mad at you about Auburn?"

Georgia shrugs. "Kind of."

"I wasn't mad at you," Chloe says. "It's just that . . . I'm kind of terrified of doing this without you. And I'm worried about you doing this without me. And I think sometimes when I'm scared it comes out like angry."

"Yeah, you do that."

Chloe winces. "Sorry. I need to work on that."

"It's okay," Georgia says. "I mean, I'm scared too. But I love you, and we're both gonna figure it out."

"I love you too," Chloe says.

It's not easy for Chloe to say stuff like that. But everything's easy with Georgia.

She picks her drink back up and says, "Now. Can I ask you something?"

Georgia nods.

"*How* and *when* did you start dating *Summer Collins*?"

Georgia covers her face with both hands.

"Oh my God."

"The *blushing*!" Chloe gasps theatrically. "She's gay, Your Honor!"

"You're so *embarrassing*," Georgia groans. "You remember in tenth grade, when I had to do that geometry project with her? I've had a crush on her since then. She was kind of like, the girl who made me realize I liked girls."

"You *never* told me!"

"I feel like I *did* mention that she was pretty before, but that always inevitably became a conversation about how she was friends with Shara, and how Shara was the worst."

Chloe winces again. "Okay. Fair. Continue."

Georgia returns to her nachos, fighting a smile. "I never deleted her number after the project. I always hoped somehow she would like, feel me staring at her contact page and get a random urge to text me. And then we'd talk, and we'd fall in love and move to the mountains together and learn how to raise sheep or something."

"And is that what happened?"

"No, what happened was that you started hanging around with Smith, and she texted to ask if I knew what was going on, and then we started talking, and it was great—like, really, *really* great—and we talked about our families and how much we didn't want to leave them to go to college even though we have a lot of things we want to do, and we figured out we're both going to Auburn . . . and then she asked if I wanted to get Sonic with her, and she bought me tater tots, and then . . . I kissed her."

Chloe gasps. "*You* kissed *her*?"

Georgia's grinning fully now. "I did."

"Oh my God!" Chloe punches the air. "What did she do?"

"She was like, 'What happens if I buy you a bacon cheeseburger?'"

"*Ohhhh my Gooooood.*"

She hears about how Summer is majoring in premed and likes banana milkshakes and fantasy novels, how Summer and Ace have finally made up, how Summer's buying tickets to Hangout Fest because Paramore is playing and they both love beach camping and Hayley Williams, how Georgia is the first girl she's ever kissed but she has a gay older sister and she's known she was bi since last year. Chloe gets how they work together, actually, now that she thinks about it.

Two smart girls who wear practical shoes and don't really care about high school bullshit. They're probably going to be the only people at Hangout to actually pack an appropriate amount of water.

"I have one question though," Chloe says. "Isn't Summer like . . . kinda Jesus-y?"

Georgia shrugs. "She goes to church with her family, yeah, but not in the Willowgrove way. She has her own deal." She glances at Chloe. "Don't be judgmental."

"I'm not! But is . . . is that weird for you?"

"Not really? I mean, I grew up believing too. The last few years I wasn't so sure, but . . . I know that Summer's church is more into Jesus the brown socialist than the whole eternal damnation thing. And her parents have actually been really chill about her sister, so that's cool."

Chloe feels her eyebrows go up. "I didn't know that variety of Christian existed in Alabama."

"That's because you're not from here," Georgia points out. "All you've ever known of Alabama is Willowgrove."

"I—"

Well. It's true. Willowgrove is the first time she's been around Christianity, and so to her, that's what faith is: judgmental, sanctimonious hypocrites hiding hate behind Bible verses, twenty-four-karat crucifix necklaces, and charismatic white pastors with all the horrible secrets that money can protect.

She's never been to a church cookout or met a practicing Christian who was also gay. She's never even stepped inside a church where she felt safe. Maybe if she had—maybe if her mom hadn't been burned so bad that she never brought Chloe near Jesus until she absolutely had to—she'd feel different. At this point, she doesn't know if she ever will.

But she also knows that Alabama is more than Willow-grove. And if that's true, maybe faith can mean more than Willowgrove too.

Downstairs, the front door jingles open.

"Georgia?"

In a beam of afternoon sun stands Summer, still in her khaki uniform shorts and a softball T-shirt.

"Up here," Georgia calls out, standing up to lean over the railing of the loft. "Hey, Summer."

"Oh my God, are you okay?" Summer says. "I was looking everywhere for you, and then Shara told me she sent Chloe after you—"

Georgia rounds on Chloe. "*Shara* sent you?"

Chloe grits her teeth. "Technically?"

"We're gonna discuss *that*."

"What happened?" Summer asks.

Georgia turns back to her. "Chloe took the fall for me. Wheeler banned her from graduation."

"Are you serious?" Summer says. Chloe shrugs. "Man, that dude *sucks*."

The front door opens again, and this time it's Benjy in his Sonic polo and visor speeding into the shop. He skids into the nearest table of books, topples a display of mystery novels, and shouts up to the loft, "What *happened*?"

Summer turns to him and says, "Chloe took the fall for Georgia so Wheeler banned her from graduation."

"*What?*" Benjy gasps. "Also, hi, Summer, lots for you to catch me up on, but—*what*? Can he *do* that?"

"Wheeler can do pretty much whatever he wants," Summer says.

"But—isn't the church board in charge of him? Has any-body told them?"

"I really don't think the Willowgrove church board is going to be that upset about this," Summer says grimly. "If anything, they'll be into it."

The door bangs open, and Ash storms in.

"What happened?" they demand.

"Wheeler banned Chloe from graduation because he thinks she was the one making out with girls in the bathroom," Benjy tells them.

*"What?"*

BANG. The door, again, before it's even all the way shut from Ash. It's a good thing Georgia's dad replaced the frame last year, though Smith Parker throwing the whole thing off the hinges would really have been the perfect end to this parade of dramatic entrances. Close behind him, Rory's scowl is extra sour. Chloe sighs and volunteers to take her turn. "I—"

"We know what happened," Rory interrupts.

Chloe stares. "How?"

"I texted Smith," Summer says. "I just wasn't expecting him to show up like, immediately."

"Well," Smith says. "When I'm pissed off, I go fast. You good, Summer?"

"I'm good," Summer says. "Are you?"

"I just think it's bullshit," Smith blurts out. "I mean, Chloe doesn't do half the stuff that some of the guys on the team do. She doesn't even do half the stuff that the kids in the *marching band* do." He pauses. "No offense, Chloe."

Chloe frowns thoughtfully. "Tough, but fair."

"And like," Smith goes on, "if that kid had seen Summer, she'd be banned from graduation too. And Summer's never broken a rule in her life, and I know that because I haven't either, because we *can't*, because me and her have to be perfect to stay on everyone's good side, so there's no room for anything. There's no room to be *anything* except this one specific version of yourself that Willowgrove likes, and—and it's so blatantly fucked up. All of it. And Wheeler doesn't even try to pretend it's not, because he knows nobody is ever gonna step to him." Smith is on a roll now, striding over the books Benjy spilled to pace the front of the store. "Like, my little brother likes football too, and he knows the same way I know that Willowgrove is where you go to get into the SEC, but what if he comes here and he likes boys, or finds out he's *not* a boy, or whatever—I'm not gonna let them do this to him too. It's *fucked up.* It's fucked up how they make us feel about ourselves, and we put up with it because we don't think there's anything we can do about it. We put up with it for so long that we don't even know who we are, only what they want us to be. And I don't want to put up with it anymore."

It's the first time she's ever seen Smith lose his temper. This must be how he lights up the field in overtime. He's incandescent.

"When my sister left for college," Summer says, "she told people about Willowgrove, and they couldn't believe it. I mean, even sometimes my church friends can't believe it. Like, it's not like this everywhere. It doesn't have to be like this here."

Chloe ducks down to the loft ladder. "It really doesn't," she agrees.

"I wanna do something," Smith says. "But I . . ."

He doesn't finish the sentence, but they all know the rest of it. Rebellion is not exactly a luxury Smith Parker gets to have.

"I'm down," says Rory, jaw set. "I vote we steal the Bucky the Buck statue out of the square and drop it on Wheeler's car."

"That's," Smith says, "not exactly what I had in mind."

"Why? It's not that hard to take a statue down. All you need is a truck and some chains."

Benjy asks, "How do you know?"

"Who do you think threw the Jefferson Davis statue in Lake Martin in the first place?"

Ash pokes their head out from behind Benjy. "That was *you*?"

"For legal reasons, I'm joking."

"What if people outside of False Beach knew about what it's like at Willowgrove?" Summer says. "What if we could put Wheeler on blast somehow? Maybe the church board doesn't care now, but we could—we could put the pressure on them. Make them change things to save their reputation. There's nothing they hate more than bad PR."

"It'd have to be big enough that the church board can't ignore it," Georgia says. She thinks for a long second. "What if *none* of us go to graduation?"

"Like a boycott?" Benjy asks.

"That's a better idea," Summer says, "but I think it would make Wheeler way too happy if none of us showed. Kinda his dream ceremony."

"What if," Chloe says, wheels turning, "instead of just a boycott, we do like, a protest graduation? Like, we host it ourselves, and we won't have diplomas or anything, but we can still *have* a graduation."

"That could work," Summer says. "We could have it at my dad's dealership, at the same time as the regular ceremony. It's right across from Willowgrove, so everyone will see us."

"We can make signs," Ash suggests.

"We can call the TV news people," Benjy adds.

"We need more people though," Georgia points out. "If we're actually gonna make a statement."

"Bet," Smith says, and he pulls out his phone.

The way Willowgrove has always worked, from what Chloe has seen and heard, is that there are enough students comfortable with the way things are to create the feeling that you're the only one who doesn't belong. It can be hard, when all the rules claim to be good and moral and godly, to feel like you can challenge them without admitting something bad and wrong about yourself. And if you can get past that, it's a free-fall into small-town gossip, and you never come out the other side with all your best intentions intact.

But that's a world where Willowgrove royalty doesn't call you on the phone to say you're not the only one, after all.

The first person to turn up is Ace, wearing sunglasses and declaring himself ready to join whatever cause Smith is joining. Then come April and Jake, who may not care much about graduation but do care about doing things that piss the administration off.

After that: Ash's friends from art club, guys on the drumline with April, friends of the girl who got expelled for sending nudes, girls who filled out the chorus in *Phantom*, Summer's softball teammates, kids from Chloe's Quiz Bowl group who are still slightly afraid of her. Brooklyn Bennett, the world's leading fan of rules, charges in like an angry Chihuahua.

"I am the *student body president*," she says to the first person she sees, who is a nonplussed April with a sucker stick in the corner of her mouth. "If you're going to stage a protest, you have to *loop me in*."

April removes her sucker with a pop and points it at Brooklyn. "Why, so you can narc on us?"

"So I can *organize it*."

From there, it's a steady stream of people busting through

the front door of Belltower like the cavalry: baseball players, stoners, victims of runaway rumors, weebs, Tyler Miller flanked by a band contingent, including clarinet girls who Chloe always kind of suspected might be a little gay (she's heard plenty rumors about the back of the band bus). Within half an hour, at least four dozen seniors have gathered inside Belltower like a makeshift rally, nearly a third of the graduating class. Some even bring along lowerclassmen friends and siblings.

All of them are talking over one another, comparing notes on the gossip they've heard about what happened today, about times they got detention for talking about sex in sex ed or arguing in Bible class or putting a Bernie Sanders sticker on their locker.

Chloe stands next to the front counter between Georgia and Ash, trying to take in what exactly is happening. All she ever wanted was to launch a revolution at Willowgrove. Somehow, it looks like her graduation ban may have done it by accident.

Summer turns to Georgia.

"Is it okay if I stand on the counter?"

Georgia nods, her eyes big cartoon hearts. "Let me help you up."

"Hey, y'all!" Summer yells over the crowd once Georgia has boosted her up. "Let's talk plans!"

Summer calls her dad, then sweet-talks the butcher across the square into giving her a roll of paper while Georgia digs pencils and paint out of Belltower's back storage room. Ash gathers it all at the center of the floor and gets to work designing a banner to hang up at their ceremony, big enough to be read from across the two-lane highway: CHANGE THE RULES

AT WILLOWGROVE. On a second roll of paper, Summer and Chloe dictate their demands while Ash writes them down. Chloe picks the first one: FIRE PRINCIPAL WHEELER.

It turns out Brooklyn has the number for a *Tuscaloosa News* editor because *of course* she interned there last summer, so they give her the number for a False Beach TV news reporter, and within five minutes, she's contacted every local news team in central Alabama. The story: a contingent of Willowgrove Christian Academy students are boycotting their own graduation ceremony in protest of the school's code of conduct, and also, yes, they *are* speaking to the student body president, thank you very much.

In one corner, Benjy rounds up April and Rory to discuss a plan for procession music. In another, Jake and Ash are painting shapes on each other's faces. In between, they all travel in shifts to Webster's next door, where Ace stubbornly insists on paying for Chloe's double scoop of strawberry with sprinkles and marshmallows. He claims that it's the Southern gentlemanly thing to do when you've kissed someone, even if it was months ago in character as an opera phantom. He passes Chloe her cone and then takes an ungentlemanly lick of Smith's scoop of butter pecan.

Jake pulls out a Bluetooth speaker and puts on a shockingly good playlist, and the whole thing becomes a sort of haphazard rally-meets-party. Chloe looks around Belltower, and she sees things she's never seen before. A softball girl hitting it off with a clarinet girl. Benjy asking Ace how big his biceps are. Brooklyn clumsily talking to April, who sits on a table in front of her looking deeply amused and poking Brooklyn's knee with the toe of her sneaker. There's something in the air, like a collective release of tension.

She passes a sponge to Ash and says, "This is nuts, huh?"

Ash nods. They've already got paint splattered up the side of their neck, matting tufts of ginger hair together. "The coolest."

"Where did all of this come from?" she says. "Like, has *everyone* secretly been waiting for a chance to overthrow Wheeler? I definitely thought it was only us."

"Yeah, it seems that way sometimes," Ash says. "You know what it reminds me of?"

"What?"

"MMORPGs."

Ah. A classic Ash tangent. Chloe can't wait to see where this one goes. "Say more."

"So, everyone is running around the same world doing the same quests, but all of them are on different timelines and at different points in the story," Ash says. "Like you could meet up with a friend, and at the exact same point on the map at the exact same time, you might be able to see a character that they can't see, because that character's already dead at the point of the game where your friend is playing."

"Uh-huh."

"Or maybe you're on a mission to save a villager from a bunch of giant squirrels in the forest outside town, but nobody else can see that villager, because they're not on that mission." Ash looks up from their work to smile at Chloe. "It's not that they *choose* to let the villager get mauled by squirrels. It's just that they're on a whole different quest."

"So, to be clear," Chloe says, "the giant squirrels are high school trauma."

"Yes," Ash says simply. "Now, can you bring this glitter to Georgia?"

Chloe takes the can of glitter Ash presses to her hands and stands up.

She looks around for Georgia, but instead she sees Smith helping a junior get an ice cream stain out of her shirt. Two band kids strategizing how they're going to explain this to their parents. Summer smiling like she's at a pep rally. People who never talk in class.

There must be a lot of giant squirrels she can't see, she realizes.

Shame is a way of life here. It's stocked in the vending machines, stuck like gum under the desks, spoken in the morning devotionals. She knows now that there's a bit of it in her. It was an easy choice not to go back in the closet when she got here, but if she'd grown up here, she might never have come out at all. She might be a completely different person. There's so much to it here, so much that nobody tells anyone about.

So, if she's the only one in the class of '22 who's really *out* for now, if her existence can provide cover for half her graduating class to stand up for something without saying things about themselves they can't yet say, that's enough. That's plenty.

"So," Benjy says when Chloe finds Georgia next to him, "I know things have been crazy, but I just wanted to say: Oh my God, Shara Wheeler is in love with you, and Georgia has been secretly dating a member of the homecoming court. Like, *what* is going on? Also, when do I get a hot person?"

"I saw you flirting with Ace," Chloe counters.

"Yeah, he's like, Dodge Truck Month–level straight," Benjy says dismissively. "I'm not wasting my time."

"Benjy, come lie down over here and let me trace you," Ash calls over.

"*Why?*"

"It's *art.*"

Benjy sighs but trots off.

"Yeah, uh," Georgia says in a low voice, looking up from her paint. "At what point are *we* going to talk about the Shara situation?"

Chloe concentrates on dipping her paintbrush. "What about it?"

"Mainly, why you're not currently making out with her."

"*Why,*" Chloe says, nearly upsetting the can and ruining the whole banner, "would I be doing that?"

"What, am I supposed to pretend the girl she was talking about in her Live wasn't you? Even Benjy put that together, and he's not the fastest on the uptake."

"I mean, yeah," Chloe confirms begrudgingly, "but I'm not going to date her just because she announced that she likes me."

"So, you're saying you don't like her."

"Why would I like her? She's not a good person!"

"Should I remind you of the several occasions on which you have testified that you think she's hot?" Georgia says. "Or maybe I should go get the Monster Fucker Collection from behind the desk? It kind of sounds like *she's* the megabitch of your dreams."

Being known the way Georgia knows her is really annoying sometimes.

"Okay, fine, I'm *attracted* to her," Chloe concedes, "but I'm not going to *date* her. In fact, I am *refusing* to date her, as a power move."

"Chloe, I love you, but that is the stupidest thing I've ever heard. You're still doing things based on what she wants, not because it's what *you* want. That's like, the opposite of a power move."

"I feel like we're losing track of the point," Chloe says, refusing to respond to that, "which is: She's not a good person!"

She shoots a hand out and grabs one of Rory's ankles as he passes.

"Can I help you?" Rory says, frowning down at her.

"Tell Georgia that I'm right, that Shara isn't a good person."

Rory contemplates this, then sits between them. He's eating a cup of mocha chip ice cream with a tiny pink plastic spoon, and when she looks at him, she realizes he's flipped his septum barbell down.

"Explain," he says.

"I want you to tell Georgia about the things she's done to you and Smith."

"Which things?"

"See?" Chloe says, waving a hand at Georgia. "How about the time she faked sick on Smith's signing day?"

"You mean because she knew she was going to break up with Smith," Rory says, "and she didn't want him to have to edit her out of the pictures?"

"She—" Chloe rewinds what Rory said. "When did she tell you that?"

"When I was helping dye her hair."

"You—what? Why?"

"After she got back, she snuck out to my house because it was the only place she could go without her parents noticing, and she said she was afraid everyone was gonna be staring at her at school, so I found some old dye and told her we could give them something to stare at. I got the idea from what you told me about dress code violations, actually."

"Okay," Chloe presses, "but what about how she made you and Smith jealous of each other on purpose to make you hate each other even more?"

"That, uh. Wasn't really what that resulted in."

"She blackmailed Dixon."

"Dixon sucks though."

"She blackmailed *Ace*."

He pauses, looking up from his ice cream. "Yeah, okay, that one does suck. She's weird about people knowing what she actually cares about."

"She ghosted her boyfriend of two years instead of breaking up with him like a normal person," Chloe says.

Rory points his tiny spoon across the room, to where Smith and one of the theater girls are having an animated conversation. "I have finally decided that Smith and Shara's relationship is none of my business."

"She's *mean*."

"Sometimes," Rory says, returning to her. "Sometimes you are too. I still think you're cool though."

*That* strikes Chloe momentarily speechless. Rory shrugs, pats Chloe once on the shoulder, and rises to his feet.

"Okay," Chloe says to Georgia once Rory is gone and Chloe remembers how to talk, "but surely *Summer* must still hate Shara. She broke Summer and Ace up for literally no reason."

"Is that what Ace told you?"

Summer, who has apparently slipped behind them unnoticed under all the chatter and music, sits in the spot Rory vacated. She crosses her legs so her knee touches Georgia's.

"He said that you freaked out when you caught her leaving his house," Chloe tells her.

"Oh my God," Summer says, rolling her eyes. "That is *not* what happened. I mean, I did get mad at him about that, because it was weird as hell, but I had been trying to break up with him for like, a week, and he kept dodging me."

She glances over to the picture book corner, where Ace has knocked over a display of novelty socks with one of his beefy shoulders. "He is just . . . way too chaotic for me. Total sweetheart, but a hot mess."

Georgia nods, and Chloe realizes she must have already heard all of this. If she had actually talked to her about the Shara thing earlier, she could have understood so much more so much sooner.

"So," Chloe says, "if that's not what you fell out with Shara over, then what is?"

"I tried to come out to her," Summer says, "and she freaked and jumped out of my car before I could finish. Like, a *moving* car. I thought she was a homophobe like her dad. Obviously, *now* I know what was up. One thing about that girl, she is gonna bail before anyone can make her think about being gay."

Chloe finds herself struggling to argue with that.

"So, you're not even mad at her for ghosting you when she ran away?" Chloe asks.

"No, I am," Summer says, pushing her braids over her shoulder. "But she also helped save my girl today, so."

Summer and Georgia slip away to chat about the call she had with her dad about using the dealership for the ceremony, but Chloe keeps sitting there.

She's surrounded by a bunch of noisy, awkward, trying-their-best Alabama kids planning a protest against every instinct that Willowgrove has given them, and she's thinking about Shara tearing across campus to catch Chloe before it was too late this afternoon. What would she do all that for, if not—

No. If Shara really cared about anyone but herself, she'd be here. She'd have stopped her dad herself instead of making

Chloe do it. Maybe it was her last shot at getting Chloe out of her way. It worked, didn't it?

She just doesn't believe she's wrong about Shara. She can't. Everyone who matters is here. Shara isn't.

*This,* Chloe thinks for the first time since she left California, *this is where I belong.*

Around sunset, people start clearing out. The shop closes at nine on weeknights anyway, so Georgia shuts down the register while Summer rummages through the books behind the counter and Benjy and Ash discuss a Bojangles run.

"Has anyone seen my keys?" Chloe asks.

"Nope," Benjy says.

"Did you check the loft?" Georgia asks. "Maybe you dropped them while we were eating."

Chloe makes her way to the ladder at the back of the store and climbs up. Sure enough, there they are behind some antique bird guides.

As she reaches for them, she hears a familiar voice drift up from below.

"I told you," Rory says. "There's no point reading the manga when I can watch the show."

She peeks over the railing and sees Smith and Rory, standing close together by the shelf of graphic novels. She hasn't seen them in at least half an hour, so she assumed they had left when she wasn't looking, but they must have slipped quietly into the stacks.

"Man, you're missing out on *so much* though."

She can't see Rory roll his eyes, but she can basically hear it. "Whatever."

Smith gives him a friendly shove, and they drift toward the space under the loft. Chloe's moving for the ladder when she hears Smith say, "Can I ask you something?"

Rory's voices wobbles slightly when he says, "Sure."

"Did you really flood the bio lab on frog week?"

A pause. "When'd you figure it out?"

"Last week, at the lake."

"It was dumb." Rory sounds genuinely embarrassed. "I knew you didn't even think about me anymore, but . . . I don't know. You really didn't want to dissect those frogs."

Smith says seriously, "I never stopped thinking about you."

Oh, shit.

Is this *the* moment?

She has to get out of here, fast—but when she glances down the ladder, she realizes they've moved to a spot that makes it impossible for her to leave without interrupting them.

Her friends are waiting for her up front, and she really doesn't want to spectate on this, but it's taken Smith and Rory so long to get to here. What if she kills it, and they never get there again?

"Do you know what this is?" Smith asks. His voice is a moonbeam in the low light at the back of the store. Chloe chances a peek—he's pulled out a small leather Moleskine.

It looks identical to the songbook on Rory's desk, the one Chloe got a glimpse of back when this all started.

If Smith starts reading love poems to Rory, she'll never be able to look either of them in the eye again.

She squeezes her keys in her hand to stop them from jingling and shuts her eyes. For the rest of her life, she vows, she will simply insist that she didn't see or hear anything.

"Is that—?" Rory starts. "It looks like the one you gave me."

"I never really told you how I picked it out," Smith says.

There's a faint creak, like he's leaning back against a shelf. "My mom wanted to get you a shirt for your birthday, but I told her you liked writing songs and you couldn't write lyrics down as fast as you could think them up. So she said my gift should be that I'd transcribe your songs if you sang them to me, and she let me get a pack of leather notebooks, and I gave one to you and kept the other one. I've never used mine, but I couldn't get rid of it."

"I still use mine," Rory says.

"I know," Smith says. "I saw it in your room."

Rory's smirk is audible when he says, "I guess I got attached to the aesthetic."

"Stubborn ass."

"Takes way longer without you though."

A pause. Another creak of a shelf.

"Can I hear one sometime?" Smith asks. "One of your new songs?"

"That depends," Rory says.

"Depends on what?"

And with all the courage in his noodle-y body, Rory says, "Depends if you don't mind that they're all about you."

Chloe has to stop herself from pumping her fist like the end of *The Breakfast Club*.

It's silent below, except for Summer talking to the iguana in the tank by the front of the store and Ash snapping their art kit back up. Then, after a few seconds, just long enough for a nervous first kiss, Smith laughs.

"Chloe!" Georgia calls out from the front of the store. "Let's go! I gotta lock up!"

"Oh, shit," Rory whispers, and there's the shuffling sound of them hustling out of the shelves together, muffled laughter and light grunts from elbows thrown. She still can't see them.

They could be two lonely seventh graders with notebooks full of song lyrics, or they could be two almost-adults who haven't laughed like this together in years.

"Coming!" Chloe calls. She can't stop smiling.

# FROM THE BURN PILE

Personal essay exercise: Smith Parker

Prompt: What is a moment in your life
that you felt truly yourself?

When we stopped running.

Written on the back of the same paper,
in the same handwriting

You look like sun in moonlight
You're faster on your feet
You're five years back, you're wrong, you're right
You're impossible to me

I've been up here waiting for you
Maybe I should have guessed
Give us five more and it's still true
You'll always be my best

R. H.

# 21

There are five school days after finals but before graduation, when the rest of the student body is reviewing for exams, but the seniors are expected to show up to school every day to do nothing. Allegedly, it's a requirement that was created in the 2000s after one senior class used the time to execute a senior prank so elaborate the entire gym floor had to be replaced. Now, they have to be supervised.

Like Dead Week, this weird in-between week has a nickname, created by past Willowgrove seniors and handed down through the years. Chloe hates it.

"I'm not calling it that," Chloe says on Monday morning, on the breezeway outside C Building. "It's gross."

"But it makes so much sense," Benjy says. "It's a pointless space between two important things."

Ash spreads their hands in front of them like a marquee and says, "*Taint Week.*"

Chloe sighs. "Somehow this feels like Ace's fault."

She pushes the stairwell door open, but before she can reach the next set of doors, Dixon Wells comes bursting out of them. Georgia throws a soccer-mom arm in front of Chloe's chest before they smash into each other.

Dixon is red-faced and swearing, his Logan Paul hair flying in every direction, and he bolts past them down the stairs and out of sight.

"Not too late to stop being a dick, Dixon!" Georgia calls after him.

"*Geo*," Chloe says. "That was *spicy*."

Georgia shrugs, catching the door on the backswing. "Somebody has to tell him."

Benjy steps into the hallway first, then stops so suddenly Ash and Chloe pile up behind him.

"Jesus *wept*," he says.

The entire hallway is crammed with students and white as a blizzard. Every locker, every bulletin board, every classroom door—all plastered with paper. Half the student body is there, passing sheets around and pulling folded pieces out of their locker vents and trampling them underfoot. Every page seems to be covered in different configurations of small, black type.

Overhead, the morning bell goes off, but nobody cares.

Chloe rips a page off the nearest bulletin board.

We can certainly make that arrangement for your son, it says, and as for the amount, $15K seems a bit low. What you're asking would involve a lot of logistical support on our end to make sure this is done right, and the school doesn't lose its status as a test center . . .

"Oh my God," Georgia says, crowded against her shoulder. "No way. No *way*. Are these—?"

"Wheeler's?" Chloe asks. "Is he actually talking about an—?"

"*Admissions scam?*"

"Isn't that—?"

"A federal crime? Yeah, uh, I'm pretty sure it is."

Chloe sets off down the hall in a frenzy, snatching up every page she can.

The papers are copies of emails, hundreds and hundreds of emails between Wheeler and parents of students. Payoffs and bribes and under-the-table deals to boost the scores of kids taking the ACT at Willowgrove.

She *knew* Mackenzie couldn't have made a 29.

Now she knows what Wheeler's been spending hours on in his office after everyone else goes home for the night. *And* why Wheeler wouldn't want the police involved after Shara ran away, and why he was so threatened by people trying to dig into his family— Wait.

Was Shara *involved*?

She grabs another page, and another, skimming as fast as she can.

—balance owed—

—answer key—

—my daughter—

There.

We need to discuss discretion. There's no need to keep your child looped in if his participation isn't required. My daughter still has no idea I had Carol raise her final grade last year, and that's for the best. If they feel they've earned this, they're motivated to keep working hard and stay out of trouble.

She scans back up to the sender to make sure she read what she thinks she did.

It's from Wheeler, and he's talking about Shara's grade in Ms. Rodkey's class last year. The class in which she edged Chloe out by a single percentage point.

"Holy shit," Chloe whispers.

He just admitted to having Shara's grades changed.

Which means Shara is disqualified from—

"I think," she says, staring at the paper so hard, her vision goes blurry, "I think I won valedictorian."

By lunch, every single student at Willowgrove has at least one page of Principal Wheeler's emails, which definitively prove that he conspired with the richest parents at Willowgrove to scam their kids into college in exchange for a lot of money and a higher ACT score average to lure in new students.

Dixon, whose dad paid at least $30,000 total to have a proctor look the other way while an Auburn senior with a fake ID took the test under Dixon's name, has ghosted completely. Mackenzie was spotted melting down in the bathroom, swearing to everyone within earshot that she had no idea her parents paid to have her answers switched with someone else's. Rumor has it Emma Grace told her that if she wanted people to believe things she says, she shouldn't have lied about giving her best friend's crush a handjob at her birthday party.

And Shara—Shara never shows up to school at all. Chloe imagines her in the Wheeler mansion, handing her mom a cucumber water and a Xanax while they meet with the family attorney.

Could she really not have known?

At lunch, Ash asks, "Who do you think did it?"

The choir room is a lot more full than usual, since Georgia invited Summer and Benjy invited Ace, and Ash has somehow convinced Jake and April to stop by and watch them play *Breath of the Wild* on the Switch they snuck into school. On the top row of the risers, Rory and Smith are having an animated discussion about either poetry or *Dragon Ball Z*—it's impossible to tell.

"My money's on Brooklyn Bennett," Benjy says. "Total Brooklyn move. Plus, she has means *and* motive."

"Nah, it was that kid with the tube socks," Summer says. "The walking YouTube algorithm. He's obsessed with ACT scores and loves conspiracy theories."

"Drew Taylor?" Ash says. "He doesn't have the range."

"What even happens now?" Georgia asks, reaching over to steal one of Summer's Doritos.

Ace, who has been doing wall sits for five minutes straight, pauses mid-squat to say, "Dixon said his dad is going to handle it because he's a lawyer. Are you allowed to be your own lawyer? Is that a thing?"

"Yes, that's a thing, Ace," Georgia says patiently.

In Willowgrove fashion, the well of gossip is bottomless. Apparently, Wheeler's barricaded himself in his office and is only speaking to legal counsel, entirely ignoring the Willowgrove church board that runs the school and presides over the administration. Nobody knows if he's going to get arrested or get fired or what. Cracks are forming in the Wheeler empire, and the craziest part is, nobody knows who put them there.

Chloe notices, though, as they scatter into the hall and toward sixth hour, that there's one person who doesn't look surprised at this news at all.

She cuts out of seventh hour early—no way in hell is Rory staying the whole day during Taint Week. In-Between Week. Whatever.

She catches him reversing out of his parking spot, and he has to slam on the brakes to stop his back bumper from taking Chloe out at the knees.

He sticks his head out the window. "Jesus Christ, Green!"

"Did you do it?" she asks him directly, coming around to

his window. "Wheeler's emails?"

"What?" he says. "No."

She eyes him: one hand fidgeting on the steering wheel, elbow propped up a bit too casually on the console.

"I don't believe you," she says. "What aren't you telling me?"

He sighs, dropping his head against the headrest.

"Do you know how I got this car?" he finally says.

Always with the cryptic questions. Rory is like a bag of right angles with a secret.

"We've been through this. Rhetorical questions only work if you don't have to explain why you're asking them."

"Do you want me to tell you what I know or not?"

"Okay," Chloe groans.

"So," Rory goes on, "my stepdad gave it to me. He's never given me a gift my whole life, but last year he springs this sweet-ass vintage convertible on me out of nowhere. Sus as fuck. So I went through his office when he wasn't home, and I figured out that he bought the car off his brother in cash since all of his shit was about to get seized, because he got caught paying off the principal of his kid's school for ACT answers."

"Okay . . ."

"So, when we were in Wheeler's office looking for Shara's note," Rory continues, "I saw some papers in the desk, and they looked kind of like what I saw in my stepdad's office. So I took some pictures, and when Shara got back I . . . may have, uh, asked her to look at them to be sure."

"But—why Shara? Why wouldn't you give it to somebody who could actually do something about it?"

Rory waves a hand and jerks his chin at her in a sort of *duh* gesture. "Shara did do something about it."

"She—" There is no possible way what Rory's suggesting

is true. "You think Shara threw her own dad—and *herself*—under the bus?"

"She was the only person I told," Rory says with a shrug. "I didn't even send her copies of the pictures, so I guess she got her hands on the originals. But I don't care what happens to Wheeler, or anyone in those emails. You know I don't give a shit about the ACT. I just thought Shara deserved to know."

Once, Chloe considered herself better than people like Rory, who act like they've beaten the system by choosing not to care. But it's obvious from the look on Rory's face that he does care, in different ways about different things. Maybe pretending is its own high school survival strategy.

"But why would she do this?" Chloe asks.

"Why are we boycotting graduation?" Rory asks. "Same thing, different approach."

He shrugs again and turns his music back up.

"Anyway," Rory says, shifting out of park. "I got plans. Bye."

He leaves Chloe standing in the parking lot, speechless.

All Chloe can do is get in her car and drive home.

At a red light, she thinks about how Shara could have taken what Rory gave her to the grave.

Shara could have let her dad keep terrorizing teenagers from the Willowgrove throne until he retired, and it would have been easy. Collect college tuition, have an expensive wedding to some guy in a camo tux, settle down for a long, comfortable life as the queen of False Beach, the heiress of the perfect family.

That's what everyone expected of her. It's *certainly* what Chloe expected.

But instead, Shara logged into her dad's email and printed

every receipt she could find. She plastered the school with them to make sure he couldn't hide it. The church board may not care if the principal is a bigot, but it'll be harder to make this go away.

She did it even though she knew she'd be taking herself down with him.

When Chloe gets home, she goes straight to her bedroom. She changes out of her uniform, and then reaches for her nightstand, where a creased, grass-stained pink card waits. She hasn't opened it, but she couldn't quite stop herself from salvaging it from the flowerbeds.

Chloe,
I threw it away because it meant too much to me. I hope you understand.

Yours,
Shara

P.S. As a graduation gift to you, I promise this is the last card you'll ever get from me. I'll leave you alone. Cross my heart.

She sits down on the bed.

Somewhere, glowing in Chloe's mind, Shara is tearing apart a library trash can and telling her parents a lie about a broken clasp in PE class. She's praying alone in an empty sanctuary. She's drawing the blinds so nobody can see her faking sick while Smith is on TV. She's shredding the sheet music she read for Ace while she uploads a stock photo of a mission trip that never happened. She's covering her own tracks. She's coming all the way to Chloe's house to leave one last card, smoothing the tape onto the glass with her finger, letting her go.

Shara doesn't throw things away because they mean nothing

to her. She throws things away because they mean too much.

It's a standardized logic and reasoning question: If it's true that Shara did the terrible things in her notes, and it's also true that Shara can only tell lies, then the terrible things must be only part of the story. The other part, still hiding behind all the smoke and mirrors and studied indifference, is somebody who cares. A lot, in a very specific way, about a few, select people and a few, select things.

If there's one thing Chloe knows, it's the danger of being yourself at Willowgrove, in False Beach. Everything she likes about herself is a liability here. You hide the things that matter most before anyone can use them against you.

That's what Shara did. That's what Shara does.

Finally, *finally,* she gets it.

Shara isn't a monster inside of a beautiful girl, or a beautiful girl inside of a monster. She's both, one inside of the other inside of the other.

And that truth—the whole truth of Shara—leaves no room to pretend anymore. *Neither* of them did all this for a title. That's what Chloe was afraid of her friends seeing. That's where the trail led. That's why she couldn't let it end.

"Oh my God," Chloe says out loud. Her brain is overheating, probably. "I'm in love with a monster turducken."

# FROM THE BURN PILE

Comments from Shara's ninth-grade report
card from her English teacher, folded up very
small and forgotten in an old binder

Shara is an absolute pleasure to have in class. She is well-liked and punctual, follows directions, and often volunteers to lead the class in prayer. She is an exceptionally bright student with insightful and clear thoughts on the readings, though getting her to share them in class is difficult. She was also happy to tell me what brand of shampoo she uses when asked for advice on achieving shinier hair. All in all, a perfect example of the type of young lady every Willowgrove girl should strive to be.

# 22

The ugly dolphin fountain looks different from last time—still ugly, but now it's also overflowing with thick clouds of lilac-scented suds. Someone put laundry detergent in it. Even rich kids get bored, Chloe guesses.

She doesn't head straight for the house. Instead, she loops around Rory's driveway, ducking behind the Beemer and slipping unseen to the front door. She rings the doorbell, waits thirty seconds, and jabs it two more times.

"Yo, *chill*," Rory is saying before the door is even open, and when he sees Chloe, he rolls his eyes like, *I don't know who else I expected.*

"I," Chloe says. She forgot to prepare a cover story. "I need to borrow your ladder. For, uh. My gutters."

"Your gutters?"

"Yeah. My gutters. They need . . . adjusting."

Rory sucks on his tongue, nodding slowly, then leans back into the house and yells, "Smith!"

Smith appears at Rory's shoulder, a bit rumpled and in a radiantly good mood, until his eyes land on Chloe.

"Oh, hey, Chloe."

She stares at him. He stares at Rory. They all stand there,

staring at one another. Looks like those "plans" Rory mentioned were six feet of quarterback.

"Chloe needs to borrow my ladder," Rory says.

"Oh, uh, okay," Smith says. "Want me to bring it out to your car?"

"Actually," Chloe says. "I was, uh. I was gonna bring it right back. I just need to bring it, um, next door."

"Next door?" Smith says.

"Yeah."

"You—oh. Okay."

"But I need help getting it over the fence."

"For gutters," Rory adds.

"Uh-huh."

And then Smith laughs, and Rory's laughing too, and Chloe's own laugh comes out high-pitched and terrified. It reminds her of that first Monday at Smith's locker, trying to avoid the fact that they were all chasing the same girl. It's kind of surreal to realize she's the only one still running.

"Okay," Smith says.

Smith blessedly doesn't say anything else as Rory leads them past the living room, which is messy with snacks and hastily jettisoned throw pillows, or as he heaves the ladder over the fence. It's not until she's at the top that he calls after her, "Hey, Green!"

She stops and looks, and he's standing there in the grass, biting back that sunshine smile of his. Ten feet behind, Rory is hovering near the patio furniture, pretending not to watch.

"Good luck," Smith says.

Chloe swallows a hysterical sound and *salutes* him, of all the stupid things. Off to a great start. She tips herself into Shara's yard before she can embarrass herself further.

When she climbs up to Shara's open window, she can tell Shara's really back, because the room looks less like a meticulously arranged movie set and more like an actual human teenager lives in it. Finals notecards and paperbacks spill across the desk, and three dresses have been laid out across the bed like she's trying to choose one. On the bookshelf, the infamous box of pink stationery has been crammed between a book of devotionals and the copy of *Emma* from Belltower. The only thing missing is Shara.

Then there she is, coming in through her bedroom door, fastening an earring. She's halfway into a white sundress. Chloe gets the briefest glimpse of a lacy bralette she once saw in Shara's underwear drawer, and then they make eye contact and she falls off the ladder.

Chloe hears a faint *Oh my God*—can't tell if it's her or Shara, maybe both—before a hand catches her.

Above her, Shara hangs out of the window, eyes wide, hair falling around her face, cheeks flushed. Her knuckles are white around Chloe's wrist, and Chloe has to swallow another hysterical laugh.

"I'm good!" Chloe says. The toe of her sneaker finally finds the rung again. Shara's expression pinches into an incredulous mix of relief and exasperation, like maybe she should have let Chloe break an arm. "I'm fine! Thanks for the assist, but I got it!"

Together, they pull Chloe through the window. As soon as she hits the carpet, Shara retreats to the walk-in closet and emerges in a fuzzy pink bathrobe.

Chloe opens her mouth to speak, but Shara shushes her, pointing to the open doorway. It's not just open, Chloe realizes. The door has been taken off the hinges completely.

"What are you doing here?" Shara whispers.

Chloe grunts to her feet, pitching her voice low. "I need to talk to you."

"I meant, what are you doing in my literal bedroom window?"

"Took the back way." Suddenly Chloe wishes she hadn't been in such a hurry that she left in her grubby after-school clothes. She's going to have the most important conversation of her life so far in a *Godspell* cast T-shirt and Benjy's gym shorts. "I, uh, figured I should probably avoid your parents."

"Probably smart," Shara concedes airily. "We can talk, but I'm supposed to be leaving for Bible study with my mom in like, ten minutes."

"Even with the whole . . . uh, thing with your dad?"

"She's counting on everyone being too polite to bring it up." Shara shrugs. "What did you want to talk about?"

Chloe takes a breath. "Was it—Rory said—was it really you? Did you leak your dad's emails?"

Something like disappointment flickers across Shara's face before it settles into unimpressed aloofness, as if someone in class raised their hand too fast with a painfully obvious answer.

"He deserves it, don't you think?" Shara says, tugging her robe around her.

"Obviously *I* think he does, but like . . . he's your dad."

"Chloe, if you think he's hard on *you,* you should come to dinner sometime."

There's a pause as Chloe takes that in. She can see it's more complicated than that. Shara looks tired, like she's lost some sleep over it. The pink in her hair is fading faster than it should. Chloe wonders how many times her parents have made her wash it.

"Is that why you did it? To get back at him?" Chloe asks.

"Or was there another reason?"

"There were a lot of reasons," Shara says, glaring at her missing bedroom door. "I guess, though, if you're *asking*, I hadn't decided if I was gonna do anything with what Rory gave me until I heard what my dad was gonna do to Georgia. And then what he did to you."

Once she's said it, she turns back to Chloe.

"Is that all?"

"Yes," Chloe says. Of course it's not. "I mean, no, there's— why didn't you come to Belltower on Friday?"

"My parents took my phone when I got back," Shara says. "I didn't know about it."

"Oh," Chloe says. When she puts it like that, it does seem obvious.

"And even if I *had* heard," Shara goes on, "I promised to leave you alone."

"*Oh,*" Chloe repeats. "Right."

Shara tilts her head back, realizing. "You never read that card, did you?"

"No, I did," Chloe says. "Like, twenty minutes ago."

Shara purses her lips. "So you're here because—"

"Because I know what it means," Chloe says. "Although, it does feel worth mentioning that you could have gotten the same thing across by kissing me like I told you to."

"Sorry, what part of you sitting on my chest screaming at me was supposed to make me think that was actually a good idea?" Shara says.

"Okay, but—school last week," Chloe says. "You could have—"

"I kissed you first," she points out. "Twice."

"But those times didn't count," Chloe says. "They weren't real."

"They were," Shara finally admits. "I just . . . didn't know it at the time."

"So you were following me around last week, because you—"

"Because I was trying to work up the nerve to do it right, but you kept acting like it was still a game." She sounds the way her handwriting looked in the wrinkled postscript: worn out. "So if you came here to reject me, do it already. It'll give me something to ruminate on during Bible study."

"That's not what I came for," Chloe tells her.

Shara blinks. "It's not?"

"Technically, that was part of the plan at one point," Chloe confesses in a rush, "when I thought you were still— But, no, I—I came here to tell you that—that—"

She didn't have time to prepare what she was going to say. She feels like the spine of a book about to crack and spill out all the love story guts.

How does she say this?

"That my best mornings are the ones when I pull into school right after you, because I know you'll have to watch me walk past your car."

What.

"What?"

"Or, no, it's—that time I had to peer edit your essay in AP Lang?" She can't believe she's going to admit all this, but she doesn't know how else to explain it. "I still remember it. Like, entire sentences from it, because I was trying so hard to come up with notes that were smarter than what you wrote, so you'd go home and think about it. I've found out your locker number the first week of every year, so that I'd know exactly how many times a day I'd pass it."

"Chloe—"

"Shut up, I'm not finished," Chloe says, and Shara shuts

her pretty mouth. "Sophomore year, when we were lab part-ners, I'd go to the bathroom every day before chem and fix my hair because I knew that was the closest I'd ever be to you, and I—I wanted to be as much of a distraction to you as you were to me. Do you get it? I wanted you to *see* me."

Shara doesn't say anything, only nods. Chloe has to swal-low a smile. It's a rush—the feeling of explaining something about herself that feels insane and being met with *Yes, of course*.

"So then, when I read your notes and I realized that you *did*—that you saw me, that you thought about me so much, that you *noticed* me—God, I thought I'd won. But it didn't feel the way it was supposed to. And that *pissed me off*. And I couldn't figure out why it wasn't enough, and then I read your last card and I realized that I didn't just want you to see me. I wanted *someone* who sees me, and I wanted it to be *you*, because I think I always knew you were the only one it could be."

After a long pause, Shara says, "Can I talk now?"

"Yes."

"So. To summarize. You're not rejecting me."

"Correct," Chloe confirms. "In fact, if you kissed me right now, I would probably die."

"Really this time?" Shara says.

"Really."

"No more games?"

"I promise if you promise."

"Okay," Shara says.

She steps closer. Chloe can feel the warmth of her body now. She wonders if Shara can feel hers too.

"Okay, then. Wow."

The fuzz of Shara's robe brushes against Chloe's skin.

"Wow," Chloe agrees.

When Shara lifts her hand, Chloe sees it splayed open in the grass outside her bedroom window. She (slowly, tentatively) touches the side of Chloe's face, and Chloe feels the cool press of a sailboat railing. She could close her eyes and hear the fluorescent hum of elevator lights. Shara searches her face with the wary, reverent interest of stumbling upon a poem in an English textbook that breaks your heart open in the middle of class. Chloe knows that feeling. She knows Shara knows it too.

She tips her head forward, and Shara kisses her. Chloe puts her arms around Shara's neck and kisses her back.

They're standing in Shara's bedroom, but they're two blocks over at the clubhouse. She's in Benjy's T-shirt, but she's in black chiffon and lace with her hair set in waves. Shara's in her bathrobe, but she's in a tiara under a dance floor chandelier, and there's the distant, dreamy echo of a slow electric guitar, and they're swaying to the last song of the night. Shara sighs, and the balloons drop.

It's a prom night they never had, and she's found the only person like her in a small town the size of the world, and they're alone in a quiet room kissing in front of God and everybody.

Someone calls Shara's name from downstairs.

"Let's go!" Shara's mom yells. "We're supposed to be bringing cookies! We gotta stop at the store on the way to church!"

Shara breaks off, eyes wide.

Chloe whispers, "My car's around the corner."

One second of consideration, two, and then Shara calls out, "I'm almost done with my hair! Hang on!"

She throws off her robe and grabs a pair of sneakers, spinning around to show Chloe the open back of her dress.

"Zip me up."

When Chloe reaches for the zipper, her fingertips graze warm skin, and her heart is five million bits of stage glitter swirling in an overture spotlight, and then Shara's stomping her sneakers on and climbing over the windowsill. She pauses at the top of the ladder and looks back at Chloe.

"Are you coming or what?"

"This was literally my idea!" Chloe hisses, but Shara's already out of sight.

# FROM THE BURN PILE

Rejected drafts of Shara's final card
for Chloe, scribbled in the margins of
her notes for the Chem II exam

Chloe,
You win. I hope that's what you wanted.

Chloe,
Of all the things I've tried to hide under my pillow, you've got to be the
most persistent.

Chloe,
There was this one weekend, a million summers ago, when I sat on the
shore drinking a frozen limeade, and I realized the only thing I wanted
to look at was the way the sun hit the girls swimming in the lake.
   The problem has always been this: When I look at you, I taste lime,
and I see light on water.

# 23

They jump the fence and take off running.

Shara's fast when she wants to be, which Chloe probably should have expected. They clear Rory's yard in seconds. As soon as they're around the corner, Shara grabs her hand, and Chloe nearly shouts a laugh at the feeling of Shara's fingers between hers. This is really happening, huh?

The dolphin fountain is overflowing now, spilling laundry suds all over the pristine grass and puddling around Chloe's tires.

"Where are we going?" Shara asks her.

"My house!" Chloe says, out of breath. "My moms have pottery class in Birmingham on Monday nights."

"Okay," Shara says. She releases Chloe's hand, breaking for the driver's side. "Throw me the keys."

"It's my car," Chloe points out.

Shara flips her hair over her shoulder, like that's irrelevant. "I'm fast."

She's never considered "getaway driving" as one of Shara's skills, but she has to admit, Shara's been good at everything else she's tried to do so far. She loops around to the passenger side and tosses the keys over the hood.

"Don't wreck it or it's my ass."

Shara catches the keys in one hand and rolls her eyes. "I'm a great driver."

And then she's sliding into the driver seat, stealing the sunglasses out of Chloe's cup holder and putting them on.

It takes half a minute for Shara to turn Chloe's hand-me-down Camry into a music video. She rolls the windows down and takes the right turn out of the country club toward Chloe's house without asking for directions, and she's right—she is a good driver. She stays perfectly between the lines. One hand on the wheel, pink hair flying, knees apart under her church dress. They pass a car with a missing headlight, and Shara slaps the ceiling.

Chloe wonders how a month away turned Shara into this, but when Shara shoots her a look over the top of her sunglasses, she remembers that Shara's always been this person. *This is what I've been trying to tell you,* she wrote on a card stuck under an auditorium seat. Shara's not nice. Shara's so many more important things than nice.

Then they get to Chloe's house, and there Shara is, standing in Chloe's kitchen, next to Chloe's mama's boob painting. Titania winds around her ankles before slinking out of the kitchen.

They're alone. This is real.

Chloe realizes that she's never actually been the one to kiss Shara first. She doesn't know how to do it.

"Do you—" Chloe says. One of the crystal wind chimes is turning in the window, and the light falls across Shara's face in a Botticelli swipe from cheek to jaw. "Do you, um, want something to drink?"

"Do y'all have sweet tea?" Shara asks.

Chloe beams a telepathic thank-you to her mom. "I do, actually."

She pours two glasses. She even gets Shara a straw and a little paper cocktail napkin out of the junk drawer.

"Well, aren't you a nice Southern hostess," Shara says, watching Chloe add ice cubes to her glass. Chloe glances up and finds her smirking.

When Shara looks at her like that, all airy and sly, it makes Chloe think of the first time her mama brought home an icebox pie. It was strawberries and cream, her mom's favorite, and the whole thing seemed to be a feat of mechanical physics. It didn't make sense how the strawberries held effortlessly together when you sliced it, or how the cloud of meringue sat weightless on top. She remembers studying the layers from the side and having the inexplicable thought, *This is a Shara Wheeler kind of pretty.*

God. *Shall I compare thee to an icebox pie?* Couldn't be gayer if she tried.

"I'm so stupid," Chloe realizes out loud.

"No, you're not," Shara says. "You're very smart. That's our whole thing."

"But you—this—ugh," Chloe says. "It's so—*obvious.* How come I didn't figure it out sooner?"

"Took me a while too," Shara says, and Chloe pushes the sweet tea out of the way and kisses the smirk off her lips.

They leave the glasses sweating on the counter and drift to Chloe's bedroom, where Shara spends ten minutes touching everything. She examines the framed photos on the dresser and desk and scrutinizes the skincare products on the bathroom counter and flips through the NYU brochures.

"I don't understand why anyone needs this many editions

of *Anne of Green Gables*," Shara says, thumbing the green spine of the '90s edition Chloe inherited from her mama, and Chloe rolls her eyes and sits on the bed.

"You're so nosy," Chloe says, as if she minds.

"At least I didn't break into your house to do this," Shara says, "unlike some people I could mention."

She gives Chloe that look again, and Chloe groans.

"Rory."

"Smith, actually."

"Whatever," Chloe says. "Can you come back over here?"

Shara's face goes serious.

"I'm, um," she says. She looks at Chloe on the bed. "I'm gonna need to take it slow."

"That's fine."

"I'm not saving myself for marriage or anything, if that's what you're thinking," Shara adds, so defensive that it sounds like a lie. "I'm just not ready for the other stuff."

Chloe's brow furrows. "I wasn't planning on doing any other stuff?"

"You weren't like . . . expecting that?"

"Did you think I was?"

Shara looks away, shrugging. "Kind of."

The answer startles a laugh out of her before she can cover her mouth, and Shara's instantly glaring.

"Sorry, sorry!" Chloe says. "But, Shara, you've known me for four years. When have I *ever* given you the impression that I'm getting laid? I've never even dated anyone."

Shara folds her arms unhappily. "Yeah, but you're from LA and your moms probably actually explained stuff to you. And you're so . . . confident."

"Okay, well," Chloe says, beginning to count off on her fingers. "One, you can't tell anyone I said this, but being from

LA does not mean I'm cool or know anything about anything. Two." She holds up a second finger. "Yes, my moms did explain different kinds of sex to me, but it was such an embarrassing conversation that I don't even remember most of it. And three." A final finger. "If I seem confident, it's because I have to. You, of all people, know what I mean."

Shara considers this, then edges toward the bed.

"Okay," she says. Her knees brush against Chloe's, white eyelet lace skimming skin.

Chloe takes Shara's hand and lays it against the side of her neck, and Shara's palm presses into her skin.

"Don't be nervous," Chloe says. "Just like, pretend I'm the AP Calc test."

Shara's glare flickers back. "I should have let you fall out the window."

"I have scratch paper," Chloe says, "you can check my desk—"

Shara's hand drops from Chloe's neck to her shoulder, and then she's pushing Chloe down on the bed and kissing her, one hand pinning her to the mattress and the other on her waist. It's the first time Shara's kissed her with both intent and confidence, and it's about as thorough and heartstopping as can be expected of a perfectionist with a competitive streak.

Chloe's never been kissed on a bed before. It's her first time feeling the corner of a throw pillow wedged under her head while the mattress springs push her back up into someone else's body. She's never kissed anybody like this.

She's glad it's Shara. Nobody else would have felt important enough.

"You know," Chloe says, "there's a lot we still need to talk about."

Shara props herself up on a pillow. "Like what?"

They've made out for—well, Chloe doesn't know how long. It felt like a long time. There's a faint red mark blooming on Shara's neck, which is probably the coolest thing Chloe has ever seen in her life.

"Do you want to start with the way you full-on staged your own disappearance to sabotage my academic career," Chloe says, "or would you rather discuss how you may have sent your dad to federal prison?"

"He has a very expensive lawyer," Shara says. "He'll be fine."

"Okay, so the first one, then."

Shara sighs, ducking her head into her own shoulder so her hair falls across her face. "I don't know what else you want me to say, Chloe. Do you really want me to apologize?"

"It's more that I want to know how you feel about it now."

"I feel . . . less confused," Shara says slowly. "This has all been real informative."

"So, you don't regret anything?"

"I don't know. There's still this part of me that thinks I've ruined my whole life. But there's another part of me that thinks ruining my life sounds kind of nice." She pauses to think. Chloe can admit it now: She loves watching Shara think. "I could have done better by Smith and Rory. That's the one thing. But I already knew they both deserved better than me."

"You're not—"

"I wasn't fishing for a compliment," Shara says. "I'm not bad. I'm bad for *them*."

Chloe bites her lip. "And for me?"

Shara turns her head so that they're inches apart on the pillow, nose to nose, eyelashes almost brushing.

"How'd you say it?" she says. "You were the only one it could be."

Warmth bubbles up from the pit of her stomach. Her mouth pops open to speak, but nothing comes out.

"Why do you look so surprised?" Shara says irritably. "You're like, *the girl*."

"What girl?"

"*The* girl," Shara says. "You know everyone is scared of Chloe Green, right?"

"Yeah, because I'm a bitch."

"That," Shara says, smiling when Chloe pulls a face, "and also because you showed up one day from California and did whatever you wanted. Nobody at Willowgrove knows what to do with that. I sure didn't."

Shara thinks she's The Girl? But *Shara's* The Girl. What do you say when The Girl tells you that you're The Girl to her?

Before she can guess, the front door rattles open.

"Chloe?" her mom's voice calls from across the house. "You home?"

Shara jolts upright.

"I thought they had pottery class?"

"They do!"

The house is small enough that even if both her moms stopped to drop their shoes and bags at the door, at least one of them should be to the living room by now. Shara jumps out of bed, and Chloe shouts out a preemptive, "Hey! You got back fast!"

"Yeah," says her mama. "The last part of the class was bisque firing. What kind of amateurs do they think we are? We figured we might as well come home for dinner— Oh!"

Her mama freezes in the doorway.

The scene: Chloe, wedging herself into the doorway, smiling through smudged makeup. Shara, near the desk, *Mrs. Dal-*

*loway* upside down in her hands like she's in Chloe's room to discuss Virginia Woolf and nothing else. Her mama in clay-splattered chambray, buffering.

Chloe's mom appears over her mama's shoulder and says, without a moment's hesitation, "Oh, hi! You're Wheeler's kid, aren't you?"

"We were studying," Chloe says.

"Finals were last week, Chlo," her mom points out.

"I should go," Shara says.

"You don't have a car," Chloe reminds her.

"Tell you what," Chloe's mom announces in that broad voice she has when she's about to recalibrate an entire situation. "I got the stuff to make spaghetti and a half gallon of strawberry ice cream from Webster's in the freezer. Why don't you stay for dinner, and Chloe can drive you home after?"

"*Mom*," Chloe hisses. It's *way* too early for Shara to experience her mama's weird hemp tea or the bad DeNiro impression her mom does when she cooks Italian.

But to Chloe's surprise and horror, Shara says, "Okay."

And the next thing Chloe knows, Shara's helping with the sides while her mom whips up a quick red sauce and Chloe boils the pasta, and they're all pretending it's normal and not absolutely the most bizarre thing that's happened in Chloe's entire life.

My moms walked in on me and Shara hooking up and convinced her to stay for dinner and now Shara is making garlic bread and my mom is telling her about how I punched a mall Santa when I was five, she texts Georgia.

"Top five Chloe moment," her mom concludes.

Georgia immediately texts back, SLDJFASDLAFAKLSAS NO followed by, SHARA??? FINALLY????? HOW??????? in rapid succession. And then, summer is losing her mind rn.

What happens next is her fault. While she's occupied with her phone, she misses her chance to intervene when Shara asks her mom, "How did y'all meet?"

"No, Shara, don't—" Chloe attempts, but her mom has already dramatically put down her wooden spoon.

"The year was 1997," she says.

"Oh God," Chloe moans.

"I was a bright-eyed, nineteen-year-old ingenue fresh out of Alabama, bartending to pay my way through trade school, and there was this waitress, Jess, and she was the most beautiful girl I had ever seen in my entire life. Perfect button nose. Killer smile. Eyes like a forest at night, like something you want to wander into—"

"Mom, *please.*"

"—and I'd never been in love before, but I saw her in her little apron, and I felt what I had been waiting my whole life to feel. And it only took me six months to work up the nerve to ask her on a date."

"And then she tried to kiss me at the end of the night and found out I didn't realize it was a date," her mama interjects.

"And so we got to have a *second* first date, and we've been living life like every day is our first date ever since."

Chloe turns to Shara to mouth an embarrassed apology, but Shara only smiles a little and returns to the bread with her face slightly pink. She remembers what Shara wrote in her first note, that she'd heard the stories of Chloe's mom before she ever met Chloe.

First Georgia, now Shara—come to the Green house, teenage queers of False Beach, for the first non-depressing glimpse of your future.

They eat dinner, and then, over bowls of ice cream, her

mama asks, "So, Shara, where are you going in the fall?"

"I'm actually thinking about taking a year off," Shara says, catching Chloe by surprise. "For a while, I felt like I should stay here, but I—I've been thinking that might not be a good idea for me anymore. I don't know where else I would go though. It's like, the whole world is here."

Her mom nods thoughtfully, setting down her spoon.

"You know what's wild?" she says. "When you're born and raised in False Beach, you think Webster's is how strawberry ice cream is supposed to taste. You can go to the fanciest ice cream parlor in LA or New York and have the most incredible scoop of fresh, artisanal strawberry ice cream in the world, but it's still gonna be disappointing, because it doesn't taste like the only strawberry ice cream you had for the first eighteen years of your life, when you were learning what ice cream was supposed to taste like."

Shara nods slowly, turning the melting lump of ice cream in her bowl over and over with her spoon.

"But when I left," Chloe's mom goes on, "I figured something out real quick: It's *not* the whole world. Just because everyone here knows who you are, and everyone talks about everyone else's business, that doesn't mean it's impossible to be the person you know you are. There are things out there for you that you haven't even thought of yet, that you don't even know *how* to think of yet. Who you are here doesn't have to be the same as who you are out there. And if the person you feel like you have to be in this town doesn't feel right to you, you're allowed to leave. You're allowed to *exist*. Even if it means existing somewhere else."

No one says anything, but Chloe's mama reaches over to rest a hand on her mom's.

"Anyway," her mom says, "you wanna hear my DeNiro impression?"

"*Mom.*"

Before they leave for Shara's house, she puts the necklace in her pocket. When they hit a red light, she hands it to Shara.

"I would apologize for being a freak and keeping it all this time," Chloe says, "but you've done weirder stuff, so let's call it even."

Shara stares down at it as the light turns green.

"How did you know it was mine?"

"I, um." Chloe keeps her eyes on the road. "I saw you. You didn't notice me, but I was in the library that day."

"Oh," Shara says. "That's embarrassing."

"Can I ask you something?" Chloe waits for Shara to nod and continues, "What made you decide to get rid of it?"

Shara is quiet, and when Chloe glances over, she's latching the chain around her neck.

"It wasn't like anything happened," Shara says. "My parents gave it to me when I turned thirteen, with this whole letter about how it represented me becoming *a woman of Christ.* It was like wearing a little travel-size version of their expectations. And everyone could see it, and I couldn't control what they thought it meant to me, and I didn't want anyone to think the way I love God is the same way other people at Willowgrove love God. It was just—it was too much. I knew my parents would notice if I stopped wearing it, so it had to go."

"You came back for it though," Chloe points out gently.

"Yeah, well," Shara says. "Sometimes I come back for stuff."

They pull up to Shara's street, and Shara's dad is waiting on the front porch swing in his Willowgrove polo, looking serious as an altar call. Last time Chloe checked, he was supposed to be in handcuffs. Maybe he's already out on bail.

"I guess they noticed I left again," Shara says.

"Do you think he knows what you did?" Chloe asks.

"Maybe," Shara says. "But he's got bigger problems than me right now, so maybe I can get out of False Beach before I have to deal with it."

Shara slips the necklace under the neckline of her dress and straightens her shoulders, and Chloe realizes this is Shara when nobody's looking. Born so smart and so curious and so fucking proud that not even Jesus could convince her she was wrong. Saved by God first and her God complex second. Going through hell and painting pink nail polish over it.

"You're kind of a badass," Chloe says. She's trying not to look too impressed, but she knows it's not working, because Shara's mouth tugs into that satisfied smirk.

"Wow, you're like, obsessed with me," Shara says.

Chloe turns her face away. "Bye."

Shara laughs and kisses Chloe hard on the cheek before she goes.

# FROM THE BURN PILE

Teacher self-evaluation written by
Jack Truman, choir instructor, scrapped and
accidentally mixed in with a packet of sheet
music eventually burned by Benjy

I think a lot about the movie *Tremors*, starring Kevin Bacon. It's about a bunch of rednecks fighting giant sandworms in the desert. In the first twenty minutes, Kevin Bacon finds some guy's hard hat on the ground full of brains, because the director needs the viewer to see the brains, and Kevin Bacon has to be the one who sees it because he's the star of the movie. But in the real world, if you happened to see somebody's brains by accident, it would mess you up. The whole movie would be about the fact that you saw somebody's brains.

By the time the average Willowgrove student is my age, that feeling you felt when you saw or heard something really bad might not be such a big deal anymore. It's just finding the brains. It's the bad thing that had to happen to move the plot forward. You're so busy shooting sandworms with an elephant gun that you're not even thinking about the brains, even though they're what scared you enough to go get an elephant gun in the first place. But when you're in high school—when you're only twenty minutes into the movie—the brains are everything.

Whenever I think about God's plan for my life, I think it's to keep some kids from seeing the brains. Or at least showing them something in the desert that isn't brains. A cool cactus, maybe. I don't know. Metaphors are hard. I'm not the literature teacher.

# 24

"You are *not* wearing a flannel to graduation," Chloe says.

Rory pulls a face at her and the black dress shirt she's holding up, unearthed from the depths of his closet.

"It's a protest graduation," Rory says. "Why does it matter what I wear?"

"Because Smith is gonna want to take photos, and you're gonna be mad if you look stupid in them."

He sighs, then snatches the shirt out of her hands. "Fine."

"You should wear it with that chain you like," says Shara's voice.

She's in Rory's window, where the morning glows around her through the flowering dogwood and crepe myrtles, and under her burgundy graduation gown she's wearing the same simple white sundress she wore in Chloe's bed. Chloe can't believe she's dating someone who comes with her own reel of cinematic entrances.

(They *are* dating, right? They haven't technically had the conversation, but trying to ruin someone's life because you're too attracted to them has to count.)

"Hi," Chloe says.

"Hi," Shara says, and then she looks at Chloe in that intense way she does, taking in her burgundy lipstick and the green dress she picked out carefully from a secondhand store in Birmingham. Pink blooms in her cheeks.

"Jesus, are you done checking her out?" Rory says.

Chloe's jaw drops. "*That's* what that is?"

"Shut up, Rory," Shara says, pretending to fight it when Chloe pulls her in to her side.

All of their respective friends are scattered this morning. Benjy's at home explaining to his parents why exactly he's not attending his own graduation ceremony, and Ash had to pick up a last-minute shift at the paint-your-own-pottery studio where they sometimes work on summer break. Georgia and Summer are already at the dealership helping Summer's parents, as evidenced by the seventeen nervous meeting-the-parents-who-kinda-know-but-don't-know texts Chloe's fielded this morning. April, Jake, and Ace are all probably still asleep, which leaves—

"Oh damn, it's a party," Smith says from Rory's bedroom door.

Maybe it should feel weird for the four of them to stand in the same room like this, but it's not. It's just . . . funny, like how it's funny now that Shara lived on a boat for a month or that Rory and Smith ever thought they were competing for Shara's attention and not each other's. High school is over, and everything is ridiculous.

Rory hands Smith a white dogwood blossom and says, "I got you these. I thought you might like to wear one or something."

"Is that why you were on the roof this morning?" Shara says. "I was wondering."

"They're fresher if you get them off the tree than the ground, okay?" Rory mumbles.

"I love them," Smith says, grinning as he takes it. "Thank you."

He spends a minute fussing in the mirror on Rory's closet door, trying to get the flower and cap to work together with his hair. He's been growing it out for a month now, and it's grown fast into short, dense curls.

"Hang on," Shara says. "I have an idea."

Smith lets her take his cap from him, and she produces a few hairpins from her dress pocket. She folds the elastic under and passes him the pins, pointing out the most strategic places for him to pin it into his hair.

"There," she says, plucking up one of the flowers from the desk and tucking it behind his ear.

Smith turns to examine himself in the mirror again. He tilts his head from side to side, and then he catches Shara's eye over his shoulder in the reflection and grins. She smiles back.

"Needs more flowers," he concludes.

"More flowers," Rory repeats with a nod before climbing dutifully out of the window.

He returns with two fresh handfuls of dogwood and crepe myrtle blossoms in white and pale pink, and Smith carefully twists them through his hair until it looks like there's a garden growing straight out of his scalp. At his request, Chloe smudges a hint of gold eyeliner around the corners of his eyes. By the time they're done, he looks like a god of the forest in white Air Forces.

Rory stares at him from across the room with wide eyes, like he's never seen anything quite like him before. None of them have, really. There's nobody like Smith Parker.

\* \* \*

At the dealership across the highway from Willowgrove, Brooklyn descends on them with a clipboard before Chloe's even shut the door of Rory's car behind her.

"Do we all have our caps and gowns?" she asks. "Again, do we *all* have our caps and gowns? Rory?"

"It's not even a real graduation, Brooklyn," Rory grumbles.

"Not without caps and gowns it's not," Brooklyn says. It looks like it's going to be a standoff between an unstoppable force (Brooklyn's dedication to micromanaging anything that can possibly be micromanaged) and an immovable object (Rory's refusal to do anything he is told to do, ever) when Smith appears over Rory's shoulder.

"He has it," Smith says, cheerfully slapping a folded gown and mortarboard against Rory's chest. "Forgot it in the car."

"I'm not wearing it," Rory says.

"Yes, you are," Brooklyn argues.

"It looks cute on you," Smith says.

"Ugh." Rory rolls his eyes so hard that his whole head goes around in an annoyed circle. *"Fine."*

"Good," Brooklyn says. She spins, cups her hands around her mouth, and yells, "They got theirs!"

Summer, who is standing on top of an ice chest in the middle of the lot with a megaphone in one hand, says through the crackly speaker, "Thanks, Brooklyn, but you really don't have to take this job so seriously."

"Agree to disagree!" Brooklyn yells.

Georgia's standing next to Summer's ice chest with a tank of helium. Summer leans over and holds the megaphone in front of Georgia's mouth.

"Hey, Chloe," she says into it.

Brooklyn puts them to work. Most of the cars have been moved to the back lot to make room for a small stage and a single mic stand, the former on loan from Summer's parents' church and the latter from Rory's A/V collection. Ace and Smith and all the other jocks are tasked with the manual labor of setting up chairs and tables, while Ash and the art club kids hang up signs and Benjy directs some of the choir contingent in assembling a balloon arch.

Across the two-lane highway, the rest of the class of '22 starts pulling into the student lot, posing for pictures outside the auditorium in their caps and gowns. A few of them stop to stare over at the dealership, where a pink-haired Shara is on Smith's shoulders, hanging a sign that says BLESSED ARE THE FRUITS with FRUITS in glitter glue. That's got to be one of Benjy's.

This is part of it, after all. There will always be people who like Willowgrove the way it is. The Mackenzies and Emma Graces and Dixons, the Drew Taylors, but also the quiet kids who feel safe there. Some of them have been in so deep for so long, they'll always be happier like this. Some of them are too scared, or didn't want to have that conversation with their parents. Some of them will reconcile these two sides of the highway in their hearts years from now.

Chloe's starting to understand. She can climb on a stage in a parking lot and try to change something, but she can't decide the rest for anyone else.

While Brooklyn has the assigning and assembling and decisive pointing covered, Summer plants herself in front of the local TV news crew as soon as they arrive. Her dad stands at her shoulder while she aces the interviews and smiles her pretty, dimpled smile. When asked, he explains that his business is happy to provide a place for anyone to stand up for something.

"Ever thought about being a politician's wife?" Chloe whispers to Georgia as they tie off balloons. "Summer's kind of crushing this."

"Nah," Georgia says. "If I wanted that, I'd date Brooklyn."

Chloe glances across the lot to where Brooklyn is shouting at a bunch of band kids. "Yeah. That girl is going to be a White House intern before she's old enough to buy beer."

Georgia laughs and starts measuring out ribbons. "Where are your moms, by the way? Didn't you say they were coming?"

"Yeah," Chloe says. She glances at her phone. "They should have been here by now. I wonder—"

Before she can finish the sentence, her mom's work truck comes trundling up to the lot.

There are cardboard boxes sliding around the bed, and when it pulls up closer, Chloe can see three people in the cab. Her mom parks beside the TV news van and climbs out in her nicest pair of coveralls, followed by her mama, and then—

"Is that Mr. Truman?"

Chloe passes her balloon off to Georgia and jogs over.

"Sorry we're late!" her mom says, circling around to the back of the truck and unlatching the tailgate. "We had to pick some stuff up at the last minute."

"Mom," Chloe says, "*what* did you do?"

Mr. Truman reaches into the bed and slaps one of the boxes.

"She knows a guy who has access to the school on weekends," he says. "I'm not saying that guy is *me,* but, you know. Always helps to know a guy." He picks up the box and grunts. "Jesus *Christmas,* this is heavy."

Mr. Truman and his imminent back sprain shuffle away as Chloe's mama joins her at the side of the truck.

"We did something very cool," she says. Gently, she rearranges a piece of Chloe's bangs. Chloe scrunches her nose and puts it back. "Your mother is very hot and daring. I want you to know that."

Her mom finally slides the remaining box up to the tail-gate and opens it.

"*Mom*," Chloe gasps when she sees what's inside.

The box contains two dozen thick, burgundy leather envelopes, each one embossed with the Willowgrove crest in white. Her mom takes out the topmost folder and opens it.

It winds her to finally see it in real life. The fancy gothic font, the shiny gold seal, the ridiculous, beautiful full name her moms picked out for her.

THIS CERTIFIES THAT CHLOE ANDROMEDA GREEN
HAS SATISFACTORILY COMPLETED THE COURSE
PRESCRIBED BY THE ALABAMA STATE BOARD OF
EDUCATION FOR THE ACCREDITED HIGH SCHOOLS—

"This is why y'all asked for the names of everyone who was coming today?" Chloe demands. "I thought Mama was going to make personalized cookies again."

"Oh, I did," she says, producing a Tupperware of frosted sugar cookies. "The diplomas were Jack's idea. Helped to have a list though."

Chloe looks over at Mr. Truman, who's huffing and puffing as Shara helps him set the box of diplomas down on the stage, and back to her moms.

"I love you so much," Chloe says, folding herself into her mom's arms.

"I love you too, coconut," her mom says thickly in her ear. "I'm so proud of you."

"Don't make me cry," Chloe says. "I spent forever on my eyeliner."

Her mom sniffs. "God, you are your mother's child."

"Hold that for one more second," her mama says. "I almost got a good picture."

"Mama, *stooooop*."

After Rory shreds "Pomp and Circumstance" on his Flying V, before Mr. Truman starts handing out diplomas, he leans into the microphone.

"I'd like to—" A squawk of feedback. "Lord in heaven. I'd like to invite someone up to say a few words. The valedictorian of Willowgrove Christian Academy's class of 2022: Chloe Green."

A sound rushes up to her ears, and it takes her a second to identify it: a round of applause. She's had a lot of fantasies of this moment, but this isn't part of most of them. She always expected everyone to sort of tolerate her at the podium. But when she looks around, Georgia is whooping through cupped hands, and Smith is pounding his feet against the ground, and somewhere in the back, her moms are blasting an air horn.

She turns to her left, to Shara, who's looking at her like she did on the bow of that sailboat, like the logic of the world all comes down to Chloe being there and she'd be disappointed to see anyone else.

"Make it a good one," Shara says, and she pushes Chloe to her feet.

From the makeshift stage, Chloe can see it all. April and Jake with their feet up on the chairs in front of them, Brooklyn fussing with the tassel on her cap, Ash's glue-and-glitter-decorated mortarboard flashing in the sun, Summer fanning herself with a paper plate, Smith's and Rory's shoulders pressed together in the front row, the TV cameras, her moms huddled by the news vans with Summer's parents.

She reaches into the neck of her gown and pulls a sweaty sheet of loose-leaf paper out of her bra. Last night, around midnight, she finally figured out what she wanted to say and scribbled it down in the nearest notebook she could find.

"Hi, guys," she says into the mic. "I'm Chloe, obviously. Um. I've imagined this moment a lot. Pretty much every day, actually. I don't even know how many drafts of this speech I've written, but I ended up scrapping them all. None of the old versions were right, because they were written for a different place with different people in it.

"A lot of those drafts were angry or had a lot of curse words or were just kind of mean, which I'm not really sorry for, because Willowgrove can be pretty mean, so I think it's fair. But I've learned more about Willowgrove in the past month than I have in the past four years, and that's not really the speech I want to make anymore.

"When I first moved to False Beach, I was pretty sure I was smarter and better than anyone in Alabama. I found my friends, and I decided those were the only people at Willowgrove worth my time. I was convinced that I knew, with absolute certainty, who did and did not deserve a chance. But then, about a month ago, someone kissed me."

She looks out at the crowd, to where Shara's smiling a soft smile under the Alabama sun. She sent Shara the speech last night for her notes, so she already knows most of what Chloe's going to say. She even ghostwrote a line or two.

"It's a long story—like, really long—but the short version is, that kiss brought people into my life who I'd never even spoken to before, and I discovered we had more in common than I ever would have guessed. I learned that there are jocks who love theater and stoners who know a lot more about the world than I do. I learned that a lot of us—a lot more than I thought—are doing whatever it takes to survive in a place that doesn't feel like it wants us. I learned that survival is heavy on so many of us. And on a personal level, I realized I'd gotten so used to that weight, I stopped noticing how much of myself I'd dedicated to carrying it.

"A lot of high school is about figuring out what matters to you and what doesn't. For some of us, popularity matters. For others, it's grades or dating or extracurriculars or our parents' opinions or all of the above. Sometimes, it's a question of whether anything that happens in these four years matters at all. And it does, but not in the way a lot of people think.

"High school matters because it shapes how we see the world when we enter it. We carry the hurt with us, the confirmed fears, the insecurities people used against us. But we also carry the moment when someone gave us a chance, even though they didn't have to."

She glances up at Georgia.

"The moment we watched a friend make a choice that we didn't understand at first because they're brave in a different way."

She finds Mr. Truman in the crowd, sweating rings in his dress shirt.

"The moment a teacher told us they believed in us."

Benjy and Ash both smile back when she looks at them.

"The moment we told someone who we are and they accepted us without question."

In the front row, Smith and Rory are easy to find.

"The moment we fell in love for the first time."

She drops her eyes back to her paper.

"Most of the things we're feeling right now are things we're feeling for the first time. We're learning what it means to feel them. What we can mean to one another. Of course that matters. And this, here, right now—even if nothing changes, even if all we can do today is prove that we exist, and that we're not alone—I think it matters a whole fucking lot."

She flips the page over. Almost done.

She takes one last look out at the crowd, and she thinks that this can be what it means—even only in part—to be from Alabama.

It's her mom welcoming every one of her friends into their house without hesitation, Georgia hiking out to the cliffs to read a book from Belltower, Smith with flowers in his hair and Rory yanking down street signs, the stars above the lake and midnight drives, hand-painted signs and improvised spaces in parking lots. All the things that people can make False Beach into.

None of the people she loves in this town are separate from it. Benjy grew up on Dolly Parton. Ash named themself after Alabama ash trees.

And Shara—Shara's an Alabama girl no matter what color she dyes her hair, and she's always been an Alabama girl, every second she was breathing down Chloe's neck. An Alabama girl outsmarted her with Shakespeare. An Alabama girl kissed her life into chaos.

She used to imagine lying to her future NYU classmates, telling them she never left California. Now she imagines telling them this.

"So, that's the main thing I wanted to say," Chloe goes on. "I also want to say thank you to a few people. To my friends, Georgia, Benjy, Ash—thank you for being my place here when I didn't have anywhere else.

"To Smith and Rory, I will never stop feeling lucky to have gotten to know you."

The last line on the page says, *To Shara,* but that's all. She never could figure out what to say.

"And to the girl who kissed me," she says, "I have done some of the best work of my life because of you. And I know you have done some of the best work of your life because of me. I don't know a better way to explain what love means to two people like us."

After the diplomas, while everyone's squeezing together for photos and Chloe's moms are busy wrangling her friends for a group shot, after the news crews have gotten their footage but before they've finished packing their cameras and big spongy microphones, Smith sidles up between Chloe and Shara.

"I got a question," he says.

"Flowers still looking great," Chloe says promptly.

"Appreciated," he says. "What exactly is the church board planning to do about your dad, Shara?"

Shara sighs and shrugs. "I think they're trying to throw enough money around to make it go away. They hired a legal team to shut down anybody who tries to post about it anywhere, and the only cop I've seen around my house is Mackenzie Harris's dad, so."

"So, in other words," Smith says. He squints into the sun, eyes flashing gold. "If something's gonna happen, the story has to get out of False Beach."

"I guess so," Shara says.

"All right," Smith says as he leaves them, "I'm gonna go win somebody a broadcast journalism award."

Smith Parker is always, always a quarterback. He's a strategist. He plans five steps ahead. So, he's subtle about swaggering up to a camera guy and slapping palms like they're old friends. It looks natural when he leans in and says something to the guy that Chloe can't hear, finishing off with a smile. Nobody would ever know what he's done. Certainly not whoever updates his ESPN profile.

It takes another minute for the cameraman to whip around, grab his reporter, and yank her into the van.

They peel out of the dealership, cutting a U-turn in the middle of the highway to screech into the Willowgrove parking lot, gunning straight for the auditorium.

The nearest reporter, one from Birmingham, turns to his crew and says, "Pack y'all's shit up *now*."

When the auditorium doors swing open and grads come streaming out of the building, the crews are waiting. Principal Wheeler steps out of the air conditioning and directly into a mob of microphones.

From Chloe's side, Shara shades her eyes with her hand and watches.

"Well," she says, white teeth glinting, "bless his heart."

# FROM THE BURN PILE

Note from Chloe's mom to her
on her first day of school

Chloe,
I promise I will let you go wherever you want to go, as long as it makes you
happy. I promise I will stand up for you against anyone who tries to make
you feel small, but only if you ask me to. I know you prefer to take care of
yourself, and I believe that you can.

Show them you're not someone to fuck with.

All my love,
Mom

# 25

DAYS UNTIL FALL SEMESTER
COMMENCES AT NYU: 100

The bonfire comes later.

One of Willowgrove's oldest senior rites of passage is a bonfire in the cow pasture near campus the day after graduation, set up by the student body president and a few volunteers from the 4-H club. Everyone's supposed to bring all their notebooks, leftover exams, homework packets, study guides, C-minus essays, and assorted high school debris they never want to see again, and burn it.

Of course, the Class of '22—Willowgrove's finest—doesn't do things the way they've always been done. (And lately Brooklyn has been busy getting sunburnt in the spectator section of the skate park.) So, it's not until four weeks after graduation that the bonfire finally happens.

For Chloe, it's been four weeks of sneaking over Shara's fence when her parents are meeting with their attorneys, jumping into Shara's pool in her underwear, and high-fiving Smith when they show up at the country club at the same time.

She keeps Georgia company on her shifts at Belltower and gets poison ivy foraging with Ash and falls asleep on Benjy's bedroom floor, but in between, it's a Shara Wheeler highlight reel. Shara tucking herself into the window seat in Chloe's bedroom. Shara making snarky comments about Chloe's randomly assigned NYU roommate. Shara floating on her back in the lake. Shara waving to Rory from her bedroom window. Shara tentatively suggesting a double date with Georgia and Summer, *if you think they'd like that, nothing fancy, it's whatever, does Georgia like me, actually never mind.* Shara pretending not to get mad when she comes in dead last on their mini-golf double date with Georgia and Summer.

Shara saying the word "girlfriend" for the first time on the hood of Chloe's car, out on the cliffs by Lake Martin, under a parachute sky.

The bonfire is their first event as an official couple. Chloe spent seven hundred of the last forty-eight hours on Face-Time with Georgia, trying to find the right outfit for Unlikely Girlfriend of Renegade Prom Queen. In the end, she settles on a black overall dress over a striped tank and her coolest sunglasses.

When she picks Shara up, she's in a tied-up white T-shirt and cutoff jean shorts, which is an effortlessly perfect outfit for Daughter of Principal Fired in Disgrace After Viral Local News Meltdown Video. Or maybe it's just a perfect outfit in general.

"What?" Chloe says when Shara looks at her too long at a red light.

"Just this." She pulls Chloe in by the back of her neck and kisses her hard over the console.

She pulls away as soon as the light turns green, settling back into her seat. Chloe tries to play it cool when she turns back to the road and hits the gas, but she has to press her knuckles to her lips to stop smiling.

Out in the cow pasture, the crowd is smaller than it usually is for this—probably because the text threads used for DIY graduation were the same ones used to organize it. There are a few new faces of seniors who walked across Willowgrove's stage but still wanted to come with their friends, but mostly it's the same crowd. Summer's backed her truck into the clearing, and there's a playlist blasting from her sound system as someone starts passing around marshmallows and sticks.

At the center of everything, a pile of logs towers higher than Chloe's head, and as the sun starts to set, the first match drops.

Between rounds of Coke and Sonic Slushes and White Claws, everyone takes their turn throwing things into the fire. Smith, who showed up with Rory in a barely buttoned shirt and shorts, dumps a Winn-Dixie bag of old tests. Georgia torches her notebooks. Jake throws his whole backpack in. Brooklyn burns a single paper with a C circled in red at the top.

"You gonna burn anything?" Rory asks, sidling up next to Chloe.

"Yeah," Chloe says. "I have some stuff."

He shakes out his hair, watching Smith and Shara a short distance away. Shara's already bought tickets to see him play when football season starts.

"You seem happy," Rory says. "Or like, the Chloe version of that. You don't seem like you're actively plotting anyone's murder."

"Thanks," Chloe says. By now, Rory knows she takes that type of thing as a compliment. "You seem happy too."

"Yeah," Rory says, septum ring glinting in the firelight. "Ready to hit the road."

She saw him and Smith packing up the Beemer yesterday when she was sneaking into Shara's yard. Smith's off to College Station for preseason training soon, but before that, they're road tripping up the coast to visit Rory's older brother, then back down to Texas to drop some of his stuff off at his dad's before he moves in. He's thinking about applying to a community college in Dallas now that Smith has convinced him to start seeing someone for his dyslexia, but first he's spending a year going to DIY shows and working on his music.

There's something horribly romantic about it, she thinks: Smith Parker broadcast across television screens in burgundy and white, taping up his hands, touching his fingers to his lips and raising them to the sky, and Rory in the bathroom of some grungy concert venue, watching the game on his phone and writing lyrics about someone who runs and runs and runs.

Benjy's still going to Tuscaloosa in the fall, and Ash is packing up for Rhode Island. Last week, Georgia finally scored a cheap car from Craigslist, and Chloe helped her practice the drive to Auburn and back. Ace is going to Ole Miss, Brooklyn's going to Yale, Jake's going to UA Birmingham, April is going to UNO.

She takes a slow lap around the fire, trying to see everyone. It's strange to know she'll never see some of them again, and some will stay in her life long after her moms have donated the last of her uniforms to Goodwill. She lets Ace squeeze her into his continent of a chest and promises to sneak him a video of the first Broadway show she sees. She screams along to a song with Smith. She links arms with Georgia to dance and sends up her only prayer of the past four years: May they always come back to each other.

Finally, she circles back to Shara. She's sitting in the grass near the fire, watching Ash and Ace argue the ideal level of marshmallow doneness while she roasts her own.

Chloe feels that familiar tug into another world, one where Shara's a siren disrupting a long voyage or a princess with secret letters tucked into her chemise. But the thing she unfurls in her mind is Shara, just like this, but two years from now.

Shara with her hair growing out but still pink, driving them across the desert to California, yelling complaints about the water pressure from a cheap motel shower. Fighting over books, over who stole whose sweater, fighting for real the way she knows they will and furiously reconciling in the back of Chloe's car. Smooth legs tangled up with hers, perfectly buffed nails scraping her shoulders. Georgia texting Shara jokes that Chloe doesn't get, her mom showing Shara how to check her oil, Chloe's life mixed up with Shara's until everything tastes like vanilla and mint.

And she imagines herself from Shara's point of view. Her fingers on a lecture hall desk, a MetroCard in her wallet, her shoes up on the fountain's edge in Washington Square Park. Her laugh in profile and a swish of dark hair as she leads Shara by the hand through an NYU dorm for a weekend visit. Sleeping two in a twin and eating french fries on the floor, working at this thing between them that only they really understand.

Difficult, frustrating, razor-sharp, feather-soft Shara, leaving lilacs on her pillow in the morning.

She doesn't really know if she'll get to have any of that. Shara hasn't decided what's next yet. There's still time for her to enroll for the spring semester at Bama, the only school her parents will agree to pay for, but it would come with a lot of strings. Shara hates strings.

When they're alone, she talks about applying for student loans and running away to study in France or Italy or China, or riding the Trans-Siberian Railroad, or going on *The Bachelor* so she can live on Instagram sponcon. Once, she half joked she might find whatever crappy waitressing job she can in New York and sleep on Chloe's couch. She'll figure it out. She's the smartest person Chloe knows. She has time.

And, at least until the end of the summer, she has Chloe. That much Chloe knows for sure.

She sits down at Shara's side and drops her bag onto the ground between them. Shara's preoccupied with a smoldering marshmallow.

"I have a question for you," she says.

"No, I didn't mean to burn it," Shara says. "I'm not perfect."

She laughs, reaching into her purse. "Actually, I was going to ask if you think I should burn these."

Shara glances over, and there in Chloe's hand are her cards. Some are worn down at the edges from being carried around. One has a matcha stain on it. All of them are monogrammed pink artifacts of a Shara who would rather tear her own life apart than tell the truth, even to herself.

Chloe's grown attached to them, to be honest, but this isn't a game anymore. Feels weird to keep the pieces.

Shara says, "Burn 'em."

So Chloe does.

Under the curl of smoke, Shara reaches over and smears melted marshmallow down the length of Chloe's nose.

"Ah!" Chloe gasps while Shara laughs. "Why!"

Shara grins an extremely self-satisfied grin, which is something Chloe is still getting used to. Shara has so many more expressions than she did before. It's like she's unlocked Shara Premium.

"Because it's funny."

"I hate you!"

"Can't believe it took you four whole years to finally say that to my face," Shara says, settling back on her elbows.

"I can only say it because I don't mean it anymore," Chloe counters. She turns onto her side so she can lean over Shara and smear the marshmallow into the sleeve of her shirt.

"I think—ugh, gross—I think you still mean it a little bit," Shara says, squirming away as Chloe tries to pin her down. "That's what makes this work."

Shara gives up the fight and lays her head down against the grass. Chloe could swear the sunset shifts on the horizon from powder blue to coral pink, the exact color of Shara's cheeks and lips and hair, and of her sugar-sticky palm, which lies open on the ground above her head.

They've never hated each other, not really. It's more like recognition. Shara tilts her chin up to the sky, narrowing her eyes even as she starts to smile, and Chloe sees someone just as stubborn and intense and strange as she is, snapping exactly into place. The thing Chloe likes more than anything else: a correct answer.

One delirious summer doesn't feel like nearly enough time for this.

Technically, though, eighteen years isn't a lot of time either.

Chloe covers Shara's hand with her own. She laces their fingers together and squeezes, and then she kisses Shara into the grass.

# ACKNOWLEDGMENTS

I feel inclined to begin this by saying that I am not Chloe Green, and Chloe Green is not me. I grew up in and around environments much like False Beach and Willowgrove, which made writing this book quite the emotional roller coaster, but Chloe's story is by no means autobiographical. To be honest, I didn't know enough about myself or the world at eighteen to be a Chloe. I think I would describe myself as an Ace sun, Georgia moon, Chloe rising.

I wrote this book for the Chloes of the world, but also the Smiths and Rorys and Georgias and Benjys and, yes, even the Sharas. I know intimately that the Bible Belt contains some of the best, warmest, weirdest, queerest kids you'll ever meet, whether or not they even know that last part yet. If you're one of those kids, I wanted this book to exist for you. I think if it had existed for me back then, a lot of things in my life would have been different. I wanted to write a book to show you that you're not alone.

(And also that you deserve ridiculous, over-the-top high school rom-coms about teenagers like you, just like the straight kids have! Don't let anyone try to convince you otherwise!)

I have a tremendously long list of people to thank for

making this book possible, but I'll try to keep it brief this time. Sara Megibow, my absolute superstar of an agent, who is as tireless and patient as she is great at her job, and who approaches every conversation with the kind of humanity we desperately need in this business. Vicki Lame, my editor, who allows me to follow my gut to so many strange and wonderful places. My assistant, Abby Rauscher, who literally keeps me sane. The team at Wednesday who put so much work into this book, including Meghan Harrington, Devan Norman, Alexis Neuville, Brant Janeway, Erica Martirano, Jeremy Haiting, Christa Désir, Melanie Sanders, and Vanessa Aguirre. Christina Tucker and Matthew Broberg-Moffitt, my authenticity readers. Kerri Resnick, who masterminded the cover, and Allison Reimold, who captured Shara's likeness and nightmare vibe.

I also have to thank all my friends who graciously and generously read early drafts or talked through plot ideas or did writing sprints or simply told me they thought what I was working on sounded interesting—you literally kept me going. There were times when the only thing that pushed me to my word count was the thought of getting to share an excerpt at the end of the day. You know who you are. Thanks especially to Anna Prendella, who gave such sharp, illuminating, extensive, and frankly feral feedback throughout the revising process that she should be canonized.

To Sasha (*New York Times* bestselling author Sasha Peyton Smith!!! No, I'll never shut up about it.), thank you for your bottomless well of patience, for Margaritaville, and for always being down for a Plot Problems FaceTime call. Can't wait to do this together forever. I was definitely your dad in a past life.

To Kris, for all those months of 2020 when it was just you,

me, the pets, this manuscript, and never-ending terror holed up in Brooklyn's most cursed fourth-floor walkup, thank you. You are my fiercest supporter, and I genuinely don't know how I would do this without you. I love you a stupid amount. Keep leaving hair ties all over my apartment.

To my family, with my whole heart: Thank you, I love you. I would be nowhere without y'all.

To every reader who has stuck with me since day one, and every reader who is beginning with this book, thank you endlessly for giving me the opportunity to keep doing this.

And, finally, let's hear it one more time for queer kids in red states and conservative religious communities. I love y'all so much. It may feel sometimes like nobody knows or cares that you're there, doing your best to get through it, carrying all that weight, but I know it. So many of us queer adults who've come out the other side know it. We're here for you whenever you're ready. You're going to be loved and known and cared for in ways you can't even imagine yet. And you're going to have some wild stories to tell at Gay Friendsgiving one day. Take good care of yourselves until then.

Wait, actually. One more.

To Chloe Green. Thank you for everything you've taught me.

Read on for new bonus content,
including character sheets, an
early draft of the calendar timeline,
assorted notes and a page with
Casey working out how
to structure a scene . . .

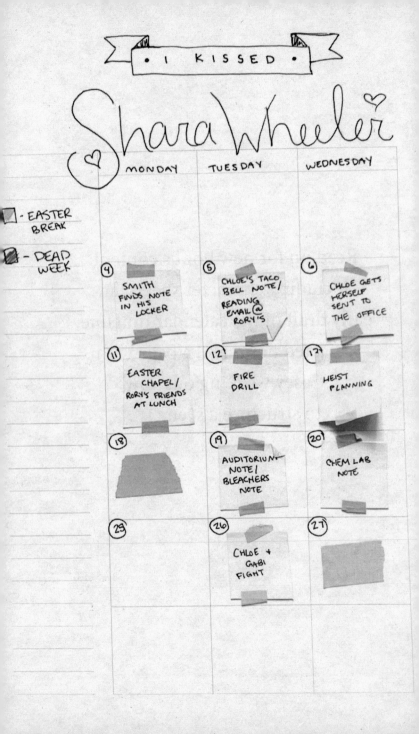

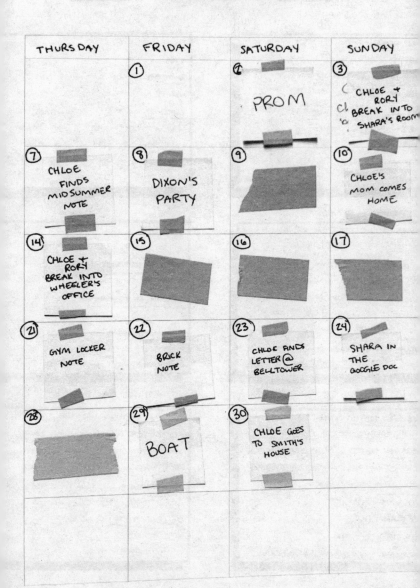

# SHARA

**FULL NAME:** SHARA ELIZABETH WHEELER
**AGE:** 18
**PLACE OF BIRTH:** FALSE BEACH, AL
**DATE OF BIRTH:** OCTOBER 24
**BIG 3:** ☉ SCORPIO ☾ LIBRA ↑ LIBRA
**MBTI:** INTJ
**ENNEAGRAM:** 3W4
**SEXUALITY/GENDER:** CIS LESBIAN
**RACE/ETHNICITY:** WHITE

**HAIR:** LONG + BLONDE, SHINY + PERFECT
**EYES:** GREEN
**BODY TYPE:** THIN W/ SUBTLE CURVES
**HEIGHT:** 5'6
**FEATURES:** BIG EYES, LONG LASHES, FULL LIPS W/ NATURAL LIP FLIP, OVAL FACE, STRIKINGLY BEAUTIFUL IN A WHOLESOME WAY
**AESTHETIC:** SOFT CHURCH GIRL, PASTELS FEMININE, SIMPLE

**HOBBIES:** READING POETRY, BULLET JOURNALING, MAINTAINING HER REPUTATION
**INTERESTS:** SKIN CARE, PHOTOGRAPHY, BEING ADORED
**FAVE MEDIA:** SHAKESPEARE, MARY OLIVER, TAYLOR SWIFT, MIDSOMMAR, SIXTEEN CANDLES, FLEETWOOD MAC, EMMA, GONE GIRL, LITTLE WOMEN
**SOCIAL MEDIA:** EXTREMELY CAREFULLY CURATED INSTAGRAM WITH 20K FOLLOWERS

**FAMILY:** TWO PARENTS, ONLY CHILD, MOM (HEIDI) + DAD (BRETT)
**PARENTAL RELATIONSHIPS:** EXPECT HER TO BEAR THE FAMILY LEGACY, LOTS OF PRESSURE
**SIBLING RELATIONSHIPS:** NONE
**CHILDHOOD:** HIGHLY ANXIOUS CHILD, ALWAYS ON A PEDESTAL, PASSIVELY BULLIED BY HER PARENTS

**POSITIVE TRAITS:** DRIVEN, RESILIENT, INDEPENDENT, CURIOUS, SECRETLY KIND
**NEGATIVE TRAITS:** IN DEEP DENIAL ABOUT HER TRUE NATURE, DISHONEST, MANIPULATIVE
**BIG WANT:** TO WIN VALEDICTORIAN TO SEAL HER PERFECT IMAGE
**BIG FLAW:** OBSESSED WITH MAINTAINING HER PERFECT IMAGE
**WORST FEAR:** BEING SEEN OR VULNERABLE

**TALENTS:** WRITING, ACADEMICS, PIANO
**PECULARITIES:** ALWAYS WEARING ESSIE BALLET SLIPPER
**RAINY DAY:** DOING A FACE MASK, STALKING CHLOE'S FINSTA, MAKING SPREADSHEETS
**DREAM DATE:** LONG DRIVE, PINK LEMONADES, SUNSET GAZING
**COLLEGE PLANS:** LOL

# ·CHLOE·

**FULL NAME:** CHLOE ANDROMEDA GREEN

**AGE:** 18

**PLACE OF BIRTH:** LOS ANGELES, CA

**DATE OF BIRTH:** JANUARY 2

**BIG 3:** ☉ CAP ☾ LEO ↑ ARIES

**MBTI:** ENTJ

**ENNEAGRAM:** 8W7

**SEXUALITY/GENDER:** CIS GIRL, BI

**RACE/ETHNICITY:** WHITE

**HAIR:** DARK BROWN BOB W/ BANGS

**EYES:** BROWN

**BODY TYPE:** AVERAGE, BUSTY

**HEIGHT:** 5'6

**FEATURES:** STRONG BROWS, HEART SHAPE FACE, ANGULAR JAW, USUALLY WEARIN DRAMATIC EYELINER

**AESTHETIC:** DARK ACADEMIA FEMME, EUROPEAN INSPIRED

**HOBBIES:** READING (FICTION + FANFIC), LOOKING @ SHARA'S IG,

**INTERESTS:** THEATRE, FASHION, FANTASY NOVELS

**FAVE MEDIA:** SHAKESPEARE, PHANTOM, T&T, HADESTOWN, SHE-RA, LOK, LORDE, PHOEBE BRIDGERS, LES MIS, LOTR, EURO HISTORY

**SOCIAL MEDIA:** TIKTOK SKITS, SOMETIMES ENGAGES IN QUEER DISCOURSE ON TWT

**FAMILY:** TWO MOMS, VAL + JESS, ONLY CHILD

**PARENTAL RELATIONSHIP:** VERY CLOSE W/ BOTH MOMS, SUPPORTIVE PARENTS WHO ENCOURAGE WEIRD INTERESTS

**SIBLING RELATIONSHIP:** NONE + HAPPY ABOUT IT

**CHILDHOOD:** CRUNCHY GRANOLA HAPPY HOME, LOTS OF ART, MANY GAY AUNTS + UNCLES, ALWAYS ENCOURAGED TO BE HERSELF

**POSITIVE TRAITS:** HIGHLY INTELLIGENT, SELF-MOTIVATED, AMBITIOUS, CLEVER, RESILIENT

**NEGATIVE TRAITS:** ELITIST, STUBBORN

**BIG WANTS:** TO PROVE SHE'S BETTER THAN WILLOWGROVE

**BIG FLAW:** THINKS SHE ALWAYS KNOWS BEST

**WORST FEAR:** FAILURE

**TALENTS:**

**PECULIARITIES:** MONSTER FUCKER BOOKS

**RAINY DAY:** READING AT HOME WHILE LISTENING TO BROADWAY OST,

**DREAM DATE:** BOOKSTORE BROWSING, FANCY DESSERT, MUSEUM VISIT

**COLLEGE PLANS:** FULL RIDE TO NYU

# · SMITH ·

**FULL NAME:** William Smith Parker

**AGE:** 18

**PLACE OF BIRTH:** False Beach, AL

**DATE OF BIRTH:** April 29

**BIG 3:** taurus ☉, cancer ☾, aqua ↑

**MBTI:** 2w3

**ENNEAGRAM:** ENFJ

**SEXUALITY/GENDER:** nonbinary bisexual

**RACE/ETHNICITY:** Black

---

**HAIR:** short w/ fade

**EYES:** brown + sparkly

**BODY TYPE:** graceful athletic build

**HEIGHT:** 6'2

**FEATURES:** good looking, broad nose, sticking eye shape with sharp inner corners, nice cheekbones, powerful eyebrows with defined arch

**AESTHETIC:** soft jock, secretly loves flowers + glitter

---

**HOBBIES:** reading poetry, running, beating his sisters in Smash Bros

**INTERESTS:** football strategy, house plants, guys who play guitar

**FAVE MEDIA:** Frank Ocean, Dragon Ball Z, Naruto, Danez Smith, Lil Nas X, Brockhampton, Taylor Swift, SZA, LOU, dumb stuff on YouTube

**SOCIAL MEDIA:** not really active but he accounts for scouting reasons

---

**FAMILY:** 3 younger sisters, parents still very much in love & supportive

**PARENTAL RELATIONSHIPS:** they believe in him + spend a lot of money to help him accomplish his dreams

**SIBLING RELATIONSHIPS:** closest with the one who bonds with him over having big dreams

**CHILDHOOD:** always loved football + had a natural gift for it, grew up in public school, family fairly religious

---

**POSITIVE TRAITS:** kind, gentle, warm, good-natured, empathetic, curious, open-minded, pragmatic, generous

**NEGATIVE TRAITS:** doesn't always stick up for himself, preoccupied w/ others' opinions

**WANT:** to fulfill his dream being a great football player

**FLAW:** sacrifices his happiness to fit in

**WORST FEAR:** letting himself down

---

**TALENTS:** football, charisma, writing

**PECULARITIES:** loves candles

**RAINY DAY:** playing mario kart while listening to music

**DREAM DATE:** big dinner, brownie sundae, making out by the lake

**COLLEGE PLANS:** drafted for ~~FSU's~~ A+M football team

# ·RORY·

**FULL NAME:** Rory James Heron
**AGE:** 18
**PLACE OF BIRTH:** False Beach, AL
**DATE OF BIRTH:** February 27
**BIG 3:** pisces ☉ sag ☽ scug ↑
**MBTI:** ISFP
**ENNEAGRAM:** 4w5
**SEXUALITY/GENDER:** cis guy, gay
**RACE/ETHNICITY:** biracial (white + Black)

**HAIR:** shaggy, curly, dark w/ highligh
**EYES:** hazel, mostly brownish
**BODY TYPE:** gangly but strong-ish
**HEIGHT:** 6'1
**FEATURES:** model jawline, big nose, wide lash-rimmed eyes, bushy eyebrows, full lips, secret septum piercing, nerdy hot
**AESTHETIC:** sad boy chic, lots of flannel, many pairs of Vans

**HOBBIES:** songwriting, organizing pranks, jamming w/ friends
**INTERESTS:** classic guitar technique, cute animals, sticking it to the man
**FAVE MEDIA:** Tyler the Creator, Jimi Hendrix, One Piece, Zelda, horror movies, shoegaze, Steve Lacy, Bojack, Get Out
**SOCIAL MEDIA:** only account is a finsta for shitposting

**FAMILY:** divorced parents, lame step-dad, cool older brother
**PARENTAL RELATIONSHIPS:** strained relationship w/ mom, close w/ Dad but he is distant for work
**SIBLING RELATIONSHIPS:** super close w/ his older brother, misses him a lot while he's at college
**CHILDHOOD:** ugly duckling, huge nerd, loved at home but struggled to fit in at school until he met Smith ♡

**POSITIVE TRAITS:** sensitive, creative, funny, romantic, poetic, loyal, deep, devoted
**NEGATIVE TRAITS:** withdrawn, quick to anger, holds a grudge, dishonest w/ himself
**WANT:** to find true love
**FLAW:** gives up on himself before the world can
**FEAR:** being abandoned

**TALENTS:** guitar, songwriting
**PECULIARITIES:** prefers cinnamon gum
**RAINY DAY:** staring moodily out the window like a music video
**DREAM DATE:** staying in to listen to music, cuddling, ~~talking~~ talking about the universe
**COLLEGE PLANS:** hasn't even applied

Shara Wheeler is a princess. From an early age, her looks and her ~~pers~~ parents' status ~~at~~ in False Beach set her up to be beloved. A highly intelligent and perceptive child, she quickly picked up on this. It was also something her parents pushed her toward and actively cultivated in her. She ~~bears~~ bears the entire weight of her family's legacy at Willowgrove. In her childhood, anytime she would act in a way her parents didn't approve of, she would be punished by having the love and attention they lavished on her abruptly taken away. All these things taught her that the best way for her to get what she wanted in life — her parents' approval, the acceptance of her peers, the concealment of her sexuality, first place in everything, was to deliberately ~~construct a perfect~~ ~~Alabama~~ princess around herself. The older she got, the more afraid she became of existing in the world without this protective barrier, and the harder she worked to both maintain it and keep it separate from her real, private self.

At the start of the book, Shara has reached a precipice — her biggest lie — that she got into Harvard — is coming home to roost. She believes the only way to ~~stop this~~ and maintain her reputation ~~is~~ to win valedictorian, and she has to beat Chloe to do it. Staging her own disappearance is her attempt to distract from the collapse of her lies, bolster the Shara mystique, and sabotage Chloe's last run at valedictorian by sending her ~~on~~ on a wild goose chase.

Unbeknownst to her, she has ~~a~~ a repressed, underlying motive: she ~~has~~ had a crush on Chloe since freshman year and ~~this is~~ her last chance ~~to have~~ Chloe's undivided attention before they graduate and never see each other again

## LIBRARY SCENE

after the encounter after the English exam, Chloe realizes she can make Shara chase her and provoke Shara into making a move on her again so she can reject her this time

Chloe daydreaming in detail about Shara kissing her again — and then rejection of course

• very short montage of horny traps / 1-2 grafs

• Chloe witnessing Shara + Smith talking at Smith's locker, which annoys her — more evidence of Shara having things handed to her

• Chloe loudly announcing to a confused Brooklyn that she's going to the library to study

• Chloe waits in the library for Shara, and when Shara shows up, she begins laying on a comically thick seduction act

> • before this let's have Chloe go to the bathroom to prepare using every single thing she's learned about Shara

### NOW WHAT?

• need to figure out what subject they're studying
• need to build up tension — maybe flashcards?
• Chloe flashing the crucifix
• mirroring Shakespeare flashback
• Shara almost touching Chloe's hand and then freaking out

# HOW DO CHLOE + SHARA ADDRESS SHARA'S CONFESSION?

## WHAT SHARA WANTS TO DO:

she thinks her confession should have convinced Chloe of her sincerity + now she wants Chloe to take it from here b/c she doesn't know how to proceed

## WHAT CHLOE WANTS TO DO:

she wants to maintain the upperhand and realizes that Shara's confession gives her that power — she has become something Shara wants but can't have, so it's her turn to be chased. she comes to school furious and ready to torture Shara. Chase me, bitch!

however! Shara is mostly just weirdly lurking around all week — she does not know how to pursue Chloe to her face — insert brief montage of Chloe going through finals week while Shara lurks, Chloe keeps waiting to see the girl who did the clues, wants Shara to try again so she can reject her — basically traipsing around a vampire exposing her neck so she can jam a stake into her heart

ed up with waiting, she tricks Shara into following her to the library for a study date, where she throws every possible thing + Shara to try to provoke her into making _ move — Shara freaks out + leaves.

# ABOUT THE AUTHOR

Sylvie Rosokoff

Casey McQuiston is a *New York Times*-bestselling author of romantic comedies and a pie enthusiast. She writes books about smart people with bad manners falling in love. Born and raised in South Louisiana, she now lives in New York City with her poodle mix/personal assistant, Pepper.

# Adult Psychological Problems:
# An Introduction

# Contemporary Psychology Series

*Series Editor*: Professor Raymond Cochrane
School of Psychology
The University of Birmingham
Birmingham B 15 2TT
United Kingdom

This series of books on contemporary psychological issues is aimed primarily at 'A' Level students and those beginning their undergraduate degree. All of these volumes are introductory in the sense that they assume no, or very little, previous acquaintance with the subject, while aiming to take the reader through to the end of his or her first course on the topic they cover. For this reason the series will also appeal to those who encounter psychology in the course of their professional work: nurses, social workers, police and probation officers, speech therapists and medical students. Written in a clear and jargon-free style, each book generally includes a full (and in some cases annotated) bibliography and points the way explicitly to further reading on the subject covered.

**Psychology and Social Issues:**
**A Tutorial Text**
Edited by Raymond Cochrane, *University of Birmingham* and Douglas Carroll, *Glasgow Polytechnic*

**Families: A Context for Development**
David White and Anne Woollett, *Polytechnic of East London*

**The Psychology of Childhood**
Peter Mitchell, *University College of Swansea*

**Health Psychology: Stress, Behaviour and Disease**
Douglas Carroll, *Glasgow Polytechnic*

**Adult Psychological Problems: An Introduction**
Edited by Lorna A. Champion, *Institute of Psychiatry*, *London* and Michael J. Power, *Royal Holloway and Bedford New College*, *Egham, Surrey*

*Forthcoming titles:*

**On Being Old: The Psychology of Later Life**
Graham Stokes, *Gulson Hospital, Coventry*

**Food and Drink: The Psychology of Nutrition**
David Booth, *University of Birmingham*